EMBR

P. C. VORSTER

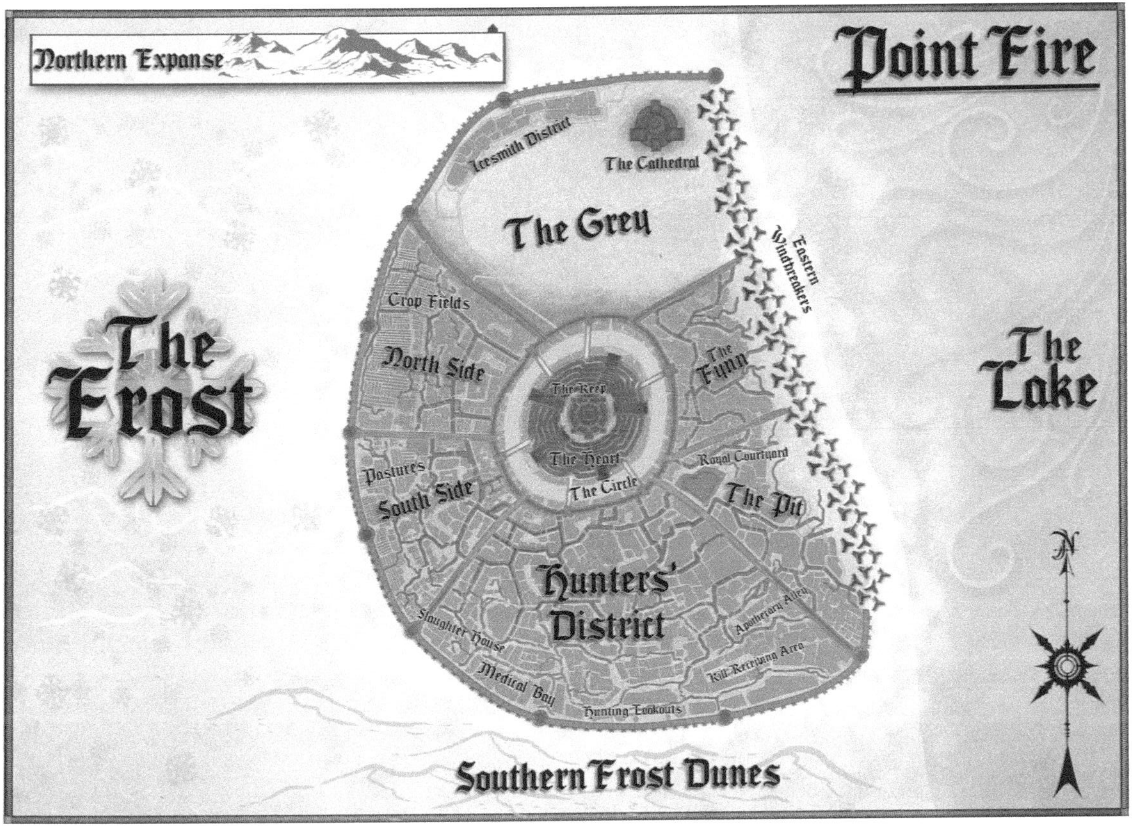

Point Fire
Northern Expanse
The Frost
The Lake
Southern Frost Dunes
The Grey
Icesmith District
The Cathedral
Eastern Windbreakers
Crop Fields
North Side
The Funn
The Keep
The Heart
The Circle
Royal Courtyard
Pastures
South Side
The Pit
Hunters' District
Slaughter House
Medical Bay
Apothecary Alley
Kill-Receiving Area
Hunting Lookouts
N

I

The god of this World is waiting.

The hazy ice dunes remained silent. On the four, perhaps five, undulations that were visible at this range, nothing moved. Avenir lowered his pocket telescope and chuckled soundlessly. His target, it seemed, knew how to conceal himself.

Things have become far more entertaining.

With one fluid movement, he covered his eyes with the ice gauze and slid from his scouting location down the back of the dune. Curling himself into a tight ball and shifting as much of his weight as possible onto the small of his back, he felt himself rapidly gaining speed. He had practiced this motion countless times with his father, who had always scorned him for leaving too large of a *breath*: the brilliant spray of ice an inexperienced Hunter might create while sliding down frozen terrain.

Avenir did not have to look back to confirm that he was leaving no such trace. Years of grueling training had come with their benefits.

He was wearing full scout gear: soft-sole boots, a dunerobe, and a matching white fur hood. The heavily insulated material covered his entire head, save his eyes, which were now shielded with the ice gauze. Deviant bits of frost and snow ricocheted off of it. The getup camouflaged his figure almost completely against the dullness of the dune's terrain. If someone, or something, were to look directly at him from a distance, they would see nothing but an ice mirage flitting playfully down the incline.

As the snowy curve flattened out, he slowly unfurled his body, taking great care not to touch the ice with anything other than his back. Unnecessary ground-contact at this speed would likely result in a visible *breath*. He would be spotted instantly and be as good as dead.

Still gliding rapidly down the dune, he readied his ice pick, double-checked his balance, and swung it sharply back over his head. Stopping a slide was the most dangerous part. In order to minimize stirring up a misty trail of snow behind him, his halt would have to be near instantaneous.

The pick thudded quietly into the dune, sending up a small puff of glittering particles. His momentum shifted immediately. It felt like he was being pulled apart. His shoulders threatened to break free from their sockets.

The maneuver came to completion. Adrenaline pulsing through him, he lay motionless, gazing at the grey sky above. It was as if he had never even moved. He had successfully held his *breath*.

Father would be proud.

The strong can be crippled by lies. The proud can be crushed. The deceitful can be exposed. The quiet can be shamed. Yet, a council of these together is near insurmountable. Such is the Knotted Rope. Its strength does not lie in its material - True strength can only be found in its braid.

Avenir tucked the pick back through its beltloop. He was now in the valley between the two ice dunes. In this location it would be nearly impossible for his adversary to spot him. He checked his other loops to make sure that none of his equipment had become dislodged during the slide. Thankfully, his telescope had survived unscathed and his Shard still hung snugly in its worn leather sheath. Avenir suppressed a smile.

Aren is still too young to receive his first Shard. But that cheeky little bastard doesn't need a weapon to kill.

His father, after giving Avenir his first one, had explained how to use it:

"Think of it as something that cannot, and will not, fail you."

Avenir unsheathed it — its length just over a hand long — and carefully crept up the next ice dune.

"'Nir! Don't touch the point!" Father had said, "That thing can pierce bone like it's snow."

Cresting the dune, Avenir thought of his younger self marveling at the strange weapon his father had given to him. Back then, he had always known that the Hunters used them, but he had never been able to see one up close. Even his father's had been hidden away in a locked cabinet.

The weapon was shaped like a short stalactite and was the deadliest tool the Icesmiths in the Frost could create. It shone a dull silver in the dreary light.

The process by which a Shard is made was painstakingly slow and tested the patience of even the most steadfast Icesmiths. To achieve the near-perfect sharpness of a Shard, an Icesmith would first have to get their hands on a coveted and rare metal — Frost Ore — found only

within the deepest chasms beneath the northern expanse. This metal would then be smelted down in their workshop, with the entire process taking up to a month. Every day, the Icesmith would take the superheated metal and force it to drip slowly over a thin mold. Almost like a real stalactite, the Shard would slowly grow longer...sharper, and finally, when the point was thin enough to pierce other metals, it was sawed off at the base. A dark leather grip completed the infamous weapon of the Frost.

Avenir eyed his own. Each Shard had the would-be-wielder's family crest imprinted on the metal near its grip. On his own was a circle with the letter "N" carved over it. The top right segment of the "N" was arrowlike in its shape, resembling a north-pointing compass. The crest of the *Novari.*

The Council of the Seven Masters, the gods of old, was Good. Perhaps it is true that in separation they lacked perfection, just as men do, but such was the strength of the Council. Each master had absolute wisdom in his realm: Fire, Ice, Air, Water, Earth, Light, and Darkness. This Wisdom alone was not sufficient.

Avenir kept his head low as he scanned the new horizon the dune had provided for him. The cloud-muffled hue which some of the older citizens still called "the sun" was already beginning to set.

This game of cat and mouse had lasted over six hours. Flakes of the Frost were now whipping at the ice gauze strapped over his eyes.

His stomach tightened. A storm would soon be upon the dunes, and when it arrived, both he and his target would have greater problems on their hands than facing sharp weapons or ambushes.

*　　　*　　　*

4

Avenir lay prone on the crest of the dune. He could no longer see the glimmer behind the clouds. It had been completely enveloped by the billowing masses of Frost particles. He shimmied vigorously from side to side, digging himself deeper into the snow. He needed to get as low as possible: even his protective clothing would not endure the wind lash of a Frost Storm.

Within moments, the Frost flakes were beating furiously against his face. The light far above had become a mere memory, and it was increasingly difficult to tell land apart from sky. He remained motionless on the top of the dune, virtually invisible due to the constant spray of ice rushing over the crest.

"Ten...no, fifteen minutes," Avenir muttered to himself, estimating the time he had left before he would be forced to flee the area.

He had endured more storms than most who lived in Point Fire, so he knew he could likely push himself further than his adversary was willing to.

Still, I have to stay calm.

By now, the bitter cold of the storm had managed to writhe its way through the crevices in his dunerobe, and the urge to shiver began to gnaw at his muscles. All of his senses were turning shades of blue and grey. The ice within the Frost had a nasty habit of overpowering all sound and vision.

His stomach was fluttering. No single Hunter had ever managed to remain motionless as long as he could, but it seemed that the person he was playing this game of frozen chess with had no grievances about braving the danger of the storm.

Since he made his initial time estimate, Avenir had slowly been counting the seconds in his mind. Seven minutes had already passed, and still there was no indication of suspicious movement. Given the current state of the storm, this was to be suspected, but he knew that his target would soon panic and make a mistake.

There was another, though the masters refused to call him a god. Legend describes him as a mere mortal, a human who strove to achieve divinity. His name has been lost to the fray, but his occupation remains infamous: The Blacksmith. To keep the Evil - an emptiness that not even the master of Darkness can comprehend - out of the Knotted Rope, the Blacksmith sought to create weapons that would have no equal. It is said that he forged them across a timespan so vast, entire ages were no more than an Angel's Breath in the wind.

Unfathomable works of perfection, he offered his crafts to each of the Seven Masters.

"Come on, you coward," Avenir gritted through clenched teeth.

He no longer felt the cold. The numbness had worked its way into his body as far as it could go. Yet, he had never been so... *alive.* The adrenaline flowing through his veins suppressed any feelings of terror that his body was aching to convey. He remained motionless.

Eleven minutes. Is my adversary still breathing?

A streak of panic flashed across his heart.

No, I can still sense a presence.

He could feel the eye of the Frost Storm approaching quickly. Had he not been wearing full scout gear, he would have already been transformed into a frozen sculpture.

Twelve minutes.

He tightened his grip on his Shard, reassuring himself. The moment his target made a desperate move to escape, he imagined slinging his Shard like a dart, quickly incapacitating him. Unfortunately, there would not be enough time to retrieve his weapon, and he would have to beg his Icesmith to make him a fourth.

Thirteen...Fourteen...

Avenir smiled grimly. He had always known that he would probably perish out in the Frost, as all Hunters did, but so far he had never even come close... and he intended to keep it that way. But as the seething Frost pierced his skin, he could not help but recall his mother describing a death out on the dunes.

"They say that when someone is about to die in a Frost Storm, everything becomes deathly silent to them. A long time ago, one of the Icesmiths told me of the day he almost perished. All sounds of the storm vanished away into nothingness. He said it became so eerily quiet, he could even hear an ice mouse skittering away in its tunnel beneath the snow."

Avenir laughed out loud. The maniacal sound was instantly sucked away by the screaming winds. The storm was still wailing like a child, so at least he could not hear the ice mouse...yet.

Fifteen minutes.

The gravity of the situation was beginning to weigh heavily on his mind.

This madman...

Even though he struggled against it, the first sliver of terror finally managed to writhe its way through the wall of adrenaline. He knew that they were both lying motionless on the dunes, but he had never encountered this level of determination. Avenir was usually the one who the other Hunters had looked up to in terms of endurance.

Could I have finally met my match?... Sixteen.

It was beyond his time limit for retreating, but he had no intention of leaving. He had to discover, and ideally take down, whoever else had the guts to stay in the storm this long.

Twenty.

"Damn it all," Avenir breathed through chattering teeth.

For the first time, the creeping fear that this was someone who would best him tightened its cold hands around his throat.

Previously, he had been counting the seconds with ease, but now they slogged by. Every tick of time tortured him, but also gave him a brief boost of strength as he tried his best to remain motionless. Pain

shot up and down his extremities. If he did not move soon, he would be at risk for frostbite.

Twenty-three.

The eye of the storm was almost upon him. He needed to move. Guilt and embarrassment flooded his body.

How could I ever hope to become like Father...like a true Hunter?

Tears froze halfway down his cheek as he achingly climbed out of his deepened foxhole. He began his shameful retreat down the dune.

He could only hope that his adversary was feeling the same fatigue and would not be able to mount an attack. If he did, Avenir would be all but helpless. His fingers were so cold he could barely hold onto his Shard.

As he reached the bottom of the valley, he stopped and cried out in anguish. Avenir turned around and looked back up the hill.

"You need to be better. A lot better," he whispered to himself.

"If you make it out of here alive," said a nearby voice.

He felt something tighten around his ankle. He looked down in disbelief. A small glove was curled around his foot. The arm it was attached to was protruding out from the snow. Avenir sank to his knees and watched in amazement as the boy, no more than ten years old, emerged from under the powder.

"Looks like I have my first win, 'Nir," Aren gloated loudly from behind his ice gauze.

II

The most ancient and primal Weapon was a shortsword cloaked in fire - Embr. It was a tool that could only be wielded by the truly brave, as it was rumored that it would consume in flame any who harbored a hint of cowardice in their heart. It was named the True Weapon: an artifact of Destruction, and Rebirth. This Weapon was bestowed upon the Master of Fire.

The second legendary Weapon was a frigid stiletto - The Needle of Tears - an instrument so cold-hearted, no Master except that of Ice could even bear to gaze upon it. The Weapon was believed to be near useless unless the wielder had experienced a terrible and personal loss. This Weapon was bestowed upon the Master of Ice.

The third Weapon given to the Seven served as the vessel for all Hope that was possible, and it was named as such. A simple, dull-painted bow, it glowed bright when hearts swelled with inspiration. The legends tell of this bow turning the tide of all losing battles and summoning roars of melodious praise. A battle decided with the bow witnessed no further casualties, and all who took part were forgiven. This Weapon was bestowed upon the Master of Air.

Avenir could not believe that they were able to make it out of the Frost Storm unscathed. He had led his brother through what seemed like an eternity of snow flats until his body felt ready to collapse.

Now that they had reached the edge of the storm — the tiny shards of ice were no longer slashing at their dunerobes — Avenir whispered a silent thanks to their mother, who had insisted that they put on full scout gear before leaving the gates.

Aren had remained quiet during the flight from the storm, but Avenir knew that his brother was struggling to contain his gloating. Giving him a playful clap on the back, he suppressed his pride and broke the silence.

"Where'd you learn to stay under the snow like that?"

Aren immediately perked up and replied, eyes gleaming, "Sen showed me how!"

Avenir scoffed loudly.

That old bastard.

Sen had once been their father's closest friend. He was a gruff old Hunter, a man whose skills were among the best that Point Fire had to offer. After their father's disappearance, Sen had taken it upon himself to be their guardian, and although he claimed to never play favorites, Avenir knew that he harbored a certain love for Aren's unpredictable nature. His brother had always been popular with the other children for it, too.

It was a surprise to most people, Avenir included, that the two of them were indeed related. Perhaps it was in some way due to the lasting shock of their father's disappearance — something Aren could not remember, given his age — but Avenir had long since developed into a lover of rules and stability. In more ways than one, Avenir took after their father, and Aren after Sen.

"How'd you get the old guy to teach you something ridiculous like that?" asked Avenir.

"Easy." Aren laughed carefully, still conscious of his brother's jealousy. "He seemed bored one day, so I asked if we could go outside the walls. That's when he showed me."

"Sen really does play favorites, then."

"Not really," Aren quickly replied, sensing his brother's increasingly annoyed tone. "He must have been *really* bored."

"Yeah, well…" Avenir trailed off.

It hurt to speak. The frigid temperatures of the Frost Storm had blistered his throat. He did not *want* to talk anymore either.

They trudged through the snow for another hour or so. Avenir's dunerobe was tattered at the edges and his boots were becoming increasingly uncomfortable. Some snow had found its way inside them, and small blisters were beginning to form on his heels. The gauze on his eyes was also frozen over.

Every time he glanced over at Aren through the hazy gauze, he found himself becoming more and more irritated. Because his brother had stayed underneath the snow during the storm, his clothes were still unscathed, if a little damp.

The moment Avenir had spied that tiny arm protruding out of the snow, the hand clutching his ankle, he had felt utterly defeated. This was the first time his little brother had gone to these lengths during their so called "Hunter Games," a pastime that was originally Sen's idea.

Good practice, he'd said.

Usually, if a storm happened to hit the area they were in, Aren would immediately reveal himself and urge Avenir that they head back home.

What had changed?

Even though he had known that they were in great danger at the time, his pride had forbidden him from losing to his younger sibling. Thinking of this, a wave of guilt washed over Avenir.

If we had died out there, Mother would have no one.

Rivulets of freezing water dripped from the ice gauze and trickled over his cheeks.

"Are you actually crying?" Aren laughed, catching him off guard by shoving him in the ribs and sending him sprawling.

Avenir fell face first into a large heap of snow. He lay there for a few seconds, stunned. His head now underneath a cold layer of

powder, a grin forced its way across his mouth. He jumped up and swiveled around toward Aren, faking rage.

"What will Mother say when I tell her you died on the dunes?"

He lunged towards his brother, whose mischievous smirk was instantly replaced with childish terror as he tried to dodge out of the way. Aren was not quick enough and Avenir tackled him over the edge of the dune they had been walking on. The boy shrieked loudly as the two of them tumbled down the incline, ample snow leaking in underneath their dunerobes.

"Did Sen teach you *this* technique?" Avenir yelled.

Tears of laughter were now also streaming down Aren's face, mixing with the melted ice.

A solid thud, and a harsh clip over the ear, brought their laughter to a quick halt.

"What are you two scoundrels doing?" a gruff voice barked.

Avenir found himself face to face with a grizzled, ancient man. He had deep emerald eyes and a patchy beard that covered the majority of his visage. A messy distribution of ice chunks was scattered throughout his shaggy grey hair.

Tark, the elder blacksmith of Point Fire.

Regaining his bearings, Avenir noticed that they had just rolled into the blacksmith's sled, tumbling it over to one side. Aren quickly climbed out from underneath the apparatus and sheepishly joined his older brother, pulling his brown hair back into a small ponytail. He had inherited the style from his father: it had always been one of his go-tos. Avenir preferred to keep his short, citing it as an advantage when out in the Frost.

"Besides knocking some of the ore out of my sled, you've worried your mother sick," Tark grumbled, bending over to pick up some of the spilled materials. "She told me that you were both late, and that I should keep on the lookout for delinquents the likes of you. Had to pull *this* damned thing out here to boot, prevent it from being raided."

"Please, Elder." Avenir rushed to help pick up the ore and load it back onto the sled. "We ran into an unexpected Frost Storm... and things got pretty rough, so we took care in coming back."

Aren nodded in agreement.

"You think I don't know what you two get up to on the dunes?" Tark asked rhetorically.

Aren stared at his feet, avoiding eye contact with the old blacksmith.

Avenir quickly spoke up. "Do not worry Elder, I would never let anything happen to family."

He fished the last of the ore out of the deep snow and dumped it back onto the sled. Tark's eyes softened, and he placed a hand on Avenir's shoulder.

"Of course, 'Nir" – then adding quietly so Aren couldn't hear – "...just like your father." The man beckoned to Aren, pointing as he spoke, "The Point's just behind that dune over there; get back to your mother. Who can blame her for being worried? The Frost seems to be getting worse and worse every year."

The brothers thanked the old blacksmith and briskly jogged to the edge of the dune. Point Fire lay in the distance, its dark stone walls silhouetted against the ice of the Frost.

Point Fire was technically an ancient castle, although it seemed more fitting that it be called a city, since it stretched almost as far as the eye could see. Built on the shores of an endless lake frozen beneath millennia of ice, the castle stood proudly as a beacon of hope against the harshness of the Frost. A brilliant amber glow infused the clouds around the city, high above the imposing blackness of its outer walls.

As they made their way towards it, Avenir reminisced on the folk stories his parents used to tell him about their home. It was rumored that Point Fire had once been an ordinary castle: the residence of a powerful lord who oversaw the lands adjacent to a magnificent lake. Yet, when the realm froze over, the only surviving structure was the castle itself, and all the peoples of the neighboring lands were forced to move in with the lord himself. This mass immigration necessitated an expansion of the castle's grounds, and over the centuries the fortress grew to become a sprawling mass of black parapets and interlinking buildings. He and his brother were now approaching the southern tip of this metropolis.

Instead of having a single large entryway, as most castles of old were rumored to have had, Point Fire boasted innumerable small gates and nondescript doors set into its looming black walls. But the ordinary members of the population rarely used these portals. It was common knowledge that the Frost outside the city walls contained nothing but roaming animals for the Hunters. For most sane people, the Frost was a place to be avoided, not explored.

Due to the lack of any neighboring inhabited territories – or rather any signs of life at all – all trade and commerce was conducted within the boundaries of the castle between the different districts of Point Fire. Six locales surrounded the central area of the city defined by the Keep, the original lord's ancient palace. The Hunters', Crafts, Agricultural, Livestock, Cultural and Icesmiths' districts made up the rest of the settlement. Each was large enough to be called a self-contained kingdom, and each had its own appointed landlord. The two brothers knew every district like the backs of their hands.

Of course, these districts had other more popular names by which they were regularly referred to. The Crafts district was named after the legendary architect of Point Fire's outer battlements, Therach Fynn. He had been a genius stonemason, responsible for building the ominous black walls that that now lay before them. Ironically, these looming, protective walls would never serve any real purpose, given the lack of any other known human settlements or threats.

The Agriculture and Livestock districts were simply called the North and South Side, respectively. Somehow, these names were interchangeable, because without the stone wall dividing the two areas it would be difficult to tell where the sickly grazing pastures ended, and where the wilting plantations began. The earth in these areas had turned all but a greyish hue.

Fittingly, "the Grey" was the name given to the district of the Icesmiths, because that was the only color that could rationally describe it. This area stood in direct opposition to "the Pit," the self-deprecating name given to the Cultural district, a place that always bustled with over-activity. The Hunters' district was simply called as it was. Hunter was a name powerful enough.

Avenir could now make out the finer details of the southernmost districts as they continued down the slopes towards the stonework city: the stark contrast between the quietness of the South Side and the brightness of the Pit, and the smoky tendrils rising from the Hunters'. Behind these areas, the Keep shone outwards like a ruby beacon.

The king of Point Fire resided in the Keep with the rest of the royal family, ensuring that all the districts interacted favorably with one another. The current monarch, Luxus II, who had been the ruler of Point Fire for over half a century, had not yet conceded any signs of weakness. Citizens looked up to him as a symbol of stability, something in great demand as of late especially with the conditions in the Frost worsening with no foreseeable end.

Avenir smiled widely as he admired the orange light leaking out into the sky from above the city's walls. Point Fire was kept warm through the endless winter by a single source of power: the legendary sword, Embr. Held deep within the bowels of the Keep, the Great Weapon was confined to a large, crystal-lined chamber from which countless fireproof pipes and heat aqueducts emerged. These outlets spread across the city and served as the sole lines of warmth and energy for every need in every district.

From what Avenir could remember from his childhood schooling, the Sword had been sealed in its holding chamber ever since the onset of the Frost, countless centuries ago, and had never been disturbed. The sheer amount of heat generated by the Sword was capable of melting stone instantly, and thus it had always remained encased in its crystal prison at the center of the city.

Avenir continued to lead Aren down the incline of the expansive snow flats towards Point Fire. The sight before him, as always, was awe-inspiring. He could trace the red lines of crystal-enclosed warmth spreading out from around the massive Keep. They crept down the walls as large steaming arteries that spilled into a branching network of narrowing capillaries which lined the streets of the city, entering every home and workshop around the districts. The contrast between the orange of the glowing heat lines and the pitch black of the palace's stone walls was a dizzying sight.

The Keep served as the living powerhouse of the city. It was a strange construction, having only one entrance. No other windows or doors could be used to reach open air once inside the building. Avenir could not recall the exact reason why, but he knew part of it had something to do with the immense amounts of heat travelling upwards from the Great Sword below its foundations. One opening anywhere on the building, and copious amounts of rising warmth would likely ruin the perfect air circulation that existed inside the palace. Just keeping the interior at a livable temperature required thousands of hours of work, with apprentice Hunters shuttling tons of ice from the Frost to be used as coolant. Avenir was more than glad to have put that stage of his life behind him.

At last they finally reached the edge of the castle walls. Gazing down their length, Avenir pulled his father's portal key out of his belt.

"Looks like Tark is the only one outside the walls today," he said.

"Yeah, besides us," Aren chirped.

Avenir slotted the rusted key into one of the various copper doors that lined the outskirts of the city.

"Let's get back to Mother."

Their family, though they had once lived in the Hunters' district, now stayed in a small fort within the Fynn. After their father disappeared, their mother could not bear to remain with the other Hunters.

The Hunters' district bordered the southern outskirts, and Avenir smiled as they entered into it through the small opening. Although their mother had begged them not to follow in their father's footsteps, both Avenir and Aren knew that it was inevitable that they join his profession. Besides, Avenir was terrible at making things or herding animals, and Aren was too much of a wild child to think of doing anything else.

A familiar and poignant smell enveloped them immediately. The telltale odors of animal oils, salves, and poison houses wafted over them. Avenir inhaled deeply, taking in the stench. There were few smells that he loved as much as this.

The district was infamous for being the most dangerous of the six, but he had long since become accustomed to it. Things were only dangerous, he believed, when one did not expect them, and he had by far enough experience dealing with the various undesirables in the area. Yet, he still held Aren close. Although he was a Hunter prodigy in the making, his brother was still a child.

It was unusually quiet in the outskirts that day, and the only other people they passed were a group of six Hunters gearing up for a short expedition.

Leaving at dusk. A short run.

The burly men and women nodded in Avenir's direction as they walked by. But when they spotted Aren next to him, they broke into hearty laughter.

Aren shouted in response, "How's it going Julnd? Hey Viktor!"

The Hunters all smiled widely, displaying their yellowed teeth.

"Running around in the Frost with your brother again, I see," one remarked.

"Yup," Aren beamed. "And I beat him in a Hunt Game too!"

Suddenly feeling a bit ashamed, Aren turned his head towards Avenir, scanning his brother's face for signs of anger. He was blushing bright red but managed not to say anything.

"Maybe someday you'll have to take care of *him*," Julnd teased playfully.

17

Avenir found his voice, "He's still got a long way to go before that happens."

Viktor pursed his lips, "Straight-edged as always."

Avenir forced a laugh and tugged at Aren to follow. The Hunters turned back to their sleds and continued to take inventory.

This far out from the Keep, the heat lines were only about a finger wide, and as a result, the entire area was colder than most others. Avenir had learned to love the cold air enveloping the Hunters' district, and he guessed that Aren felt the same. Life near the center of the city was suffocatingly warm. It was too...artificial.

When he was younger, Avenir and his brother had loved to find an especially thick line of heat emerging from the central Keep. They would follow the glowing orange tube as far as they could. Usually they would end up at the outskirts of the Hunters' district – the area they were in now – but sometimes they found themselves far into the North Side, a section of the castle grounds that most people avoided.

Because of their childhood travels, and much to the anxiety of their mother, the two brothers had earned themselves a respectable amount of fame — more likely infamy — throughout the castle's territory. It was now almost guaranteed that someone would notice them and smile, or wave warmly, or frown in annoyance.

Aren yanked on Avenir's tattered dunerobe. "Hey, can we go check out Yugo's shop?" Avenir game him a look. "I promise I'll be quick," Aren added knowingly.

He was nodding his head in the direction of a house-sized stone block jutting out from the side of some eroded greyish-black walls. Bronze-cast lettering was hammered into the granite near the entrance: *"Yugo's Poisons."*

Avenir sighed in exasperation, corralling his brother away from the rusty door.

"No. You know that Mother is probably getting more worried by the minute. Can you at least act your age until we get back?"

Aren echoed his brother's sigh, allowing himself to be pulled away from the grim storefront.

"Can we at least stop by the Heart? I haven't been there in ages." He jabbed his brother in the ribs. "Plus, it's on the way home, so it doesn't really matter anyway."

"Fine. But if Mother is in bad shape, you are *not* blaming this on me."

The two continued through the Hunters' district, appreciating the sights and smells that clung to the men and women who had dedicated their lives to the protection of Point Fire. Though Avenir had begged their mother many times to allow their family to move back to the area, he could understand her reluctance. The district, although somewhat hearty, would certainly prove too much for a long-grieving widow.

As of late, the mood around the city had been severely dampened. Now having firsthand experience of one of the newer, more frequent, and more merciless Frost Storms, Avenir could feel the glumness invading his own mind. For the past two years, the storms had been coming with no end in sight. The age-old pattern of relative stillness broken by sporadic blizzards had long since come and gone. In the Hunters' district, which lay directly adjacent to the horizonless wastes of the Frost, many had already come to fear the increasing cold. Although still very much alive, it was almost as if the area's once head-numbingly vibrant atmosphere had been smothered by a blanket of snow.

The heat-lines had thickened to about the size of a person. They were nearing the Keep, and Heart, of Point Fire.

"When last did you get a look at it?" Aren questioned.

Avenir furrowed his brow. "Years ago, probably. I went more often before Father left.

Aren frowned as well. He hated it when his older brother called it "leaving" instead of "disappearing."

Aren forced a smile. "Well, good then. Maybe they've built some cool upgrades or something–"

"We're here," Avenir interrupted. "Keep close."

In front of them swirled a throng of people. Merchants hawked their wares and beautiful temptresses slinked around the shadows of the dark walls, beckoning tired Hunters towards them. Their jewelry glinted in the light of the now-swollen heat lines. The worn black stone of the Hunters' district had already morphed into a reflective obsidian color. It shone brilliantly among the commotion.

All around them, people were exchanging various amounts of a bright orange liquid, a substance that most citizens simply called "Blood." The currency had earned its name through the manner in which it was created – by "Bloodletting" the heat lines.

The largest heat lines near the center of the Keep leaked at a slow, albeit constant rate. If harvested correctly, evaporation of the superheated fluid within could be avoided, allowing for the distillation and production of Point Fire's only currency. The entire process would cool the substance, creating the easily dividable legal tender used all around the city.

Of course, some people had tried forging their own Blood illegally. However, the harvesting process itself was extremely intricate and required large amounts of expertise and specialized machinery. If done imperfectly, the resultant Blood would be dull in color, and would therefore also ruin any "true" Blood that it was mixed with. Dull Blood was essentially useless in all but the shadiest transactions, not to mention that illegally cutting heat lines was a grievous crime, punishable by death. The royal family ran a tight economic ship, and their treasurers ensured that the levels of Blood in the city were always kept in check, taxing or rationing the populace as needed.

Most citizens wore small gourd-like containers around their belts, transporting various amounts of the liquid. While some had separate vats of it at home, most had their wealth stored in the Central Vault of Point Fire. There, they could deposit and withdraw Blood as they wished, with the bulk of the currency being housed in enormous and heavily guarded storage tanks.

On the streets, Rich nobles might display two or three gourds, sometimes made of unique tempered glass so as to flaunt their wealth. Peasants carried small leather pouches that were almost empty.

Avenir had always loved the glow of Blood as a young child. It had been somewhat surreal, yet satisfying, to watch the adults pay for food, clothes, or rent, as they poured the bright orange elixir into a recipient's gourd. He could still vividly recall the first time he saw a shopkeeper receive a large amount of Blood.

The man had hurried back behind his counter, greedily emptying his profits into one of many glowing storage vats. The currency was perfect: easily divisible with standard measuring units, yet fragile enough to ensure that none of it went to waste.

The noise levels around the two brothers was escalating rapidly. The bottleneck creating the milling crowds lay just ahead: a sixty-foot tall dark iron gate bolted wide open, permanently welcoming anyone inside. They had reached the portal to the Circle.

III

The fourth Weapon came to be called Whispr. Like the Master who wielded it, it was the smallest of the Seven. What it lacked in force, it made up for in form. The point of the blade was known to be so sharp that the instrument would simply fall out of existence if dropped. This Weapon was bestowed upon the Master of Water.

The fifth Weapon was a ceremonial greatsword. Named Prayr, it was a tool so intricate that any attempt to use it towards violent ends would shatter it instantly, rendering it useless. It thus became known as the instrument of piety: a symbol of the peace to be kept in all realms. This Weapon was bestowed upon the Master of Earth.

Its vengeful brother, the sixth Weapon, was an aspect of holy rage and chaos: a warhammer known only as Eclipse. No mortal man could bear to look upon its vengeful glory. This Weapon was bestowed upon the Master of Light.

The final Weapon - that which was given to the Master of Darkness - has never been seen, not even by the other Six Masters.

The sprawling area surrounding the Keep slumbered during the day and came alive as the decades-fading sun set behind the city's walls. Roads coming from each of the six districts' iron gates flowed into a

23

wide highway that encircled the royal palace. At nighttime, the Keep pulsated brightly, like the beating heart of the castle, sending its warmth down the closed heat-lines to their furthest reaches.

The enormous highway, or the Circle as it was called, served as the marketplace and trading center for all districts, as well as the primary entertainment hub of Point Fire. The air was always oppressively warm there, a by-product of its proximity to the Keep. Carts and stores from each district lined the outer lip of the ring, while gambling houses, taverns, and bureaucratic halls densely populated the inner lip. The royal palace rose into the skies at the very center of the Circle, surrounded by the pulsing orange moat of heat-lines. Multiple arched stone bridges spanned the width of the glowing moat, leading to the Keep's looming iron gates.

After elbowing their way through the masses of marketgoers at the outer lip, the brothers began to traverse the Circle. Luckily, due to the recent Frost Storm, the inner area had become slightly less populated. People had taken cover inside the various stores and gambling houses or simply retreated to their homes around Point Fire. Avenir knew that very soon these endless crowds would be making their way back for further indulgence.

Aren had already broken free of his older brother's grip and was scurrying back and forth between the Hunters' storefronts that lined the nearby walls. The young boy loved the Circle: he was much more of a people-person than Avenir.

"Come look here!" Aren shouted, hidden by the milling crowds.

Avenir groaned and began pushing through the throng towards the sound of his brother's voice. He found Aren hunched over, eyes fixated on multiple pairs of Hunting boots neatly displayed on the ground. The expertly crafted articles of clothing were made from a tight white leather. A man was looming over his brother. He had noticed that Aren was not carrying a Blood gourd and was making sure that this potential thief did not run off with his merchandise.

Aren turned to Avenir. "Please can we get these! I heard this guy say that these boots are the lightest ones to ever come out of the Hunters', plus they aren't even that expensive..."

He trailed off when he saw Avenir's expression.

Avenir turned to the man. "Sorry, but we really must be getting home."

The man sniffed at them as Avenir dragged Aren back into the crowds towards the center of the Circle. The sky had already turned dark, and the entire marketplace was now lit by the pulsating warmth of its center.

Avenir found himself becoming slightly nervous: they would be going back to the Fynn across the bridges, a route he had not taken for many months. There, beneath the Keep, is where the Heart – and the Great Sword – of Point Fire lay.

The place reminded him too much of their father, and since his disappearance, Avenir had tried to keep away from the area underneath the royal palace. Usually he kept to the edges of the Circle, absent-mindedly eyeing the various commodities for sale.

Today, however, he felt a strong pull towards the city's hidden center. Perhaps it was just a feeling of obligation: some urge to pay respects to his father. Or maybe it was because he was still freezing and wet, and he knew that the excessive warmth there would at least dry him out.

The population inside the Circle had already increased notably, and the clamor and bustle of the night was once again approaching its peak. Avenir quickly lead Aren past the gambling houses on the Hunters' segment of the inner lip, and onto one of the bridges that spanned the moat of heat lines.

Aren gazed back towards the Circle. "It's funny how no one else ever goes on the bridges."

Avenir followed his gaze. It was true, most commoners tended to avoid the Heart of Point Fire. Those who typically used the bridges were members of royalty returning to the palace, politicians, or the occasional red-cloaked priest.

25

The Great Sword in the depths of the Heart had once held a significant religious following, but over the millennia of Point Fire's existence, most folk had come to think of the weapon as nothing more than coal to a fire. The heat provided to their homes and crafts was now a commodity taken for granted. Even so, the Church of Embr had managed to stay active somehow, with a few of the priests bringing the Sword weekly offerings to be burnt.

Avenir had read somewhere that the Heart had once been akin to a religious tourist attraction. People from all over the city would come to pray to the burning chamber. It used to be heavily guarded, as one would expect given that it was the principal source of heat and power for the city. But the royal guards stationed there had thinned in number drastically over the years, mirroring the decline of religious zealotry. The current grand total of guards actually *within* the Heart was now zero, with the only remaining security attachment consisting of a couple of men near the small trapdoor entrance. The least they could do was to make sure that the few people who did go down there were not carrying excessive weaponry or explosives. There was no written history of a disturbance occurring within the Heart for obvious reasons: attempting to even approach the Great Sword within its crystalline chamber would result in quick and fiery death.

The stone arches that made up the bridges had a certain blunt beauty to them. They cast unwavering cubic shadows which cut against the orange light. Aren skipped ahead, marveling at the pulsing heat lines down below. Avenir had already taken off his dunerobe and shouted for Aren to do the same. The warmth coming off the lines at this distance was not something to scoff at. Avenir had always imagined that this is what "sunlight" would feel like if the perpetual grey skies of the Frost ever decided to open up.

When they were about halfway across the bridge, the brothers passed by a group of lesser landlords and members of the royal family. Their customary garb shone dark black, drifting hauntingly against the subdued oranges around them. The group was arguing intensely among themselves and did not even bat an eyelid when the boys passed them.

They were now far enough towards the Keep that the cacophony of the Circle had been reduced to a dull roar. The imposing palace at the center of the moat rose high above them, an impeccably crafted mess of dark, spiraling towers. A distant smokestack marked the pinnacle of the castle. Far below, at the building's base, lay the foundation of the Keep: a regal obsidian dome which housed the royal court. The insignia of Luxus — a roaring carnelian fire — was engraved everywhere on its walls.

And far beneath this dome, Embr lies, burning.

"Alright, fine. Let's check it out. But we have to be quick," Avenir said begrudgingly.

Avenir stopped right at the base of the Keep and searched for the entrance to the Heart. After spotting it – a tiny black trapdoor off to the side of the royal court – the two quickly lifted it open and crept inside. The guards nearby turned towards them but did not seem to care.

Underneath the trapdoor sank a seemingly bottomless spiral staircase lit by rows of evenly spaced torches. Aren immediately began scuttling downwards, his footsteps ringing out loudly on the thin metallic platforms.

A few hundred steps down he almost collided with a priest, who grabbed him by the collar and was about to give him a violent clip over the head when he saw Avenir appear above them.

"Master Avenir, please keep your...brethren in check," he hissed, letting go of Aren's nape.

"Yes, Your Grace." Avenir bowed his head.

The priest smiled, his rotting teeth glinting in the flickering light from the sconces. He brushed past Avenir and continued his ascent. When the metallic footsteps no longer echoed above them, the two brothers continued downward. Avenir glared at Aren, who turned away sheepishly.

"Yes, I know. I didn't even see him in this light," Aren whispered, and then added, "I'm actually glad I didn't – he was pretty ugly."

Avenir laughed, and playfully punched Aren on the shoulder. "Watch your mouth, young one. This is sacred ground!" he chuckled sarcastically.

A few years before he disappeared, their father had become a devout member of the Church of Embr, and because of this the priests had always held a soft spot — if such a thing even existed in their hearts — for Avenir. Aren, given his wild nature, did not receive a share of their affection. Avenir secretly hated the priests, but ever since his father's disappearance he had forced himself to recognize the usefulness in maintaining a good relationship with them. He did it out of respect for his father's memory, and nothing more. Still, he hated the sickeningly courteous conversations with the occasional priest arriving on their doorstep.

As they neared the bottom of the staircase the temperature levels increased rapidly. Sweat was already dripping off Avenir's nose. Yet surprisingly, it did not seem as sweltering as it had been years ago.

"I think it actually got *cooler* down here," Avenir said, half seriously. He was breathing heavily from their extended descent.

"*I* think you're just recovering from your death in the Frost Storm," Aren jeered.

Avenir ignored this.

They passed through an open portcullis at the bottom of the stairwell. This entryway opened into a central chamber: a cavernous but somehow claustrophobic room with no windows, except for a few viewing panes facing into the Inner Sanctum. The air was filled with the hiss and quiet power of a blaze too powerful to imagine. They had arrived at the Heart.

The Heart of Point Fire was awash with orange brilliance, and the light from the flames within the Inner Sanctum writhed on the dark walls around them. A grey bouquet of freshly picked Frost Flowers lay on an offering plate near the entrance. It was a gift presumably left by the priest. The delicate petals were already cracked and wilted.

Shielding his eyes against the oppressive heat, Avenir made his way over to the viewing panes. The Inner Sanctum was the oldest constructed chamber in Point Fire, and the crystal panes showed it. Centuries of exposure to the breath of onlookers had dulled the clarity of the panels, their edges now waxen and sullied. He leaned over and moved his hand from side to side in front of the viewing pane. The fire inside followed it, mimicking every motion. It made him feel like some sort of powerful demon.

Aren was also staring through the panels. He was waving his arms around like a buffoon, making the flames dance in jagged circles.

"It's so cool," he whispered.

It was difficult to determine what *exactly* lay at the center of the Inner Sanctum due to the sheer volume of wild flames that leapt around inside. However, when there was the occasional break in intensity, one could just make out the edges of the Great Sword. Multiple raised clear crystal pedestals trapped it in a fierce grip, but even so, the outline of the Sword seemed to be vibrating with fury. It was easy to imagine that at any moment the weapon would triumphantly break free.

Unfathomably hot pyres of energy rushed out of the blade, bombarding the walls with muffled anger, and hiding the Weapon behind a shimmering haze. The hilt of the Great Sword glowed white hot behind the tumbling inferno.

After a few minutes of admiration, Avenir spoke up, "Sometimes I still can't believe something like this exists." He looked down from the panes, pointing at the archaic inscriptions below them. "Do you believe the stories?"

Underneath the selection of viewing panels were spaces for equally ancient bronze plaques. The first five were still present, but the final one was empty. It was rumored to have been stolen by a thief many years ago. The unfinished summary of the Knotted Rope's history was transcribed on the rest of them: the only written accounts of the Church of Embr's faith. The rest of it had been passed down over generations as an oral tradition. Avenir glanced at the first:

The god of this World is waiting.

He snorted. Though the Weapon itself was clearly the work of a supernatural being, he had never encountered or believed in a *god*.

Aren managed to peel his eyes away from the Great Sword, and began to read the fourth plaque, which was closest to him, out loud.

"There was another, though the Masters refused to call him a god. Legend describes him as a mere mortal – a human who strove to achieve div..." he paused, struggling to read the next word, "...Divinity? His name has been lost to the fray, but his occupation remains infamous – The Blacksmith."

"Maybe that's Tark," Avenir joked.

Aren giggled. "Makes sense. He *is* pretty old."

Avenir walked over to the fifth and last remaining plaque. He was sure that the sixth one had still been there when he had visited this place with his father, but he could not remember the words exactly. He wiped his brow. His undershirt was already damp from sweat. Even though he doubted the truth of these accounts, the words written on the fifth had always given him an uneasy feeling:

The Legendary Arms bestowed upon the Masters brought with them a Golden Age of happiness, peace, and balance. The Seven Masters, as a result of their newly gained glory and power, forgot the benevolence of their Weapons' creator. Being forgotten, emptiness and jealousy grew within the heart of the Blacksmith. He was once again alienated from the council, its members refusing him entry.

A time came when the Weapons dulled, worn down from timeless ages of use. The Masters demanded that the Blacksmith return their instruments to their original splendor, and he obliged. Burning with silent rage, he cursed the Weapons, and when the Masters greedily grasped their newly refined tools, their souls were enslaved within them, causing the Weapons to fall to the realm of mortals. The Blacksmith found himself to be the last free deity, a mortal turned immortal, a single being remaining to command the will of the Knotted Rope. This being, turned divine, turned omnipotent, rests alone, undying, at the Pinnacle of Existence. He alone holds the Knotted Rope.

Avenir's eyes wandered from the empty sixth space back to the Great Sword. The Weapon was still bucking against its shackles, and for a split second Avenir felt himself considering the ancient stories to be true.

A god, trying to escape.
He shook off the idea.

"Let's get home."

IV

"**W**here have you lowlifes come from?"

A young woman Avenir's age stood curtly in front of them, blocking their path across the bridge leading away from the Keep. Tight-fitting black leather armor hugged her thin frame. A dark robe studded with the royal insignia was draped over her shoulders. Delicate piping filled with bright Blood lined the robe, casting a brilliant light around her.

Literally wearing her wealth.

Two shining rapiers hung at her waist. Avenir sighed.

I have no time for this.

He bowed his head. "Good evening, Your Highness. We were simply paying a visit to the Heart, but we must be going, our mother must have become very worried due to our prolonged absence."

Her eyes narrowed, and she let out a forced chuckle. She had a perfectly attractive face, one that could only belong to royalty. Her bright green eyes shone out from under the straight sable hair which fell neatly around her neck. Contrasted against the orange light cast by the heat lines below them, and the robe around her shoulders, she looked like a shadowy apparition.

"Please. Drop that tone of voice. It hurts my ears to listen to someone who always sounds like they are groveling." She eyed Aren, who was hanging back behind his older brother. "Silent as usual," she sneered.

"What do you want, Luna?" Avenir said, dropping his formal tone. "I'm serious about needing to get home."

"Nothing *really*. I just found myself wondering why two of Point Fire's most infamous *Hunters* are crawling around my castle."

She put a special sarcastic emphasis on the word *Hunter*. Luna was the only daughter of the king. Aren hated her, Avenir tolerated her.

"We just got back from outside the walls. On our way home, we thought it would be nice to try and get a look at Embr. That's all."

Avenir nudged Aren and started walking back towards the Circle. Once again, Luna moved in his way to stop him.

"I haven't said you may leave yet," she barked.

"What would you like us to do, then?" Avenir asked, stifling his annoyance.

"Spar with me. Consider it a toll for being on royal grounds. You are a *Novari* aren't you?"

She unsheathed and tossed one of her rapiers towards Avenir, who instinctively caught it. She knew that mentioning his family name would get a reaction from him.

"This is ridiculous," he said under his breath.

Avenir noticed that the bridge guards had their eyes trained on him. It was not the first time that Luna had pulled a stunt like this. The princess raised her hand and signaled to the guards.

"Don't worry about them," she smiled.

A situation like this was the last thing that Avenir wanted. Ever since they were children, Luna had always held a personal grudge against him, given his natural talents in the areas she dreamed to excel in. Twenty years later, the reason was even more obvious: he (as well as Aren) was well known and loved in many of the districts for his prodigy-like adaptation to the Hunter profession. Luna, on the other hand, had always been a black sheep, an outcast of the royal family.

Unlike most of her counterparts, including her brother Luxus III, she had devoted herself to a life of combat training. Everyone knew that her father, the king, had constantly begged her over the years to instead pursue a career in politics, but it seemed that she had the correct intuitions in terms of her true talents. She herself was a combat prodigy and had long since outclassed even the highest-ranked royal guards, many of whom were now onlookers to this spectacle on the bridge.

Avenir prided himself on his aggressive swordplay and general, open combat. His father had trained him well. In plain sparring,

however, he was severely outmatched. He struggled to remember when he and Luna had last gone head to head.

Behind the tavern, perhaps?

Aren nervously moved off to the side of the bridge.

"Let's see what a *Hunter's* son can do," cajoled the princess.

Assuming a parrying stance, Luna launched forward with the rapier. Avenir barely had time to react, spinning sideways and feeling the blade whisk past his hair. He knew that Luna would not kill him, but she certainly would not mind giving him another serious injury. The scar just beneath his ribs tingled from the memory.

He stole a quick glance at the instrument she had thrown him. It was a masterwork of blacksmithing: a fine royal rapier commissioned only for the highest of guard ranks. Thin rivulets of orange semi-precious stones were inlaid along its blade.

He tightened his grip on the hilt. She had chosen her weapons carefully – rapiers heavily favored nimble combatants, perfect for someone of her skill level and build. Luna had already reset her stance and was tensing for another deadly lunge.

Since she had given him no time to adopt the correct defensive posture, Avenir knew he had to get out of range to buy time. Her rapier rushed towards his chest. He dropped directly onto his back, knocking the wind out of his lungs, and rolled towards the edge of the bridge. Jumping back to his feet, his body aching to recover from the shock, he adopted the closed stance that his father had taught him. It was a simple, yet effective defensive strategy, achieved by turning one's body completely sideways towards the opponent and focusing solely on parries. He had no intention of harming a member of royalty.

Throughout their various violent interactions over the years, Luna had always held this unspoken advantage. If Avenir so much as scratched her, the royal guard would be holding their blades to his throat within seconds.

Luna smiled, sensing his lack of malice, and launched into an all-out assault. Though Avenir had been blessed with Hunter's Vision, he had to concentrate immensely to even see the blade moving. Sparks flew as he parried each jab, the royal rapiers glinting orange as they danced though the night air. After the eighth parry, Luna tilted her rapier at an unusual angle, and before Avenir could react to this shift she punched him squarely in the face, making sure to use the pommel to maximize the damage inflicted during her follow-through. Avenir reeled to his side, struggling to maintain his stance. Blood dripped from his nose.

"'Nir!" Aren yelled, nervous.

"I'm fine," Avenir spat.

By now, a small group of people had gathered around them. Guards stood solemnly on the Keep's side of the bridge as the commoners and marketgoers began to gather on the Circle's edge.

"I've got half a Small of Blood that he makes a comeback!" proclaimed a beady-eyed merchant, daring the other onlookers to take his bet.

"Ridiculous! Luna wins. Two Smalls!" another man countered.

Avenir could tell Luna loved the attention.

"Well that was pretty embarrassing," she crooned. "I take it you haven't been punched in a sword fight before?"

Avenir smiled coldly. "Don't worry about it. If you didn't have your royal friends watching, this fight would already be over."

Luna's expression changed immediately. "I'll send word to the healers that they are going to be needed *very* soon."

Avenir made a quick backwards glance. She had him near the edge of the bridge. Aren was still behind her, standing timidly next to the opposite railing.

Without warning, she began jabbing again with the rapier. Although they were all deadly in their own respect, Avenir knew that these jabs were merely probing movements. She was testing his defenses, and when she found the weak point, she would put her full effort into a single finishing strike.

As their blades continued to clash, Avenir found himself being pushed towards the edge of the walkway. He would have to gain a new position, or she would find an easy opportunity to land her finisher. Between parries, he managed another glance to the side. The small group of spectators had already grown into a crowd, with adults and

children alike cheering and gazing in wonder at the spectacle before them. Because of this, his lateral movement paths had become completely cut off. There was no way to conduct the fight other than head-on.

Luna's face was cast in a state of confident bliss, bordering on the maniacal. She continued her relentless assault, the silence of her jabs interrupted by the screeching noise of Avenir's blade.

His body was completely fatigued. The Hunter's Game in the Frost Storm had finally caught up to him, and his arms and legs were aching terribly. Now within arm's reach of the railing behind him, he found himself slowing down. Luna noticed the weakness in his defenses. Avenir steeled himself, preparing for the worst. In one swift movement, she crouched, hugging the ground, and jabbed upward at a blinding pace. It was a carefully calculated attack – there was no space to the sides of her target and the only way to dodge an attack of this style was to either shift backwards or counterattack. She knew that Avenir would not do the latter, and he was up against the rails of the bridge. He was trapped.

Acting purely on instinct, Avenir jumped diagonally upwards in retreat. Time slowed to a crawl as he saw the walkway of the bridge pan out from under him. Either by sheer luck, or the grace of the Seven, when his feet came back down, they landed firmly on the moat's railing. The heat lines far below pulsed steadily. He teetered for a few moments, then regained his balance. The crowd erupted into a roar of applause.

Avenir gasped. "That's it right? You've won, Your Highness."

The risky jump had given him a surge of adrenaline, but he knew his fatigue would soon catch up again.

The princess did not appear satisfied. Avenir had just successfully won the heart of every person in the crowd. Even the guards had perked up and now spoke quietly amongst themselves about his death-defying maneuver.

"This is combat. It only ends when one of us can no longer stand," Luna stated bluntly.

At these words, one of the guards, presumably the highest ranked, moved forward to intervene.

"If you interrupt this, there will be consequences," she snapped.

And then, to everyone's horror, Luna jumped onto the same railing. Her glowing black cape billowed upwards from the heat waves below. The entire bridge was now filling with people, and there was a bloodthirsty hum of fear and excitement in the air. Avenir was no longer certain if death was off the table. Luna seemed to have gone insane, driven by the mob that was now cheering her on. He needed to get off the railing, and fast.

"Let's test his balance!" Luna called out to the crowd, egging them on.

She quickly jabbed her blade in Avenir's general direction. He parried it easily but miscalculated the resultant change in his center of gravity. His right foot left the railing and for a few moments he swayed on the brink of death. At this point, the crowd was out of control. Guards were flooding out of the Keep, responding to the increase in noise and activity around the royal grounds.

Luna waited for him to regain his balance, savoring the moment. She gave him no further time to rest and jabbed again. This time he did not parry, and he ducked beneath the sharp point. Each movement they made was echoed in the cheers of the spectators.

Avenir had had enough. He retaliated with his own rapier, a quick riposte. The attack was weak due to his lack of energy, and Luna nimbly hopped backwards to avoid the strike... but it had given him the time he needed. Before she could counterattack, he leapt off the rail back onto the walkway. As he turned around, he saw Luna on her haunches ready to pounce.

"You've lost!" she cackled.

Luna jumped off the railing in a magnificent arc. At its apex, she pulled her sword-arm back as if she were holding a javelin, tensing her muscles to deliver the final blow. The noise of the crowd mimicked the arc, now at its peak. Avenir knew he would not be able to dodge in time. He braced himself for pain and closed his eyes.

39

The moment passed and he felt nothing. The crowd had become completely silent. He opened his eyes and his jaw dropped. Aren stood between Avenir and Luna, his gloved hand firmly gripping the shaft of a rapier – the one that was pointed at his older brother's chest. In his other hand was Avenir's Shard. The point was touching Luna's neck. Like a lazy stream, a small rivulet of blood appeared and slowly wound its way downward. Luna immediately let go of her weapon. Aren did too. The clang of metal on stone echoed in the silence.

The crowd went berserk. They rushed forward towards the brothers, screaming and applauding. The swell of people was partly cut short by a unit of royal soldiers who beat them back. Two guards already had their swords pointed at Aren's throat, and another pair of weapons was heading for Avenir's. Luna wiped the blood off her neck with a gloved hand. She was fighting back a look of utter surprise. Avenir dared not make eye contact with her.

"Let... them go," she stated in a flat tone.

She turned her back and strode off towards the Keep, her black, yet glowing cape flowing behind her. The guards obeyed, lowering their weapons. The crowd instantly engulfed the two brothers.

V

"**F**inish your soup, Aren."

They were sitting around the wooden table in the kitchen. Aren stared at his bowl, stirring its contents guiltily. Their mother, who was sitting across from him, was fuming.

"By the way," she added, "you are not leaving this district for at least another month."

Aren groaned loudly. Avenir snorted and shot his younger brother a look of mock-grief. Although he did feel some of Aren's disappointment, part of him was glad that their mother was coming down as hard as she was. Aren was lucky that he had not been seriously injured or thrown into the dungeon. He did look miserable enough, though.

"Mom, please!" Aren whined. "I didn't even do anything!" He turned to Avenir, "'Nir should also be trouble – *he* was fighting her the whole time!"

Avenir laughed incredulously. "But I didn't *injure* the *princess.*"

After the abrupt end to the episode with Luna, countless cheering children and laughing merchants had swarmed the two boys. Public duels weren't a terribly rare occurrence in the Circle, but it was not every day that the princess herself was caught in one of them, not to mention that the duel was brought to a close by a ten-year-old.

Eventually, when the inspired onlookers began to dissipate, the brothers had made their way back to their home district – the Fynn – as fast as possible. Though he had thanked him at the time, Avenir had warned Aren that their mother would most likely place the blame solely on him. It seemed now that Aren had forgotten this warning and was acting childish again.

"What am I going to do in the Fynn for a whole month? There's nothing interesting in this place."

Aren was still sulking, twiddling the soupspoon in his broth.

"Stop complaining and eat your dinner. You will be helping us weave containers down in the eastern quadrant. You will also be going to school, in the Pit. It should make for a nice change," their mother explained angrily. "Aren, have your soup before it gets cold."

Aren shot Avenir a dirty look – his older brother was fighting to suppress his laughter. It was a rare occasion to see his mother selectively angry at Aren, and he was savoring every moment of it.

Their mother noticed and smiled a warning. "Do you want to help weave too, 'Nir?"

Avenir choked on his broth. This time it was Aren's turn to laugh.

Her expression became serious. "Before you can laugh any more, Aren, you need to think long and hard about what you've done. You could have been killed. I expect a sincere written apology to the princess by dawn."

"She started it! Plus, I had to help 'Nir..." Aren whined, looking at his mother.

He was starting to get on Avenir's nerves.

"Just do it, okay?" he interrupted.

Avenir finished his last gulp of broth – some sort of snow hare and vegetable combination – and left the table, placing the bowl in the cleaning area. The window above the washing trough overlooked the center of the Fynn, a colorful flea market with various carpets and baskets scattered between stalls. Like Aren, he did not really find the place appealing, but he had to admit that they had been truly fortunate in their living assignment.

Due to the unchanging nature of the city's architecture, every man, woman, and child in Point Fire was assigned a residence at some point in their lives. The castle-like structure had its limitations, and one of them was little to no room for further expansion. With the Frost Storms worsening over the years, the landlords were forced to proclaim that any further thinning out of the heat lines could prove dangerous to those in the outskirts. To prevent overpopulation, strict regulations were enforced by a royal decree: a maximum of two children per household. But, exceptions could always be made in the case of an unexpected lull or boom in citizen numbers.

It was unusual for a whole family to move like they had done, but due to their father's elevated rank among the Hunters, their mother, and Sen, had managed to negotiate a more-than-comfortable living space with the king.

Avenir returned to the table and kissed his mother on the cheek. "Thanks for dinner. Sorry for coming home so late."

Aren was fiddling with his dune robe clasps. He looked up. "Mom, when can I get my own Shard?"

Their mother frowned. "No more talk of weapons or fighting." Her face softened, and she added, "Let's see how well behaved you are for the next month."

Avenir slapped Aren on the shoulder as he left the kitchen. He climbed the ladder that connected to their bedroom above. He and his little brother shared a cramped space in the attic. Even though their home had a spare bedroom, it was located underground, and after an extreme amount of complaining, Aren had eventually convinced their mother to force Avenir to share the loft. Neither of them wanted to sleep in the basement.

Avenir fell hard onto his bed, a simple wooden cot. He lazily traced the tiny heat lines in the wall with his fingers. He was exhausted. Although the company of his brother did annoy him from time to time, he still loved the attic room. On days like this, when their mother made a really good meal, the space would fill with the aroma of delicious food. Falling asleep was the easiest thing in the world when all you could smell was cooked meat. Downstairs, he could hear Aren complaining again.

As soon as they got home, their mother had given them a fierce talking-to. The news of the duel had already made its way around the city by that time. His mother had then taken Aren into a separate chamber and scolded him for injuring the royalty. The whole time Avenir could hear Aren complaining that "He didn't mean it" and that "He did it to save 'Nir."

He felt sympathy for his brother's situation. Had the roles been reversed, he most definitely would have also intervened. However, Avenir was not so sure that he would have been able to pull it off as flawlessly as Aren did. In all his years of dueling, fighting, and Hunting, he had never seen someone grab a rapier like that. Not only did it require inhuman speed, but it also meant that Aren had been willing to risk serious injury. He must have gripped the weapon so hard that the blade stopped moving as soon as his hand closed.

Avenir never wanted to admit it out loud, but that boy was a true Hunter. If he continued in his training, he would be without equal in Point Fire. Part of him was proud of his little brother, but another part was jealous. It felt sadly ironic that Aren, who had never known their father – the legendary Hunter of Point Fire – could grow up to best him.

Someone blew out the candles in the kitchen and the attic turned dark. The heat lines now looked like incandescent spider webs, tracing their way intricately along the walls. Avenir rolled over; he could hear his brother coming up the ladder. By the time Aren reached the top, he had already fallen asleep.

VI

Things went quiet during the following month. Aren was off at school in the Pit, learning about Point Fire's long history, and Avenir continued with his regular routine. All the while, the city itself was getting colder. Everyone felt it. The heat lines in the outskirts, especially those in the fringe areas like the Hunters' district, pulsed with a lower intensity than before. Even Avenir felt a frigid chill rush through his body one morning, when he was fetching some Frost hares from the market. It was the first time in a long while in which the true cold of the Frost had touched him *within* the walls of Point Fire. Still, there had not been a Frost Storm for a few weeks, though people feared the next one to come.

As for the royal debacle on the bridge, surprisingly little was made of it. Apart from the occasional whisper of passersby when Avenir escorted Aren to school, most people either did not seem to remember it, or even care. Luckily for Aren, they all had Frost Storms on their minds.

Avenir was sitting on the dreary stone wall separating the Livestock from the Agriculture districts: the division between the South and North sides. He had just walked with Aren to his school in the Pit – an exceedingly boring, rectangular hunk of masonry – and had decided that he deserved some time off.

Besides the Hunters' district, and the endless expanse of Frost outside the walls, this was Avenir's favorite place to unwind. It could only be accessed by shimmying up between two adjacent forts and then traversing a semi-perilous shingled roof...but the destination was well worth the risk. Besides being a perfect hiding spot, the thick segment of dividing wall offered a beautiful view of the grey plantations to the north and the grazing fields to the south. Yet, the best part was that the wall itself served as one of many physical aqueducts for an arterial heat line travelling outwards from the Heart. Avenir could lie here for hours, enjoying the pulsating warmth coursing beneath the black stone. It baked his skin softly through the thick material of his dunerobe.

A major Hunt would occur within the fortnight, and he could already feel the premature excitement building up within him. Sen had personally invited him to join the other tasked Hunters.

Aren was still too young to participate in a full-blown excursion. The principal duties of the younger and more inexperienced Hunters involved checking the daily small-game traps and lures. Although mind-numbing, this job was integral to the food-supply of the city, providing well over thirty percent of it. Avenir thanked the Seven that he had grown out of this responsibility.

Due to the recently increasing risk of disease and starvation that the strange onset of extreme coldness presented, almost twenty Hunters had been recruited to take down as many animals as possible and to bring them back to Point Fire. This time there would be no room for smaller catches like snow hares. Frost Flyers and even wild Sabers were now the targets of choice.

Avenir could vividly remember the first time he saw a Flyer moving at full speed. His father had passed him his telescope and told him to look carefully along the crest of a particularly oblong dune. Both he and his father possessed Hunter's Vision, but even with this rare talent, he had struggled to make out the beast that lay at the dune's peak. It looked sort of like the animal he had learnt about in history lessons — something called a "horse" — but with claws instead of hoofs and lacking rear legs. That, and it spanned tens of feet.

"Watch this. It may be blind, but its ears are unmatched in the Frost," his father had whispered, before clapping his hands as softly as he could.

Though Avenir had been focusing entirely on the strange animal, he had almost missed what happened next. In the blink of an

eye, the Frost Flyer's front claws gripped deeply into the snow, and after a brief tensing of muscles, it launched its entire body forward at a speed too fast for regular vision to track. Tiny wings were spread out near its back. The last Avenir saw of the beast was a white blur disappearing over the dune.

Over the years, he had seen his fair share of Flyers, but this was the first Hunt he had heard of that designated the species as a principal catch. He rolled onto his stomach, enjoying the heat rising from the black stone beneath him. Gazing over the grey fields to the north, he could only just make out where the next wall began.

It was easy to forget just how large Point Fire was. One could even mistake the far northern wall for a dark mountain range on the horizon. He let his eyes drift down along the northern barricades. On the western edge of the city lay the Frost, and as he shifted his gaze further east, the view of the frozen Lake came into focus. He had always found it amusing that no one, neither royalty nor commoner, knew which expanse of ice was greater in size, the Frost, or the Lake. For all they knew, the Lake could be the *real* Frost. The only difference was that absolutely nothing lived out on the Lake.

Avenir's eyes stopped on a tall structure just west of the infinite body of ice, skirting the interior of the Point's furthest boundary.

Thin. Lonely.

It was the Cathedral – the founding monument of the Church of Embr. His father had paid regular visits there and had sometimes brought Avenir along with him. And, now that he thought about it, he had not returned since his father's disappearance.

Aren has yet to set foot inside the building.

He wondered if it was perhaps a good thing that he had avoided contact with most members of the Church for the better part of seven years. But since the recent encounter with the priest in the Heart, part of him wanted to know more, to find out the reasons for his father's involvement with such a suspicious organization. Even his father had acknowledged the eerie nature of the Church of Embr. He had always made fun of the way the priests dressed – their long crimson robes and ominous hoods – but when questioned about his personal allegiance to them, he always had the same response:

"One day you will understand."

Avenir sat up, stretching his back, which was sore from all the heavy carting he had done in the past month. Carrying carcasses between the districts was certainly taxing on the body, but not so much on the mind. He had decided he would pay the Cathedral a visit.

A break from the regularity will do me some good.

Avenir deftly slid down a segment of arched stone. Rejoining the bustle below, he made his way northeast through the dimly lit streets.

It was about an hour's walk to the palisade surrounding the Grey – the Icesmiths' district. He had managed to finish off his daily duties...or at least enough of them, to ignore the guilt of slacking for a while.

As usual, this area was near deserted. The only purpose anyone could have for coming this far would either be to visit the Icesmiths, a group of isolationists not known for their hospitality, or to travel to the Cathedral, the eerie bastion of a dying religion. Neither option was very appetizing.

Avenir steeled himself against the cold as he pushed his way through a battered copper gateway set into the northern palisade. There were no intact locks remaining here. They had all eroded a long time ago, and no one had bothered to fix them.

To his surprise, he found his heart beating faster than it usually did, even compared to a Hunt in the Frost. Something about the Cathedral had always frightened him, though he could never place his finger on exactly what it was. He knew it was not the appearance of the priests which, though menacing, only really startled small children. It was something deeper.

Uncertainty, perhaps. The ghost of my father.

After walking some distance over the harsh expanse of grey ice, he could now make out the Cathedral more easily, which lay further still to the northeast. The building, which had once been a beautiful monument to the Fire that powered the city, was now a shadow of its former self. Parts of the tower were crumbling, and many of the intricate upper flourishes had long since eroded.

The Cathedral was known for being the only structure which stood completely separate from the other constructions within the city's walls. It was the only place of dwelling that had no heat lines connected to it.

Since the creation of the Cathedral, the priests inhabiting it had consistently refused offers from the royal family to have heat lines installed. They believed that using the power of Embr for their own comfort was too indulgent, gluttonous even. Consequently, they lived in a frigid sanctuary where the only sources of heat and light came from handcrafted torches and furnaces.

And unlike the rest of Point Fire, which had been built in an oppressive and brutalist style with asymmetrical forts, imposing flying buttresses, and square black towers, the Cathedral was architecturally fluid. Up close it looked like a pyre of black flames reaching for the dismal clouds. The place of worship truly matched the element embodied by its god.

*   *   *

Flakes of ice swirled around Avenir's ankles and kicked up behind his dunerobe. In the distance he could now see red specks milling around the base of the Cathedral. They were likely priests going about their daily business. Beyond them, farther to the west, he could just make out the workshops of the Icesmiths: ugly cubes which lined the farthest possible segment of the northern wall. Directly to his east stood multiple ominous barricades against the winds from the lake. Dolosse like these lined the entire eastern border of Point Fire, beginning all the way at the bottom edge of the Pit. The winds coming from the endless expanses of the lake were known for their particular ferocity, but luckily for all those who lived in the eastern portions of their districts, they happened to be periodic and predictable, appearing every six months in a sickening monsoon of ice.

49

Avenir had a hunch that the red-robed figures had noticed his presence; they were all slowly filing back into the Cathedral. He had hoped to approach the chapel discretely to avoid commotion but must have stood out like a sore thumb against the flat expanse around him. He gauged the moving figures as a group of maybe one hundred priests. A single red outline split from the rest and made its way towards him.

When he was within earshot, Avenir called out to him, "Your Grace. I am just here to visit. There is no need for a welcoming party!"

The figure waved in a dismissive manner but did not respond. Avenir quickened his pace. The last thing he wanted was to get on the wrong side of the Church. He was not certain why they were reacting this way to the arrival of a single person, but he felt that they should not be kept waiting.

Avenir recognized the robed figure as the priest they had met on the staircase to the Heart.

Similar gait and height.

Aren had not been exaggerating when he had described the man as ugly. Short, rotting yellow teeth added to the grotesqueness of his aged face. His weathered eyes drooped downwards at their edges.

"Master Avenir, we've been expecting you."

Avenir suppressed his shock. "You must be mistaken. I have just come to pay a quick visit. Unless one of your brothers spotted me on the way here—"

"There has been a development," the priest interrupted curtly. "Please follow me."

The ancient priest turned and began walking back towards the Cathedral. Avenir hesitated, estimating the possible risk of the situation. Deciding that the priests posed no real threat, he followed.

The Cathedral loomed over them. The numerous reflective black flames that made up its structure glinted in the heavily overcast light.

"Please come in. The others are waiting." The priest motioned with his arm towards the main entrance.

The door itself was covered with brilliant metalwork etchings and depictions of fire. Avenir obliged, removing his hood in a gesture of respect as he stepped through the entrance.

Unsurprisingly, the interior of the building was freezing – almost as cold as the expanse outside its walls. The priest shuffled loudly past him and down one of three doorways. The one he had chosen was marked with the word "Worship" in embellished writing and led to a long tunnel flanked by torch sconces. The doorway furthest to the right was labeled "Caverns," and the central one "Apartments." Avenir strode past the eerie torches at a brisk pace. The lack of natural light in this place was making him uneasy. He could understand why a young child would hate coming here.

But why was it never this ominous to me as a child?

The tunnel opened abruptly into an echoing amphitheater. Row after row of hard wooden pews were stacked upwards towards a distant ceiling. An oratory pedestal stood, as if stranded, in the middle of the chamber. The room itself was well lit by thousands of torches that lined the walls. There were no windows, and the cold metallic boundaries of the chamber eliminated any semblance of warmth that the multitudes of naked flames may have provided.

Avenir spotted the priest he had met outside taking a seat among the first few pews. With a startled jump, he discovered that the rest of the seats were all filled with crimson devotees. Countless red-robed priests sat side-by-side, filling the entire space. They were all watching him. Somehow, he had not detected the presence of hundreds of people. Avenir's hand instinctively fell to his Shard, which was tucked under his dunerobe. Based on the relative distance between him and the tunnel, he calculated a three second escape time. He tensed his legs.

"Please, Master Avenir," a deep voice boomed, "there is no need to be afraid."

A man who had been sitting in the first row stood up and walked towards the pedestal nearby Avenir. His footsteps were achingly loud amidst the complete silence of the other priests. He had shoulder-length black hair as well as an exquisite beard which was trimmed to a sharp point.

A man of neatness to the point of vanity.

He appeared too young to be a priest, but Avenir had sensed a deep wisdom in his voice.

Stepping onto the raised platform, he spoke again, "First of all, welcome back, Master Avenir! You may not remember me – we used to play as children – but know that we will always do our best to make you feel at home in the Cathedral."

The man smiled, showing off his perfect teeth. They glinted in the torchlight.

It's Kreymar.

During the few times that Avenir had come to the Cathedral with his father, there had always been one other child his age to play with: an orphan boy by the name of Kreymar. They used to play hide and seek in the various nooks, crannies, and hidden areas of the building, though his father had always forbidden him from going to the Caverns below. Yet, the man now standing in front of Avenir might as well have been a complete stranger. He still had the black hair of his younger self, but his build had changed completely. The robes which loosely flowed around the other priests hugged this man's frame tightly, betraying the exceptional physique underneath.

Perhaps a life amidst the Church of Embr is harder work than many think it to be.

"Kreymar?" Avenir questioned, astonished. Then, realizing that the man was now most likely a member of the Church, he added, "Your Grace."

Kreymar grinned again. "So, you do remember! Exceptional memory, just like your father." He waved his hand casually. "We can catch up on pleasantries later. You will see that we have more important matters to attend to."

Avenir could not believe that the man was conversing so easily in front of the hundreds of other priests staring right at them. They all remained silent.

"Brother Segur, please step forward," Kreymar boomed.

Another robed man seated in the front pew instantly obeyed and walked towards the platform. The hood of his robe was covering

his face entirely. He stopped next to them and turned to face Avenir. Kreymar lifted the hood off the other priest. Avenir had to stifle the urge to recoil in disgust. The man's face was grossly disfigured, with half of it burnt down to the bone. The blackened flesh on his jaw gave way to reveal a grimacing set of teeth underneath.

"Brother Segur has been blessed," Kreymar whispered.

He covered the man's face again with the hood. Avenir remained quiet, fighting the urge to run.

"For years Embr has remained silent," Kreymar continued, "but it appears that the Great Sword has finally begun to...*whisper* again. It speaks softly, but with *conviction*." Kreymar turned back to Segur. "Read us the message."

The monstrosity named Segur dug into his pockets to reveal a scrap of paper with writing scrawled over it. In a raspy wet voice, he read what was written on the parchment.

"Darkness. West. Damnation. Seven Years." He paused and looked Avenir dead in the eyes before uttering the last word, his face twisted in perpetual agony. "Novari."

"Thank you, Brother."

Kreymar motioned towards the priest's seat, and Segur sat down. He turned back to Avenir, who was clearly stunned at the mention of his family's name.

"Brother Segur was worshipping at the Inner Sanctum two days ago when the Sword spoke to him," Kreymar explained. "Words of great power bring with them great pain, as is expected, but fortunately our brother managed to record a few of them during the ordeal. It has remained silent for the past seven years, but it seems that Embr has maintained its obsession with your family." A tingle ran down Avenir's spine, as he sensed the words that would come next. "Your father most likely left at the call of a similar message."

Avenir forced himself to interrupt, speaking loudly so his voice echoed around the chamber. "What do you mean *most likely?*"

Kreymar paused, choosing his words carefully. "Borea never told us the exact details of the messages he received from the Great

Sword. However, he did show the marks of exchange — not nearly as bad as Brother Segur's of course — but marks all the same."

The 'accident' at the Inner Sanctum. Could it be?

A deep, boiling anger began to build within Avenir.

How can they expect me to believe such childish tales? But if there is some truth to them, then father...

"You're lying! The gods do not exist. It is only us here. Us and the Frost!" Avenir blurted out.

For the first time, a slight murmur swept its way around the amphitheater. Kreymar's eyes narrowed as he raised both hands. Silence returned to the room.

"It matters little whether you believe us or not... for the time being. We are simply telling you what we know, and it is clear from Brother Segur's message that your family is implicated in our city's destiny."

Avenir turned to leave. He had had enough of the priests' babble. It was now clear to him that the Church of Embr had no idea what transpires in the real world. Their desperate fanaticism had finally gone too far.

Brother Segur had probably tried to get inside the Inner Sanctum in his lunacy. How else would he get an absurd injury like that? And then writing that false message for dramatic effect...please.

Kreymar moved closer and placed a hand on his shoulder. Avenir tensed the muscles of his right arm, ready to deflect any type of attack.

"Master Avenir, you may be leaving for now... but there is no way you can escape the clairvoyance of the Great Sword. It has chosen your family, and we must therefore pledge our allegiance to you." He slipped a small item into Avenir's pocket. "Take this as a symbol of our servitude, so long as your family lies in Embr's favor. He who carries it shall receive our protection." He let go of Avenir's shoulder. "Farewell."

Avenir turned and walked quickly out of the cavernous room and back down the tunnel. It was only there that he took the item out of his pocket and examined it. It was a crimson medallion. An intricate image of a flame was carved into its forefront. He had half a mind to throw it to the ground, but he did not want to further anger the members of the Church – who knew what consequences *that* could unleash.

Kreymar's voice echoed behind him, sinister. "We wait for you."

Avenir regretted coming now.

To think father conversed with such lunatics...

Kreymar's words echoed in his mind: *"...left at the call of a similar message."*

He shook his head clear and pulled his hood tight as he passed through the thick metal door back out to the expanse of ice. The wind hit him hard. Steeling himself against the drafts coming from the Lake, he left the Cathedral, flakes of ice swirling around his boots.

VII

"Aren, wait for me!"

A dwarfish boy burst through the school's outer doors, tripping over his own feet. Aren was already scrambling up the side of the building walls towards the roof. Using the irregular stonework for hand and footholds, he worked his way higher and higher. The other boy reached the base of the wall a few seconds later and followed Aren's path of ascent.

His month of school was almost over. Aren had hated it. Any type of learning other than practicing his Hunting skills usually gave him a piercing headache, or so he claimed. The teachers had not taken his excuses too seriously.

But I guess just one month isn't too bad.

Most children were forced to attend school for an entire year, but Aren's mother had been remarkably lenient when it came to his distaste for formal education.

If I had been trapped like this for that long, I would have probably gone insane.

Avenir, on the other hand, had always said that he had actually liked school; it was an opinion that was beyond Aren's comprehension.

He reached the roof with ease and stood up on his tiptoes as he surveyed the surrounding area. The Pit, the smallest district of the six, made up for it with its eccentric beauty. This particular school was located right next to a cluster of glassblowing workshops. Colorful vases and candleholders littered the shelves crowding the streets below them. The workshops also imparted the area with a comfortable layer of warmth year-round, as the artisans honed their crafts to perfection. Aren was not personally interested in the trinkets and luxury objects produced in the area, but his mother had dragged him around the place many times.

Most of the studying that Aren had done over the past month was focused on the history of Point Fire. When they had come to the lesson on the Heart of the city, Aren had bragged excessively, exaggerating to the other children about how he had been there multiple times. Even their teacher, Ma'am Scallier, had never been to see the Great Sword in person. Most people preferred to avoid the royalty... and the priests.

They had just finished the module on the Walls themselves, but Aren was sure that he knew the layout of the city better than anyone, even the teachers. As soon as Ma'am Scallier had finished the lesson she had flashed a knowing look of warning directly towards Aren. Exploring the walls was one of the many taboos that Aren had boasted about.

"Hurry up Udar," Aren shouted over the edge of the walls. "We don't have a hundred years!"

"Wait... I'm almost... there."

A tiny hand had reached over the edge and started to grope around for something to hold. Aren walked over and grabbed it, pulling the small, yet chubby, boy up and over the side of the school roof.

Since the beginning of his time at school, Aren had made it his daily ritual to scale the walls and explore the surrounding area during each free period. About halfway into the month, he had noticed a tiny boy trying to follow him... and struggling. When he had finally caught his breath, the boy introduced himself as Udar, the son of a locksmith in the Fynn. He wanted Aren to show him around, and to teach him how to do the things he had become infamous for, like defeating members of royalty in hand-to-hand combat. After one look at him, Aren knew that he could never hope to excel in any physical capacity, but the boy had begged him, and he finally agreed to show him what he could.

Soon, the two of them started going everywhere together. Aren had even tried to take him to the Heart, but Udar refused to go any further than the moat bridge.

On one occasion, they had found an abandoned section of the city near the southern end of Point Fire, right below the Pit. Aren had spotted an ancient-looking copper door in the side of one of the crumbling walls. Unfortunately, when he tried it, the door had been locked. Udar had smiled shyly and proceeded to deftly pick the mechanism. They did not find anything spectacular inside – just a few old bowls – but Aren had been stunned by the other boy's magnificent skill. After that moment, they became best of friends.

Udar brushed some grime off his robes. "I swear that climb gets harder every time."

"Maybe you've just gotten smaller," Aren teased.

Udar laughed quietly. "You're not that tall yourself, you know."

Aren ignored this and scuttled over to the opposite edge, keeping his head low. Any students spotted climbing in restricted areas were sure to end up in a world of trouble. He had not been caught yet and was not keen on breaking that streak today. Udar followed suit, joining him at the overhang.

"Where to?" the small boy whispered excitedly.

Aren squinted his eyes as he scanned over the jutting roofs and outcroppings in the immediate area. A long strip of flattened stonework caught his attention.

"We don't have that much time today. I think Ma'am wants to start class kind of early. What do you think about trying to get inside that glassblowing warehouse?"

Udar's eyes lit up. "Lead the way."

Aren tucked the ends of his robes tightly into his pants. "Alright, let's see what we can do."

Peering over the ledge again, he made sure that no one was watching from the streets. Satisfied, Aren hopped over a gap to another roof. He landed without making a sound. Udar bit his lip and looked down. A fall from this height would result in a few broken bones... at best.

"Come on!" Aren hissed. "How many times have you done this?"

After pausing for a moment, Udar jumped. He made it over the gap easily, but when he landed on the opposite roof's tiles, a loud crack echoed outward from the impact. Aren grabbed him by his robe and pulled him prone. He glanced over the adjacent ledge. Somehow, no one had heard the noise.

"Land on the balls of your feet," Aren groaned, "...if you don't want to get caught."

Shaken by the bad landing, Udar quickly nodded in agreement. They were now outside the school's grounds. Leaving the boundaries was not really an issue, but leaving by rooftop... that was another deal altogether.

They crept over the top of the building towards the place Aren had spotted. The flat roof of the warehouse was not too far away. Aren estimated that they would be able to make it over in about three or four more jumps.

Things went smoothly, and stealthily, for the rest of the journey. Though Udar was still a novice climber, he was a fast learner, and he tried his best to take Aren's advice to heart. His petite frame worked in his favor, allowing him to remain out of sight even in the case of the occasional error. Once they made it over the top of the warehouse's smooth surface, they took a quick break.

"I've seen this building from the ground a few times. It looked pretty cool," Aren said as he crawled to the edge and squinted downwards. "I think there are openings just below us."

Udar shimmied over and joined Aren in his gaze. What looked to be the edges of a windowpane protruded outwards from below.

"Alright. Make sure my feet don't slip."

Aren tipped his entire body face first over the edge. Udar almost screamed in terror. Then he noticed that the tops of Aren's boots were serving as anchor points on the roof. The rest of his body lay vertically downwards along the side of the warehouse. Aren's face

was against the wall. Udar gulped and hastily clamped his hands over Aren's soles to make sure that his feet did not slip. He could hear his friend fiddling with the window down below. A quiet creak came next.

Aren gasped. "I got it. You can let go."

"Are...Are you sure?" Udar's voice was trembling.

"Don't worry, I won't die. Quick, before someone comes."

Udar forced himself to let go of Aren's feet. They instantly disappeared over the edge as Aren swung his body around, heels over head. Udar suppressed a cry, first of fear, then of admiration. Aren was now holding the bottom of the window - which was open - and his feet were below him, placed against the black stone walls of the warehouse. He slithered in through the opening like a lizard.

"There's shelving just below the window." Aren's voice called out from inside the building. "No one's here. Okay, lower your feet to me - I'll pull you in."

"How's that supposed to work?"

"Udar. Just trust me, come on."

Udar sighed heavily and lowered his legs gingerly towards the top of the window. Aren had the tendency to forget that normal people were not able to pull off ridiculous feats of agility. A pair of hands appeared under Udar's feet, providing a stable base.

Aren's voice followed. "Put your weight on my hands, I'll bring you down."

Slowly but surely, Aren lowered Udar to the windowsill. Once his feet touched down, Aren yanked him roughly through the window and into the warehouse. Udar landed with a thump, and nearly panicked when he saw how high up they were. Aren's hand clamped his mouth shut.

"Check it out!" Aren hissed, eyes glowing.

Below the tall stack of shelves they were sitting on, lay row after row of neatly packed glass containers. Intricate and brilliantly shining vases stood to attention, stretching across the entire warehouse. Most of them were various shades of orange or red, but some were glassy black and reflected the other vibrant colors in sparkling rainbows.

"Do you know what these are?" Udar peeped.

"Let's just say that if we break any, we're dead," Aren whispered.

He flipped himself over the edge of the shelf they were sitting on and clambered down to the floor of the warehouse. Once at the bottom, he double-checked to make sure that no one was within earshot.

"These are royal ornaments!" he announced loudly.

He began walking up and down the rows of glistening glass.

Udar slowly climbed down the shelves. His hands were trembling – one wrong move and the entire shelf would come crashing down. He was sweating profusely by the time his feet finally reached the ground. Udar stared incredulously at Aren, wondering how his friend had done that so easily.

"Took you long enough." Aren was cantering back towards Udar, tossing a small ebony-colored jar between his hands.

"What's that?"

"I found it over there. Maybe they were defects or something? Had cracks in them. I'm sure they won't mind if someone *disposed* of them. I got one for you as well." He patted his dunerobe pocket.

Udar's eyes bulged. "You can't take it! If someone finds out it was you, the royal guard will punish your family, even if it is some kind of defect!"

"That's a lot of '*ifs,*'" Aren laughed. "I'll just make sure no one finds out. Hey, let's go check out the rest of this place."

Aren took off down one of the aisles. Udar followed. The inside of the building was indeed cavernous, boasting multiple chambers and backrooms. After a short while, they discovered a separate area which housed a large selection of decorative glass orbs. Most of them displayed the royal insignia of burning carnelian flames. Others looked more like private orders, with the names of various stores and businesses inscribed on them.

"This really is something," Udar said, amazed by the vast amount of wealth contained within the building.

"Yeah," Aren laughed. "What even are these?" he said, running his hand over a set of spherical ornaments.

"No idea. Maybe the royal children only get to play with *glass* balls," Udar joked. "We should get going soon, though. I think our break period is almost done."

"Good idea, I think the window was this wa–"

A door creaked open loudly in the distance. Aren immediately hit the ground, hiding behind a particularly eye-catching selection of glass balls. Udar remained stunned, his eyes widening. Aren grabbed his robe and pulled him down.

"Stay here. I'll see who it is."

Aren silently crawled out of the room and disappeared into the main chamber of the warehouse. Within seconds, he was back.

"We have a big problem. It's Feather."

Udar whimpered at the mention of the name. Feather was the school bully: a hulking monstrosity of a child who enjoyed making smaller children like Udar cry for mercy. He also enjoyed boasting about his family's wealth. Aren's opinion was that the boy's ridiculous name probably gave him some sort of inferiority complex.

"Well, I guess we know where all his family's money comes from," Aren whispered.

"How can you be so calm? If he catches us, we're as good as dead," Udar said, feeling like sobbing.

Aren placed a hand on his shoulder. "It's okay, we'll get out of this. You'll see."

He felt bad for his friend. Being the smallest, and weakest-looking boy at school, he had received non-stop attention from Feather since the very first day. After he became friends with a certain young Hunter, however, Feather had completely ignored Udar. Aren knew that the bully was frightened of the reputation he had garnered. After all, the news of his victory over princess Luna had spread like wildfire among the younger citizens of the city. Most of the children knew about it, and without a doubt would have embellished the tale further. Even so, if Feather caught them here, skulking around what was most likely his family's warehouse, they would indeed be as good as dead.

Aren furrowed his brow. "This is what we're going to do. There's no way out through the main doors: he's right there. I'm going to distract him and you're going to move into the next room over and pick the lock. I saw another door over there, maybe it goes outside...you should be okay picking a lock from the inside, right?"

Udar remained silent.

Aren squeezed his shoulder and whispered again. "Right?"

Udar nodded. "Right."

"When you hear a loud noise, go."

Aren crawled out the room again and took cover behind a rack of ochre vases.

Udar, you have to do this.

He scouted the rest of the warehouse through a gap between the glassware. Feather was at the far end of the building. The boy was cheerily running his hand along the rows of objects as he walked slowly towards where Aren was hiding.

I have to think of something before he gets any closer.

He thought about tipping a row of the vases over, but something as drastic as that would only be needed as a last resort. Large-scale destruction of soon-to-be-royal property was not something he wanted to add to his list of infractions.

Feather was getting closer. Aren could hear him humming a non-descript tune as he fidgeted with the edges of the vases.

Is this what someone like him does on their lunchbreaks?

Aren's arm brushed against the two small jars stored in his robe pocket.

That's it.

He pulled one out and readied his arm to throw. If he messed this up it was all over.

These better actually be defects.

Taking one last glance through the gap to make sure that Feather was occupied, he launched the jar across the building. His heart was beating furiously. If Feather saw the jar flying through the air, he would be able to trace the trajectory back to its origin.

The object sailed across the warehouse silently, undetected, and out the window they had initially climbed through. Aren let out a sigh of relief.

63

The brittle sound of breaking glass pierced the air. Through the gap, Aren could see Feather's face morph from a look of startled surprise into a mask of anger. The hulking boy turned and jogged out the front entrance to see what had happened.

Aren heard a shuffling noise behind him: Udar was crawling as fast as he could around the corner of their hiding spot towards the other room.

"You can stand up. We have about twenty seconds," Aren hissed.

The duo got to their feet simultaneously, Aren running for the main door and Udar for the side room. When Aren reached the front entrance — a large sliding gate made from sturdy iron — he carefully peeked around the outer edge. Feather was bent over about a hundred feet away, inspecting the shattered glass. As he had guessed, there was no way they could make a run for it from here. If Feather spotted even one of them, it would be enough. He would tell his father and that would be the end of them.

Aren moved back into the warehouse and quietly pulled the main door shut. He closed the latch on the inside and locked it. Pulling one of his own lockpicks out of his pocket, he shoved the thin metal needle into the keyhole, intentionally jamming the internal mechanism.

This should prevent any key getting in from the outside. For a while at least...

Without looking back, he sprinted across the warehouse. When he was about three-quarters the way across, a shrill voice rang out from behind him, accompanied by a rattling of the latch.

"Open up! There's no way out! I might not kill you if you let me in!" Feather paused. "I'll tell my father!"

Feather began shaking the door with such force that it rattled at its hinges. Aren ignored him and kept running. He was not scared of the boy, but he did fear the punishment that the royal family would dole out if they were caught.

He turned the corner into the room where Udar should have moved. He spotted his friend kneeling next to the outer door, fidgeting furiously with the lock.

"How much lo-"

"Shh!" Udar snapped.

It was clear that Feather's screaming had made him even more nervous. Aren was feeling the pressure as well: it would not be long before Feather gave up shaking the front door and searched around the edges of the building. The lock popped open with a satisfying click. Udar gasped in relief.

"Follow me and close the door behind you," said Aren.

The main door was still rattling, so he knew they were still in the clear leaving from this back entrance. Aren rushed outside and looked for an access point to the nearby rooftops. He spotted a cramped alley lined with wooden crates. He moved over quietly and motioned for Udar to hurry. When the small boy caught up, he boosted him up onto the crates. Aren ran up the opposite wall and jumped off at a perpendicular angle. His fingers caught the upper edge of one of the crates near Udar. He paused to listen. Feather was no longer shaking the gate.

We have to move faster.

The overhang of an upper rooftop lay just above and opposite to them, across a six-foot gap. Aren did not hesitate. Leaping forwards, his hands found their grip at the far stone's edge, and he pulled himself up. He pointed back to Udar, feverishly gesturing for his friend to do the same. Udar ran across the crates and jumped. His eyes were screwed shut as his arms flailed around, blindly searching for a handhold. Aren managed to grab a hand and pulled him, monkey-grip, onto the roof. Udar was breathing heavily. They scuttled over the tiles and out of sight. Feather's cries soon melted into the background noise of the streets below.

Aren and Udar made it back to the school courtyard with a few minutes of breaktime to spare. Aren laughed loudly.

"I've never seen anyone try to make a jump like that with their eyes closed!" he said between chuckles.

"Yeah thanks, I would have been dead if you hadn't caught me." Udar paused. "I think I might take a break from our adventures for a while."

"Oh, come on. You'll feel better soon. Let's get inside."

Ma'am Scallier stood at the entrance to the school, making sure that all the children returned on time. She, like always, was dressed in an uncomfortable-looking uniform. Her face was stuck in a permanent scowl. When they passed her, she sniffed in surprise.

"Aren, I'm surprised you made it on time for a change." She turned to Udar and smiled, a rare occurrence. "Don't let him get you in trouble."

"Yes Ma'am," Udar answered politely.

Udar had admitted to Aren when they were first getting to know each other that he had purposely been a teacher's pet during the first few weeks – he had needed at least *some* sort of protection from Feather.

They ducked indoors and made their way to the main classroom. There were multiple schools in Point Fire, and each one only taught a single class of students. Though this particular academy was not at the top of the rankings, it was still an enormous privilege to attend it: one of the many benefits of having a highly ranked Hunter as a father. In total, there were just under fifty students in Aren and Udar's class.

They took their seats near the back of the lecture room. Various other children were milling about and making their way inside. Aren had not really been able to make friends with anyone other than Udar since the bridge debacle. Most of the others had become scared of him, or did not want to be associated with someone that dangerous. Ma'am Scallier herded the last of the students into the room and began the lesson.

"We will continue our module on the history of Point Fire by focusing on its neighboring geography." She pulled a weathered map down from a ceiling cabinet, displaying it to the class. "As you all know, when the Great Frost set in, countless people were forced to move out of the other territories. The lucky ones managed to make it east, creating and adding to Point Fire. The unlucky ones were never heard from again, lost to the blizzards of history. The lands they left behind make up the area of what we now call The Frost. It is a barren wasteland, but not one necessarily devoid of life... animal life that is. We do believe that Point Fire is the last remaining *human* settlement. Let's start with the southeasternmost portion of the Frost, right adjacent to our city, since it is quite simple. Most call the region: 'The Dunes.'"

Aren already found himself zoning out.

This information could have been interesting to me... if I was a baby.

He had lived his whole life in the Hunters' district, often exploring the nearby Frost, so he probably knew more about it than even Ma'am Scallier. The other children, however, had no idea what lay outside the walls. Point Fire, or even their own district, may as well have been the entire world.

"...The long and short of it is that there is nothing out there, or at least nothing within reach. Many Hunters have tried and failed to find any evidence of human life in the Frost, and we have no written record of neighboring lands far to the east. The only thing we *do* know is that in ancient times, before the onset of the Frost, those areas had once been rich in agriculture, and provided most of the sustenance for the entire territory. Let's move on here–"

The door burst open. An exhausted Feather stood panting at its opening.

"Sorry Ma'am." He was breathing heavily. "Someone broke into my father's storage and I was looking to give them a right beating when–"

Ma'am Scallier slammed the desk with her palm, bringing Feather's sentence to an instant halt.

"There will be no excuses in my class. Perhaps the Master would rather listen to them. Off with you!" She walked across the hall and closed the door in his face. "Unbelievable."

Aren grinned in Udar's direction but found that he was fast asleep in the back corner, his head resting on a raised hand.

The teacher continued. "Let's move on here." She raised her ruler and circled an area to the east of Point Fire on the map, "Does anyone know what this is?"

A girl with red hair in the front row raised her hand,

"It's the Lake, right near the Cathedral."

"Good. This is known as the Lake. Quite a simple name, but we can all agree it gets the job done. The air over the Lake is much colder than it is over the Frost, and as a result absolutely *nothing* lives there, not even animals. A few years ago, a group of Hunters attempted a search for any form of life at all... and came back empty handed. Half of their pod died to frostbite. The Lake, as of recent, has become a forbidden area, not to mention that its banks have never been accurately defined. What is mysterious is that we *do* have ancient accounts of lucrative trade agreements being made with eastern civilizations, but no records of the civilizations themselves. We can only assume that once upon a time, before the Lake turned to ice, faraway kingdoms conducted trade with our current territory over the water. Now, who can tell me where the coldest place within the Point is?"

Aren's had shot up. "That's easy. Outside the walls!"

Some of the other students giggled in response.

"Very funny, Aren. Actually, the area *underneath* the Cathedral – a place known as the Caverns – is the coldest location in Point Fire. This may be due to its close proximity to the Lake's edge. Not that anyone would really want to go there for *that* reason... a holiday at the Lake" – A cynical chuckle echoed around the classroom – "The Caverns have long since frozen over completely."

*   *   *

After what felt like an eternity, they finally heard the Master ring his bell upstairs. Aren packed up his things and joined Udar on the way out. Feather was still fuming as they passed him in the hallway.

"Still feeling sick from today's adventure?" Aren asked once they were outside.

"No, no. I'm fine now. I think I just got a little bit nervous, that's all."

"You ready to do it again tomorrow?"

Udar snorted. "I'll have to ask my stomach first."

Aren laughed and was about to leave, when he remembered the second ebony jar he had taken.

"I almost forgot. You should have this. Maybe keep it in your room as a cool souvenir of our adventure... but I don't think you should show your mother."

He handed the small container to Udar.

"Really? Thanks!" Udar beamed, tightly gripping the glistening defect.

VIII

Avenir pulled out a stool and joined the counter at the bar. It was the day before the Big Hunt. Most of the other Hunters who would be going were also seated around the tavern, reacquainting themselves with each other. He counted eighteen of the twenty who were tasked for tomorrow, including himself. Sen had said he would be on his way.

The barman slid over. "'Nir! Haven't seen you here for a while! You part of the Hunt?" His thick beard and bushy eyebrows moved in unison as he spoke.

"Yes, I'm quite excited. I've never been on something this important before." He paused, studying the other Hunters. "Worried about the risk, though. Even Sabers are on the hit-list this time." He noticed the barman was not wearing Hunters' gear. "You're choosing not to come, Darch?"

"Ach, I'm getting too old for that kind of thing. Remembering everyone's favorite drink is work enough for me." He pushed a tankard of steaming aged cider over the counter to Avenir. "Drink up. Warmest thing you'll touch for a while, from the looks of it." He nodded towards the door. "Frost's acting strange lately."

Avenir scoffed. "Thanks."

Darch slid away, attending to the other customers. Avenir turned to further survey the rest of the crowd. Those chosen for the Hunt were easily distinguishable from the regular tavern-goers. Many were already wearing full scout gear, their ice gauzes hanging at their cheeks. Most of them would not sleep tonight. Hunting pods usually left Point Fire well before dawn and many preferred to be completely awake as they left. Avenir was wearing his full gear as well, but he would make sure to get enough sleep. His father had always told him that a good rest was far more valuable than an alert start.

He was just about to doze off in his chair, dreamily watching a group of men playing cards, when Sen ducked through the tavern entrance. Standing seven feet tall, the leader of the Hunters was nearly impossible to miss. Avenir immediately stood up and walked over to greet him.

"'NIR!" Sen's voice boomed, drowning out all other noise in the tavern. "HOW ARE YOU?"

Two regular tavern-goers sitting near the door almost jumped out of their seats. Some women sitting at a nearby table burst out into hearty laughter, their Hunting gear rattling on the table. Other Hunters in the tavern joined in.

Sen was a giant, and the highest ranked Hunter in Point Fire. Everything he did or said was too loud, but in a friendly sort of way. He was beaming as he slapped Avenir on the back, knocking the wind out of him.

"Been... managing..." Avenir sputtered.

Sen burst into roaring laughter. Avenir's ears were ringing. Before he could ask what was so funny, Sen grabbed his shoulder and led him back towards the rear of the tavern. He steered Avenir towards a table where two other male Hunters were sitting.

"Here we go!" he shouted, as he let go of his vice grip on Avenir. "You boys will be working in a pod for tomorrow's hunt, randomly allocated. There's a fourth member but it looks like they would prefer a good, long, REST!"

With the last word, he raised a tankard – *where did he get that?* – towards the rest of the tavern. The men and women all raised theirs and gave a cry of approval. The towering Hunter pulled a chair out from under the table.

"Piet, Soljan, this is Avenir, Borea's son," Sen introduced him.

At the mention of his father's name, the two men raised their drinks in approval. Avenir quickly sat down. His father's name still brought back unsettling images of priests, and red robes. He had since tried to keep these out of his mind. Sen left the three of them, setting off across the tavern as he organized the other pods. His voice trailed after him like the echo of a Frost Storm.

The man named Soljan leaned back in his chair, balancing it at a careful tilt. He was remarkably slender and had uncut grey hair. His eyes were shifty and darted around in the dim light of the tavern.

He's likely our tracker.

The other man, Piet, broke the ice. "Been 'earin few rumors flyin round 'ere 'bout you fightin wit royal blud."

Avenir studied the man before answering.

Thick accent. Ties to the westernmost slice of the Hunters' district. Most likely from a poor family.

Piet had long brown hair, but it was roughly pulled into a tight bun on the top of his head. A strong jawline complemented his protruding brow. His massive hands gripped his tankard, which was at least double the size of a regular one.

"Yes, I had an interesting duel with Princess Luna on one of the bridges."

"I 'eard ye stuck a Shard to 'er neck."

Soljan answered before Avenir could, "Actually, I believe that was his brother. You know...little Aren." His voice was soft, almost feminine.

Higher accent. An eastern Hunter. I've heard tales of a master tracker before, orphaned at birth in the east.

Piet laughed boisterously. "That littl' rascal!"

Avenir could not help but feel jealous.

How does Aren even know these guys?

"I heard Avenir over here pulled a stunt no one's ever seen, though. Hopped right onto the guard rails. Sounds like something out of a children's fantasy," Soljan continued.

Avenir's pang of jealously instantly vanished.

Piet laughed harder. "If I wer ta try somethin like dat," he paused, searching for words. "Ma big tank woulda fall'n right off!"

He nudged Soljan, who was not laughing as loudly as Piet wanted. Soljan increased his volume accordingly. After Soljan stopped his forced chuckling, Avenir leaned forward in his chair.

"So, who's the fourth?"

"No idea!" Soljan shouted over Piet's laugh. "We've all been randomly allocated, as Sen said. I guess we're just going to have to find out tomorrow and make do with whoever it is."

"I see. How are we specializing tomorrow? I assume you are the tracker." Avenir sent a nod in Piet's direction. "Muscle?"

Soljan nodded in agreement. "A fair assessment. That would make you and our absent friend the killers. Wouldn't have guessed it at first – is this your first Big One?"

"Yes. I normally go with my brother to Hunt small game and teach him the basics."

"Well, let's pray to the Seven that tomorrow is successful."

Soljan raised his tankard again and downed the rest of his ale. Piet was still giggling to himself – if one could call the guttural noise he was making a giggle.

Sen reappeared next to them, holding a chair in his right hand like it was a twig. He slammed the piece of furniture on the ground and took a seat.

"I see you boys have already exchanged family secrets!" he joked. "'Nir! You like your pod?" He was practically yelling.

Avenir tried his best to match Sen's volume. "Looks like we're going to be an effective unit, even if the fourth doesn't pitch up! We've got a rather good assortment of skills!"

"That's what I like to hear!"

Sen downed the entire tankard in a heartbeat. He motioned with one finger for everyone to get closer. Avenir and the two other Hunters moved their chairs in. For the first time in an awfully long while, Avenir heard Sen speak in a lowered voice.

"Listen up boys, tomorrow *has* to succeed. Failure is completely and utterly off the table. Most people don't realize this, but we are about six failed Hunts away from the beginnings of starvation. Counting the last Big One, which was not successful by any stretch of the imagination, it could even be five."

This news came as a surprise to Avenir, but he believed it. The storms and the accompanying drops in temperature had indeed been

worsening. Even more worrying was the inexplicable cooling of the heat lines near the fringes of the city.

Sen continued, "The last Hunt didn't fail due to a lack of skill. No, it seemed as if the Frost itself wanted us to fail. *That* is why we are upgrading to higher-risk targets – we need to bring back as much as possible. That is also why there are twenty of us. The twenty best Hunters in Point Fire."

He slammed his hand down on the table in pride. Then, he seemed to remember that he was supposed to be talking quietly and leaned in again.

"That makes five pods of four. Any more would be too risky and any less would be useless."

Avenir appreciated Sen's forthcoming nature about the direness of the situation, but he wished he had not heard anything that the veteran Hunter had just said.

If even Sen is getting this serious, the situation must be far worse than it seems.

The massive Hunter started up again, "One final word before I leave: never forget that we are alone. Completely alone. In all my years as a Hunter – and believe me, I have gone deeper into the Frost than many would even dare – I have never once encountered even the hint of human life. I don't mean to frighten, but rather to inspire. The Hunters are the first and last in line to protect this city. The royal guard protects the few; we protect *all*. Feel proud of your profession and know that every living person in Point Fire needs you. Many over the Few."

With those words Sen smiled broadly and left the table, bellowing at Darch to bring him another tankard.

"You heard the man," Soljan said, combing his grey locks with his fingers. "Let's get this done."

IX

The house was completely silent when Avenir woke up. Nothing stirred. It still felt like the dead of night. He rubbed his eyes, straining to see in the darkness of the attic. Aren was sleeping quietly in his bed. He rolled out of his own and sighed. He was not exactly nervous, but part of him just wanted to get back into his warm cot and pretend that he had overslept. He hastily dressed, putting on his full scout gear. Before he climbed down the ladder, he stood beside Aren's bed and placed a hand on it.

"Be back soon."

He descended soundlessly into the kitchen. A small parcel lay on the table – a meal his mother had prepared for him to take with on the Hunt. He thanked her silently, promising his return.

Taking stock of his equipment, he performed a last-minute checkup. He touched each piece as he counted through his tools. His pocket telescope, ice pick and Shard were tucked tightly into his dunerobe's loops. A short spear was fastened to his back by a leather strap. He was more comfortable fighting with a sword, but he realized that it would be virtually useless against the type of game they were Hunting. A final weapon – his father's hunting bow – hung over his shoulder. The shortbow was nothing special, a weapon made of tense frostwood marked from years of use, but Avenir had always marveled at its reliability. It had never failed his father over the decades, and it had never failed Avenir since he began using it seven years ago.

Shrugging his shoulders to get them warmed up, he wrapped a quick-draw arrow belt around his torso. When he was done preparing, he closed his eyes and inhaled deeply. For the first time since he had been a child, he felt like he was finally following in his father's footsteps.

Someday they might even lead somewhere.

"'Nir?"

Avenir turned around. Aren was standing sleepily at the bottom of the ladder, rubbing his eyes.

"Hey, you're up early. You should get some more rest. Go back to bed."

Aren walked over and pulled Avenir's Shard from his belt. He stabbed the air playfully.

"You must be joking. On the day my brother kills some Frost Flyers? Not on your life."

Avenir snatched the Shard out of his brother's hands and shoved him playfully.

"If they don't get me first."

They laughed quietly. Waving, Avenir turned and ducked out the door.

The walk to the edge of the Hunters' district was uneventful. The few other Hunters who had chosen to sleep in their homes slowly filtered in to join Avenir as he progressed through the city. He recognized most of them from the tavern…at least the ones who had already been assigned to other pods. Minimal words were exchanged. There was no need, and it was still too early to strike up a conversation.

They eventually reached the portcullis at the outer fringe of the Hunters' district. The man at the front of the makeshift column moved forward to unlock it with his own rusty portal key. The rest of the Hunters followed through, single file.

Awaiting them was a swirling mess of people, Hunters and commoners alike, who were all getting ready for the event. Even though Avenir had been a spectator to multiple serious Hunts, it still always surprised him how many people were involved.

Apart from the obvious ones – the Hunters themselves – countless other citizens were assigned important roles to play, such as watchperson or medic. Watchpeople, who were positioned in towers on the southern wall, were responsible for spotting either returning pods, or pods that had made a successful catch. After a catch, the pod responsible for the kill would have their designated tracker fire a Flare of Embr into the sky. The watchperson would then send the signal for a group of rookie Hunters to leave on retrieval. Of course, depending on how far the pod had travelled outwards into the Frost, and the size of the animal, the muscle of the pod may have already carried the catch a significant distance back to the city.

Avenir had been on many of these retrieval missions as a child. He remembered them fondly. Everyone would start cheering when a flare lit up the distant grey sky. He could still feel the excitement he had experienced every time, as he squabbled among the other young Hunters for the right to help with retrieval. They would bring the animals back on a sled and run it all the way to the walls of Point Fire. Butchers from the South Side would then take their meaty treasure and begin portioning it into smaller chunks for storage. And all the while, festivities would run wild in the district.

The Flares of Embr were mastercrafted. Each one was made of hardened residue that had shed itself off the Great Sword in the Heart. Icesmiths were good for more than just creating Shards: they would also periodically visit a special chamber behind the Sword's Inner Sanctum to harvest this residue. To even open the door to that room required incredible resolve, and infallible equipment. After harvesting, the Icesmiths would then seal the residue in small pipes covered with the same crystal that lined the Inner Sanctum. Once opened, the Flare of Embr would shoot out violently and explode at a distance, erupting into a brilliant shower of sparks.

Avenir spotted Soljan at the other end of the commotion and made his way over to him. Halfway there, a nearby medic noticed his full scout gear and wished him luck. Avenir thanked the woman. He shuddered when she turned away to her duties again; the mere thought of having to call a medic made his blood run cold.

Medics were usually recruited from a pool of second-string Hunters. The reason for this was to give them hands-on experience in the field. Avenir had the luck of being talented enough to avoid being in that position for long, but he also had the misfortune of being summoned to the Frost more than a few times on his required shifts.

Assistance Flares were a rare sight to behold, but when their dark cloud appeared over the dunes, the entire district fell silent. These flares were near identical to the others, but also contained a payload of compressed charcoal that dyed the sky an ugly black when the flare exploded. A medic team would instantly be dispatched. While they were gone, everyone inside the walls remained on edge, waiting to see whose son or daughter had been either injured or lost.

On one of Avenir's medical summons, he had rushed out with four other Hunters, carrying medical supplies towards the cloud. It had not been too far, about a five-minute sprint, but by the time they reached the site it was too late. A startled Frost Flyer had sliced a young man's legs clean off at the waist.

"Morning, Avenir," Soljan sang. "It looks like you've managed to get a good night's rest." He dug into his pocket and revealed two flares, one Regular and one Assistance. "For you. I already gave Piet his. We're still waiting on the fourth to arrive."

Avenir jammed the flares in his belt. "You manage to get any sleep yourself?"

Soljan laughed. "I've never slept before a Hunt, and don't plan on starting a new ritual now. It keeps me alert out there." He nodded towards the outer wall.

An impossibly loud yell broke out of the crowd behind them. Avenir did not need to look to know who it was.

"'NIR!"

Avenir held out his hand before Sen had a chance to wind him again.

Shaking his hand with enough force to kill a small animal, Sen proclaimed loudly, "I see my favorite pod has arrived!"

Avenir threw a look at Soljan and quickly added, "I'm not sure we have a full pod today. It looks like our last member may have gotten cold feet."

"Don't you worry," Sen beamed. "Their arrival is almost certain."

With that he left Avenir and Soljan, moving back into the crowd and barking orders at an alarming volume. They exchanged a look.

Soljan shrugged. "Let's go find Piet."

They elbowed through the throngs of people that were now flooding into the area. Vendors from each district had already begun to set up their stalls. The familiar smell of oils and brine soon filled the air.

Besides live duels, a Big Hunt was the highest level of entertainment in Point Fire. Children chased each other beneath the legs of merchants hawking their wares, who fumed angrily when their items were knocked onto the street. Two ladies sang ancient folk tales beneath a newly erected tarp. At their feet sat an upturned hat containing a half-empty gourd of Blood. The Hunters' district had already awoken from its brief, nightly slumber.

They found Piet leaning against the outer wall, tankard in hand, flirting with some young women. When the burly man saw the rest of his pod approaching, he grinned and introduced them.

"Chardon, Fior, meet ma boys for tha day – Soljan and Avenul."

Soljan snorted at the mispronunciation.

"It's Avenir," Avenir corrected.

Piet looked surprised for an instant, then waved it off.

"Bah! Out there wer' all tha same anways."

Avenir smiled at his response. Piet would make the perfect muscle for the group: a man with nothing on his mind but his job.

"And... there will be no more of that for you." Soljan swiped the tankard out of Piet's hands.

The girls looked shocked, then snickered when Piet started laughing.

"Ah need somthin ta keep ma body warm out ther. Ye know how cold it's bin getting," he guffawed.

Soljan remained stone-faced. "Agreed. But we also need you alert... and alive."

The set-up of the district ran for another half-hour. It was still completely dark over Point Fire.

It seems even the light would prefer to sleep late in this weather.

After Soljan managed to shoo Fior and Chardon away, the three Hunters went through a full equipment check. Their gear set was identical except for one item that varied among them according to their specialization. Avenir, the killer, had his father's bow to fire at targets from long distances. Soljan, the tracker, had a pouch filled with lures and traps, and Piet, the muscle, had a sturdy-looking sled. All three of them carried a spear.

When they were satisfied that everything was ready, they joined the growing congregation of selected Hunters gathering at the center of the area. Snowflakes had begun to fall heavily: a grim indication of the conditions outside the walls.

Sen was standing on a raised platform off to one side, overseeing the whole process. In a few minutes, eighteen of the twenty elite Hunters were standing ready with the rest of their pods.

"Where's the damn fourth?" Soljan muttered, visibly irritated.

Avenir shrugged. "Wherever they are, we need them to get here right now, or we are going to have a serious lack of kill capacity out there."

Avenir had barely finished his sentence when a royal trumpet blared at the rear of the crowd of spectators. A dark coach with brilliant carnelian inlay crawled slowly through the masses. Carried by four members of the royal guard, it wound its way towards Sen's platform. More guards skirted its edges, keeping the spectators at a sword's length. When it reached the edge of the raised wooden structure, the side door swung open and Luna stepped out, her obsidian-colored hair flowing behind her.

"So," she announced loudly to the gathering of Hunters, "Who are my partners?"

X

Avenir stood frozen in shock. He scanned the faces of his other pod members. Soljan and Piet seemed to have also connected the dots and were having a similar reaction.

"Ah think um gunna throw up," Piet said blankly.

Sen appeared to be oblivious to the crowd's reaction, which was equally incredulous.

"Your Highness. Although I am sure your father will regret allowing this... we welcome you as a new Hunter!" His voice rang out over the masses of people watching. He turned back to Luna, speaking more quietly, if that were even possible for Sen, "However, we would like to politely ask that next time... you don't arrive tardily."

Luna laughed. "You must be a lunatic if you think I'm going to hang around with this rabble for more than ten minutes."

Sen forced an awkward smile but said nothing.

Luna pressed on, "So. Where is the lucky pod?"

This time it was Sen's turn to laugh. His roar echoed off the walls.

"I'm sure you will find yourself quite familiar with one of them."

He pointed towards Avenir, who looked like he was about to keel over. Luna's eyes widened in absolute horror. Her face began to glow a bright red.

"Ye match the color of the royal crest!" A lone voice in the crowd chirped.

Every single citizen, except those of Avenir's pod, burst out laughing.

Luna exploded, directing her anger towards Sen, "Listen here, you washed up old man. I demand I be assigned to another group! If this does not happen, and happen right this instant, I will get my father to disband this entire useless group of trash you call the best 'Hunters'. That, or you will be thrown into the dungeons."

All noise stopped. Only Luna's jagged breaths could be heard, each one accompanied by a tiny puff of vapor.

Sen had had enough. He took a few steps step closer towards Luna, so that his chin almost rested on top of her head. What came next was an order so thunderous that it could even be heard in the adjacent districts:

"Royalty or not, you are now a Hunter by your own word. That makes you my *subordinate*. Now get yourself in order and join your pod!"

Luna looked like she had been struck by lightning. The members of the crowd were shaken too, their ears ringing in the resultant silence. She wobbled off the stage and found her way next to Avenir, who was also recovering. The guards dared not interfere.

"Now then," Sen continued, dusting off his dunerobe to help calm himself down, "Let us bow our heads in a moment of silence, honoring the Great Sword."

Everyone obeyed. No more convincing was needed to keep everyone quiet. After a few seconds, Sen vaulted off the wooden stage and joined his own pod.

"Happy Hunting! Many over the few!" he yelled cheerfully.

The tracker in his pod unlocked a portal and the other three members followed. The waiting crowd, which had still been recovering, suddenly lurched into action and broke into boisterous cheering and applause.

Avenir's pod was the last to leave. They had watched the other groups depart, one by one. Avenir and Luna were trying as hard as possible not to make eye contact. The final member of the other pods ducked through the outer portal.

Soljan mustered up his courage, and barked loudly, "Let's go, we can't let the others have all the fun!"

The crowd echoed a cheer of approval. For a split second, Luna's eyes met Avenir's, and without wasting another moment, she followed Soljan, who had already ducked out of sight. Piet scoffed and slapped Luna's back, sending her hurtling through the portal. The big man squeezed through after her. Avenir was about to follow when a loud child's voice cut through the crowd,

"Wait! That's my brother! That's my brother!"

Aren pushed his way out through the front of the mob. He was glowing with pride. He ran over to Avenir and hugged him, though to many it looked like more of a tackle. The crowd let out a happy cheer. Avenir ruffled Aren's hair, and with a final wave to the spectators, he too exited the city.

The cold hit harder than Avenir expected it would. No sooner had he made it through the small door than the frost flakes had already begun slashing at his cheeks. He grimaced and pulled his ice gauze tight. Luckily, he had the foresight to wear an extra vest, or else frostbite would have been a real danger. Luna was catching up with Soljan and Piet, who had already pushed ahead. She was wearing mastercrafted Hunter's gear, consisting of pure white robes and perfectly tailored snowshoes. After a few feet's movement, she virtually vanished into the swirling ice.

At least she's taking this seriously.

Only her head – the black hair cutting a swath through the falling snow – remained visible. She raised the hood of her robe and disappeared completely. Avenir closed his eyes. This was the Big Hunt for which he had waited for.

And she was spoiling it.

Although Aren was the best brother he could have asked for, he had always longed for a moment in which he could let his own talents shine. He knew that Aren was a far better instinctual Hunter than he was, but it took more than raw instinct to become the best. One also needed a still mind, and a willingness to wait...to plan. And after all his waiting for this moment, it appeared that this expedition would turn out to be disastrously chaotic.

He could still hear the crowds cheering from inside the dark walls. Remembering what Sen had told their pod about the state of the Frost, he steeled himself and jogged into the whiteness after them.

He found his pod thirty feet further into the snowfall. They were all hunched over, looking at a damp map that Soljan was trying his best to shield. They had their hoods drawn and ice gauzes strapped, rendering them near invisible to an untrained eye. The tracker looked up and nodded.

"Good. I was beginning to think you had already lost your way." He glanced in Luna's direction. "Thanks to the antics of our princess, we'll have to do a quick recap of the hunting plan out here."

Luna remained silent.

Soljan continued, "Sen informed me that most of the pods will be heading west or northwest. That leaves only one direction for us to go. I'm fairly certain that *most* of us," he looked condescendingly at Luna, "have had some experience hunting in the Southern Dunes." Avenir and Piet nodded. "Our general orders are to bring back at least two hauls of large game. Since we are heading to the Dunes, however, we have more cover, and therefore have the obligation to bring back more than that. Anyone object?"

"Can Piet handle the extra weight?" asked Avenir, eyeing the sled.

Piet grunted loudly in affirmation. Soljan chuckled and checked his pouch.

"I've packed more Flyer lures than Saber ones. I recommend we target Flyers first..."

"Get on with it," Luna snapped, interrupting the tracker. She stood up, looking down on the rest of the pod. "You lot can waste all the time you want but let me make one thing clear – I do not listen to the recommendations of commoners."

With that she turned and strode off, heading southward.

Piet immediately sprang up and was about to go storming after her when Soljan laid a hand on his shoulder and spoke, his voice quiet and colder than ice, "Piet, let us not forget why we Hunt. Even people like her need us."

Avenir readied his spear, gripping it tightly in both hands. "After her then," he said bluntly.

XI

They caught up to Luna with relative ease. Soljan moved to take the lead and set them in a brisk jog towards the Southern Dunes. They ran with their spears raised, wary of an ambush. For a while, Luna moved in parallel apart from them, carving a lonesome track in the snow, but eventually she fell in line behind Soljan, making a point of being in front of Avenir and Piet. Avenir laughed under his breath.

Royalty or not, no one could simply carve their own path in snow this deep, unless of course that person was an expert tracker.

Soljan clearly knew his way around the Frost, and within ten minutes they were nearing the foot of a monstrous dune. The crest of the ice-mountain was towering, so much so that it blocked some of the snow falling towards them from the sky. This dune put his and Aren's practice area to shame.

Soljan stopped at the base and crouched down, motioning for the others to do the same. Luna remained standing, gazing up at the dune.

Arrogance? No. Perhaps wonder?

For a split second, Avenir felt unusually proud of his profession.

If even members of royalty are stunned at the sight of a dune like this, perhaps this is truly where I'm meant to be.

Soljan spoke again, ignoring Luna's inattention and breaking the silence of their short run.

"We're at the northeastern fringe of the Dunes. If we're lucky, no other pod thought to come this close to the Lake. If that's the case, Frost Flyers may be right over the top. We're going to scale this side and take positions at the crest. Avenir, I'm going to need your Hunter's Vision once we're dug in."

Avenir nodded in agreement. "Alright. Everyone take a final equipment check," he said.

He strapped his spear onto his back and switched it for his father's hunting bow. He rubbed the smooth frostwood with the thumb of his glove. The motion helped clear his mind and still his tense and shivering muscles. Soljan looked in his direction and motioned silently with his hand towards the dune, indicating it was time to get going.

Before following Soljan and Piet up the incline, Avenir shuffled over to Luna, who was still gawking at their surroundings.

After a brief moment, he spoke, "Your Highness, we must work together if we want to live–"

"I'll live and die on my own terms," she hissed.

She unstrapped her bow. It was a magnificent whitewood piece made by a royal weaponsmith. Ornate tales describing countless successful Hunts snaked around its hardened arches. Without another word, she made her way up the dune, making sure to keep her distance from the other two. Avenir felt the beginnings of loathing flare up in his chest. Gripping his own bow tightly and creeping up towards Soljan, he somehow managed to suppress his rage.

When they were near the crest, they fell prone and leopard-crawled slowly to the edge. Luna did the same, some distance off to their right.

Soljan dug into his pouch, looking for the correct lure. Piet joined them at the crest. The wind had picked up a bit, and the ice flakes in the air were forming lazy tornadoes that rolled off the edge of the dune. Piet and Avenir shuffled from side to side, digging themselves into makeshift foxholes for shelter and camouflage. The tracker produced a small black vial from his pouch and rolled over to the rest of his pod, creating his own foxhole in the process.

"I found this little beauty at Yugo's place. He claims that pheromones like these are as rare as they come. And strong too," said Soljan, whispering barely loud enough to be heard.

He passed the vial over to Avenir, who opened it to take a whiff. The odor was repugnant, smelling of rotting flesh. Avenir gagged and offered the vial to Piet, who vigorously shook his head.

Soljan snickered quietly before explaining. "It's a concentrated stress signal. Frost Flyers release it out of their dorsal glands when they're in danger. It must have been a real battle to acquire something like this... that's what the price suggested at least." He squinted his eyes and looked out over the endless dunes that lay before them. "Damn, my eyes aren't what they used to be. Avenir, you're up: what are we looking at?"

Avenir scanned the area, taking in every detail. Aren had always complained that Avenir's vision gave him an advantage when hunting. Since his victory against his older brother, however, Aren had toned down his moaning. Only two people in Point Fire still possessed true Hunter's Vision: Avenir, and Sen.

While normal Hunters could only see rough outlines and dull colors in the harshness of the Frost, those gifted with Hunter's Vision could pinpoint objects down to the size of individual snowflakes. In addition to this, Avenir had always been able to guess the exact locations of living creatures and their movements in the Frost, almost as if the surrounding snow were betraying their existence. It was for this reason that his inability to detect Aren underneath the snow came as a grievous shock.

There are other gifts besides pure visual acuity.

There was no evidence of any recent movement on the dunes directly ahead of them. The snow lay soft and undisturbed by any life. The uppermost layers of powder rose and fell gently in the gusts of wind.

A brief puff of ice caught his eye on a distant dune. If he had blinked, he probably would have missed it. He concentrated on the area where the white particles had been disturbed. The snow remained static. The dune of interest was beyond the range of regular eyesight, and even Avenir found himself straining to see clearly. Giving up on using his raw visual power, he carefully pulled his pocket telescope from his belt and pointed it at the location. His father had always warned him about relying too heavily on what he had called "artificial sight." Using a telescope to achieve better focus at range came with significant dangers. One of these dangers was the lack of peripheral vision, a necessity that could easily draw the fine line between the life and death of a Hunter.

The telescope gave him what he was looking for. At the crest of the faraway dune was a small undulation, too miniscule to see with the naked eye, but just large enough to kick up puffs of snow carried by strong winds. A Frost Flyer had slept there, in a foxhole much like their own.

"It seems like a Flyer decided to take a rest on that far dune not too long ago," Avenir whispered happily, passing the telescope to Soljan.

The tracker fixed the scope on the same location and confirmed Avenir's finding.

"I can barely see it, but I believe you. Still, it seems the Flyer was not the only creature that decided that this would be a good place to sleep." Soljan suppressed a laugh and nodded towards Piet, who was lying face down in his foxhole. "We will need his strength when the time comes," he continued. "For now, let us do our part." He handed the black vial back to Avenir. "Let us see how well Sen has trained you."

Avenir pulled an arrow out of his quick-draw loop and carefully applied the pheromone oil to the entire length of the shaft, trying his best not to retch.

"That means that if I mess up Sen's to blame, right?"

"Of course."

Avenir nocked the arrow and pulled the strong fiber as taut as possible. Carefully assuming a crouching position, he exhaled calmly, and let it loose. The bow sighed in relief as the arrow cut itself a clean trajectory over the dunes. Avenir kept his eyes fixated on the small projectile, making sure not to lose it amongst the falling snowflakes. It sank soundlessly into the shallow undulation on the distant dune.

"Perfect," Soljan breathed through his gauze.

Avenir nocked another arrow and lay down next to the tracker once again. He glanced over at Luna, who was in her own hole further down the crest of the dune. Soljan nudged Piet awake. They waited.

*　　　　　*　　　　　*

Avenir's heart was racing. He had seen movement near the faraway undulation. Soljan had not noticed it yet. He gently touched the tracker's shoulder, notifying him of his observation. Soljan nodded back towards him, a signal that it was now up to him, the killer of the group.

Slowly, like the probing antennae of an insect, two long feelers crept over the crest of the undulation. Then, with near unimaginable speed, a magnificent male Flyer mounted the dune. He sniffed around the site where the arrow had landed, his feelers furiously waving as they searched for the source of the pheromone.

The creature's beauty was staggering. Its length was almost dragon-like in regality and its long dull-white fur swept into the air behind it. Avenir could feel the sweat trickling down the nape of his neck. It had only been around half a year since he last saw a Frost Flyer, but its beauty and power still made him nervous. However, this time it was different. This time, his mission was to kill.

The Flyer's feelers found what the animal had been searching for. They wrapped themselves around the base of the grounded arrow and carefully extracted it from the snow. Large puffs of steam billowed out from the creature's nostrils.

Taking great care to make no noise as he moved, Avenir assumed a crouching position again and readied his bow. Only a headshot would kill from this distance. A direct hit to the heart would probably slow the beast down, but a spear would be needed to finish it off. There was no use for poison when hunting Flyers – they were known to resist even the deadliest of toxins. Not to mention, they were probably capable of killing a person in a few seconds, meaning that even the fastest-acting poisons would still allow a relatively high degree of risk.

He trained his arrow above the creature, adjusting for the wind. The projected arc would fall directly on the head of the Flyer.

It's still not accurate enough.

Sweat rolled down his back. Avenir collected himself. To guarantee the kill, he would have to shout right when the arrow was about to hit the target. That would force the Flyer to turn towards him and create a larger impact point. Making sure he was aligned well, Avenir held his breath.

A royal arrow, shimmering orange against the white snowscape, planted itself firmly into the creature's head. The Flyer let out an ear-piercing shriek and turned to face them. Luna's happy snort wafted towards them on the wind. The Flyer was shaking its head vigorously. Vapor billowed angrily out of its nostrils.

"If that arrow does not kill it, we are all in great danger," Avenir breathed as he readied his spear.

He could see the Flyer's front claws digging deeper into the snow, a sign the beast was about to jump. Even with his Hunter's Vision, a Flyer pouncing from this distance might be too fast to track.

At the last possible moment, the Flyer let out a pained sigh, steam escaping sadly from its snout, and flopped down onto the snow. Dark rivulets of blood trickled down its jawline.

A sharp giggle echoed across the Frost. Shocked, Avenir turned to Luna, who was standing triumphantly with her bow in hand. He dropped to his knees, the danger of what had just happened finally sinking in.

"I'd like to see one of you land a shot like that," Luna sneered.

Avenir was breathing heavily. "You don't understand, if that arrow was not–"

"Avenir, let me handle this," Soljan interrupted.

The tracker removed his ice gauze, revealing a stone face. He strode off towards the princess, each step more menacing that the last.

Luna removed her gauze in kind and extended her hand regally in a welcome of the man's praise. She had not yet sensed the anger in the tracker's movements.

Soljan raised his hand and slapped her. The sharp crack rang out in the resulting silence. Luna stumbled and sank down to one knee. Soljan towered over her.

"Royalty or not, if you ever put the pod in jeopardy, attempting something like that again, I *will* kill you. This is not some sheltered royal archery range. If you make a mistake, or act on your own, you will have the blood of the pod on your hands, and your own on the dunes."

He spat into the snow in disgust, and returned to where Avenir sat, fixing his gauze back around his eyes.

*   *   *

In the hours following the clash between Soljan and Luna, the group trekked further southeast down the sides of the dunes facing the Lake. Soljan halted the pod once he had found a suitable location to have a brief rest. On the way, they killed an additional two Flyers.

Avenir had fired the killing shots, bringing down the two young cubs on separate occasions. The cubs did not even come close to the extravagance of the first beast, which had turned out to be an adult bull.

Piet stopped pulling the sled and breathed a deep sigh of relief. Some newly fallen snow slid off the dead Flyers' wings.

"This 'ere is right killin' me back," Piet groaned. "Soljan, can we use tha flares now? The nice 'uns of course."

Soljan shook his head. "We are too far away from the district to fire flares. However, given the size of our first catch, I am satisfied with bringing home just four kills. We can try for one more."

"I agree," Avenir added. "We should not let our pride get the better of us. We already have far more than was asked for. Thoughts, Your Highness?"

Luna sniffed and looked away. Soljan let out a long sigh and dug into his pouch. He pulled out their lunch: a few strips of dried hare meat heavily preserved in rock salts. Avenir wished he had saved some of his mother's food from earlier. Still, the members of the pod, even Luna, ate their rations ravenously. From the position of the light behind the clouds, Avenir guessed that it had just passed midday. Even if they had wanted to Hunt more animals, there would not be enough time to get back to Point Fire before dusk.

94

Part of Avenir felt pity for Luna. He understood that she, like him, would go to any length to prove herself, to set herself apart from the rest of her family. Yet, he could not forgive her for putting their pod in danger, an act that would usually warrant strict punishment.

Think about this later. For now, just make it back to the Point.

Piet finished the last of his meat and coughed loudly.

"I'm gunna go take a piss," he grumbled as he slouched away to a large ice formation.

Avenir checked his supplies. He had seven arrows remaining: way more than enough. His spear, though he had used it as support stick on their long walk, showed no notable signs of wear. He glanced in Luna's direction, who was also taking inventory. Of course, she still had nine arrows to spare. The first one had been used for the kill on the bull Flyer. She was carefully polishing the gleaming whitewood bow which lay on her lap using a bright piece of fabric.

Luna broke her long-standing silence, "Do you enjoy ogling at my kit that much?"

Avenir quickly looked away in embarrassment. He felt a sharp jab in his back and was surprised to find Luna offering him her bow.

"I requested the royal weaponsmith to craft me a bow using the finest wood available. You can take a closer look if you want; I actually prefer dark oak."

Avenir took the bow from her and held it up to the dim light trailing through the clouds. Even in the relative dreariness of the Frost, the bow shimmered like water.

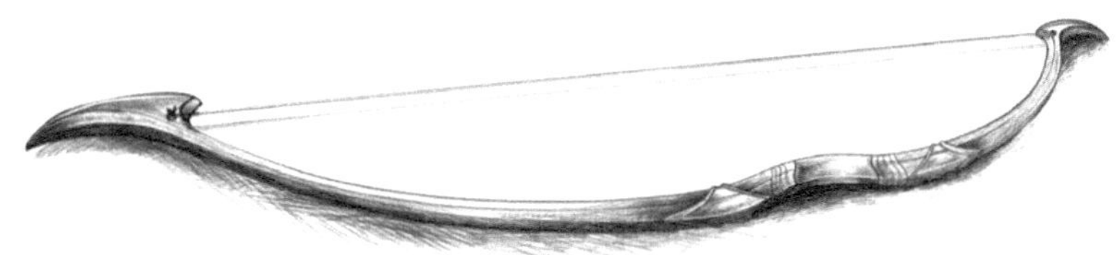

"I would like to see yours too, if you don't mind." Luna nodded towards the hunting bow slung around his shoulder.

"Of course, Your Highness. Please be careful with it – it was my father's."

He passed the bow over to her, glancing at Soljan. The tracker was sitting off to the side. The man shrugged in indifference.

"I would much prefer a bow like this," Luna said curtly. "It has a history. Substance. Mine is empty, a weapon with no soul."

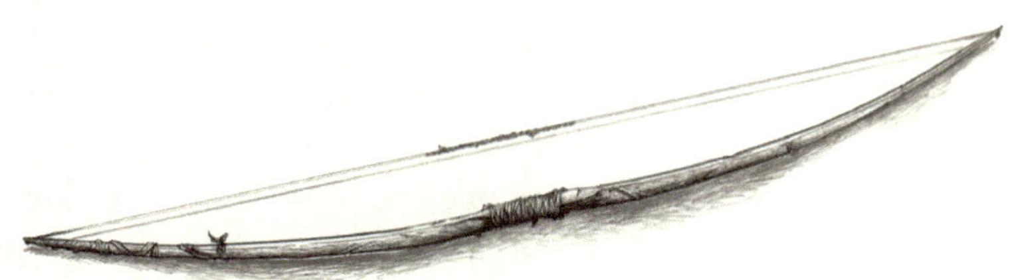

She traced her finger along the various marks and scratches lining the wood. They were etchings that could only be garnered over a lifetime of Hunting. Avenir looked at the bow in his own hands. It was indeed beautiful, but Luna was right. Something about it seemed off, as if the bowstring were too tight and the curve too perfect. For a brief instant, his sense of pity returned.

"Hey!" a terrified voice echoed in the wind.

Instinctively, Avenir drew and nocked an arrow into the whitewood's bowstring.

"Sabers! At least two of 'em!" came Piet's next phrase.

The muscle's massive frame came crashing out of the ice formation. He was waving his spear frantically. From what Avenir could tell, he was unhurt.

"I saw 'em. They wer' watchin' me from tha ice," Piet gasped.

Like Avenir, Luna and Soljan had already assumed a battle stance, weapons drawn. The four of them fell into a tight defensive formation, each facing outward towards the surrounding dunes. Avenir took stock of their situation. They had made camp in a deep valley surrounded by dunes and ice, an ideal location to remain hidden. Now, however, it seemed like they had also chosen the perfect place to be ambushed. Piet had relieved himself on the northern edge of the valley near the ice formation, so that meant the most likely avenue for escape would be further south, over the dunes.

"I didn't see any tracks nearby. They must have been sleeping right inside that ice formation," Soljan breathed.

Avenir sprang into action, the years of his father's and Sen's training kicking into gear:

"We have to move south now. If they decide to circle all the way around..." he trailed off before barking, "On me, and stay low! Spears upward in case they pounce. Luna, watch the rear."

Avenir shuffled quietly through the deep snow. Soljan and Piet followed him at his flanks, weapons at the ready. The sigh of a released bowstring sounded behind him.

"Barely missed one. It's moving by the ice. Your bowstring is too loose," Luna hissed.

Avenir did not bother turning around. He led the group further south, with Luna backpedaling at their rear. They were almost at the edge of the valley. All they had to do was get over the crest of the nearest southern dune and the Sabers might decide to leave them alone. However, if they remained in the basin much longer, and the creatures decided to attack together, they would all be as good as dead.

A large feline visage appeared over the ridge of the southernmost dune, less than thirty feet away from them. Avenir's heart stopped. This was the worst possible scenario. These Sabers, or this one at least, were apparently much faster than he had guessed. But it did simplify their options. The large catlike head quickly ducked behind the dune.

It's waiting for the others to circle around. To get closer to this side of the basin.

Sabers were a terrifying species to go up against. Not only were they exceptionally powerful, but they also possessed an uncanny pack intelligence.

"Everyone, on my go, we attack the Saber directly in front of me," Avenir ordered.

"I'll keep watch on our backs," Luna huffed.

Soljan and Piet grunted their agreement.

Without wasting another second, he yelled, "GO!"

Summoning all the strength in his legs, he powered his way up the dune's incline. Piet and Soljan followed behind him closely, their spears still poised to thrust. Avenir crested the dune within seconds. To his horror, *two* ice Sabers were lying in front of him, ready to pounce. Before he could curse, the larger of the two bristled and leapt towards him. Instinctively, he fell backwards onto the snow, spear point raised towards the beast. The creature sailed right over him.

"Soljan!" Avenir barked, "keep that one occ-"

Before he could finish his order, the second Saber was upon him, jaws snapping, searching for his neck. His spear was flung to the ground. By some miracle, he managed to jam the side of Luna's bow into its mouth, stopping the gnashing teeth an inch from his face. He could smell the acrid breath of the Saber, gusts of it blowing over him with each successive attempt to end his life.

The beast finally managed to snap the whitewood. The two halves of the weapon, still connected by the bowstring, flopped uselessly over his chest. Avenir had stopped thinking at this point. His body, trained over the years, knew that the fight would be over within a second. Pure instinct guided his actions.

In the next heartbeat, Avenir performed a motion he had perfected with the help of his father. His hand dexterously unlatched his Shard from his belt, as he rolled over to the right, still in the prone position. The Saber emitted a high growl of surprise when, after its predicted killing bite, its jaws were filled with snow and not flesh. Its eye swiveled to face Avenir. Its whiskers shivered as it realized what was about to happen. The Saber tried to pull its head away, moving with all its might.

But it was too late. Avenir was already thrusting his arm with pinpoint accuracy. His eyes were focused, dead in their purpose. The Shard glinted dully as it pierced the side of the Saber's neck. Like an ice pick cutting through freshly landed snow, it bore a silent path though the flesh of the beast, until only the dark leather grip remained visible.

The Saber's eyes bulged as it struggled for control of its body. Avenir seized the opportunity and rammed his boot as hard as he could upwards into the midriff of the feline beast. It grunted and teetered off-balance as the force of the kick carried it sideways.

The Saber refused to die easily. As the last of its life was being sapped away, it lurched towards Avenir's legs. His kick had been hard enough to put a small amount of distance between him and his adversary, but the Saber's long legs allowed one of its claws to reach. Avenir could only watch in horror as, in slow motion, the longest claw on the Saber's paw hooked into his thigh. Excruciating pain shot up his leg and knocked the air out of his lungs.

By now the beast was already dead, but its bodyweight carried it further as it crumpled, putting strain on the flesh-buried claw. Avenir could feel it digging its way across his leg. Desperately, he grabbed the paw of the animal with both hands, stopping the creature's roll. Cursing, he roughly unhooked the bloodied point from his leg. Behind him, he could hear the shouts of his companions, and the growls of more Sabers.

XII

When Avenir turned around, his eyes were met with a gruesome battle scene. The Saber that had leapt over him lay mangled in the snow with its innards torn out. Clearly someone with immense strength had dealt the killing blow. A quick glance at Piet's spear confirmed this.

In front of his pod members was a scene only found in Hunters' nightmares. Three more Sabers circled just out of range of their spear tips. Back in the ice formation beyond, two additional shadows slunk towards them. Miraculously, his companions appeared unhurt.

Piet and Soljan had formed a ragged two-man phalanx in front of Luna, who was using her now-meagre supply of arrows to keep the Sabers at bay. One of them had an orange shaft protruding from its shoulder. It was still tensing its muscles, ready to pounce at any moment.

Avenir was astonished. He had never heard of Sabers fighting this desperately. They were usually cautious hunters, always luring out the weakest of targets. He sprinted over to the rear of his pod's formation.

The situation within the Frost must be as bad, if not worse for the animals. They're starved.

Without turning, Luna shouted fearfully, "Avenir, if I don't make it out of this, I will make sure your family lies in the gutters!"

"Shut up!" Soljan yelled. He jabbed his spear at a Saber making a lunge towards him. "We need to think!"

As if on cue, some of the Sabers back in the ice formation began to move closer towards the group. They too began to circle slowly, playing a game of territorial chess.

"Shite!" Piet cursed as he waved his spear, trying his best to keep the Sabers grouped in front of him.

Avenir was crouching deadly still, his mind working furiously, calculating their escape. Every scenario he played out in his mind ended up with them being overwhelmed and overpowered - as if they were playing the chess game against a board full of rooks. Surely there was no possible strategy to win. His mind trailed on this idea — *a board full of rooks* — desperately thinking of any way to survive.

Rooks are straightforward pieces, powerful but predictable. Yet, they hide a secret weapon. There is a defensive move wherein the king and rook switch positions, castling the king in the corner. Castling.

Avenir found himself coming to a plan, a last hope forming in his consciousness.

"Everyone, do you have your flares?" he shouted over the rising growls.

The pod quickly assented in unison.

"Launch all the flares you have at your feet. Use the smoke as cover and find a high structure in the ice formation!"

The Sabers were becoming more aggressive, the nearest two biting at the tips of the spears as the others crept to the sides. Luna unleashed a quick volley of arrows, but to no avail. The Sabers had become wary of her and nimbly dodged the projectiles.

"Listen! You must find a structure to defend, a castle! Only then can you possibly hold out against this many!"

Luna's shrill voice responded, "What do you mean '*you*'? Are you just abandoning us?!"

"No. I'm going to get help from the *real* castle," Avenir barked.

Soljan murmured nervously, "Sen taught you well after all. We're ready."

Avenir did not hear him, but it made no difference. He sucked air into his lungs and yelled as loud as he could.

"GO!"

Soljan and Piet dropped to one knee immediately and deftly brought out their flares: one Regular and one Assistance. Luna cursed and followed suit. Without another word, they flipped the latches in

each of their hands. Multiple deafening thunderclaps erupted and vibrated within the basin, loud enough to make the Sabers leap backwards in fear. The primary Flare charges shot outwards awkwardly and lodged themselves in the underlying snow as their secondary fuses burned. Avenir prayed that they were short.

After being startled, the Sabers became enraged and assumed a pouncing position. Before they could launch themselves, the Flares of Embr ignited. Another cacophony of booms echoed, this time accompanied by rapidly expanding clouds of ash and sparks. The black coal from the Assistance flares mixed brilliantly with the showers of fire from the regular ones.

The basin had effectively been turned into an erupting inferno. Visibility and awareness had been reduced to worse than zero. Avenir could faintly hear the feline beasts whimpering from within the smoke, but he knew that their fear would not last long. Trusting that his pod had already begun to run towards the ice formation in search of a suitable defense point, he turned and began to sprint back towards Point Fire, trying to ignore the searing pain in his thigh.

*   *   *

Part of him feared that one of the Sabers had been smart enough to follow him, but deep down he knew that their blood-thirsty instincts would force their concentration on the closer, and larger prey – the rest of his pod.

He had been running flat-out for almost ten minutes now, and pain was shooting through his right thigh. Many times, he almost gave up, but the thought of his companions falling to the Sabers in the ice formation made him grit his teeth and push through the agony. He snuck a quick glance down at his leg. It did not look good. From the thigh down, his once-white dunerobe and pants were soaked in blood, with some of the crimson dripping down onto the snow. Grunting in frustration, the safety of his pod on his mind, he soldiered on.

After another minute he found he could just make out the dark shape of Point Fire on the horizon. By some miracle of the Seven, the conditions had cleared.

This will have to do.

He knew that if he ran for any longer, he would be putting both himself and his pod in further danger.

Fainting now would likely result in everyone's death.

He achingly pulled the Assistance flare out of his belt and aimed it towards the city, making sure to approximate the right angle. He needed to make absolutely sure that the flare traveled as far as possible.

It must be seen.

Whispering a final prayer to whoever may be listening, he unhinged the latch. An ear-piercing *CRACK* erupted from the capsule. His eyes strained as he traced the dimming payload arc towards the horizon. At the peak of its trajectory, the flare boomed again, expanding into a sickeningly black miasma. Avenir slumped onto his knees, his palms falling to the snow. He could feel the warm blood spilling from his leg.

"Please make it in time," he whispered, as he fell face first into the cold embrace of the Frost.

*　　　　　*　　　　　*

His father sat in a chair across the room. Avenir smiled.

Finally.

"I've missed you so much," he sobbed, tears welling up in his eyes.

The look on Borea's face meant he felt the same.

Avenir began to run, arms open.

All at once, black clouds snaked their way around his father's seat, quietly enveloping him. Avenir picked up his pace, but his father's chair seemed to be sliding away, moving to match his increased speed. Borea's eyes showed a sudden change of emotion. Happy tears turned to outright rage, as his mouth twisted into a wicked smile. A final

103

emotion, fear, struggled to the surface of his visage. Avenir found himself sprinting, arms held out, pleading with the dark clouds to stop what they were doing. His hands were young, those of a child. The last of the clouds snaked around his father's face, completely enveloping him.

Avenir stopped sprinting and fell to his knees. He was going to vomit. Tears streaming down his face, he searched the black mass ahead for signs of his father. Two slits of red light opened where his father's eyes should have been. A low hum invaded his ears, filling his mind with evil droning. Thundering noise echoed in Avenir's chest, then in his soul.

The sound was alive. But not alive in the sense that *he* was alive. It was parasitic, a black hole of fear, rage, and above all else, jealously and envy. The sound consumed him.

Aren's face came into focus. He could feel unimaginable hatred bubbling up within him. The tiny amount of jealously he felt towards his brother exploded, turning him almost feral. He tore at the image of his brother, screaming. The silhouette of the man in the chair was doubled over in laughter, red eyes gleaming. The man was controlling him.

"That's my brother. That's my brother!" came a distant voice.

He sobbed. The words revived some deeper part of him. He saw Aren running through a crowd, young eyes beaming.

"That's my brother!" he shouted, pointing towards Avenir.

Then, in a flash, the hatred disappeared. Jealously was replaced with a more powerful feeling. Perhaps it was unconditional love.

The black figure that had once been his father snapped upright. The thundering stopped. The vibrations in his chest ceased to exist. With a howl, the chair, and his father, shot off into the dark.

*   *   *

"He's coming to."

"AND?"

"He seems to be in a stable condition."

104

"GOOD. That's my BOY!"

Avenir opened his eyes into narrow slits. That inanely loud voice could only belong to one man. Someone else was kneeling beside him. A young healer.

She has beautiful eyes.

The world was moving by slowly. Flakes of satisfyingly cold snow found their way onto his cheeks. His mind felt foggy. As he returned to reality, so too did the pain in his leg. He groaned loudly.

"It's okay," the healer cooed. "You're on a sled back home. We're almost at the Point."

"Myyy... po..d. Sa...ber." The words came out sluggish, unintelligible.

"Don't exert yourself. You've lost a lot of blood."

He tried again, "Are... th.......ey...?" he trailed off as he slipped back into unconsciousness.

*　　　　*　　　　*

When Avenir finally came to, he felt strangely warm. He was now tucked into some sort of cot. The heat was making him dizzy. He struggled to sit up. The location was now familiar – the medical zone in the Hunters' district. He was in one of the emergency cabins.

The memory of the rest of his pod shot through his mind like an arrow. He jumped to his feet. His right leg failed him as pain ripped through his thigh. Avenir fell awkwardly onto the bedside cabinet, bruising his rib and knocking over some medicinal containers. They rattled onto the ground loudly. The pain gradually subsided. He could feel powerful drugs busy working their magic.

The door to the room ripped open with immense force, nearly breaking off its hinges. A giant of a man lumbered in.

"'NIR! What in the name of the Seven happened out there?!"

Though hearty, Sen's voice was unabashedly filled with relief. He marched over to where Avenir was struggling to stand. With one powerful motion, he swept him up like a small child.

105

"Aghh!" Avenir gasped, the sudden movement causing another jab of pain.

"Oh, calm down. It's just a little stab!" Sen bellowed.

He did, however, make sure to hold Avenir more lightly.

"Where's my pod? Please tell me they made it. If I hear..." Avenir gasped, waiting for the pain to lessen.

Sen carried him out though the door. The tough cold outside was a welcome sensation. The medical zone was isolated from the rest of the district by a thick wooden palisade, so no crowds could gather there. Avenir was relieved.

Two figures were making their way towards them through the light snowfall.

Soljan and Luna.

The tracker rushed over, his grey hair flowing wildly behind him. For the most part, he appeared completely uninjured. But, Avenir did notice a slight limp in his right leg. He also looked strangely clean – he and Luna must have bathed already.

"Avenir! We made it!" he hugged the young man in Sen's arms. Avenir moaned. "Sorry, sorry," Soljan apologized.

The tracker released him carefully and stood back, a renewed appreciation for life splayed across his face. Luna kept her distance and remained silent. She had redonned her usual royal robes, which cut her as a black figure against the snow. She too appeared unharmed.

Soljan emphatically continued, speaking quickly, "That was without a doubt the longest half-hour of my life. By the mercy of Point Fire, they decided to send *very* capable Hunters," he nodded in Sen's direction. "Otherwise we would all be Saber food right now."

Avenir choked out a laugh. Admittedly, what would have been twenty minutes for reinforcements to arrive was quite impressive, in fact near impossible. When he had been running assistance as a medic, he probably could only have made it in thirty, minimum. Avenir's respect for Sen grew immensely.

Who else could have been sent? Runan?

"We are all happy to be alive," Soljan continued. "Except..." he trailed off, face clouding.

Piet.

Avenir forced himself to ask the question, pushing through a mixture of fear and still-raw lungs from his wild sprint in the Frost,

"Where is he?"

"He'll make it."

Worried, Avenir looked up at Sen, who smiled back.

The massive man spoke warmly, "Let's go see how he's doing."

With Sen in the lead – Avenir still in his arms like a small child – the four of them made their way across the medical zone. They arrived at another wooden lodge, much like the one Avenir had been in. This one, however, was swarming with medics, and worryingly, surgeons wearing bloodied aprons. At the sight of Sen, they all turned, relief breaking out on their faces.

Before Avenir could wonder why the medical staff would appear relieved at the sight of a Hunter, the answer became clear. An empty ale tankard careened through the open doors to the lodge before finding its rest in a pile of snow. A medic followed the mug, ducking for cover.

"Oi! Stoph slackin'! Ah need mor!" Piet's drunken voice raged inside.

Avenir laughed loudly, then groaned in pain as he was reminded of his leg's injury. Sen carried him inside. Piet lay haphazardly in his medical cot, one leg dangling off the side. He was severely inebriated. He was also missing an arm.

Soljan explained, "The Sabers decided at some point that the bigger, tastier-looking body was worth the risk. They all turned on him. We had a good vantage point but one of them managed to sink its teeth into his arm." He glanced towards Luna. "She's a real piece of work, but without her he'd probably be missing more than that."

Luna sniffed. Avenir thanked her.

Piet finally noticed Sen and stood up immediately, swaying wildly. "Sen! Avenul! Where hav' you guys bin?" He lurched forwards.

This sent the surgeons into a state of panic. They swarmed around the injured man, begging him to return to his bed. Sen strode

over, shifting Avenir so that he could hold him in only one arm. He slapped Piet heartily on his good shoulder.

"What a day! You'll be surprised how many people are waiting to see you outside! For now, though, you must rest up! How are you going to Hunt again if you don't get better?"

With these last words, Sen used his free hand to shove Piet back into his cot. Piet tumbled off-balance and landed with a loud thump among the sheets. As he lay there, dazed, the surgeons seized their opportunity. A large needle filled with heavy sedatives was quickly injected into the man's arm.

Soljan chuckled. "We should go. He needs his rest. Knowing him he'll be back in the Frost within the month."

They all turned and left, leaving Piet behind. He was still blubbering nonsense, his body confusedly fighting off the combination of ale and drugs.

"Plesh. Ah need mah ale. Where are mah girlsh? Fior? Chardon?"

"Beast of a man..." Luna muttered under her breath.

"Yet you saved him," Soljan added.

"I protect my subjects."

It was dark when they returned to the wooden palisade back to the central area of the Hunters' district.

"We hadn't yet left the medical bays," Soljan explained. "We needed to make sure you and Piet were okay."

"Well!" Sen laughed, "You'd better get ready!"

With a powerful motion of his free arm, he threw open the doors. An excited crowd was waiting. Some of them were grasping lit torches, the light illuminating their exhilarated faces in the dark. They had probably been there for a long time, given that all the other pods must have returned a while ago. The people erupted with joy and pride when they saw the survivors of the last pod. Someone had constructed an oversized weapon rack-like structure, from which the spoils of their Hunt hung. Avenir was still curled in Sen's arm like a small child.

"Ready?" A voice rang out from the gathering.

Avenir tracked it to a man standing near the structure. He was the mirror image of Sen, only slightly slimmer and more sinewy.

Runan.

The man pointed to the first catch, farthest to the left on the strange construction.

"One!" he hollered.

The crowd echoed his call. Each catch was announced with another shout, the excitement level rising with each successive number.

"Two! Three! Four! Five! Six! Seven!"

A woman's voice quipped a shrill joke above the noise,

"There's one for every Master!"

The crowd erupted into boisterous laughter. Runan walked over to the pod, smiling broadly. He then turned back to the crowd, raising his hand to reveal a cluster of medals.

"By Avenir's hand, son of Borea, one Saber and two young Flyers! We have chosen an Obsidian!"

Avenir could feel tears of happiness welling up in his eyes. The mention of his father, and the pain in his body, did not help. Runan slowly lowered the glinting black medal over Avenir's head. On each of its two sides, the royal insignia was welded onto a brilliant amber stone. An obsidian medal was the highest honor one could receive for a Hunt. Runan moved over to Luna.

"By Luna's hand, daughter of Luxus II and second heir to the royal throne, one Saber, and one bull Flyer! We have chosen," he paused. "An Obsidian!"

Though she tried to hide it, Avenir noticed a genuine smile creep its way onto her face. She thanked Runan as he lowered the medal.

"By Soljan's hand, son of Frost, one Saber! He's a tracker, by the Seven!"-the crowd burst into laughter - "Surely an Obsidian is warranted?"

Everyone roared with approval as he lowered another black medal. Soljan's weathered face beamed. Runan held up the final medal. Like the others, it was a shining obsidian. Everyone held their breath in knowing anticipation.

"The fourth and final medal will be given to Piet, son of Fane," Runan's voice was building, getting louder. "By his hand, one bull Saber. The largest of them all! And a royal seal of courage for sacrifice in the Hunt!"

Triumphantly, Runan raised the last medal for all to see. It dangled in the wind, the dark black and amber colors reflecting in the light. Attached by a ribbon to its base was another smaller insignia. The tiny secondary medal shone a bright crimson as it rotated within the glow of the surrounding fires. Avenir had seen very few of these in his life. Or at least, he had seen very few hanging around a living person's neck. They were usually awarded posthumously. Few survived a grievous injury like Piet's and returned to Point Fire alive. Runan pocketed the medal, signaling the end of the announcements.

"The Many over the Few!" he shouted.

On cue, the crowd enveloped them. Sen kept a watchful eye and batted away any celebrators who got too close to Avenir's leg. Soljan and Luna laughed along with their admirers.

"'Nir!"

The familiar voice of a young boy called out to him. Aren rushed over to meet them.

"I'm holding him, the hero!" Sen boomed, giving Avenir a painful jostle.

With his free hand, Sen roughed up Aren's hair. The little Hunter was ecstatic. He had already planned to ask Avenir if he could borrow his medal so he could show it off to everyone at school.

"Is your leg okay?" he asked nervously.

"It should be fine. Give me another month or two and we can get back onto the dunes."

"With your leg hurt, maybe I'll win even more than last time," Aren teased.

A few days ago, this little quip would have greatly annoyed Avenir, but right now, it made him love his brother even more. Making it back in one piece, and knowing that the others were safe, made him – for once – genuinely happy.

As the festivities died down, butchers from the South Side continued carrying away the fresh corpses of the animals. They had already paid the Hunters' Association through Sen and he would go on to pay the Hunters themselves. Once most of the butchers left, he presented Avenir with his payment. Avenir ogled the large gourd of Blood in his hands. This was the first real Hunter's Blood he had ever received.

And by the Seven is it a large amount.

He could use it to rebuild half their house, and maybe get some elite dunerobes for himself and Aren. Naturally, a large amount of it would be spent on supporting their mother; Avenir could already sense her worry and anger at his injury. She was most likely still waiting nervously at home: she could not bear to pass the time in the Hunters' district with the rest of the crowds.

After helping to move the last of the catch – the heavy bull that Piet killed – Runan walked over to where Sen, Avenir, and Aren were standing. He leaned on his older brother's shoulder.

"Now *that* Hunt was something to remember." He laughed curtly. "I thought our pod had it made with three. But *seven*? That may very well be the largest catch of the last century, ey?"

Sen puffed out his chest. "Easily! Do you want to ask who trained him?"

"No thank you," Runan laughed. He turned to Avenir, "Your pod provided food for a thousand families today, maybe more. It could last them a long time, too. With the Frost getting worse, it's just what we needed."

"I'm just glad everyone made it back in one piece," Avenir said. "The biggest piece, I mean," he added, thinking of Piet.

Sen provided Avenir with a crutch and urged him to go home to his mother. Avenir did not think that a single crutch would be enough, but at least he had Aren to lean on.

Opening the portcullis, they exited the fringe of the Hunters' district.

"Hey."

111

Avenir stopped, searching for the voice that had spoken. Luna stood to the left of the portal, casually leaning amongst the shadows against the black stone wall. She was dressed in royal garb, with her dark hair covering most of her face. She threw something towards Avenir, who instinctively caught it with his free hand. It was his father's hunting bow.

"It helped me out during the fight. I thought I should give it back to you."

Avenir bowed in gratitude, stifling the pain in his thigh. He noticed that the princess was tapping her foot. She clearly felt uncomfortable. Luna donned her royal hood.

"I just wanted to say thank you. It was a good strategy. We would have died otherwise. Don't worry about my bow, it's replaceable."

With those words she turned and vanished into the milling crowds, her right hand tightly clutching her medal.

XIII

The last week of school was agonizing for Aren. While he had at least *slightly* enjoyed the modules on the history of Point Fire, he almost did not make it through the others. Grammar was by far the worst. He could not believe that being able to write was even necessary for life in Point Fire. He had let Ma'am Scallier know his opinion, and was promptly sent on the first in a long line of visits to the Master's office. His mother would have burned him alive for this if he were not already getting relatively good grades. He did not find the work especially difficult. Even so, it was frustrating to him that he would most likely never use any of the skills he learnt.

During the final class on the final day, Aren could have sworn that he was going to have a heart attack. He sat next to Udar at the back of the class, tapping his foot at one hundred beats per minute. He had actually confirmed this number: the extent of his boredom was immeasurable.

The last bell rang. He jumped up so quickly and so loudly that Udar fell backwards in his chair in surprise.

He rushed forward to where Ma'am Scallier was sitting at the front of the class. He grabbed her hand and shook it vigorously, as he slurred out a quick mess of words.

"Thank you so much for the great classes I had a good time I'll be sure to tell my mom it was great."

And with that he was out the door. The teacher could not help but smile.

Aren stared at Udar in disgust when the tiny boy finally walked out of the building.

"What have you been doing in there?" Aren complained. "I've been waiting here for ages!"

"Oh, calm down, I had a lot of books to pack."

"It doesn't matter anymore. Don't you see? We're free!"

Udar sighed. "No. *You* are. You're some kind of wild child. A Hunter. I actually have to go back to school soon. My mother's making me do it."

Aren scoffed. "Well, we have time now."

"Time for what?"

Aren scanned the walls surrounding the school mischievously. Udar groaned. Whenever Aren got like this, he knew they would be in for something dangerous.

*   *   *

Within the hour, Aren and Udar stood shivering in the cold, their thick robes tightly wrapped across their chests. Behind them, a copper door in Point Fire's northern palisade stood ajar.

"Remind me why we're going to the Cathedral?" Udar groaned.

Aren pulled his hood tighter. The winds coming in from over the Lake were especially brisk today,

"The priests are all at some kind of ceremony in the Heart right now," Aren stated, matter-of-factly. "I heard some of those creepy guys talking about it this morning before school, when I was on my way to help out with the lures."

"What's that supposed to mean?"

"Isn't it obvious?" Aren began walking out over the barren ground towards the distant structure. "No one's home, so we can take a look around. I've always wanted to check it out."

Udar was still standing at the door, shifting his weight uncomfortably.

"I think I'm going to sit this one out," he muttered.

Aren sighed, trotting back to his friend and pulling him by his robes. "Trust me. I've come *super* prepared. Even if they catch us sneaking around, they can't do anything to us. 'Nir gave me this."

114

Aren produced a small crimson medallion. He handed it to Udar.

"What's that?" Udar asked nervously.

"No idea. I found it in his drawer. But he said it was something that would protect anyone from the Church."

"So, you *stole* it?" Udar asked again, eyes bulging. He timidly turned the medallion over, revealing the intricate engraving of the flame.

"I'm just borrowing it for now. It's a safety measure," Aren said quietly.

"Aren..."

"Come *on*. Remember how much fun that place with the royal vases was?"

"Fun? I don't know if...." he trailed off, pondering exactly how *fun* that experience had been.

Aren jumped at the opportunity, prodding Udar under his ribs. Udar jumped, trying to stifle a chuckle.

"I knew you liked adventures!" Aren announced triumphantly.

Udar exaggerated a sigh and returned the medallion to Aren. With renewed courage, the two set off over the icy expanse.

Aren had been dead right about the priests' absence, somewhat surprising even himself. The area around the Cathedral was completely devoid of typical activity. No priests missed around the base of the structure, like he had often observed them doing from afar. In the distance, the obsidian architecture of the building glittered sadly, alone in the cold air.

They reached the main entrance with no complications. Aren could barely contain his excitement as he tried to prise open the heavy doors. They stubbornly resisted his efforts.

He turned to Udar. "Please tell me you remembered your set."

Udar grinned. He produced a small satchel from his pocket. The contents clinked softly inside.

"Yes! Let's see you work your magic," Aren said proudly.

115

Udar shuffled over to the doors. Intricate images of fire were carved over every inch of the sturdy metalwork. The small boy began fiddling with the single oversized keyhole.

After almost thirty minutes, Udar started to become visibly frustrated. He had gone through his entire arsenal of torsion wrenches and hook picks, but to no avail. Aren sat off to the side, making trails in the snow with his finger. Udar sighed, exasperated, and sat next to Aren.

"I don't understand it. The lock is either too old for me to understand, or there just isn't any mechanism at all."

"I thought you were the greatest lock picker in the Point," Aren teased.

"I am! Even my father thinks so, and he's seen and *made* basically every high-grade lock in the city."

"Obviously not *every* one. They clearly don't want people getting in here, do they?"

Udar lay back in the snow, pondering. "It's not that. It's almost as if no key could ever work in that hole. It feels virtually empty."

"But I've heard 'Nir talk about the Cathedral. He's definitely been inside! I'm pretty sure he could get in whenever he wanted to... when he used to go with Dad," Aren pouted.

It annoyed him greatly that when he finally decided to explore the one building only Avenir had seen before...it had ended up being inaccessible.

Udar perked up. "Maybe there's a secret back entrance or something? A door that only members of the Church – and I guess your brother or father – could find."

Aren regained some hope, thinking of the inconspicuous trapdoor that lead to the Heart.

Yes! Maybe something like that?

Springing to his feet, he began to earnestly circle the border of the obelisk-like building. The architecture remained consistent around its circumference. Gargantuan black flames appeared to grow straight from out of the earth, spiraling and twisting towards the heavens.

For the good part of an hour, the duo analyzed every nook and cranny between the obsidian flames of the Cathedral's exterior. Aren even tried to dig a small tunnel in the snow underneath the walls, but quickly realized that that would be a fruitless endeavor. Eventually they found themselves standing back at the engraved entrance, panting and disappointed. Aren cursed. Udar looked somewhat relieved. Aren took a few steps back and glared at the dark structure.

What could Dad and Avenir know? It must be something that all the priests know as well.

Suddenly, Aren shrieked. Udar jumped up in shock, glancing over to make sure everything was okay.

"Look, look!" Aren gibbered.

He was pointing excitedly at the entrance gate.

"Nothing's changed," Udar said as he gazed at the door for the umpteenth time. "It's just like before."

"No. Look carefully at the engravings!" Aren beamed.

Udar was getting annoyed. Aren was acting like he had made an amazing discovery, but for the past hour he had just been moping around, complaining about Udar's lock picking skills.

"It's the *same*," Udar said incredulously.

"It's the *Heart*," Aren explained. "The engravings are a picture of the Inner Sanctum in the Heart."

"You mean the place where the heat comes from?" Udar asked, not really sure what Aren was talking about.

With these words, Aren realized what the secret was. It was something that probably only he, Avenir, and all the current Church members knew: the structure of the Inner Sanctum. Most, if not all, of the other citizens of Point Fire – people just like Udar – had never been to the Heart. Perhaps in a bygone age, when the Great Sword was universally worshipped, this type of information would have been commonplace.

Aren ignored Udar and studied the great metal door. The grooves and etches of the cast metal flames swirled and twisted in an unpredictable fashion. Just like the real Inner Sanctum, it would have been near impossible to make sense of the flaming patterns. However,

Aren had also noticed six evenly spaced squares near the base of the gate.

The six ancient plaques.

If he remembered correctly, Embr lay directly above and in-line with the fifth plaque.

The scary one.

He strode over and placed his hand on the square representing the plaque. It was only about a foot off the ground, just below Aren's knees. He carefully traced his hand vertically upwards, feeling the cool metal of the engravings under his fingers. When he had reached about shoulder height, the temperature of the metal began to change. The cool black carvings became increasingly warmer. At eye level, Aren could no longer touch the metal. He had found a single point between the intricate sigils that was searingly hot. Strangely, though, it looked just like the rest of the door. Udar had been watching in silence, and curiously touched the area Aren had been examining.

"OW!"

He jumped back in pain, rubbing the tips of his fingers furiously against his dunerobe. He eyed Aren, who had taken a tinderbox out from his dunerobe. He scoffed as the other boy fiddled with the esoteric item. Sometimes Udar forgot that his friend was indeed a young Hunter. Aren struck the flint and raised a naked flame to the precise point on the doors. At first, nothing happened, and Udar was about to laugh out loud. Then the hot point on the door began to glow a dull orange. With a deep groan, the metal gates swung ajar.

"YES!" Aren jumped, waving his arms. "Udar, did you see that?"

Udar was too stunned to speak.

Aren was yelling, elated, "That was AWESOME! It was just like some old mystery. Udar, we just unlocked something ancient! I can't wait to tell 'Nir that I also know the Cathedral's secret!"

Udar joined Aren with a whoop. "I've never seen anything like it!"

Before he could speak another word, Aren grabbed him by his robe and pulled him inside the dim interior.

XIV

Avenir chewed on a tough scrap of rabbit skin he had just purchased from a stall on the outer edge of the Circle. He turned his gaze to the center of the bustling ring where the Keep lay. As usual, the whole area was bathed in an orange glow, courtesy of the thick moat of heat lines surrounding the royal palace.

His recovery had been swift over the past month, especially with no Aren to bug him. He had spent most of his time at home with his mother, helping around the house when he could, sleeping when he could not.

Cursing, Avenir limped towards one of the bridges. He was in a foul mood now. Earlier that morning, a priest had come to their door. Avenir's heart had stopped at the sight of the man's red robes. Luckily, his mother had been out in the Fynn doing errands.

The priest had relayed a simple message: "Master Kreymar requests your presence at the Inner Sanctum at noon, Master Avenir. It is of paramount importance."

Thinking of the message, Avenir became even more annoyed.
I thought I said I wanted nothing to do with them.

He realized that Kreymar had him cornered. He had almost lost it at the mention of his father when they last met, so the head priest knew that Avenir would not be able to resist a summoning like this. Regardless, he had already decided that this would be the last time he ever interacted with the Church. Even the occasional sight of the priests was now enough for him to recall painful memories of his father. He wanted nothing more than to erase this connection in his mind.

Trying to disguise his injury, he hobbled over one of the bridges at the Circle's center. As he began to cross, two red-robed figures emerged from the crowd and kept in step with him, like bodyguards.

"Please get away from me," Avenir said bluntly. "My business is with Kreymar, not you."

"We will show you the way," one of them answered quietly.

Avenir stopped walking. "I know the way very well, thank you. Now, if you don't stop following me, I will simply turn around and leave."

The men nodded, eyes glaring. Avenir turned and walked over the bridge, faster than before, making sure to show no signs of weakness in his leg. He found the black trapdoor – the entrance to the Heart – and quickly slid underneath.

As he rounded the final turn in the descending spiral staircase to the Heart, he was met with what appeared to be the entire congregation of the Church. Hundreds of priests were packed into the chamber, all equally solemn. Despite the heat, they were still wearing their full crimson robes. A voice called out, coming from an area nearer towards the viewing panes.

"Ah, he's here! Excellent."

Avenir recognized it as the voice of Kreymar and made his way towards him through the throngs of priests, making sure to avoid all other eye contact.

The head priest welcomed him, extending his right arm in a formal gesture. Avenir immediately noticed several severe burns along Kreymar's skin. The sight made him feel exceedingly uneasy. Noticing Avenir's weary gaze, the priest pulled his sleeves forward, hiding his wounds.

In an almost embarrassed tone, he explained, "Yes, I have been marked by Embr as well. Such is the reason for this fateful ceremony."

With those words, Kreymar flourished his hands towards the rest of the assembly gathered around them. The other priests remained ever silent.

"Kreymar, please," Avenir said, trying to keep his voice steady. "Tell me what you wanted to say, and then I will leave. I am not suited for this life like you are. My place is out in the Frost, not here."

Kreymar smiled knowingly. "You will soon learn that those two places are converging."

Something about Kreymar's tone made Avenir feel light-headed.

Or perhaps it's the sweltering heat in here.

Avenir knew that he would not be able to defend himself if the priests tried to do something to him. They were simply too many. Kreymar noticed his unease.

"Do not worry, Master Novari. Embr has found you in good favor. The Church, on the other hand..." he trailed off as he studied the burn marks on his arm, "...after Brother Segur made contact with the Great Sword – and partly due to the ominous nature of his message – I found I had to converse with Embr myself. I do believe I was able to make successful contact." Kreymar's perfect face darkened into a deep frown. "The message, this time, was clear."

"Just tell me." Avenir was tired of these vague, foreboding babblings.

"The only way for you to believe us is for me to show you."

With this, Kreymar raised his unburnt arm. Instantly, the rest of the congregation kneeled where they had stood, heads bowed in prayer. Only Avenir and Kreymar were left standing. Avenir's hand instinctively darted to the Shard on his belt. Ignoring him, Kreymar turned to face the viewing pane and pointed his arm towards it.

"Lord Embr, show us your fire. Show us your resolve," he beseeched. "I have done as you asked, I have brought the Novari."

Avenir unsheathed his Shard and made a break towards the spiral staircase. The other priests ignored him; their heads were still bent in intense prayer. He had only made it halfway there when a blinding burst of light stopped him in his tracks. All of the heat had somehow left the chamber. He turned around slowly, fear gripping his soul.

A torrent of fire was erupting *through* the viewing panes, linking onto Kreymar's arm. The light and power of the flame was so extreme that the priests nearest to Kreymar had been blown sideways, parts of their bodies turned to ash. Sweat rivulets were streaming down the hooded faces of the rest of the congregation.

Why can I not feel the heat?

Avenir felt as if his eyes were betraying his other senses. The room was a comfortable temperature, cool even. He could see that some of the priests had started screaming, desperately trying to smother the flames growing in sheets over their bodies. Their voices seemed far away, subdued. Bewitched, he walked slowly towards Kreymar. Flames were blackening the man's left arm, but he seemed undeterred. His dark hair was billowing outwards.

Nvi.

A single word, undecipherable and ancient, resounded from Kreymar's mouth.

Novari.

The word was spoken again, this time in his own tongue. It scathed Avenir's mind. It was as if the meaning itself was coming from within him.

He was close enough to Kreymar to see the man's face. His eyes were glowing a deep amber. Smaller flames licked out of his mouth as something spoke through him.

Novari. You have been chosen.

Avenir was now standing right adjacent to the head priest, whose arm was still extended, enveloped in fire. His skin was waxing and melting.

I am weakening. Point Fire will... follow. You... must prevail. Borea will fight. When they leave, you... must join them. There is no time. My... latent power... will provide life for a year. Take my... prison. If you are brave... my soul will remain inside it.

Avenir was enraptured. The voice was terrifying, yet beautiful. All the other priests, save Kreymar, had fled the room. The few that had attempted to stay now burned as glowing corpses.

Without warning, the fire in the Inner Sanctum erupted into an apocalypse of pure energy. Blinding white light bathed the Heart's chamber. Kreymar's silhouette stood dark against the holy blaze.

Off to the side, the heavy door to the Inner Sanctum swung open, a blasphemous sight. The energy that had been trapped inside the sanctum flooded out and danced savagely around the two remaining humans. Somehow, they remained untouched by the blistering inferno.

Instinctively, as if he were being instructed what to do, Avenir walked towards the opening, stepping over the crumpled and burning bodies of two priests. Moments later, he was within the Inner Sanctum itself, with nothing but his dunerobe to protect him.

While part of him was completely aghast at what was taking place, something else was subduing the fear in his mind. He was being guided. Being told that whatever was transpiring *had* to be completed. Still, deep inside, he wanted to leave. He wanted to call out to his mother in fear.

The flames in the Inner Sanctum gave way to reveal the Great Sword, which had melted through its age-old crystal shackles. It no longer shone with intense fire. All its former power had been distributed to the air in the sanctum around him. It was almost as if the remaining energy in the Sword had been dispelled from the Blade. Avenir grabbed its hilt. It felt unceremonious and awkward. He left the sanctum quickly, with the door shutting behind him, seemingly of its own volition. Embr spoke its last words through Kreymar, as the remaining fury within the blade dwindled.

An ember to the fire of Rebellion.

The tornado of fire detached itself from Kreymar's arm and retreated back through the viewing panes into the Inner Sanctum. The hole in the glass through which the pyre of flame had escaped melted in on itself, magically repairing the age-old window. Where the Great Sword had once been, a holy fire still surged. The chamber had returned to its normal state. It was glowing once again, ever bright. An unknowing eye peering through the viewing panes would never suspect that the Sword was no longer there.

The fire that will be gone within a year.

The usual roar of the Heart returned to Avenir's ears as soon as the flames retreated. As all other sounds came back, so too did a sense of dread. The trance-like state which seemed to have been induced by the Sword was now being washed away by a steady onslaught of fear and guilt.

"Kreymar!"

Avenir rushed over to his childhood friend. The head-priest was doubled over. He was clutching at his arm, or what remained of it. His hand and forearm were completely burnt away, leaving a blackened stump near his shoulder.

"It is..." Kreymar sputtered, fighting back the pain. "It is wonderful."

With a grimace, the head priest hoisted himself to his feet. He flashed Avenir a smile – a genuine one. Ignoring the still-burning bodies of the priests surrounding him, he placed his remaining hand on Avenir's shoulder, gripping it fiercely.

"Do you realize what has just happened?" Kreymar's eyes were fiery, joyous. "We are the first witnesses to a new era. No. I am merely the witness. You are the flagbearer."

"No. No!" Avenir managed to sputter. He raised the Great Sword. "Take it back."

Avenir held it towards Kreymar, who simply shook his head. Avenir could feel a deep rage beginning to burn inside him. Kreymar lowered his hand from Avenir's shoulder.

"It is already done, Master Avenir. You cannot deny your own eyes. You–"

Avenir roared, throwing the Sword with all his strength. It ricocheted loudly off a viewing panel and fell to the ground. He ignored the pain in his leg. Kreymar was stunned for a second, before rushing over to where it fell. Once there, he knelt over the Blade, making sure it was unharmed, but too afraid to touch it. Avenir stormed over and grabbed the hilt roughly, picking up the Sword again. He could not bear to see Kreymar looking upon it with such admiration.

"How can you say this is wonderful?" Avenir growled angrily. "Look around you. Do you not care for these men? Did you not know them? And, if I'm not mistaken, Point Fire's only source of heat just extinguished itself!"

Kreymar held his gaze. "Yes, of course I cared for them. But they joined the Church knowing their lives meant nothing in comparison to our mission. They came today knowing that Embr might speak. Embr is our *god. Embr* has decided that this is the right path to take. You must have heard it too. That fire there–" he pointed at the Inner Sanctum with his remaining hand "–will remain for a year, powering this city."

"But now it's all but dead, your god," Avenir spat. "You spoke its words yourself. You know what it said."

"Yes. I remember, and I do not intend to forget. Which is why–"

"I do not care why. All I know is that this god – or demon for all I know – does not value life."

With his free hand, Avenir took out his Shard. He raised it, tensing to strike at the Blade of Embr, which he rested against the nearby viewing pane. He did not know whether it would do damage, but he promised himself he would try his best to destroy it.

"Real or not, I cannot listen to something like this–"

Kreymar moved with unnatural speed, barreling into Avenir, and knocking both weapons out of his hands. The two of them fell hard onto the stone floor. Even with his injury, Kreymar possessed formidable strength. Avenir tried scrambling for the Great Sword. Within a heartbeat, Kreymar was behind his back, placing him in a one-armed chokehold.

"Do not be a fool," said Kreymar, struggling to control Avenir, who was thrashing wildly. "I know you have read the ancient scripts, the plaques on these walls."

Avenir was not listening and attempted a hard elbow jab into Kreymar's ribs. The priest grunted in pain but did not loosen his vice grip around Avenir's neck.

"Listen to me," Kreymar half-pleaded. "LISTEN! Embr houses the soul of one of the Seven. It is not a perfect being, but it is still a *god*. As with all things, the Knotted Rope needs its braid. I know you have read this."

Avenir had stopped struggling, instead focusing on getting air into his lungs. Kreymar's chokehold was perfect.

"Think about its words," Kreymar grunted. "About what you just witnessed. It was a prophecy. Point Fire will freeze within the year. Think about Aren. Think about Sylis."

At the mention of his mother's name, Avenir froze. He could not believe his ears. He did not want to believe his eyes. His mind was being completely overwhelmed. The two young men lay unmoving on the warm floor of the Heart. The burning flames in the Inner Sanctum roared and popped as they always had. Slowly, Kreymar removed his arm from around Avenir's neck.

The priest stood up, wincing at the battering his body had taken, and began to move around the Heart, checking on his fallen brothers. Avenir lay deadly still, taking deep breaths. With his eyes closed, he listened to the sounds of the fire. He knew that nothing would ever be the same again.

What just happened?

Images flashed through his mind. Kreymar's burning arm. The priests running. The strange sense of calmness he had... his unnatural immunity to the flames.

The voice coming from Kreymar.

Point Fire.

Aren.

Mom.

He did not want to look. So long as his eyes remained closed, the whole ordeal was nothing more than a nightmare.

He lay there for a long time, listening to the soothing sounds of the flames. Finally, he sat back up and reluctantly surveyed his surroundings. Kreymar was waiting for him, sitting with his back against the plaques beneath the viewing panels.

"I apologize, Master Avenir. I have spoken with Embr before this occasion, but I did not realize he would communicate with his full voice. I am sorry."

"So... what do we do now?" Avenir asked weakly.

Some of the bodies around them were still smoldering, adding to the gravity of his question.

Kreymar laughed cynically. "*I* will be taking care of my fallen brothers. As for you...I do not know. The message, at least to me, was not perfectly clear. Yet, this spectacle has deepened my loyalty to your family. Embr has chosen you, that much is obvious. Now... we wait."

Avenir recollected his Shard and tucked it into his belt, making sure to avoid eye contact with the Sword that lay next to it on the ground.

"Borea will fight. When they leave, you must join them..." Avenir echoed Embr's words quietly.

He forced himself to retrieve the Weapon, refusing to look at it directly. He did not want to take it, did not want to obey the orders of whatever unknown entity lay within the Blade.

But I can't just leave it here.

He placed it under his dunerobe next to his Shard, looking Kreymar directly in his eyes. "Fine, I'll play this game... for now. But if my family becomes endangered because of you or the Church, or if you bend the truth again, I *will* kill you."

With that, he left Kreymar behind with the charred bodies, his hand placed nervously over Embr's hilt. Nothing seemed real anymore. As he ran up the staircase, Avenir kept wishing, even praying, that he would wake up from this empty nightmare.

XV

Once inside the Church, Aren and Udar giggled excitedly, eyeing the potential pathways they could take. They had both agreed that the ones labeled "Worship" and "Apartments" seemed somewhat boring. Aren briskly walked down the third and final tunnel with Udar in tow.

"Caverns. Awesome!" Aren exclaimed.

"That's just like a bunch of big caves, right? It sounds kinda scary to me."

"Ma'am Scallier mentioned them remember? 'Supposed to be the coldest place in Point Fire... I guess there's only one way to find out."

After a few minutes of descending the torch-lined tunnel, they reached yet another door. Although locked, Udar easily picked it this time. Beyond it lay a cracked stone staircase. The steps descended further into the darkness; the walls were lit with more endless arrays of flickering torches. As they followed the path, their footsteps echoed softly, absorbed into the natural stone surrounding them. Shadows moved and danced into contorted and unsettling images across the walls. Aren could already sense Udar shivering.

This must be taking us very near to the edge of the Lake.

Finally, they arrived at the bottom. A red curtain was hanging over an open doorframe, obscuring what lay beyond. Flames imprinted in dark ink covered the fabric.

"This is where they perform the human sacrifices," Aren stated, matter-of-factly.

"That's not funny," Udar peeped.

"Sorry, I couldn't resist," Aren apologized as he swept the curtain aside.

The result was not what he had been expecting. He let out a startled gasp. The empty cavern beneath them was awash with turquoise light. The aura of it seemed to be emanating from within the walls themselves, bathing the area in a tranquil glow. The edges of the cavern were perfectly smooth, as if the two boys had just wandered into the center of a giant blue marble. And most startlingly... it was not cold.

"Lemme see too. Get out the way."

Udar pushed himself past Aren and stumbled onto the stone platform that was beyond the curtain. His reaction mimicked Aren's.

"Wha...what is this?" he stammered. "It's warm! There's light in here!" he paused. "Except it's blue!"

"This is awesome!" Aren shouted.

His voice echoed loudly off the smoothness on the far side of the chamber. The two boys jumped at the sound of the perfect echo, believing for a second that it was someone yelling back at them. When they realized it was in fact Aren's voice, they took turns shouting obscenities and curse words into the turquoise expanse. After recovering from mischievous laughter, Aren tried to get a better grasp of the chamber's layout.

They were currently standing on a wide, raised stone landing about the height of his home in the Fynn. From this precipice, two evenly spaced dark pathways descended to the ground of the cavern. The earth below was bare and uneven, in stark contrast to the walls that were almost artificially flat.

The cavern was mostly empty. The only area of interest was still a way off near the far border of the chamber – an arrangement of seats around a central area filled with miscellaneous smaller objects.

"Let's go check that out," said Aren, pointing to the chairs in the distance. Udar was still giggling at the echoes. He wiped a tear from his eye.

"Sounds good to me."

After descending one of the dark walkways, they ran together towards the far wall. Aren was still shocked by the warmth they were feeling. It was not really *hot* by any definition, but it was far less cold than outside — or even inside — the Cathedral. He laughed to himself.

Everyone thinks that the priests in the Cathedral are constantly braving the elements... they're probably just hibernating in here!

The arrangement of seats was less exciting in person than it had appeared to be from afar. The central area was littered with stacks of paper and ancient texts, none of which were remotely legible to the boys.

Some sort of makeshift priest classroom?

"Hey Aren, come look over here!" Udar called out.

He was standing next to the glasslike wall, the one furthest across from the curtain they had come through. Aren caught up with his friend, who was busy tracing his hand along the turquoise boundary.

"Why do you think Ma'am Scallier lied to us?" Aren asked as he joined Udar in touching the strange material.

It was warm — *a different kind of warm... not like the heat lines* — to the touch.

"What do you mean?"

"She said this was the *coldest* place, remember? This isn't cold at all."

"I don't think she was lying. Maybe she just doesn't know?"

"That doesn't make sense," said Aren, furrowing his brow. "Then the *priests* are the ones lying. I think they don't want to have anyone down here for a reason, and they make up stories to keep it that way. It's a good lie...I mean, who would ever want to come to a place colder than the Frost?"

"Beats me. *Feel* this, though. It's so nice..." Udar pressed his face against the wall. "It's almost better than a heat line!"

They explored the rest of the cavern for the good part of an hour before getting bored. Besides the setup of furniture and the illegible manuscripts, there was no real evidence of human activity. The

Caverns were a lonely, heated paradise, an escape from the reality above ground.

"Let's check out another tunnel back at the entrance," Aren suggested.

Udar seemed wary. "I don't know Aren, we've been here a while, and we don't know how long their ceremony is... I think we should leave while we can. Plus, there's no way it could be more exciting than this."

Aren pushed the red curtain aside and began making his way back to the coldness above.

"We'll be quick, I promise."

His voice faded away into the hard, earthy passageway.

Upon reaching the top of the torch-lined stairs, the boys quickly scuttled back through the tunnel and turned the corner into the opening marked "Apartments." Aren knew that they were testing their luck staying this long, but he could not give up this opportunity. This was one of the few times he had ever had the luck of hearing about a mandatory ceremony for all priests. He was not about to forgo this chance to explore an area of Point Fire which up till now had only been open to his father... and brother. Yet, something told him that even Avenir had never seen the caverns below, as he surely would have mentioned something so spectacular. He could not be certain about his father, though.

The tunnel leading to the "Apartments" was short compared to the one they had just been down. It opened right into the center of the Cathedral. Shockingly, most of the building's interior was hollow. A large spiral staircase of rusty metal traced the circumference of the space and wound its way upward, almost out of sight due to the sheer height of the spire.

Flanking this staircase were the apartments themselves: doors upon doors leading laterally to living quarters, workrooms, and other unknown places.

"This must be where all the priests stay," Udar commented, shivering at the renewed cold in the air.

"We *have* to go all the way up. Up and down, then we're done," Aren grinned.

Udar sighed as Aren lead the way up the spiraling walkway. Along the path, there was a rigid order to everything they encountered. Without fail, all the doors near the base of the Cathedral lead into areas of study, or workshops. Udar and Aren occasionally peered through the tiny windows set into the entrances, spying various desk arrangements, or cluttered writing stations.

Beyond some unmarked point, they noticed the rooms were labeled: the beginnings of the living quarters of the Cathedral. The first room they passed, which also appeared to be the largest, belonged to someone named Master Kreymar.

The higher they climbed, the more cramped the living spaces became. Name titles were no longer marked on the upper apartments. They curiously eyed the interiors of the rooms through iron bar-lined windows.

The newer priests probably stay here. Pretty terrible living conditions...

Eventually, as they reached near dizzying heights, the rooms had devolved to nothing more than jail-like cells. Udar was making sure to keep to the outer part of the staircase, as close as possible to the obsidian-colored walls of the Cathedral. Aren could handle the height slightly better, but even he did not stray further than the middle of the staircase. He wondered if and how many priests had fallen to their death.

The rooms lining the outer wall suddenly ceased to exist. The staircase however, continued, spiraling upwards into an obsidian heaven. Because of the conical shape of the Cathedral, the stairs had shrunk in width noticeably, much to Udar's horror.

"I can't go on," he mumbled, his legs shaking a bit from the vertigo.

"I can see the top... it's so close," Aren urged, trying to comfort his friend. "Look there, it's a door."

133

He pointed to what he was referring to. A small wooden hatch was set into the side of the building's shrinking walls. It appeared to be another cell where someone could live. Although it looked no more interesting than many of the other apartments they had passed, this one was unique in how far it was set apart from the rest.

"We *have* to see what that is," Aren begged. "We've made it *this* far, so we might as well find out what's at the top."

Udar croaked something unintelligible. Then he nodded sullenly, making sure to glue himself to the wall as they ascended further.

What kind of madman would want to live in a place that dangerous?

Aren was the first to make it to the door. He too was hugging the wall at this point, afraid of the dizzying drop right next to his toes.

He silently read the inscription carved into the wood.

Udar noticed a change in his friend. Aren's face had gone completely white, and he seemed frightened.

"What is it?" Udar whispered. "Is it worth going into?"

Aren tried to regain his composure as he pointed to the inscription.

"Look."

Udar delicately inched next to Aren and read the single word carved into the door.

Borea

He glanced over at Aren again, who seemed both fearful and excited. Everyone in Point Fire knew that name, even Udar. Aren tried the handle. It was locked. Udar knew what Aren would ask next.

He tried to muster as much courage as he could. "Are you sure you want me to open that, Aren?"

Aren sighed and smiled sadly after a brief pause.

"Yes. Let's find out who my dad really was."

XVI

After managing to weakly crawl out of the trapdoor at the base of the Keep, Avenir limped as fast as he could in the direction of the Fynn. Multiple priests were in the area, clamoring among themselves in fear. It had already turned to night, and he was keenly aware of the singe-marks spattered across his robes. He just had to hope that the other passersby would somehow not notice them.

The sleepy-looking guards who had been nearby the trapdoor were watching him — as well as the remaining priests — absent-mindedly, most likely believing it to be some sort of primitive, crazed ceremony. Avenir left as quickly as possible.

He stumbled back home while sheltering the once-blazing Sword against his torso. By some miracle he managed to make it back without drawing the attention of another guard, or a curious urchin.

Avenir fell onto his bed, exhausted. The harrowing experience in the Heart had sapped him of his energy...and his resolve. He felt his chest at the location where the Great Sword had been hidden. His skin was severely burned. He winced as he slowly applied some soothing balm from his mother's medicine chest. The Sword lay on his bed, singeing the covers. Avenir refused to look at it. He knew it would remind him that every law of his reality had just been broken. With a cry of anger and despair, he slammed his fist into a cabinet. A glass broke inside.

"Damn you!" he shouted, letting another reckless blow crash into the piece of furniture.

An immediate and terrible pain pleaded with him to calm down. Another glass breaking brought him back to his senses.

"Damn you," he whispered, speaking to himself.

He took a deep breath and closed his eyes. He inhaled a deep breath.

Calm yourself and think. No. You must rest. Give your mind a chance to reset. You are a Hunter. Remember who you are.

He opened his eyes and gingerly extracted the broken pieces of glass from inside the cabinet. He let them fall into a small leather pouch he retrieved from his wardrobe. He tied it around his belt.

"No one can suspect anything," he counseled himself, his voice shaking miserably.

Avenir grasped the hilt of the Great Sword without looking at it. It was still mildly painful to hold given the lingering temperature. He made his way downstairs to the underground guestroom. There, he lifted one of the floor's flagstones, placing the weapon in the hole he had once dug underneath it. A few other items populated the hole: a birthday letter from his father, an interesting skull he had found in the Frost, and a love letter from a girl he once had feelings for when he was Aren's age. Avenir almost smiled.

Thank the Seven Aren doesn't know about that.

He let the dark slab fall back with a silent thud.

Avenir immediately set out into the center of the Fynn. The first order of business was buying some replacements for the glasses he had broken, using the Blood from the Big Hunt. Glass was wildly expensive, given that sand was essentially a non-renewable resource in the Point. He cursed himself at having been foolish enough to break two. Luckily, he managed to offset some of the cost by selling the broken shards to a local scrapper. He eyed the nobles with their endless glass gourds of Blood and envied them.

Next, Avenir began searching for the item truly on his mind: a suitable scabbard for the obscenity lying beneath the flagstone. He knew it had to be a simple, and ideally boring, piece. He struck a bargain with a trusted crafter, an old friend of his father, for an unassuming leather scabbard. He did not know whether the blade would fit, so he bought it in a single size larger than his original estimate.

Satisfied, he began making his way back home. The skin on his chest was hurting again. The salve was working, but the burn had been deep. For some reason, his immunity to the heat had faded abruptly after he had left the Heart. He stopped walking.

What am I thinking? If that is truly a god, or a divine weapon, what's to stop it burning through the leather as it wished?

Avenir groaned silently.

A leather scabbard for a scalding hot weapon...Idiot.

He racked his brain for a minute and stumbled on a possible solution.

Crystal. Just like the Inner Sanctum.

Fifteen minutes later – he was running now, eager to make it back home before the rest of his family did – he found himself passing through the doors to *Yugo's Poisons.*

Yugo himself sat behind the grimy copper counter at the rear of the store. He was smelling various heaps of ingredients littered about in front of him. The man was deftly swirling a beaker fuming with acrid neon vapors in his left hand. He did not look up as Avenir entered, due to his intense focus.

The grotesque shopkeeper smiled when the fragrance he had been waiting for entered his flared nostrils. He added an ingredient – a boring-looking white powder – to the flask. The concoction fizzed loudly and then became calm, forming a substance that resembled water. The sides of Yugo's eyes creased in pleasure, but his lids did not open. The man was completely blind: his sight itself was an old casualty of his own experiments.

Losing interest in whatever he had just created, he turned towards Avenir, nostrils flaring.

"Boy, I can smell you – or even your little brother – instantly," he crooned melodiously.

Avenir had always been deeply disturbed by this man's ability to detect his scent from across the room. It was terrifying to think that there was a person in Point Fire with a sense of smell almost as sharp as his own Hunter's Vision was precise.

Yugo coughed up a giant ball of phlegm onto the floor. Then, as if he had just remembered something, he stooped over with a vial, collecting his own mucous. He lovingly stored the container on a nearby shelf.

"What do you want boy? More pheromones? I heard from Soljan that you had yourself quite the haul."

His voice was raspy and hard to understand, no doubt the result of ingesting some more of his own poisons. Avenir leaned over the counter, taking in the monstrosity of a man before him. Blemishes and craters scarred every inch of the poor soul's skin. Strangely, though, Yugo did not stink. In fact, he was immaculately clean, if one could somehow turn a blind eye towards his physical deformities.

*

When Avenir was a small child, while on an errand with his father, he had asked Yugo why he even bothered bathing so often.

"So I can smell *you*," had been the harrowing response, "... and my potions of course," Yugo had added with a sly giggle.

Avenir did not return to the store in the year following that nightmarish revelation.

*

"Fire-proof crystal," Avenir responded bluntly. "The best grade you have."

After a moment of silence, Yugo's hand shot out over the counter and grabbed the collar of Avenir's dunerobe. He moved forward and inhaled from it deeply.

"You've been burnt! Been travelling too close to the central heat-lines, have we?" Yugo accused slyly.

Avenir ripped the man's hand off his collar, terrified of the possibility that Yugo would discover what had happened. He silently thanked the Seven that Yugo was blind.

Your nose may be good, but even you can't smell fear.

He regained his composure. "Unfortunately, yes. Aren and I were sparring near one of the thicker lines and the tip of my sword opened a small hole in it."

"Oh?" Yugo smiled, amused. "Tampering with heat-lines is a royal crime, you know."

Avenir exhaled, relieved. Yugo had believed his lie.

"Yes, I know. That is why I had to come to you immediately. I must fix the leak as soon as possible, before it is discovered. You wouldn't mind keeping this a little secret between us?"

Yugo cackled in delight. Avenir knew that the man had a mischievous streak. It came as no surprise that he and Aren were great friends.

"Of course, of course," Yugo beamed, "But..."

Avenir braced himself for the clause.

"...but you have to try this poison on your next Hunt."

Yugo gleefully retrieved the flask he had been busy with earlier. The clear fluid still appeared as innocuous as it had before. Avenir let out a sigh of exasperated relief. He had expected something far worse from this disgusting man.

"What is it?"

"I call it Soul Scream," he explained proudly. "So far, I've only given it to small rodents. They whined in terror, completely frozen. Of course, I had to try it on myself. Believe me, I injected no more than a droplet... and by the Seven was it terrible. It felt evil, as if my body itself was demonic and craving its own death." Yugo's closed eyes crinkled in childlike excitement. "Lovely."

Avenir took the vial and slipped it into his dunerobe. "I'll let you know how it goes." He held out his hand. "The crystal?"

"Yes, yes. Coming right up."

The poisoner shuffled over to a wall filled with an endless array of glassware. Adopting a behavior that Avenir found very disturbing, Yugo began sniffing around in a pattern along the wall. Once he found a scent to his liking, he pulled the vessel off the rack. He did the same for a couple other vials. Eventually, Avenir found himself looking at three containers of different sizes lined up on the copper desk.

"I don't know how big the hole is you want to fix, so I'll just detail all of them." Yugo placed his swollen pink hand on the tiniest vial: a golden jar. "This small one is common liquid crystal. Easy to apply. Still has formidable fireproofing properties." He moved to the next one. "The large flask over here contains a powerful variant. Needs to be freeze dried, though. Can easily throw anything coated with this into a fire."

Avenir eyed the third and final flask: a cylindrical clay tube. "And that?"

Yugo somehow sensed his gaze and chuckled. "This's some serious stuff. Same crystal as in the Inner Sanctum. Insulated. And you better make sure you apply it correctly. The substance will never erode. Only the Seven would know why you would need something like this." Yugo smiled. Half his teeth were missing or rotting. "But then again, you are the son of Borea. It'll cost three Larges."

"I'll take it."

He pulled out his gourd of Blood and poured it carefully into a measuring unit on the counter marked "Large." Usually, the carrying gourds were designed to pour a half a Small at a time. With ten Smalls in a Medium, and the same number of Mediums in a Large, it was quite the undertaking to complete this pricey purchase. After each consecutive pouring, Yugo greedily deposited the liquid into a glowing vat behind him.

Avenir began on his way back to the Fynn, but not before making a pit-stop at the stall Aren had visited after their last Hunt Game. The distrustful shopkeeper was still there, pacing among his wares. Avenir chose the pair of gleaming white boots, paying the necessary amount of Blood.

Aren will love these. Hopefully they'll keep him occupied.

He ran home, all the while praying that Yugo would decide not to spread the details of his recent purchase or mention anything to Aren.

Once inside, he was relieved to find that neither his mother nor Aren had returned yet. He quickly retrieved the Great Sword and brought it back up to his room. The blade still resonated with an otherworldly heat.

He finally forced himself to take a good look at the Weapon. It was a completely different tool from the one he had envisioned, having seen only glimpses of the ancient instrument hiding behind the flames in the Inner Sanctum. Fire was no longer spouting from the Blade, but the smooth silver metal still retained an aura of anger. Something about the perfect sheen, and the unblemished edge, made it difficult for Avenir to pull his gaze away.

A faint red glow traced its edges. The hilt, no longer white-hot, had settled to a dull crimson. For the first time, Avenir noticed that the Great Sword lacked a hand guard. At some unknown point, the dark ruby color of the grip morphed into the silver of the blade. It was truly an eye-catching instrument. He would have to change that.

He cut some strips of fabric from the bottom of his dunerobe and carefully wrapped them around the Sword's grip. He had to make absolutely sure that no red color shone through. When he was satisfied, he prepared the items he had purchased in the Fynn.

With a feeling of apprehension, he carefully uncapped Yugo's crystal solution and poured it into the interior of the leather scabbard. The crystal was a clear color and flowed relatively easily. He let the liquid fill out the length of the sheath, before slowly rotating it, coating the whole inner surface with the sticky substance. As the poisoner had warned, the crystal set itself very quickly. Avenir sat back and smiled, admiring his handiwork. The door to the kitchen opened.

"I'm home! 'Nir? Aren?" His mother's voice drifted calmly upwards.

Jerked back into action, Avenir doused the strips of dunerobe around the hilt with the remainder of the crystal. He quickly sheathed the Great Sword in its new home. He swore silently when he noticed additional singe marks on the bed covers.

Remember to turn them over before Aren gets here.

141

He tied Embr around his waist and placed his hand on the scabbard, gauging its temperature.

Cooler to the touch. Perfect.

"I'm upstairs," he called back. "Where's Aren?"

XVII

Aren fell through the door as Udar unlocked it. Both boys had been leaning hard against the wood, afraid of getting too close to the endless drop. After untangling themselves from a puzzle of arms and legs, they took stock of their surroundings. Aren was not sure what he had been expecting, but it definitely was not this.

The cell was a complete mess. Piles of aged and rotting books, manuscripts, and scrolls — like the ones they had seen in the Caverns — lay strewn haphazardly across the floor. Rat feces littered almost every surface, mixing with a near-solid layer of grime. Startled, one of the rodents responsible for the mess darted into its makeshift home of crumpled papers.

"No one's been here for years," Udar remarked.

He immediately regretted making the statement, remembering that Borea had in fact disappeared seven years ago.

"It's okay," said Aren, noticing Udar's visible embarrassment. "I just want to find out why."

He began reading a few lines on the nearest manuscript. It was some sort of account of Hunter finances. He noticed Sen's name next to a large negative number labeled "ale" and could not help but chuckle.

"What's so funny," griped Udar, who was peering at one of the rotting piles, his nose crinkling.

"Nothing, just a Hunter thing," Aren responded absent-mindedly, as he made his way over to a desk jammed into the corner of the cell-like room.

A sad-looking window was inlaid above the decaying furniture piece, offering a breathtaking view of Point Fire in the distance. The black battlements shone brightly in the dusk, illuminated by the glow of the heat lines. Far to the right lay the Frost, a deathly grey expanse that stretched to the horizon.

None of the papers on the desk were interesting. The rotten ones were completely illegible, and the legible ones were mundane: a receipt for a purchase in the Pit, a few scrawled notes about the weights of different animals, some indistinct mathematical calculations.

"Here's something that mentions your brother," said Udar.

"What is it?" came the response, hopeful.

"It looks like a receipt for his school fees."

"Now *that's* something crazy," Aren joked sarcastically.

He began opening and closing the various drawers in the desk, eyeing the contents of each. None of them revealed scandalous secrets or adventurous details about his father. He was on the brink of giving up and was about to ask Udar if he wanted to leave when he found himself struggling to open the final drawer. He stooped down to take a closer look. Upon first inspection it appeared identical to the others. Aren gave it another tug. The drawer did not budge. Then he noticed a tiny keyhole near the edge, barely a third of the size of a regular one.

"Udar, I think this drawer needs you."

The locksmith's son crept over to where Aren was. They were both acutely aware of the diminishing light. Nightfall arrived quickly in Point Fire, and the shadows in the room had already merged together.

"Aren, we really have to go. It's getting dark."

"I know, I know. Just take a look at this first."

Udar joined Aren in his examination. He pulled out his lock picking kit, found the correctly sized wire, and began feeling around inside of the keyhole.

"This shouldn't be too hard, I think. It actually seems like something your father may have made himself."

"What are we waiting for, then?" Aren blurted.

Udar started his work on the lock mechanism, slowly massaging the pins to fall into the correct order. After less than a minute, he inserted a torsion wrench, and prepared to turn it. He suddenly froze, his face a couple of shades paler.

"Aren, move away. Right now. It's been spring-loaded. I felt the resistance change when I was about to open it. I'm going to move to the side before I do it."

Aren obeyed, darting to the edge of the cell and crouching. Udar shifted his weight carefully, making sure to keep constant pressure on the lock mechanism. When he was satisfied that he was outside the range of whatever lay inside the drawer, he completed the turning motion, diving to the ground in the process.

The motion caused a loud *POP* to ring out. Udar was lying face down in the grime, clearly expecting the worst. But Aren was watching the desk with extreme focus. He barely saw it, but he caught a glimpse of a flying object leaving the woodwork.

If only I had Hunter's Vision...

After waiting for a moment, just to make sure there was not anything else lurking at the back of the dusty drawer, he made his way to the wall at the opposite end of the cell.

A small needle sat embedded in the stone. It had clearly been released with considerable force. Using two nearby sheets of moldy paper as a makeshift glove, Aren slowly extracted the metal pin. The tip of the needle was covered in a maroon substance, dried and cracked with age. Seeing the color, and fearing the worst, Aren sniffed the top of the needle. A chokingly sweet smell invaded his nostrils.

"Snowfall," he breathed.

"What did you say?"

Udar was now at Aren's shoulder. His clothes were covered in grime.

"Snowfall. It's the deadliest poison I can think of. Can probably kill a person in less than a minute. This is really old though – probably useless now."

Udar's mouth fell open in shock. Aren buried the needle in a pile of grime and mold in the corner of the cell. Although he was relatively certain that the toxin was now inert, he still respected its killing power.

"That poison is no joke," Aren continued. "You even lose the ability to talk once it enters your blood. I've heard that Hunters use it on animals when they're worried that reinforcements are nearby."

"*Animal* reinforcements?"

"You know, like the rest of the pack of Sabers or whatever." Aren replied as he slowly crept back to the desk.

He was now acutely aware of every object in the cell.

Are there other traps?

"You know Udar, I think my dad *really* didn't want anyone to see what was in here...or even try to call for help once they got hit with that poison needle."

Aren closed his hand around the drawer's knob. Just in case, he moved his body off to the side. Udar, horrified by what Aren had told him, had bundled himself into a corner. Gingerly, Aren slid it open.

The compartment gave way without resistance, accompanied by a small puff of dust. Aren peered inside. The sight was disappointing. Inside were a couple of folded paper sheets. Yet, unlike the rest of the rotted mess littered around the cell, these were still in relatively good condition. The drawer had been sealed off completely.

Aren had expected some type of magical artifact or deadly weapon, but still somewhat hopeful, he lifted the thick-looking sheet that was lying on top of the pile. As he spread it out, he realized that it was a hand-drawn map of Point Fire and the surrounding Frost – something that Aren knew almost too well. The scale of the Frost on the map was unusually large. His heart skipped a beat.

"Udar, come look at this!" Aren said excitedly, positioning the map on top of the desk.

Udar shambled over from his defensive position.

"Isn't that the same one they showed us at school?" he said after moment's contemplation.

"No way – look at the Frost!" Aren pointed, beaming.

This map was further reaching than any other he had ever seen, and Aren had seen most, if not all, maps of the Frost...even Sen's. Usually, just beyond the Southern Dunes and to the west in all directions, the mapmakers would have drawn some form of page filler:

a bunch of billowing ice clouds perhaps, or a frilly geometrical flourish. This map however, contained other locations and written notes that stretched beyond what Aren had once thought was the unreachable horizon. His pulse quickened as he studied the map further, seeing mentions and icons of "Glacier Runs" and a "Castle" far to the west of the city's walls. Peculiarly, the area of land east of Point Fire – over the lake – was still fully uncharted.

Looking at the westernmost portion of the Frost, Aren frowned. It was almost as if someone had taken black ash and smeared it on the paper. It stood in clear contrast to the rest of the map, which was clearly labeled and drawn. A single word was written besides the ashen smear – "*Darkness.*"

A faded red line snaked eastward from this dark wipe on the map, all the way back to the walls of Point Fire.

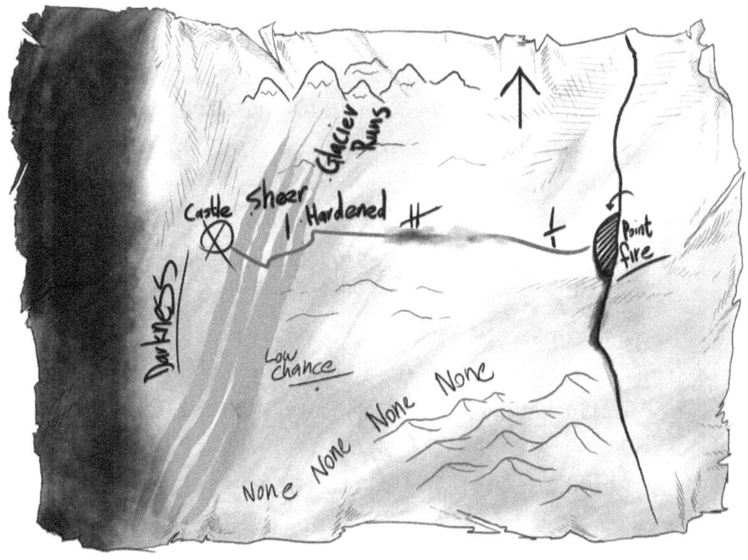

Aren closed the paper quickly and unfolded the second piece that had been lying in the drawer. This one was much smaller, and

contained only a few lines of writing, beneath which lay the circled-N Novari family crest:

South - X

East/Lake - Cathedral?

West - Darkness

Ⓝ

"Aren!" Udar whispered, panicked.

Udar had been getting bored of the map, and while Aren continued to study it, had made his way back to the entrance of the cell. He was now closing the door very slowly, his eyes wide.

"Aren, they're here!" he hissed.

Aren acted quickly, pocketing the map as well as the piece of paper. He was then surprised to discover that another object had been lying below them in the drawer. Aren immediately recognized it, heart pounding.

The missing sixth plaque. From the Heart.

He did not have the time to inspect it. He crammed it into the largest pouch inside his dunerobe.

Hopefully it doesn't rip from the weight.

"How many?" he said, creeping over to the cell door next to Udar.

"All of them," Udar shivered. "Aren, what do we do?"

Aren cursed under his breath.

"We might have to wait till it's much later. Hopefully, we can creep out then."

Udar groaned sadly and slouched over onto the wall. Aren opened the door again, peeking through the crack.

Something's wrong.

Priests were rushing in through the main entrance far below, like tiny crimson ants returning to their nest. Many of them were shouting, and Aren thought he saw a few of them carrying others as if they were gravely injured. Some of the priests had turned onto the

148

Ⓝ

staircase and were ascending it rapidly. Though this did cause Aren a small amount of stress, he knew that the cell they were in had not been disturbed in years, making it very unlikely that they would come all the way up.

They're probably just going back to their individual cells.

Even so, Aren kept an eye on them: the small platoon of crimson ants crawling in upward circles. They showed no indication of slowing down.

Surely they aren't coming here...

"Udar, look for a weapon. And try and find that needle. The poison might still be strong enough to knock a person out. Also, close the drawer."

Udar stared back, eyes wide in shock.

"You can't be serious..." he stammered.

Aren turned around. His face looked years older, and something about it terrified Udar. Udar moved back into the cell, searching frantically.

Aren fixed his eyes back on the ascending column of priests.

Only three of them now.

They were much closer. As he had feared, they were skipping the doors below: the ones leading to the smaller upper cells. With a sinking feeling, Aren could only guess which specific room they were coming for. A larger man with flowing black hair was barking phrases from the rear of the column.

Frighteningly, the priests did not appear to be afraid of the death-assuring fall. They maintained the pace of their ascent.

They're going to get here in about twenty seconds.

Aren darted back into the cell, shutting the door behind him. Udar was still frantically searching through piles of moldy paper, but to no avail.

"There's nothing here to use," Udar quivered.

"Where's the needle?"

"On the desk."

Aren retrieved the poisoned item.

"Udar, stand over here. I'll hide behind the door."

Udar had started to cry. He did what Aren said. The priests were already at the door. A key entered the cell lock. Udar began to sob loudly.

"Who trespasses here?" boomed a voice.

The next actions all happened in an instant. The cell door flew open, almost crushing Aren behind it. Two priests stepped inside and were taken aback by the sight in front of them: a tiny young boy crying miserably.

Aren emerged from behind the cell door, diving towards the nearest priest and pricking him deeply with the needle on his right hand. Before the other one could react, Aren was recovering from his roll and was already upon them, stabbing precisely with his tiny weapon. He found his mark both times: an exposed ankle and an outstretched forearm. The first of the two robed figures was already collapsing from the poison. He would be asleep for hours.

Aren was about to turn and fight the remaining priest, when a large hand closed around his wrist. The strength of the grip was terrifying. Aren struggled to writhe free of the arm, which was covered with many severe burn scars. When he realized that he would not be able to escape the iron grip, he let go of the needle, intending to catch it with his free hand. The needle fell, but before he could catch it, a powerful knee collided with his sternum. Aren doubled over, gasping for air.

"Master Aren, I do not appreciate your willingness to add to the day's casualties."

The man was missing his left arm. A blackened hole gaped through his crimson robe, which was also burnt thoroughly. These features stood in surreal contrast to his face and hair, both of which were groomed perfectly. Long black locks flowed beautifully around his shoulders.

Aren had managed to regain some of his breath and he tried to lunge for the needle that now lay on the ground. The back of Kreymar's hand caught Aren's chin. Hard. He reeled backwards, his world spinning.

"Please," Kreymar's voice was soft, cruel, "I don't have time for this. I know you may not remember me. My name is Kreymar, I run this place."

Aren could still hear Udar's pathetic sobbing.

Why doesn't he do something?

Aren realized he was flat on his back, lying on the grimy stones. Kreymar's blow had caught him completely off-guard. He suddenly remembered that he was carrying Avenir's crimson medallion. He reached into his dunerobe, desperately searching for it. Kreymar's boot collided with his ribs.

"I thought I told you. Do not try to fight me. You may look like a child, but I know of your infamy."

Pain was shooting through Aren's chest.

"Wait," he choked. "I have this."

This time, Kreymar allowed him to retrieve the medallion. Aren raised it, hopeful.

"Oh?" Kreymar crooned. He bent over and gently took the object from Aren's hand. "I do not recall any of us giving one of these to *you* personally. But I suppose these do have a certain... transitivity." He slipped the medallion into his pocket.

Kreymar continued, "But those trivialities don't matter anymore. Your bloodline is important to us now. Events have occurred that will forever change this place. Even now..."

Aren was no longer paying attention to this crazed man. His mind was racing, thinking of a way to escape. Thinking about what Avenir would do.

"...So yes, of course I will let you go," Kreymar nodded to Udar, who was still blubbering, "as well as your friend here."

A great weight lifted off Aren's shoulders. His mind slowed its churning.

"But that does not mean you will not be taught a lesson," Kreymar smiled. "Though this medallion has spared you the...customary punishment."

Treading over the two dazed priests, Kreymar approached Udar. The small boy tried to shuffle away, but the large priest grabbed

his arm and reeled him in easily. With a sickening grin, Kreymar grabbed Udar's little finger and snapped it. Udar screeched like a demon, flailing his arms and kicking his legs. Kreymar turned, ignoring the boy's whimpering. Aren's face was filled with black rage, and for a fleeting moment, the high priest paused, surprised by Aren's expression. The cold stare reappeared on Kreymar's face.

"Your turn now."

XVIII

Avenir and his mother were considering reporting Aren's disappearance to the royal guards when the boy in question crashed through the kitchen door. Avenir immediately leapt to his feet. He was still on edge from the events in the Heart, and he knew that Aren had somehow already found a way to make things worse.

"What have you done?" Avenir asked bluntly.

Aren was about to angrily respond, but then he noticed their mother sitting near the end of the kitchen table. Suddenly, the ten-year-old boy seemed to remember his age, and he burst into tears. Wailing, he ran over to his mother.

"What's happened? Aren, tell me!" Sylis cradled her child, checking for injuries.

Aren sobbed something incoherent and showed her his hand. His little finger stood at a grotesque angle. Avenir bristled at the sight.

"Where were you? South Side?" he asked.

He imagined Aren trying to do something idiotic with one of the livestock there and being bitten or trampled.

"No," Aren sniffed.

His mother had already helped him remove his dunerobe, which was dirty and wet. Aren was about to tell the truth when he realized that probably was not the best idea, given the presence of their mother.

"I had to use your red medal," said Aren cryptically.

Avenir immediately knew where his brother had been. He struggled to suppress his anger.

"I told you not to bother the Icesmiths," he lied through gritted teeth.

He glanced over at their mother, who was examining Aren's fingers. She did not seem to know, or care, what they were talking about.

"'Nir, wash Aren's dunerobe. I'm going to take him to a healer."

Without a word, Avenir grabbed his brother's dunerobe and took it to the washroom.

"Wait, wait!" Aren tried to snatch back at the robe.

"Stop it Aren," Sylis was forcing him to put on clean clothes "We're leaving right now."

Avenir could not understand why Aren was getting so worked up over the robe. Then, he noticed that the pockets were stuffed with something. One of the larger pouches contained a heavy object.

"Yes of course," Avenir answered for his brother. He shot Aren a knowing look, one that sent a terrible chill down his younger brother's spine. "I'll clean his robe *right away.*"

With a sob of defeat, Aren followed his mother out the door.

*   *   *

Aren and Sylis returned much later, during the early hours of morning. Avenir was just finishing up his dinner - a cold bowl of gruel. He and Aren avoided eye contact.

"Luckily, the breaks were clean. That's quite strange for a smithing accident, don't you think?" Sylis wondered.

"Mom, I've told you a thousand times. My hand got stuck in the machine. I could only get it out after it broke."

Aren was caressing his hand, which was now quite swollen. A splint held his fingers in place.

"Well, in any case, I'm going to send a formal complaint about the Icesmiths to the Palace tomorrow. It's absolutely ridiculous that-"

"I'll do it, don't worry about it," Avenir interrupted. "I'm heading to the North Side anyway."

"Thanks, 'Nir," Sylis looked at Avenir's meal in disapproval. "It seems you've inherited your father's cooking skills. Aren, what would you like?"

154

"Anything is okay."

Aren tried to catch his brother's eye, who quickly turned his gaze towards his homemade gruel. They sat across from each other awkwardly at the dinner table. Avenir paid him no attention, concentrating intensely on moving his dinner from side to side in the bowl.

Within a quarter of an hour, Sylis placed a delicious-smelling soup in front of Aren. The aroma of steamed vegetables and rich spices filled the room.

"Careful, it's piping hot." She noticed Avenir, who had refused to look up from his plate. "You're awfully quiet. Aren't you glad your brother is okay?"

"Yes, of course," came the mumbled response. "I had a tough day sorting out hunting equipment." He stood up. "I should get to bed."

Avenir left the table, and his half-eaten bowl of food. He ascended the stairs to their bedroom quietly. Aren watched in fear, knowing all too well that his brother would be waiting for him later. He and his mother ate their dinner in silence.

Aren made sure to wait until their mother had closed her bedroom door before ascending the dreaded wooden ladder. As he had expected, Avenir sat waiting for him, the contents of the dunerobe spread across his bed.

"Please close the trapdoor. We can't risk mother hearing any of this."

Aren obeyed. He guiltily crossed the room and lay face up on his bed.

Avenir gestured towards the items. "Explain."

As best as he could, Aren gave his brother a detailed account of what had happened earlier that day, and where he had found the items. Avenir was mildly intrigued by the description of the Caverns, but when the part about breaking into their father's cell came up, he interrupted angrily.

"How could you? How dare you! Do you have no respect for anything?" Avenir was furious but managed to keep his voice down.

Aren responded, defensive. "I *do* have respect. Don't you think Dad would have wanted us to find this?"

"You have no idea what our father wanted," Avenir hissed. The horrifying events in the Heart were still fresh in his mind.

"I know he wasn't afraid of anything, unlike *you*. If I didn't go in there today, the priests would have taken everything..."

Avenir slammed his hand on the bed. The motion did not create a lot of sound, but the violence of it silenced Aren.

"Don't call me a coward! There's a difference between being afraid and being cautious... and I think your locksmith friend knows the difference quite well."

Aren's face went white. "I'm sorry! I didn't mean to bring him..."

"Shut up. What's done is done."

In those words, Aren sensed a strange emotion in his brother. Something weary and fearful.

"Something terrible happened," Aren said. It was half question, half accusation.

Avenir sighed deeply.

Calm yourself down. Remember, no mistakes, no leaks...everyone's life could depend on it.

"No, Aren. I think something terrible is *going* to happen."

"What? Tell me!"

Avenir thought carefully, choosing his next words. "Point Fire is running out of heat. There was an explosion in the Inner Sanctum today – some sort of leak. Many priests were injured."

"I saw them!" Aren whispered excitedly. "The man who did this to me – Kreymar, I think? – was missing his whole arm!"

Avenir struggled to suppress the horror that the sound of that name conjured.

"In any case, it looks like everyone is going to freeze in about ten years," he lied.

There was no use in giving the real deadline of only one year. It would only cause unnecessary panic.

Aren's eyes widened. "Do you think Dad knew about this?"

"Yes."

"That must be why he left! You saw the notes and map, right? We figured it out 'Nir! We know why he disappeared!"

"No. No, we do not. And you cannot, under any circumstances, mention this to *anyone*."

Aren moved over to Avenir's bed, still wary of his brother's earlier bout of anger. He pointed to the dark smear on the map.

"He's there, wherever that is. I can sense it. I'm sure if we show Sen this map, he'll be able to make plans to save him."

"Don't be naïve."

Avenir had initially come to a similar conclusion after seeing what Aren had found. Yet, the more he thought about it, the more he became certain that their father was no longer alive.

If he were, he would have come back.

He knew his father had loved exploration, but even so, the idea of him simply leaving seemed too out of character, too far-fetched.

"Aren, Father is probably dead," Avenir continued bluntly. "Don't you think he would have returned by now? We can't go chasing after some pointless hope, when it is obvious that the entire city is at risk."

At this, Aren became angry. "You see? This is why you lost that Hunt Game in the dunes. You're too afraid to do anything special."

That hurt Avenir, and Aren immediately regretted saying it. Just a day ago, that statement would have cut deep, but now Avenir held a secret, a secret which somehow was able to shield his heart from jealously. The secret lay quietly in their basement, and although it was a terrible one, it provided him with a strange but unwavering sense of self-confidence.

"Anyway, I'm going to keep these things," Avenir pointed to the items strewn across the bed. "And we're going to wait."

Although he disagreed with all his heart, Aren knew that this would be the final word, at least for the time being.

"Can I see the plaque? I didn't have time before," he asked carefully.

"Sure, take a look. I'm exhausted. Hey, I almost forgot..."

Avenir reached under his bed and presented his brother with the white soft-sole boots he had purchased earlier at the Circle.

Aren could hardly contain his excitement, already forgetting the serious tone of their discussion. He ran his fingers over the silky leather. Avenir smiled and tossed the heavy plaque onto Aren's bed, before stowing away his father's other items in his dresser. He crawled into bed and fell asleep almost instantly.

After spending a good deal of time admiring his new boots, Aren intently studied the sixth plaque in the candlelight.

A fallen Master lies before you, the first of the seven. Like the others, his will is absolute. But a will does not guarantee power. Behold the prison of his soul: a tool created and exploited by men. Behold the glowing Embr beneath Point Fire.

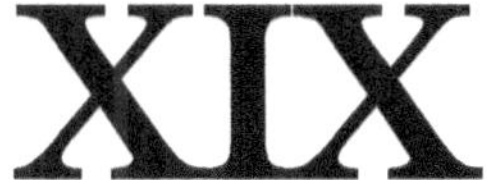

XIX

Somehow, the next month carried on in an unsettlingly normal fashion. Aren spent most of his time with Sen, learning new Hunting techniques. Avenir counted the days as he helped transport livestock to the South Side and ran errands for his mother. He carried the Great Sword with him wherever he went. Sometimes he would forget that it was there, and life would be simple. In these moments of bliss, usually when he was distracted by the task at hand, Avenir found himself actually enjoying himself. Relishing the cold mornings and seeing his breath wisp away in the freezing air as he pulled dead hares off carts.

But then he would be reminded. Often it would be a sudden occurrence, a quick surge of heat at his thigh. Other times it was by accident, his hand brushing the leather scabbard while searching for his Shard. In these moments, the terrible truth came hurtling back to him.

Did I cause the death of those priests? How much time do we have left? Why didn't you come back?

Conditions in the Frost were worsening at a higher rate, adding to his long list of anxieties. Only a small number of Hunters had actually noticed this, but he himself had become highly attuned to any slight changes in the weather. He kept thinking back to a small game Hunt just a week prior, when an unusually icy wind had forced his pod to hunker down.

"It seems like the Frost really doesn't want its hares to die!" Soljan had joked.

Even more terrifying was the barely noticeable decrease in the heat available throughout the city itself. Rumors had since begun to spread around the populace. A heat-line powering a house stove in Point Fire's outskirts would briefly die out. A blacksmith would cough in impatience as his ores took just a little bit longer to melt. Hunters had even started to wear their full dunerobes inside the taverns.

On one particularly frigid afternoon in the Pit, Avenir had overheard two women gossiping:

"...my one also went out! Franza was furious."

"It's unbelievable what those Royal snobs are doing. I heard from Gren that he actually saw some guards pouring ice onto one of the heat-lines."

*   *   *

As time went on, and another month dragged by, every person in the city was feeling a barely perceptible sense of unease. By this point, Avenir knew of more rumors than he had time to count:

The king is dead, and they are using extra heat to cremate him... There's a leak in the palace and no one can fix it... Demons have invaded the Point and are taking the heat from the guilty.

Eventually, some invisible threshold was reached, and a lunatic from the Pit vandalized one of the bridge entrances to the Keep. Angry and accusatory words painted in a white substance had been scrawled over every surface:

Luxus II has boiling-hot baths! There goes OUR heat!

At first it was hilarious to all. People gathered in the Circle, jeering and laughing at the royal guards who furiously scraped away the messages. But it was not long before the laughter turned to angry cries, when people realized that the heat was the only thing keeping their families alive. The guards made short work of the mob, dispersing them to the far edges of the Circle. But ever since that moment, a small posse of angry citizens had made it their daily business to protest in front of the bridges.

Just when Avenir was beginning to wonder if all the royal family had indeed disappeared – even Luna was nowhere to be seen – an

160

announcement was made that King Luxus II himself would address the people. The speech would be tomorrow, at midday.

*　　　　*　　　　*

The two brothers stood in front of the Keep, jostling for a better position. A raised pulpit had been erected right in front of the royal palace. Guards skittered around like teeming black ants with their armored exoskeletons clinking loudly.

Avenir was near the end of his rope with Aren's behavior. Ever since he had told him about the "explosion" in the Inner Sanctum, it was as if Aren felt that it was his obligation to tell as many people as possible. He first heard Aren spilling the beans when he happened to pass him as he was talking to a group of similar-aged children:

"No, no, no," Aren had said, thrilled. "I know what happened. A fireball erupted underneath the Keep. Fourteen dead...at *least*."

Avenir had stopped to shoot him an incredulous look. When he noticed his older brother was one of the onlookers, Aren had blushed intensely.

"Well, that's what I heard at least. Rumors and all..."

If it had not been for the abundance of other, equally outrageous-sounding stories, Avenir was sure he would have lost it then and there. He had given Aren a stern talking-to that night.

"Why is this taking so long?" Aren was getting restless.

"Be quiet."

Even with the mass of bodies that had accumulated in front of the Keep, the cold air was piercing. Embr's scabbard still hung at Avenir's hip. He wished he could just throw it away into the crowd, to forget about it somehow. But it just hung there, weighing down on his mind.

"PLEASE BOW!" a booming voice echoed out over the crowd.

161

Everyone obeyed instantly. Although most people were unhappy with the current state of their lives in Point Fire, they were not yet ready to disrespect the family who ruled their shelter.

King Luxus II appeared at the pulpit, which seemed to diminish in size under the man's broad shoulders. Filamentous grey hairs danced around his face and caught in his beard. He was wearing the ceremonial royal dress. Brilliant oranges and sunless blacks shone outwards from his figure.

"Citizens of Point Fire. I must apologize for my late arrival." His voice carried almost too far given its low volume. He was a true orator. "My bath was filling slowly today."

Avenir snorted. It took a few seconds for the joke to catch on, and soon the entire crowd was guffawing. Their laughter came from a mixture of paranoia and complete admiration. The old king raised his hands, signaling silence.

"On a more serious note, I have indeed heard your concerns and criticisms. I too have felt the effects of the increased cold. Currently, there is a palace-wide ban on excessive heat use, in case you thought otherwise" – claps of approval rang out in the courtyard – "I ask that you do the same." The clapping came to a halt. Luxus II continued, "We are indeed running on a heat shortage, and it appears as if the Frost is trying to take advantage of this."

Clever, marking the Frost as the real enemy.

"Nevertheless, if we band together, and only slightly limit our consumption for a brief period, this drought will be quickly overcome...Or so my experts have told me. Remember, we are alone here. As a tough family, we will stand united against the cold."

Luxus II raised his hands again. Thunderous applause echoed off the dark walls of the castle. And then, just as quickly as he had appeared, the leader of Point Fire was gone.

"Why didn't he tell the truth?" Aren asked, a little too loudly for Avenir's taste.

Avenir prodded him hard in the back.

"Of course, he told the truth!" he said loudly.

When they had passed over the bridge, and back through the Circle's portcullis into the Fynn, Avenir pulled Aren into a crack between two buttresses.

"Are you out of your mind?" he snapped, "What is the *matter* with you? What I told you needs to be kept a *secret.*"

"Well I can't help it if someone just lies like that," Aren pouted.

Avenir let out a long, exasperated sigh.

Sometimes I forget his age.

"Yes, *Aren.* You are the *epitome* of honesty."

"Hmph. Don't you have a Hunt or something to prepare for?"

"Yes, as a matter of fact I do."

The next Hunt was indeed soon – just two days away.

*   *   *

Avenir was polishing his father's frostwood bow, thinking about the cold. He would be in a two-man pod with only Soljan this time – just enough for a small game Hunt. Piet was still recovering from his injury. The large man had tried to sneak into a Hunting pod one day, but Sen had quickly shown him back to his quarters. Luna was still nowhere to be seen.

Aren had gone to explore the North Side. Avenir knew that his brother's friend, Udar, still refused to talk to him.

Perhaps that's why he's being so stubborn.

He smiled sadly. Aren was just like him in some ways, exploring the city or going out into the Frost when he was angry or troubled. They had probably inherited it from their father.

Avenir thought about the papers Aren had retrieved from the Cathedral. He had already memorized his father's map. What utterly amazed him was not that his father had created what was essentially a cartographer's dream, rather, it was that no one else had ever even scratched the surface of his supposed discoveries.

Was my father so far superior to the other Hunters? To Sen? And why did he keep that knowledge hidden? For himself?

163

While it did bestow upon him a strong sense of pride, the idea also brought with it a deep sense of paranoia.

Something was not right with my father.

Avenir had tried to search deep into the recesses of his memory for anything that would hint at why he had left. Still, all he could remember were flashes of a happy childhood: learning how to use a Shard, exploring, laughing at Flyer cubs playing in the distance.

Had he become colder before he disappeared? More distant?

He wracked his brain, trying to remember any details at all about the days, even months, before his father's disappearance. He came up short. His father had always been perfect, a legendary Hunter everyone looked up to. He could not even recall whether his father had ever even been injured on a Hunt...

Although there was that one time he managed to burn himself in the Heart...Had he said he brushed against the viewing panes?

At least he now knew where he had probably disappeared to, and some part of him was happy Aren had found out. What his brother had said to him had been somewhat true.

"He wasn't afraid of anything, unlike you."

He hated to admit it, but he himself would have never gone into that cell. Aren thought that Avenir did not know of its existence, but that was not the case. He had known of the cell for years, but he could never bring himself to open it. Whether it was out of respect for his father, or a fear for the unknown, he was not certain. He was certain, however, that if he *had* gone and opened that door a few years ago, he would be lying on the flagstones with a lethal needle in his chest.

*   *   *

The morning of the Hunt arrived, bringing with it a dreary grey wind. Aren could not help but wish his brother good luck, even though they had been on somewhat shaky terms lately.

"Thanks," Avenir said, relieved that his brother seemed to have gotten over their recent bout of arguing.

"What's the target today?"

164

"Only small game again. Another pod got lucky about a week ago and brought back a pretty big haul."

"I can't wait till I can actually come with."

"If the animals are still alive by then," Avenir joked cynically.

*   *   *

He met Soljan in the tavern. To Avenir's surprise, the tracker had pulled his hair into a tight bun.

"I see you're no longer wearing the 'Wild Hunter' look," he teased.

"Avenir! Have a seat," Soljan pulled out a chair. A golden ale awaited him on the table.

"You shouldn't have."

"Please," Soljan chortled. "It's about time I made a dent in our legendary payment." He raised his gourd of Blood and sloshed it around playfully.

Avenir smiled. "I've been afraid to use it," he lied. "Honestly, it was a little bit too much for me to appreciate, I think."

"Always so careful!" Soljan laughed. "That is why you make the best Hunting partner." He gestured towards the bar, where Darch stood cleaning tankards. "I hear he just received a package. Sweetbreads from South Side. Want one?"

"I'm not that hungry. It sounds good though."

"I'm not taking that for an answer. Didn't you ever learn that being hungry before a Hunt is bad luck? It's on me." He motioned to Darch with his gourd.

"What're you two fine men thirsting for?" The barman waddled towards them, still cleaning a tankard. There must have been quite a large party the previous night.

"Actually, two of your finest sweetbreads please."

"Comin' right up. That'll be one Small." Darch held out his gourd. It was an oversized sphere commonly used by shopkeepers and merchants. Soljan produced a miniature measuring unit marked *"1/2 Small"* and carefully poured out the correct amount. Once the bright

165

liquid had been deposited into Darch's container, Soljan turned back to Avenir,

"I see you're still using your old man's bow."

Darch dropped two plates of steaming food in front of them. The sour aroma of the freshly dough-wrapped organs swirled upwards in hot tendrils. Soljan ate ravenously and motioned for Avenir to join him.

As they ate, they briefly went over the plans for the Hunt. It would be a short excursion to the northwest, with the goal of retrieving any amount of small game. This category included animals such as hares, snow-ferrets, or any species of rodent. If they were lucky, they might even be able to bring home a Frost Fox.

Given their limited pod size, they were allowed under no circumstances to attempt to Hunt larger game. A single Saber could make quick work of a two-person unit.

After eating, the two Hunters thanked Darch before leaving, and began preparing their equipment and weapons. Sabers and Frost Flyers were rare in the northwest portion of the Frost, so Avenir had only packed a Shard, as well as his father's bow. Staying hidden from large game was a far better strategy than facing them. Still, the Great Sword remained on his belt.

"New sword?" said Soljan, eyeing the leather scabbard.

"Yes, just something cheap I carry around with me now. You can never be too careful with the way people have been acting lately."

Soljan could sense something strange in Avenir's voice, but he shrugged a shrug that said, "If you say so," and went back to inventorying his potions.

This Hunt did not require the use of any poisons or weapon augmentations, but Avenir had still remembered to bring Yugo's Soul Scream. He tucked the inert-looking substance into one of his dunerobe pockets.

"And that?"

"One of Yugo's newest creations. I promised him I'd try it out."

"That man has nothing but my respect. If it wasn't for him," Soljan flourished his hand in front of his pouch, which was filled to the brim with vials, "I might be out of business."

*　　　　*　　　　*

There was no real time constraint to their Hunt, but they both agreed that getting it done as fast as possible was the easiest, and safest, option. Avenir pulled his ice gauze tightly over his eyes as they left the safety of the walls. The grey wind had turned to a white flurry.

"Well Soljan, it looks like the Frost doesn't want us out here for too long anyway."

The tracker nodded, making sure that no openings were exposed through his dunerobe.

It really is frigid.

It was a rare occasion that Avenir was grateful for the small amount of warmth emanating from the scabbard on his hip.

Soljan led the way out through the exit into the Frost. It was like walking into the maw of an icy beast. If this had been a Hunt on a larger scale, it would have almost certainly been called off.

"Avenir, rub some of this on your face. It washes out well, so you don't have to take off your gloves," Soljan beckoned with a small vial. "It seems we may have slightly underestimated the chill-factor today."

Avenir obliged, pouring the foul-smelling tallow onto his gloves. Holding his breath, he massaged it into his cheeks and lips. Once he got used to the smell, it felt amazing. Like dipping his head into a warm bath.

"You see? You have the almighty Yugo to thank for that."

Soljan applied a layer to his own face and returned the vial to its pouch. He extended his first two fingers in a sign that meant "let's go" and began carving a path through the snowfall. The powder underfoot had already packed to about an arm's length deep. Avenir thanked whoever had invented the wide-base snowshoes they were wearing. Without them, moving in terrain this deep would have been near impossible.

When they were approximately two miles out, the wind really started to pick up. The constant flurry of ice painfully stung what little of Avenir's face stuck out from under the gauze. The world had been reduced to two tones: the white of the snow beneath them, and the speckled grey of the air above it. The visibility was not too bad for Avenir's eyes, but he still suggested that he and Soljan tie themselves together. Soljan agreed. Once the thin rope was between them, the tracker led the way onward.

An hour later, Soljan pulled his hand into a fist, his thumb facing horizontally: '*Stop here for planning.*'

The two of them huddled together as Soljan unfolded the white travel tarp he carried. He pulled it over their heads. With a gasp of relief, Avenir pulled off his ice gauze. His voice was muffled by the large clumps of snow falling outside their momentary haven.

"Damn. This is a rough one."

"Yes, about as dreary as they get. Would you agree that we stay here about two hours, see what comes by, and then head back?"

"That sounds perfect to me. I don't want to mess around in this any more than you do."

Soljan nodded and produced two metal anchors and a long spike. Working swiftly, he used the anchors to fix the tarp into the snow beneath them. Avenir stomped the powder underfoot, packing it tight enough to lie on. The tracker quickly sorted through his vial pouch, found what he was looking for, and promptly tossed it some distance away from their hideout. He then fixed the long spike under the front of the tarp, raising the entire length of material slightly. After untying the rope between them, the two Hunters took up a prone position underneath the tarp, close enough to each other to feel cramped. They had secured themselves a makeshift lookout, perfectly camouflaged amongst the falling ice.

Avenir lay with his bow in front of him on the packed snow, peering out through the crack beneath the tarp. All they had to do was wait for Soljan's lure to work its magic.

*   *   *

Thirty-four minutes passed before the first signs of movement. Avenir struggled to see what was causing it, so he guessed it must have been a white snow-ferret. It did not help that conditions had been slowly worsening. Luckily, he had Soljan's warm body heat — and Embr's — to keep him company.

Still, it's not as bad as that Frost Storm with Aren...yet.

169

He knocked an arrow and pulled his bow taut, still completely under the tarp. The creature appeared, its movements nonchalant. Its strangely long, furry body, and equally lengthy whiskers gave it the appearance of a pleasant and fuzzy worm. It stayed snug to the ground as it moved, practically hugging the snow with its four little paws. Avenir gulped. It was far easier killing a bloodthirsty Saber than this fragile, happy-looking ferret.

He waited till it found the vial before releasing the arrow. He fired from the prone position, and the projectile skimmed soundlessly over the surface of snow. It kicked up slow-moving tendrils of ice as it flew. The arrow-tip struck near the animal's head. The front end of its body recoiled backwards, sending its flexible body wheeling. It died instantaneously.

Avenir quickly got up from his hiding spot under the tarp and jogged over to the fallen ferret. He pulled the arrow out, was pleased to find it undamaged, and returned it to his quiver. Drops of red were sprinkled across the otherwise unblemished whiteness below his boots. The snow had melted a little where the steaming blood had landed.

"What was it? I could barely see what happened," came the tracker's voice.

"Snow-ferret."

Avenir produced the haul when he rejoined his partner under their warm tarp.

"Devilish little bastards," sniffed Soljan.

"Really? I kind of like them."

"You say that until they eat out your starch storages."

"Anyway, it left quite a mess out there. A curious fox might want to investigate."

Soljan took the limp snow-ferret and stored it in another pouch, "That...would be divine."

*   *   *

The snowfall increased relentlessly over the next hour. It was not nearly as cold as the Frost Storm though. In fact, it was getting uncomfortably warm in their tarp-tent.

"By the Seven! Soljan gasped quietly, "Are you a living heat-line?"

Avenir forced a chuckle. "No, but if you're really *that* warm, you must be getting a pretty severe fever."

Avenir felt for his belt, then for the scabbard. Fresh beads of sweat broke out on his back as he detected the small puddle that had accumulated underneath it.

Let's hope this goes by quickly. Damn this Blade.

Avenir realized he had almost forgotten about the Soul Scream. He pulled out the vial and gingerly applied the liquid to his arrow, thinking of the terrifying effects that Yugo had described. He reassumed his position next to Soljan, making sure that the tracker did not see the puddle.

*　　　　　*　　　　　*

When there were twenty minutes left in their planned timeframe, Avenir noticed the next flicker of movement. The falling snow was now cascading heavily, each flake as big as a child's hand. His earlier prediction had been correct: the bushy tail of a Frost Fox darted playfully near the bloody mess across the snow. It was barely perceptible among the waterfall of white paint that was dripping from the sky. Soljan had not noticed the animal yet.

He may be asleep. Heat can make one unusually exhausted.

Once more, Avenir pulled the bowstring tight as he observed his target.

The fox's head came into focus, a perfectly white visage with slanted markings above its eyes that gave it the appearance of being permanently grumpy. He trained the arrow between those markings. The fox cantered over to where the slain ferret had fallen. It sniffed the ground, its wet black nose twitching furiously.

171

Within easy killing distance.

Avenir's hairs stood on end. At first, he thought he was imagining it. A faint whine in the base of his skull. The sound reminded him of the feeling he got when someone shouted too loudly into his ear, or when the ring of a blacksmith's hammer was just that little bit too sharp. Then, the noise amplified drastically. A deep but somehow high-pitched squeal rose up from within his bones. The fox must have heard it too and was pawing at its ears in pain. Soljan was wide-awake now.

"Avenir, what's–"

It happened almost too quickly for Avenir to understand... or see. The only reason he noticed it at all was because of his Hunter's Vision. A faint line of darkness raced from behind the fox towards them. It was like a shadow – not the black void of night that children are afraid of – but rather, it was as if the light above had slightly changed angle, and the resultant shade had selectively lengthened in a moving line. With this strange tinted beam came a terrible wave of cold.

As the line of altered light passed over the fox, the animal wobbled, then collapsed. Within a heartbeat, the line had reached their tarp.

No time to speak. To react.

As the shadow touched them, the noise dug itself into Avenir's eyes, and pierced through his feet. It was a terrible, evil scream. He grabbed at his ears and curled into a ball. Soljan was doing the same. It felt like the sound was pouring out from his mouth, and through his very skin.

This complete hell only lasted for a few seconds. When it was over, Avenir found himself lying on the snow, sweating, and battered. The sound of Soljan's panicked gasps was all he could hear now.

"Ss... Soljan?" He struggled to find his voice again.

He felt around his body for any injuries.

Had the sound only been an illusion?

Soljan sat up groggily, rubbing his ears. He slowly turned towards Avenir. His eyes were glinting a strange shade of blue.

Something is wrong with him.

"Why are you here?" Soljan whispered, his dark eyes cutting and indignant.

"Hey, are you–"

"Imposter!" Soljan jabbed his finger at Avenir, "You take it from me and think you deserve it. You act as if you are special. You think you can see things I can't!"

His voice had reached a fever pitch. Avenir was stunned into silence. Soljan's voice lowered to a terrifying, maddened whisper.

"I should kill you right here. Spare you the future which you face."

He dove towards Avenir, who was already reaching for his Shard. Because they had both been writhing in pain from the sound, the tarp had tangled awkwardly around them, and Avenir could not pull out his weapon before Soljan was upon him, fingers clawing at his throat. His bow had somehow wrapped itself around his neck and right arm, further constricting his movement. Soljan noticed that Avenir was desperately trying to bring his Shard into a usable position. The trapper grabbed his arm, shouting triumphantly as he ripped the weapon from his hand. Avenir kicked out hard into the man's forearm. Soljan yelped as the Shard flew out of his hand, landing somewhere in the snow beyond the tarp. Avenir scrambled backwards out from under the fabric. It was still snowing heavily. His ragged breaths were muffled in the eerie tranquility of the snow. Soljan's head appeared beneath the material. He was holding his own Shard.

173

"Where do you think you're going?" he growled.

Soljan moved unusually fast, skittering out to follow Avenir. The bow was still wrapped around Avenir's shoulder. He would not be able to nock an arrow fast enough from this position.

I have no choice.

He reached for Embr. His hand closed around the warm stone-like surface of the hilt. The leather wrappings around the grip must have come off during the struggle. Still, he hesitated to use the Great Sword. Images of burning priests flashed through his mind.

Soljan was now on his feet. The tracker was oddly calm.

He's really going to kill me.

Avenir drew the Great Weapon.

XXI

The day had passed quickly for Aren, and he now lay on the edge of a towering fortress in the Pit. It was a quiet area, adjacent to the fringe of the district. It was also a place where law-abiding citizens would not dare to tread, given its precarious location. Aren, however, felt completely safe at this height. He enjoyed sneaking into places his mother called "dangerous" or "unsavory," always making sure to stay to the rooftops and parapets. Sometimes, if he got lucky, he would find and watch groups of masked men slash a heat-line and attempt to harvest some Blood.

Always unsuccessfully.

Other times, he would witness the secretive exchange of some unknown substance. Mostly, he gazed at mothers and fathers walking their children to school. There were so many worlds within the walls of Point Fire. To see them, all one had to do was climb on top of a building and wait.

This time, unfortunately, nothing of interest had happened in the streets below. It was snowing furiously. Not letting a good rooftop go to waste, Aren found a nook in the masonry and tried to take a nap. Guilty thoughts of Udar prevented him from doing so. He really felt terrible about what had happened at the Cathedral. He had tried numerous times to visit Udar's home, to apologize, but no one ever answered the door. Aren knew he should not bother trying to break in, it being a locksmith's home and all.

He thought about Avenir on his Hunt, and suddenly felt very jealous that he did not have a Shard. The age restriction on all weapons in Point Fire was sixteen, which Aren thought was quite ridiculous, given that he could probably wield them better than anyone else. Sen agreed with his opinion on this – "Children should understand what toys their parents are playing with."

He let his eyes lazily wander over the streets below. A man was sitting on a crudely paved road, his shoulders hunched against the stone walls. His clothes were filthy and there was dirt caked in his hair. Another man walked past him, consciously keeping his gaze averted. The one who was hunched over did not look up either. Aren wondered what that would feel like.

Searing pain.

A terrible ringing in his skull caused Aren to cry out. Luckily, he happened to be wedged into the stone nook, or he probably would have fallen off the roof. Tears welled up in his eyes.

Then the sensation was gone.

Aren heard pottery breaking in the distance. A woman screaming. Dazed, he looked down into the street. Both men lay on the ground, hands covering their heads. The man who had walked past the other was the first to get up. He looked around, confused. The homeless man lurched upright. He spoke loudly enough so that the sound reached Aren on the rooftop.

"Ye bastard! Men like you think yer can jus leave us 'er to rot!"

The other man was clearly surprised. Aren saw his eyebrows raise in amazement, then quickly widen in fear, as the man who had spoken moved towards him quickly. Before Aren could blink, they had fallen into a desperate brawl. The homeless man was feverishly scratching at the other's face, and when that did not seem to be working, began swinging at him wildly.

But the other one was burly-looking – the usual type of person roaming the Pit's less frequented areas – and when he had regained his resolve, he powerfully shoved his assailant away.

"Are you raving mad? By the Seven, I should have you locked up," the burly man shouted.

The homeless man clattered against the grey cobblestones. He seemed like he was hurt, but then, to Aren's horror, he sprung back up again.

"Me, punish'd? Me? We'll see about dat."

He launched himself at the other man again, who easily caught him by the arm and flung him over his shoulder onto the cobblestones. The man landed with a sickening crack.

He must be some sort of bodyguard.

"I'm warning you, you lunatic. If you attack me one more time, I *will* kill you."

The homeless man staggered to his feet.

"Then do et. Was happenin slowly anyways."

He pounced, hoisting a large piece of broken cobblestone.

Aren saw the burly man reaching for something underneath his robe. He called out frantically from the rooftop.

"Stop!"

But it was too late. A long dagger lay buried in the homeless man's chest, just above his stomach. For a few brief moments, the men were still. They both fell backward, one of them grasping at his chest in shock, the other watching. The burly man turned his head towards where Aren had called out from, then instantly back when the other man started speaking again.

"What have ye done to me?" It sounded like genuine fear to Aren. "I din' mean it!"

The homeless man stumbled towards the bodyguard.

The burly one had had enough. He kicked out hard, right at the location of the stab wound. His boot caught the dagger, driving it deeper into the other man's sternum, who stumbled backwards,

gasping. Aren hid out of sight. After looking up again and seeing no one, the burly one darted away into the shadows. Streams of blood flowed in little rivulets between the cobblestones.

*   *   *

Soljan froze when he saw the Great Sword. His eyes narrowed in contempt, and Avenir noticed a strange, primal glint in them. The Weapon crackled like a young fire being brought to life. An orange aura of light emanated out from its edges, as if a small sun lay just out of sight behind the flat of the Blade. A miniature solar eclipse had formed in Avenir's hand.

Soljan — or whatever it was the man had become — had not yet moved: he appeared to be afraid of the angry glow.

At least for the time being.

The trapper took a step forwards, unsure of himself. Avenir echoed his movement in the opposite direction. It was beginning to dawn on him that there was truly nowhere to run. Heavy snow was falling as far as the eye could see in all directions.

Soljan kept on pressuring him backwards with his Shard. This would be a fight to the death, Avenir could sense it. After a few more agonizing paces, Avenir decided to stand his ground.

There's no use running, even in this weather. Soljan could easily track me down.

He raised the Great Sword to shoulder level, its tip focused on Soljan's chest. The blade was releasing unimaginable warmth, forcing trails of sweat down his forehead, but somehow his hand remained steady.

Soljan, please. Soljan, you have to **STOP.**

As if Embr had been listening in on his thoughts, the Great Sword responded with a brief but terrifying pulse of warm light. Avenir's vision was consumed by total whiteness. The energy released was tremendous, but somehow it did not burn any part of his body. The pulse of warmth shot outwards from the blade in a circular wave, kicking

178

up snow as it traveled. The wave passed over Soljan. His eyes glazed over, and he crumpled silently in a white puff of ice.

The warmth was moving so fast that it disappeared over the surrounding dunes in all directions within a fraction of a second. All that remained was the vacuous silence of the falling snow. Avenir stood still, shocked, before he realized that his hand holding the Great Sword was bleeding. He unfurled his fingers slowly. What looked like tiny thorns had formed along the crimson grip. They retracted painfully, almost like a cat's claws, where Avenir's skin broke contact with them. A putrid wave of revulsion swept across his body. With a startled cry, he dropped the Weapon into the snow. It lay there, sizzling, and glaring at him while his blood seeped off its grip into the snow. Avenir forced himself to tear his eyes away from it and refocus on his fallen friend. The afterimages of the burning priests played again in his mind.

"Soljan!"

He rushed towards him and turned his crumpled body over. Soljan's features were caked with the freshly fallen powder, but he appeared unscathed. To Avenir's great relief, he could see small packets of snow flutter around the man's nostrils.

He's still breathing. He's okay.

He quickly re-erected the tarp and dragged Soljan's limp body underneath.

*   *   *

Aren ran away along the rooftop as fast as he could. He was frightened, terrified even. He had never seen a person die before, and the ease by which it had happened nauseated him.

He was quite sure that no one else had seen him spying from the rooftop. Still, he stole backward glances regularly, expecting to see a troop of royal guards climbing after him at any moment. Or even worse, the murderer.

None appeared, but deep down Aren knew that things were only going to get worse the further he ran into the city. Something terrible was happening in Point Fire.

179

That noise. The pottery breaking. The woman screaming.

As he listened carefully, the sounds of chaos seemed to be coming from all directions. A volley of curse words from a nearby alley. More items breaking. A child's wailing. He did not know what was happening, but he could only guess that the piercing, painful noise had something to do with it.

He managed to escape the rooftops of the Pit. He now stood on a section of ramparts that made up the outer rim of the Circle. At the center of the city, a scene of utter chaos unfolded before him.

It was like some sort of over-the-top performance by the royal jesters. People were running around like lunatics. Cries of rage and forced laughter joined together in a grim cacophony. Traders' storefronts were being upturned. Their brightly colored contents painted the cobblestones with reds and oranges. Countless brawls had broken out, with men tearing at women's skirts, as well as at each other's hair.

Aren noticed that some people, just like himself, were unaffected by whatever had happened, and stood by in horror or fought frantically to defend themselves. It was a raving den of madness. The usually hearty glow of the massive heat lines surrounding the Keep had become an apocalyptic orange spotlight. Aren saw a man mount another person, fists raised in fury. His eyes glinted bestially in the surreal twilight.

Just as the Circle seemed to be reaching a climax of fear and confusion, Aren felt a brief and intense pulse of warmth that disappeared just as abruptly as it had come. Hands that had just been raised fell to the wayside as their owners regained their faculties with uniform looks of shock and disgust.

The noise did not quiet down, however. What had once been cries of rage or sobs of fear turned to those of accusation and confusion. Royal guards, many of whom had been involved in the brawls, struggled to restore a sense of sanity and order to the Circle. Aren slumped backwards on a wall, feeling like he was drowning. He had almost forgotten to breathe.

What. Just. Happened?

*   *   *

"Did I miss the Hunt?" Soljan sat up, sputtering. "What happened?"

Tears of joy welled up in Avenir's eyes. His friend had returned.

"Thank the Seven."

Avenir fell on his backside, relieved. He sensed that the real Soljan had returned to his body, but still chose his words carefully in the minutes following their fight. He recounted almost everything, all the while focusing intently on the intonation and emotion in Soljan's responses to his story, searching for any hints that the man may still be possessed. He intentionally left out the parts concerning Embr, having already restored the Great Sword to its former state of anonymity. Bafflingly, it appeared that the tracker truly remembered none of the recent events.

"I just recall having this terrible pain in my skull," said Soljan as he rubbed the base of his neck. "It was like someone was drilling deep inside it."

"...but you don't remember us fighting?"

"Nothing. Nothing but darkness."

Those words reminded Avenir of the barely imperceptible shadow that had raced over the snow – something that Soljan also had no explanation for.

"Soljan, I hate to say it, but I think we just survived something truly evil."

"Listen to yourself, Avenir. It was probably some of Yugo's new poison that got into us somehow."

Yes...Could that be it?

Avenir glanced at the Soul Scream-lined arrow he had been ready to use. It was still wet with the liquid Yugo had given him. The vial itself had disappeared in the struggle earlier. He could only hope that its contents and vapors were still safely trapped inside. After considering the possibility, he slowly shook his head.

"Perhaps...No...I don't think that's it. Yugo described a different reaction. And if you had a higher dose than me – assuming that *is* what just happened – you would probably be dead by now. Or worse."

"So, what do you think we should do? It seems you are in a far saner position to make that decision than me."

Avenir's brow furrowed in concern. "I say we go straight back to Point Fire, to the royal palace. Report this to king Luxus." He hesitated for a second. "And maybe I'll pay a visit to the Heart."

Soljan eyes widened in surprise, but he kept his thoughts to himself. He and Avenir left the confines of the tarp and began packing up. Out of the corner of his eye, Avenir spotted a small lump in the snow just a few feet away. He knew immediately what it was, and something about the inconspicuousness of the mound made him uneasy.

"It looks like our foxy friend wasn't so lucky," Avenir said, as he trudged over to the heap.

A quick brush-aside of the newly fallen snow revealed the medium-sized Frost Fox's head. Its eyes were an unnatural shade of blue. The poor creature had died instantly.

XXII

Entering Point Fire, the two Hunters returned to what Soljan labeled as "A state of Frost Shock."

"I've only seen something like this once before," the trapper explained in a low voice, as people cowered in their homes and behind closed doors. "It was when I was a child, after the Great Ice Storm. It terrified me."

"I'm not so sure this is the same, Soljan." Avenir had noticed a strange look of guilt in many of the people's eyes. "The storm today was harsh, but many have seen far worse. We were in the thick of it, after all."

They searched for Sen at his office – if one could call it that – in the Hunters' district, with the hope of claiming the payment for their meager haul. The massive man was nowhere to be seen. Avenir noticed one of the office guards slipping a note underneath Sen's door.

"Is he out?" asked Avenir.

The guard responded as if in a daze, "Yes, I believe he was called to the Pit somewhere..."

This is a bad sign. There's no way Sen would have skipped a Hunter's payment... or missed our return.

Deciding that perhaps it would be best to try again the next day, they stored the two animal carcasses in one of various freeze-lockers near Sen's office. After making sure it was sealed shut and handing Soljan the key, Avenir spoke again, breaking the ominous silence they had shared for a while.

"Let's go home and find out what the hell happened."

"Agreed."

It was the first time Avenir could recall that he felt truly uneasy walking through a district, especially the Hunters'. He felt like some sort of outcast.

Everyone knows something I don't. They're wondering why I'm out in the open.

He made it home without greeting or talking to a single citizen. There were none of the usual conversations or the crunching footsteps across the ever-present snow. He feared the worst as he unlocked the door.

"Who... is it?" The fearful voice of his mother drifted down from his bedroom in the loft.

"It's Avenir! Mom?"

He was suddenly full of adrenaline.

Is there an intruder in the house?

"My 'Nir!" It sounded like she was choking back tears. "Come in quick! Lock the door... I was so worried!"

He did as she asked, relieved that there was not someone else inside.

He called up to her, "What's happened? Are you okay?"

"Just come up," she sounded uncertain, shaken. "Aren is here too."

This deeply troubled Avenir. It was not like his brother to be this quiet. He clambered up the wooden ladder into the attic. His mother and Aren lay in the same bed – his brother's – her hand gently cradling his head. Avenir tried to speak but could not find the words.

"It's okay," she said. "I think it's calmed down outside. We're just a bit shaken, that's all."

Aren was blushing a deep red, obviously embarrassed that his older brother was seeing him like this. Avenir noticed, however, that he did not move out from his mother's embrace.

He sat down on his bed, facing his family. They were clearly relieved that he had returned home unharmed. He mustered up his voice, having gotten over the shock from seeing them like this.

"Tell me what happened."

Aren responded first, to Avenir's surprise.

184

"I saw someone get murdered... It was terrible."

Sylis shifted her arm from Aren's head to his shoulders, giving him a quick squeeze.

"It's okay, Aren. I think a lot of people aren't feeling like themselves now either." She turned to Avenir. "All hell broke loose in the city."

Could it be?

Soljan's crazed stare resurfaced in Avenir's mind, the blue glint in his eyes. He wished to the core of his being that he was wrong in his assumption of what had happened here, too.

"I don't understand," he said hopefully.

"I had some great pain in my head, and then people just started...*attacking* each other. Luckily, I was just outside the front door, cleaning. Otherwise..." she stopped, collecting herself. "I saw old Hendril – you know, the quiet elder down the road? – beat a passerby on the street. I wanted to shout something. Next thing I know, there's this man just behind them – they're at each other's throats by now – and then he's looking right at me. He's holding a knife and *looking right at me*, and he starts running. By the Seven 'Nir, I've never been so scared in my life. I locked myself in just in time and he starts banging on the door. 'Let me in!' he says, 'Or I'll slit your little boy's throat, that brat.'"

Avenir looked at his mother, stupefied.

She continued, struggling not to cry, "He wouldn't go away, no matter what I said. I was practically sobbing, begging him to leave. I could hear terrible things happening outside...then everything went warm for a second, and it all stopped. Aren came back a half-hour after that, just as terrified as I was. He also said everything had somehow stopped in the Pit after the strange heat."

Everything fell into place in Avenir's mind. He got up briskly and ran downstairs.

"'Nir! Where are you going? Please don't–" Sylis stopped short at the sound of her son vomiting profusely in the bathroom.

Avenir gripped the edges of the toilet seat, white-knuckled, watching the last of his breakfast fall into the underground chasm far below.

It's far worse than I could have ever imagined. Did I — or Embr — just unknowingly save Point Fire from total destruction?

The sequence of events that his mother had retold all slid into place within a sickening narrative that terrified him. He felt a deepening sense of dread, far worse than the nervous sweats he had experienced after the ordeal in the Inner Sanctum.

That same shadow had hit Point Fire, and all of its citizens...

He retched again.

It was like what happened to Soljan, except with the entire city. And the saving warmth. Could it have been me? No...

He fought back a third wave of nausea.

Yes...It had to be me. Or rather Embr. Embr saved Point Fire from whatever that shadow initiated.

He cleaned his mouth in the sink, and groggily made his way back upstairs.

"Are you sure you're okay?" asked his mother.

"...Yes, I had a similar experience in the Hunters' district, not nearly as bad though. I thought it was just because the daily haul wasn't adequate."

He knew he could not tell his mother, or even Aren, the truth.

That evening, Sylis told the boys she would cook them their favorite meal: scrambled eggs and rabbit stew. While she worked, Avenir constantly checked the windows to make sure it was safe.

Slowly but surely, people were beginning to make their way back into the streets, and by dinnertime, some normal activity seemed to have been restored. There was a palpable uncertainty and uneasiness among the population of Point Fire. It was a gnawing fear that would never completely go away, a terminal illness just beginning to spread its tendrils.

After going out to fetch some additional ingredients for the meal, their mother reported back on an announcement she had heard from the royal guards:

"To all people of Point Fire. Do not be alarmed. The royal family will be looking into the strange events which have occurred, and after an official royal council meeting tomorrow, will enlighten the public."

"Doesn't seem like they know what's happening," Aren scoffed sarcastically.

He was almost his old self again. He shoveled a spoonful of stew into his mouth, wincing as it burned his tongue.

"Let's *hope* they know what's happening," Avenir corrected. "We wouldn't want something like this to occur again. If they don't know what it is, who else could? I honestly can't even come up with a reasonable explanation."

This was a lie. One that was hard to tell, but a necessary, and stomach-churning lie. Avenir had already come to a single, albeit hesitant, conclusion.

Could it be that the shadow waves have always approached Point Fire over the Frost? Could my removal of Embr from the Sanctum have allowed it – that shadow from the west – to finally break through somehow? Point Fire is the last city to exist for a reason...and I may have finally removed that "reason" from its resting place...

XXIII

Avenir knew he had to listen to what would be said at the private royal meeting within the palace.

If anyone needs to be there, it's me.

His mother had announced the previous night that she would be taking Aren to an animal pen in the South Side – the type of place he used to love going to when he was younger. Aren had groaned...but not loudly. Even *he* had to admit he was deeply unsettled and in need of a mental break.

Avenir made sure that Embr was securely fastened to the belt underneath his dunerobe before heading out to the Circle. He had a newfound sense of respect and trust for the Sword, but still could not shake the feeling of revulsion at seeing those tiny, bloodied barbs. He forced himself to stop thinking about it and made his way out into the bitter cold of the streets.

He could recall from his father's stories that the official meeting room in the palace was located at its center. He also knew that the Inner Sanctum, though now his personal symbol of paranoia, lay at the center of the Heart, right beneath the obsidian dome above it.

If there's going to be any way of sneaking into the palace, that's where it would begin.

The journey to the Circle was uneventful, as was the crossing of the bridge to the Keep and the descent into the Inner Sanctum. Few citizens were around. People were wary and afraid of each other, regardless of whether they believed the royal statement later that day would shed any light on the situation.

It would be hard to forget that your friend or family member recently tried to strangle the life out of you.

His sense of paranoia returned once he had entered the Heart, just as he thought it would. This feeling only intensified when the panels of the Inner Sanctum came into view. To the untrained eye, it still appeared as if Embr was angrily burning inside the fiery chamber. Avenir knew better.

He scanned the ancient ceiling and walls for any shafts or possible entryways to the palace above. A litany of ladders and rusty portals branched outwards from the Inner Sanctum, but from experience Avenir knew that many of these would lead to dead ends, in the most literal sense.

As his eyes fell upon a rickety-looking black ladder, Embr pulsed, almost imperceptibly. Avenir carefully unsheathed an inch of the Great Sword. The brilliant silver of the Blade was calm, as was the soft crimson lining of its edge. He raised his eyes to the same ladder. A sharp pulsing heat from the edges of the Sword started up again. In his peripheral vision, he could sense the edge of the Blade calmly phasing through different shades of orange. He sheathed the Sword again.

"Looks like you're still there, whatever you are," he muttered under his breath.

Avenir climbed the ladder that Embr seemed to have signaled to him. It led upwards into a dusty network of metallic air ducts.

He used to explore places like this when he was younger. Aren still loved to do it, no matter how much Avenir hypocritically warned him about the possible dangers involved. He chuckled at the thought of his brother exploring these same pipes, as he shuffled awkwardly down a long and winding one.

Every now and then, Embr would give off a reassuring pulse, causing Avenir to unsheathe it and check the direction that the Great Sword was intending. At some stage, he realized that he was now fully at the mercy of the Weapon's direction. It had led him down a labyrinth of jutting metal sheets and half-torn openings, and he had completely lost his bearings.

By the Seven, please do not stop working now.

At last he reached a cramped rectangular shaft with bright holes on its top side. The holes were covered by tough metal grilles. He tried

to get a better sense of what lay above him from the dim light below. Craning his neck, Avenir noticed what appeared to be an elongated table, and heard what seemed to be servants scurrying about.

It must be the royal banquet hall.

In a gesture of thanks, Avenir squeezed the hilt of the Great Sword. It did not pulse in response. He sat backwards on his haunches, leaning against the cool wall of the shaft.

"Well, looks like I'm going to be waiting here alone," he whispered as he closed his eyes.

*   *   *

"ALL RISE FOR KING LUXUS II!"

A booming voice from above jolted Avenir awake from a restless slumber. He had somehow managed to fall asleep while crouching and had to stop himself from groaning loudly when he tried to straighten his legs again.

The uniform screech of shuffling chairs echoed down from the massive chamber above. The shuffling returned as the chairs and their occupants moved back to their original positions. The powerful voice of the king broke the ensuing silence.

"So...what, in the name of the holy Seven, has happened to my city?"

The question had a dark edge to it, almost accusative.

Of course, to a king, the events that transpired must appear alarmingly similar to an attempted coup or rebellion.

None of the other people in the room, whom Avenir assumed to be the landlords and ladies of the various districts, dared answer.

The king spoke again, "Surely you, Yob, overseer of the Pit — *the true Heart of Point Fire* — surely *you* have some inkling of what is afoot?"

There was no immediate answer. Avenir could imagine the man's sweat glands working furiously.

Finally, the quiet response came, "No, Your Majesty. I do not. It happened within my own family as well," there was a creaking of a single chair as the man stood up. "I think I can speak for everyone here in that we don't understand what happened. Given the circumstances, I think we should—"

"It's evil."

Avenir instantly recognized the voice that had interrupted Yob. *Sen.*

The tone in Sen's voice frightened Avenir. It was unusually quiet.

"It's evil, plain and simple," Sen continued. "I've felt it before, once."

"Don't be ridiculous," Yob retorted. "You know very well that our city is alone in this realm. There's no time to engage in moral fantasies here..."

"Let him speak." The king's voice came down hard, like the strike of a smith's hammer.

The chair Sen had been sitting on creaked a sigh of relief as the hulking man stood before the king.

"I think I have felt this darkness before, Your Majesty." Avenir envisioned Sen's bushy eyebrows slanting in concentration. "When it last happened, I had mistakenly believed it to just be some emotion *within* me." Sen paused, thinking carefully about how to place his next phrase. "We all remember when Borea left..."

Avenir's hairs stood on end. He had just recently managed to work off the nerves and the dull fears that he had picked up with Embr...but now these feelings came rushing back.

"...but I remember better than most. We had been out in the Frost, *too* far out in fact. We had decided to scout further west, just the two of us. It was meant to be a three-day excursion. At dusk on the second day I felt something strange pass over the ice. It was like a shadow of the mind. I thought nothing much of it at the time. Borea told me he had felt it too. He left that night. Alone. I can only imagine, knowing him, that he wanted to find its source."

"And why have we never heard of this phenomenon before, Sen?" The king spoke loudly, but his voice was devoid of anger or accusation. He clearly held an immense sense of respect for the current leader of the Hunters' Association.

"I apologize Your Majesty, but I had always attributed the feeling to my own sadness, in hindsight. Especially after Borea went missing, I thought I must have misinterpreted the feeling as one resulting from his disappearance. Given the recent occurrences in Point Fire, I now believe that this shadow might have been a *cause* and not a consequence. It is certainly, in my opinion, an evil force. I felt it myself."

A great silence fell across the king's hall. Beneath this silence, Avenir fought the urge to run. He struggled to maintain control of his breathing. He was terrified. More than ever, he just wanted to go home and curl up beneath his bedsheets, praying to the Seven that he could rewind time to a period before all this madness began.

The king's voice above broke the silence again and brought Avenir back to reality.

"That is indeed troubling. We should not come to any rash conclusions, but since no one else has a logical explanation, I think we should investigate this issue further. Sen, come to my private office tomorrow at noon. Bring any Hunters you feel may have experienced similar forces out in the Frost."

"Of course, Your Majesty." Sen's seat groaned painfully as the man returned to his place.

"This is *ridiculous*," Yob's shrill voice rang out. "Surely we must take the logical approach and assume this is the work of some dissident faction? Magic...*Evil?* These abstract concepts do not, and should not affect our lives here! Your Majesty, you must know this of all people."

The king's voice echoed softly in return, "Yob, you speak as if History itself began with the Frost. You know this not to be true – that *is* what is taught in your districts' schools, is it not?"

Yob snorted loudly.

"Yob..." Sen's gruff voice warned.

The overseer of the Pit could not take it any longer, as he launched into a loud tirade.

"Am I alone here? Does no one else believe in rationality?"

He stopped speaking, and Avenir guessed the man was searching the faces of the others in the room. He must have found at least some agreeable looks, and he began shouting again.

"Yes! I believe we should perform a thorough questioning of the population, see who is–"

West.

A sickeningly perfect and powerful voice resounded across the banquet room. Avenir yelped loudly, but his voice was easily drowned out among the other startled gasps and yells from above.

Something about that voice sounded familiar.

Instinctively, his hand fell to the hilt of Embr. It was brimming with dull fire, singeing his robes through the crystal-lined straps. Somehow, he had not noticed the acrid smoke rising off his clothes, nor the pain that would normally come with it. With a feeling of despair, he smelled the smoke wafting off him. Embr was hissing quietly, almost like a cornered cat.

They're going to see it. They're going to know someone's here.

Then he realized that everything had gone dark, and the faint smell of the smoke was indeed the only sense that could give him away. At first, he thought it was a trick of the light – the smoky haze blocking the light above – but then he saw that the entire banquet hall had also gone dark. The room above had become coated with an almost artificial level of pure blackness.

As the fear of the initial shock quickly wore off, he began to hear the sounds of people shuffling around above. Objects were being knocked over and chairs creaked loudly as the members of the royal court attempted to regain their bearings.

Go west.

The clear voice sliced through the air once more. It carried a deafening timbre, but one that was somehow not painful to the ear. Avenir's hand still gripped the hilt of the Great Sword tightly, trying to muffle its glow. Subdued flames wrapped around his knuckles...painlessly. He could only hope that the people above did not notice this faint light emanating through the metal grill.

It's definitely not Embr that's speaking, like it did in the Inner Sanctum. It's something else, something that the Great Sword understands to be a threat.

Finally, the first human voice – that of the king's – rang out.

"What is the meaning of this?"

Silence followed. The whimpers of the lords and ladies chittered in the hall like tiny crickets. Small flames now crackled around Embr. Avenir could not even begin to guess what was happening above.

Go to the Salvation of Point Fire.

Impossibly, the voice had become even clearer. The clarity of the phrase was so intense that Avenir found himself mouthing every syllable, his vocal cords entranced. Somehow, it was as if the voice was all around him. It was almost as if the sound was emanating from the air itself, materializing from nothingness.

This is no human speaking.

The disembodied voice proclaimed its final words:

Send only the finest Hunters.

Something about this last phrase flipped a deep, hidden switch in Avenir's mind. He *had* heard this voice before.

XXIV

Avenir sat on his bed, waiting for the inevitable knock on his door.

The "finest Hunters," the voice had said. What's taking Sen so long?

Multiple days had passed since the otherworldly message. The official royal report given later that dreadful day had been surprisingly positive, with the king reminding the citizens of their duty to protect their families and friends against this new threat from the Frost. It was clearly in their best interests to keep the terrible happenings at the meeting hidden from the public.

However, something in king Luxus' tone had been awry, or perhaps his brow had been more furrowed than usual...and the people of Point Fire had taken notice. In the following days, the city had become deathly silent.

A loud rattle echoed from the kitchen.

That must be Sen.

Avenir rushed down the ladder from their attic bedchamber and opened the door a crack. Aren's sweaty face peered through. Disappointed, Avenir let the door fall open.

"What's with you?" Aren joked, bringing substantial amounts of dirt and dust onto the newly cleaned floor.

Avenir noticed the grime caking Aren's fingernails. Anyone looking at the boy would have no reason to guess that something terrible was currently afoot in Point Fire. He had clearly been exploring the city, as usual. Avenir grabbed his younger brother by the shirt and yanked him back to the entrance.

"Hey! Mother *just* cleaned this; at least take off your shoes! Besides, where have you been? You were out all day."

Aren roughly discarded his clothes onto the cobblestones outside the door.

"Are you kidding me?" The young boy asked incredulously. "More like, where have *you* been? The Point's gone crazy – I've been trying to see what I can find out!"

A surge of anger built up within Avenir.

What is Aren doing? The last thing I need is another person...

"I overheard Yob ordering some of his men to begin searching the Pit...as well as the royal palace," Aren continued, oblivious to his brother's irritation.

This bit of information helped quell Avenir's exasperation.

So, Yob has decided to go against the king's intuition. He still suspects that it may be a rebellion. Point Fire must be approaching a tipping point.

"That's pretty interesting," said Avenir as he picked up Aren's dirty rags and dumped them into a washing basket. "It looks like some people believe that those strange events signaled the beginning of some sort of rebellion."

"Yeah, that's what I thought at first too."

"Oh?" Avenir raised his eyebrows, urging Aren to elaborate.

His younger brother stopped halfway up the ladder to their bedroom,

"That's what I thought...until Runan told me that Sen just signed him up for a new *special* mission. He didn't really tell me what it was about, but he did seem kind of excited...and maybe a little scared, if that's even possible." Aren clambered up the ladder and into the room above, his voice trailing behind him. "Anyway, having a Big Hunt while all this is happening seems a bit strange to me."

Avenir was glad that Aren was out of eyesight because he could feel his cheeks turning a deep shade of red. A bitter mix of jealousy and confusion mingled between his thoughts.

Surely Sen would have chosen me? Is this "Hunt" because of something unrelated? No...impossible. I have to find Sen and speak with him. Immediately.

*　　　　　*　　　　　*

Avenir found the hulk of a man poring over a roughly stacked pile of papers. He was in his cabin-office near the edge of the Hunters' district. At first Sen paid Avenir no attention, his nose buried deeply in the words he was reading. When he noticed someone had entered, he barely looked up and motioned absent-mindedly to a chair nearby.

"Please, sit. I'll be with you in–" Sen's head jerked upright. "'NIR!" His booming voice almost blew the stack of papers right off the desk. He collected himself. "I apologize for not recognizing you. Things have become very...difficult for me."

Avenir pulled the chair over to the other side of the desk and sat down. Before he could begin speaking, Sen interrupted him.

"I know why you're here, my boy. And the answer is no." He did not look up from reading his papers.

Avenir was not sure if he had heard correctly.

"What? How could you..."

"'Nir," Sen spoke quietly, cutting Avenir off, "I've decided that you are not coming with us."

Avenir sat back, aghast. Sen shuffled some of the papers neatly together and finally fixed his gaze on the young man across his desk. A brief glimmer of sorrow flashed over the man's hardened face. Sighing, he moved the stack of writings back into a drawer.

"It is as I say. I can only guess as to how much you know already, especially after your eavesdropping escapade below the banquet hall."

Avenir did not react to this. He was not surprised that the greatest living Hunter in Point Fire was able to come up with this information. Sen cleared his throat.

"Out of respect, I've kept that fact a secret, but that doesn't change my decision. I cannot lose another Novari – another *friend* – to the Frost. That voice in the hall...it came out of thin air, belonging to no one present there. As I'm sure you heard me say, this is something that is beyond our comprehension. You must understand that it is better for you to remain here."

Avenir finally regained his breath.

"Sen, I have to come with."

"Absolutely out of the question. I know you and Soljan were out in the Frost when the darkness came. He told me what happened. I am not forbidding you to go due to your lack of skills. In fact, it is almost the opposite. You are a very capable Hunter, and so I need you to stay *alive*. At home. Protecting your family, as well as the Point."

"Protect them against what?" Avenir could feel a terrible anger rising up within him. "The *Evil* you claim to have felt.? You know damn well that whatever this is cannot be defended against. It must be destroyed! We must protect the Many over the Few, like you always say!"

"Listen to yourself, Avenir. A clear mind has always been your strength. Don't make the same mistake that Borea did."

Avenir shot to his feet, slamming the table with an open hand. "Don't you dare bring my father into this," he hissed. "I heard what you said in the hall: 'He left by himself.' Bullshit. *You're* the one who has always taught all Hunters never to travel alone in the Frost. Either that bit of wisdom meant nothing, or you're hiding something."

The accusation clearly struck Sen somewhere deep.

"That is incorrect," he whispered sadly. "What I said *is* true, and it is probably the thing I regret most in life."

Avenir turned his back to Sen and stifled a cry of rage. His blood felt as if it was on fire with emotion. More than that, the way everything had unraveled in Point Fire had left him stranded in a daze of confusion. Like he was in a maze filled with dead ends.

His hand patted at his right thigh, trying to cool down an area where the rage-induced heat was oddly intense.

Embr. Of Course. Sen doesn't know.

Avenir turned around quickly. Sen's eyes greeted his with a mild look of confusion. With a deep sigh, Avenir went to close the door to the office, making sure it was locked.

"Avenir, what is the meaning of this?" Sen said, frowning and slowly beginning to rise from his seat.

"I have no choice," Avenir said quietly.

He slowly, carefully, peeled back the segment of his dunerobe covering the Great Sword. The crystal scabbard hung at his side, smoldering faintly. Without hesitation, he pulled Embr free, holding it out in front of the veteran Hunter. The hilt's dark crimson was beating like a glowing heart beneath his hand. The Blade hummed with a soft power, the red lining at its edges foreboding, like a silver cloud filled with blood.

At first, Sen was dumbstruck. After a few moments of pure silence between them, he closed his eyes and fell back in his chair. The wood groaned in pain.

His voice came out shakily, in a tone Avenir had never thought he would hear.

"I apologize. It seems it was I who was acting rashly. I did not..." he trailed off, and for a moment Avenir thought he would see the man cry. Yet, Sen managed to remain calm. "I did not realize the true extent of the darkness that is facing us. Has anyone else seen this?"

"Only Kreymar, the head priest. But I can assure you he will remain silent."

"Good. If more than the three of us know that the Great Weapon has been taken from the Inner Sanctum, the Point will erupt into complete chaos. Now, tell me everything."

Avenir slid Embr carefully back into its scabbard. The Blade hissed, as if in protest. He fell heavily into the seat across from Sen.

"Of course, but this may take a while."

XXV

Avenir pulled the door to his home open and flopped into a chair at the kitchen table. His mother sat at the head, tapping her foot impatiently.

Aren must already be asleep.

The fatigue of the past few weeks had finally caught up to him. Yet, he felt as if a massive burden had been lifted off his shoulders. He had explained everything in great detail to Sen.

The first meeting with Kreymar in the Cathedral. The struggle with Soljan in the Frost. The pulse of warmth from the Great Sword...and the time limit on the life of Point Fire and all those who occupy it.

Even after hearing this information, Sen had still pushed for him to remain in the Point. It was only when Avenir attempted to give Sen the Great Sword to inspect it, and after it burned his hands severely, that the veteran Hunter understood there was no other way. It had to be Avenir. To face whatever force lay out in the Frost, they would need an equally powerful one on their side.

And I might be the only one who can wield this force.

"Well? Where have you been?"

His mother's voice was sharp but tired. She stopped tapping her foot and got up, moving towards the kitchen counter. The whistling of a kettle soon filled the air.

"I was over in the Hunters' district, speaking with Sen." Avenir replied, trying his best to mask his fatigue.

A young voice joined the conversation. "About what?"

Aren appeared at the top of their ladder, rubbing his eyes.

The sound from the kettle probably woke him up.

"Aren, get back to bed this instant," said Sylis. She poured two cups of steaming water and dropped a handful of leaves into each.

"I will, I will," Aren groaned. "I just wanted to come see what you guys were talking about."

"Nothing, Aren," this time Avenir's voice came out clearly exasperated.

"I was just asking. Jeez."

"Aren, you should go to bed. Avenir will be up there soon enough."

Aren glared at his brother, then stormed back up to their room. Avenir knew that he would just pretend to go to bed, and then go to lie with his ear glued to the floorboards above. But that did not matter anymore. He knew that what he was about to tell his mother would change all their lives anyway.

"In one week...I have to leave with Sen." The words came out more nervously than Avenir had intended.

Sylis tried to process the sentence and came up short.

"What do you mean, 'leave?' Where to? When?"

Avenir leaned back in his chair, staring at the ceiling,

"Into the Frost. I've been chosen to Hunt in a special expeditionary unit."

His mother's eyes widened in shock. She pulled out a chair and sat across from her son.

"Have you gone insane? Have *they* gone insane? Why does it feel like I am the only one who..." she trailed off, struggling to compose herself.

Avenir moved to comfort her, but just as he was about to put his arm around her shoulders, she grabbed his wrist and looked at him with tears in her eyes.

"'Nir, please tell me what's going on. It feels like no one else is seeing what is happening around us. Aren was terrified for his life just a few days ago, but now he's out exploring again..."

"Mom, you know how Aren is..."

"Of course! But that's *Aren*, not *you*! You have always been different – but now you're acting just like...your father did!"

Avenir felt a sharp pang of sadness. He could also feel Aren's guilt seeping through the floorboards above. Sylis let go of his wrist and wiped her eyes dry.

"I'm sorry 'Nir, it's just that I can't lose *you* as well. I can't describe it, but I have this feeling that something evil is happening around us. I had a similar feeling all those years ago, and just like then, I don't understand what is happening."

She let out a terrible sigh and buried her face in her hands. Avenir moved behind his mother and held her shoulders as she cried quietly. He was now painfully aware of the Great Sword hanging at his side. It was begging to be revealed. His hand fell gently onto the hilt. He was about to draw the Weapon, if only to offer some form of explanation to his mother, when he heard the floorboards creak above his head.

Aren shifting his weight. He will hear everything, and I can't trust him to keep it a secret.

His hand fell away from the Sword. He wished with all his heart that he could show it to his mother, if only to help justify what was to come. But he could not. The Point was already teetering on the brink of chaos. If even a harmless rumor got out that Embr had been removed, the city would likely fall to pieces. Such was the critical role of the Hunt with Sen: to find out what mystery, if any, lay out in the Western Frost, and then to return the Sword to its rightful place in the Inner Sanctum, all under complete secrecy.

"Mom, something evil *is* happening. Which is why I have to go with Sen. We're going to fix it. I promise I'll come back. Just believe in Sen – he'll be with me, just as he was with father. He won't make the same mistake twice."

His mother nodded her head but did not look up. Avenir stayed with her until she fell asleep at the table. She looked completely exhausted. He carried her to their parents' room and tucked her in. When he returned to the kitchen, he sat on the edge of the table and ran his hands through his hair. He was surprised to find that he was very dirty. He mumbled to himself that he would have to bathe first thing in the morning.

He sat still for a few moments, calming his mind. With a grunt of effort, he stood to his feet, and as silently as he could – so that Aren would not hear – he made his way to the underground room and hid the Great Sword under the flagstone once more.

Back in the kitchen again, he felt another pang of sadness when he noticed the two cups of tea that were still sitting on the counter. He poured the now ice-cold liquid down the drain, watching the green river disappear into its depths. He sighed again and ascended to his bedroom.

When he heard his brother climbing the ladder, Aren silently leapt back into his bed, pulling the covers over himself and closing his eyes to slits. In a few seconds, the trapdoor opened upwards and Avenir poked his head through. He moved across the room and fell on his bed. He seemed very tired.

"I know you're awake," said Avenir quietly.

Aren opened his eyes fully, getting a better view of his brother, who was lying on his back, staring at the roof.

"I know you know," Aren responded guiltily. "I had to try at least."

"Aren..." Avenir started, "What do *you* think is happening in Point Fire?"

The question caught Aren slightly off guard, and he had to think for a bit before answering.

"Sorry 'Nir. I really don't know."

Avenir laughed dryly and turned over to go to sleep.

"...but it does feel like whatever is happening isn't coming from inside the city."

"What do you mean by that?" came Avenir's muffled voice.

"I just don't think anyone here is mad enough at the king, or whatever most people are saying. It feels weirder than that."

Avenir jerked upright and moved to sit over the side of his bed facing Aren. There was the faintest hint of a smile on his face.

"Good. I knew you weren't that foolish."

"What?"

"Just listen to me for once. I happen to think the same thing. I have something I need you to do for me."

XXVI

It was five days later, and Aren stood on Udar's doorstep. He had so far done exactly as he had been asked, while his brother prepared for his excursion.

"Watch every member of the royal council. If anything happens that suggests or resembles a rebellion, lock yourself and mother inside our home, or somewhere in the Hunters' district, and wait for me to come back."

Nothing out of the ordinary had occurred so far, but Aren was beginning to doubt the coverage of his own surveillance. Up till now, he had ignored Avenir's last bit of advice:

"...get people you trust to help you."

The previous day, when Yob and Prince Luxus III were giving simultaneous speeches on opposite ends of Point Fire, Aren had finally decided to swallow his pride and find some help. And now, here he stood, waiting for his old friend to respond to his knocking.

It's been so long...

The faint sound of a latch being unhinged clicked from behind the wood and Udar's father opened the door. The locksmith towering over Aren was an old man. Wispy trails of white hair swirled around his shoulders, standing in stark contrast to the weathered contours on his face. Any other child would have been intimidated.

It took the man a moment to recognize Aren. He frowned.

"Please, leave us in peace."

He began to close the door again, but Aren stuck his foot in the crack, grimacing as the heavy door almost crushed it.

"Young lad..." The man's voice was filling with anger.

"Please sir, could I just talk to Udar for one moment?"

"He doesn't want to see anyone, and most definitely doesn't want to see you."

The locksmith tried to pull the door shut but Aren held his foot in place, trying not to wince from the pain.

"Young lad, if you do not remove your foot this instant, this could become quite painful for you," Udar's father warned.

"Please, sir," Aren repeated. "Even if I can't see him now...tell him I really need him. It's something important. Tell him this isn't just about some adventure or exploring!"

The man was getting increasingly frustrated, and was about to slam the door shut, when Udar's chubby face appeared besides his father's waist. Grunting in surprise, the locksmith allowed Udar to pass by him. For the first time in two months, Aren was face to face with the boy who had braved the Cathedral with him.

"It's okay Father, I'll come back inside soon," said Udar.

The old locksmith looked like he was going to begin on an exasperated tirade, but then he coughed loudly and disappeared into the darkness of the house.

"Hey," said Aren awkwardly.

"Hey," came Udar's response.

The two boys eyed each other, not really knowing what to do or say.

"You've gotten pretty fat since we stopped exploring together," began Aren.

Udar's face turned tomato red. Then, a twinkle of humor flashed around his eyes and at the edges of his mouth. He scrunched up his face and shoved Aren, sending him reeling.

"Shut up. I hate you," said Udar, but Aren detected the hint of a restrained laugh.

Aren regained his balance by resting his hand against a nearby wall. He turned around to see Udar sitting on his doorstep. He readjusted his dunerobe and walked back to his friend.

"I'm *so* sorry. I came back to your house quite a lot, but I could never find you," Aren apologized.

"I know, I know. No, it's my fault – I was scared," said Udar, sulking a bit.

"No, no. It's definitely *my* fault," Aren insisted. "We should never have gone all the way to the top. I got too greedy."

He sat down next to Udar.

"Looking back on it, it *was* interesting," Udar admitted. This made Aren grin, who turned to find that Udar was also smiling.

"How's your finger?" Aren asked cautiously.

"Oh, it's mostly fine now. Still a bit sore when I do work with my father."

"That's great! Mine's good as well. Maybe that church guy's done it many times. Like he knows how to break fingers so they can heal quickly."

"Let's hope not. So, what was this important thing you were talking about earlier?" said Udar, trying his best to restrain the apprehension in his voice.

"Hmm, it's a bit hard to explain. It's something my brother asked me to do..."

Udar let out a surprised chortle. Aren looked away shyly.

"I know, I know. It sounds really lame. I don't usually do what he says, but this time it feels like something is different."

Udar laughed again. "*Feels like?* Have you been around the Point recently? It's a mess."

"Exactly. That's exactly what my brother was saying. But since he's going out..." Aren paused. Avenir had told him not to let anyone know about the Hunt with Sen "...Since he's going out to the Cathedral to make sure things are okay there, he wants me – wants *us* – to keep tabs on what's going on around the rest of the city."

"That sounds exactly like something the *royal family* should be taking care of."

"And what if the trouble began inside the royal family?"

Udar's eyes opened wide in shock. "Really? What's happened?"

Aren shrugged and shook his head.

"No, nothing like that has happened at all. But something *can* happen. And my brother thinks that if it does, there won't be any way for families like ours to protect ourselves. That's why you and I gotta look around just in case."

"And if we *do* see something strange...what do we do?"

"Just let each other know. If it's bad enough, Avenir said we should hide our families someplace – I can help yours stay in the Hunters' district if you'd like."

Udar grinned. "You don't have to worry about us. You do know my father is a professional locksmith, right?"

"Do you have a secret base in your house or something?" Aren asked excitedly.

"Don't be ridiculous," Udar chuckled. "...Maybe."

Aren jumped to his feet. The prospect of discovering some new unknown part of Point Fire made his heart skip a beat.

Udar shook his head. "There's *no way* I'm showing you now. Not with my father in there."

Aren's shoulders slumped slightly. "Damn."

The idea of exploring another section of the city was beginning to cross Aren's mind when he remembered why he had even come to Udar's in the first place.

"Wow, I almost forgot," said Aren sheepishly. "I wanted to tell you my plan for how we'll keep track of people."

"Which people exactly are we talking about?"

"The royal counsel of course," said Aren, matter-of-factly.

"That is *not* what you said earlier. There is absolutely no way I'm going to be snooping around behind the king."

Aren's eyes twinkled. "Don't be silly, I'll take care of that sort of thing. I just need you to keep tabs on Yob."

"You mean the landlord of the Pit?"

"Yup, that's the one. Plus, it's nowhere near as scary as following people like Luxus or Luna."

Udar shivered at the sound of the princess's name, something that most children did not dare say out loud.

"I can definitely agree with that. So, I just have to see where he's going every day?" asked Udar.

"And what he's doing, if you can. I think checking where he is once or twice a day should be enough. But if you see him meeting or talking with anyone else from the royal family or counsel, I need you to come tell me right away."

"That sounds okay to me." Udar got up and was about to enter through his door, when he turned around, somewhat confused. "Wait, why am I doing this again?"

Aren was already halfway up the wall to the buttresses above when he responded.

"To keep your family safe!"

The young boy vaulted over a dark stone precipice and was gone. The red glimmer of the heat lines played on the walls where he had been.

*   *   *

It was the evening before his departure, and Avenir was taking inventory of his gear. His full dunerobe complete with boots, hood, and the ice gauze lay neatly in a stack on his bed. Leaning up against the wall were his ice pick and his father's frostwood bow. Twenty arrows lay in a carefully arranged pile beside the weapon. He searched through his wardrobe, found his Shard, and placed it next to his quiver. The compass-N Novari family crest stared at him from the Shard's grip.

Avenir ruffled through his dresser and found the small red vial he had purchased earlier that day. It was the most potent under-the-table poison Blood could buy, fondly nicknamed Snowfall for its ability to kill without a sound. Even Yugo had been a bit reluctant to part with it, but with a bit of rough bargaining from Sen himself, the blind man finally gave in to his greed.

Avenir stole a quick glance outside the window to try and gauge the time. He was supposed to meet Sen in his office tonight to go over the plan for the next morning. The massive Hunter had said that he

209

himself would be taking care of all provisioning and tenting. Avenir just had to worry about his own clothes and basic weaponry.

And, of course, to bring Embr.

He had stashed the Great Sword underneath the flagstone in the basement once again. He planned to retrieve it first thing the next morning.

The time for mistakes has long come and gone.

After a final run-through, he left for the Hunters' district.

Sen was in his office, packing goods into an assortment of white sacks, when Avenir arrived. He was concentrating intently on what seemed like putting small bags of food into each. Avenir pulled out the extra chair opposite his desk and took a seat, silently watching the man sort their rations for the unknown period of travel that lay ahead. Finally, Sen appeared satisfied with his assortment and roughly sat down in the other chair.

"'NIR!"

The curt and bellowing tone of his voice jerked Avenir awake from what felt like a stress-induced nap.

"Sorry, I must have dozed off slightly. I haven't been getting much sleep."

Sen put his massive hands behind his head and leaned back in his chair.

"Well, my boy, you should get to bed early tonight. Before our strange mission tomorrow."

"Strange indeed," Avenir sighed. "Tell me, who will be joining us? I guess I can assume we will not be travelling alone?"

"Of course not. Runan and Soljan will be accompanying us."

"Do we not need capable Hunters like them to stay back and help around the Point? Things have been getting dicey, especially around the royal palace."

"Do not worry about that sort of thing. I have already dispatched available teams of Hunters to watch over every district."

Avenir whistled in awe.

It seems Sen has still retained his composure amidst all this chaos.

Sen continued bluntly, "Luna will be joining us as well."

For a moment, Avenir thought he had misheard the veteran Hunter.

"Come again?"

"I know you two have your differences, but I will not budge on this issue. She is a fine Hunter and—"

"Fine Hunter?" Avenir spurted, "She is selfish and prideful. If I'm not mistaken, those are two of the worst qualities to have as a professional Hunter."

Sen ignored him and carried on, "...and I believe she is in great danger if she stays in the city."

Avenir stilled himself, struggling not to argue any further. He waited for Sen to explain further. Sen sighed and stood up. He stretched his legs and lower back, groaning at the stiffness in his muscles. He leaned down onto the table, the wood protesting.

"Yes. Great danger. I already have spies set up in the Pit and the Fynn. There are rumors circulating that she is the one responsible for the so-called 'rebellion' that failed."

Avenir scratched his face. He had not shaved in a while, and the stubble was getting to him.

Yes, I forgot most people still believe that the murders and fighting were orchestrated by someone in the city, and the most likely culprit would be someone in the royal family wishing to dethrone the king.

"I see you understand me," said Sen, studying Avenir's reaction. "There are two principal heirs to the throne: Luna and her brother Luxus. Which of the two would you blame for a rebellion?"

Avenir nodded. "I don't disagree. But surely there is some other way? A safehouse in the Hunters' district perhaps?"

"You know well enough that that won't work. She must leave the city with us. It will help clear her name."

"It's not as if I can disagree at this point..." Avenir said under his breath.

"No, you cannot!" Sen responded strongly, a hint of warning in his voice. "*I* have planned this expedition, and *I* alone will choose who comes with me."

"With *you?*" Avenir asked angrily, "Don't forget that I am the one who has the Great Sword. This expedition will fail without me."

"Careful with your pride there."

"This has nothing to do with pride," Avenir snapped. "You heard what the voice said – whomever that was. It said–"

"Bring the finest Hunters," Sen interrupted. "Yes. I know."

"No. Not that. That sentence carries no real meaning."

Sen raised his eyebrows.

Avenir continued, "It said go *west.* What do you know about that region?"

"I am not naïve, 'Nir."

"Well, let me show you something then. Aren gave this to me."

Avenir produced Borea's map from his dunerobe pocket and splayed it out on the table between them.

"Look."

Sen studied the map closely, frowning as he noticed the markings for the "glacier runs" and the "Castle" in the west.

He looked up at Avenir, "Where did you get this?"

Avenir grinned sullenly. "*I* didn't get anything. Aren stole it from a secret drawer in my father's study. The one in the Cathedral."

Sen was stunned for a second, but he did not say anything. He focused on the map.

"This is unbelievable. These markings – this 'Castle', for example – are far beyond where even *I* have ever gone."

"Yes, exactly. And look here," Avenir motioned towards the ashen smear marked 'Darkness'. "I have a feeling we will need Embr with us on this mission, as we have guessed."

Sen grunted heavily. "I apologize, 'Nir. Perhaps I should listen to you a bit more. However, you should have told me about this earlier."

"I didn't know about this either until Aren gave it to me."

Sen laughed suddenly, rattling the floorboards.

"Horrible little rascal."

"Imagine living with him."

Sen chuckled a bit, wiping a tear from his eyes.

"Could I look this over tonight? Soljan should also see it before we leave in the morning, him being the tracker and all."

"Yes, of course."

Avenir turned to leave, speaking as he reached for the door, "I guess that's all there's left to say. I won't argue further about Luna coming, but I am still warning you that it is a mistake to choose her. I'll see you at dawn."

"Until then, 'Nir," said Sen in a trancelike state, his eyes glued to the map.

*   *   *

The dim light was setting as Avenir returned home. Although the perpetually overcast clouds allowed no warmth through their thick barrier, a small modicum of illumination shone down on the city, accentuating the orange lines of sprawling warmth.

As he opened the door, the fragrance of fresh tea and hare stew filled his nostrils. Smelling the mouth-watering meal that his mother had specially prepared, Avenir abruptly broke into tears. He quickly closed the door again, before anyone inside could notice him crying. After a few moments, he wiped his eyes and entered his home.

Sylis stood at the counter, preparing the meal. She was so focused on her cooking that she barely noticed Avenir enter. Aren was sleeping on a nearby pile of linen.

"Welcome, welcome," she sang. "Dinner's almost ready. I made your favorite, seeing as you probably won't be having good food for a while."

Avenir went over and hugged his mother. Since he had smelled the stew, the unshakable feeling of dread had returned.

Everything will change again, starting tomorrow.

"Oh hey, what's up?" Aren said groggily. "What did Sen say?"

"He's just getting ready for tomorrow. Planning things."

"Who did he choose to go with you?" asked Aren perkily.

213

"I'm afraid I would have to kill you if I told you," Avenir joked. "Although you'll probably find out on your own anyway."

"So just tell me noooow," Aren whined.

Avenir ignored him and took a seat at the dinner table.

"I hope you didn't touch any of the things I put on my bed earlier."

"Not a scratch! Though I did see you got a little present from Yugo," Aren teased mischievously.

"Really, what did he get you?" asked Sylis, as she poured three hot bowls of stew.

"Just some poisons for the Hunt tomorrow..."

Avenir glared at Aren, who pretended to inspect a ball of lint.

"Oh, you mean that little red bottle? I might have used it for the seasoning," Sylis added.

Avenir and Aren shared a moment of terror, imagining they were all accidentally inhaling Snowfall fumes. Sylis laughed.

"Silly boys. I used to visit Yugo's many times with your father. Don't worry about me."

The two brothers exhaled loudly in relief.

The stew was delicious, and they all ate ravenously. Avenir savored every bite, knowing that he would be getting used to cold gruel over the following days... maybe even weeks.

"Any news from the city?" he mumbled to Aren, rabbit grease dripping down his chin.

"Nophin," Aren responded quickly. His entire face was covered with broth.

After they had drunk their tea, they spoke at length about the interesting sights they had seen in Point Fire over the past few weeks. Aren was especially excited to explain how he had discovered a new observation perch near the royal palace, much to Sylis's dismay. For the first time in a while, Avenir felt the stress of the preceding months leaving him, and for a few minutes, their family had become normal again.

The feeling was fleeting, however, and soon they grew tired. Avenir explained that he should sleep early, and bid a sad farewell to his mother, who struggled to hold back her tears. After she had gone to bed, he and Aren headed upstairs.

"Here," said Aren. "Don't forget this."

The small boy searched through his robe pockets and came up with a small piece of paper.

South - X
East/Lake – Cathedral?
West – Darkness

Avenir looked it over again, holding his breath as he read his father's handwriting.

"Well, that's where I'm going," he said wistfully.

"You have to find him. I think he's still out there," Aren said, quite sure of himself.

Avenir mulled over Aren's words as they both fell asleep.

XXVII

The first hint of dawn was creeping through the window. Usually, Avenir would have barely noticed it, but he had been lying awake for about an hour now, counting the seconds till his departure. Now that the time had finally come, his limbs felt as if they had been filled with lead. Aren still appeared to be asleep, though Avenir guessed otherwise.

He slipped out of bed silently and got dressed in his scout gear. As he was about to pull on his hood, he stole a last glance at Aren. He met his younger brother's open eyes.

"Please come back," Aren said quietly.

"No need to say that. Of course I'm coming back."

Avenir tied up his hood, put his ice pick and Shard in his belt, and slung his bow over his shoulder. He caught a glimpse of his obsidian medal hanging from the wardrobe. The memories it conjured seemed so far away, as if the medal itself were from a bygone era. He lifted the trapdoor and descended into the stillness of the kitchen.

He made sure to retrieve Embr quickly, so that Aren would not have time to creep downstairs and see it. He tied the homemade scabbard firmly next to his ice pick. He opened the door to the Point, letting in a frigid gust. He stepped outside quietly and closed the door.

*   *   *

Avenir traveled down through the Pit instead of cutting across the Circle. It was critical that no officials or royal guards noticed him. This was made even more difficult given how quiet the city-fortress had become. Almost everyone now slept behind locked doors, and only the loud pumping noise from a heat line occasionally filled the air.

Thankfully, he and Aren had passed this way many times, and he knew exactly which shadows to keep to, and which walls to climb. The empty portcullis to the Hunters' district greeted him soon enough.

This is where you prove yourself.

He ducked through the small opening and was startled to find Piet waiting for him. The giant of a man looked awkward without his arm, almost like he had forgotten to attach it when he woke up.

"Looks like yer finally 'ere," Piet said gruffly. He shook Avenir's hand. His grip was iron.

I guess your other arm got even stronger without its counterpart.

"I hope I'm not too late."

"Nah, just a lil. The others 're waitin fer ya at the edge."

Piet lead Avenir across the Hunters' district. It was surprising to him that Sen had let Piet in on the fact that they were leaving.

He is very dependable, though. Simple. A man that can always be trusted.

It was not long before they reached the southwest edge of the district. The rows of copper portals along the outer walls shone conspicuously in the light of the thinner heat lines.

"Ther waitin outside."

"Just like that? Has Sen prepared everything?"

"Jus like that."

Avenir forced a smile and hugged the big Hunter. The embrace was awkward, but heartfelt. Then, without another word, he unlocked the copper door using his father's key, and left Point Fire.

The chosen pod sat about fifty feet away, tending to and checking their equipment. The white sacks Sen had packed were strapped tightly to five identical sleds. Luna was the first to notice his arrival. He knew it was her because of the dark hair that was spilling out from the edges of her hood. She turned away and fiddled with the ropes on her sled.

The largest two outlines, Sen and Runan, turned and made their way over to greet him. Runan was the first to speak. His voice was loud, but still noticeably softer and more calculated than Sen's.

"'Nir! You ready to go on the journey of a lifetime?"

"Hey, this is a serious occasion!" Sen butted in.

Yet Avenir could detect a hint of childlike excitement in his tone. He laughed softly.

These men are true Hunters to their cores.

Avenir was eager to get moving, if only to escape the stresses of the city for a while.

"Do they know?" he asked the larger of the two Hunters.

He could only see his eyes, but he saw enough to know that Sen knew what he meant.

"Yes, I showed them the map you brought. Soljan was especially excited about it. I'm sure he won't be able to keep quiet for the next couple hours."

So, he didn't tell them about Embr. Good.

"That map is quite something! I knew your father was good, but I didn't know he was *that* good," said Runan.

Sen's brother walked back towards the others. Sen motioned towards his hip, glancing at Avenir. Avenir mimicked the motion. Sen nodded and joined the rest. Avenir followed and was guided towards his sled.

"Good morning," said Soljan. "Have things been okay around the house since we got back from our last Hunt?"

"Yes, everything's been great. Relatively speaking, I mean. My mother and Aren are safe. They're hoping I will be too." Avenir patted Soljan on his shoulder, "If they had known, they would have been glad you were the chosen tracker for this group."

He was relieved to see that Soljan seemed to have recovered from the experience with the shadow in the Frost.

Although if something like that happens again...

Avenir left to go check on his sack. Looking inside, he could immediately gauge that Sen had been meticulous in his preparation. All the provisions were neatly placed in certain locations, and all the bindings were expertly tied. He glanced over to the other members of their pod. Luna still had not said anything, and Avenir was beginning to feel a strong sense of awkwardness, so he spoke first, walking over to her.

"I was surprised to hear you would be joining us."

Luna didn't turn around as she replied, "What do you mean by that? Do you still think you're superior to me?"

Avenir fought back an internal sigh.

"No. I mean...It's just that you happen to be *royalty*."

"What a joke," Luna sniffed beneath her hood. "Sen must have told you already. Apparently, people think I care about that. I would worry about my brother far more than me if I were my father, at least in terms of this so-called *rebellion*."

"People know that you are far stronger than your brother."

Luna laughed – a short, high-pitched note. She seemed taken aback by his compliment, even though it was not spoken with praise.

"That may be true," she said, "but right now I just want to get as far away from this damned city as I can."

Sen sat down on the edge of his sled and summoned the rest of the pod. The other four members came and huddled around him, like animals cowering from the wind.

"Alright, put on your masks and gauzes. Wouldn't want you to die this early on!" Sen barked, his voice easily cutting over the cold buffets of wind. As they complied, Sen continued, "You've all had ample time to study the map, but I guess I should *rebrief* us now, in case there's any confusion, given the short notice of this task." He shifted his weight on the sled, the snow beneath it groaning in response. "This is no ordinary 'Hunt.' I mean this in that we are not simply Hunting game in response to requests from the South Side. We are hunting for *answers*... to a question posed by an unknown threat."

"And from what I understand, Luna and Avenir have also heard the voice belonging to this unknown threat?" asked Runan.

"Yes, that's right."

Avenir noticed Luna steal a quick glance at him after this bit of information.

Of course. She must have been present at the meeting in the banquet hall. She probably didn't know that I was listening then.

Sen clapped his hands together.

"In any case, we can thank our lucky stars that we have this," he said as he flapped Borea's map open, "which should make our search for answers far easier." He pointed to the map. "I think we should make our way directly west, through this area that is marked 'glacier runs.' I assumed none of you knew what 'glacier' meant either, so I did some research in the archives and found that it could refer to a large expanse of ice. It likely originates from the mountains in the Northern Expanse. Since this doesn't sound too bad to cross, I suggest we traverse this area rather than skirt around it to the southwest, which would take considerable time. Everything okay so far?"

The group nodded in agreement.

Sen continued, "This leads us to the place marked 'castle,' which of course is a must, if we trust Borea's cartography...which we do." Sen brushed at the part of the map displaying the ashen smear. "And then, only the Seven can guide us further."

Soljan stretched his back. "Well let's get this going then, before someone sees us here."

Sen nodded. "Yes, Soljan's right. As I've informed you, this mission is top-secret. No one sees us leave and no one sees us return." He smiled broadly. "Which means no more Flares of Embr to save us, and no more rescue teams."

"Finally, a real Hunt," Luna said quietly.

"Yes, you could call it that. The Many over the Few!"

*   *   *

The first two hours of pulling the sleds were grueling. Every jolt of the harness yanked at Avenir's joints and begged him to stop moving. They were walking in single file, with Sen leading the column. Second in tow walked Runan, then Luna, then himself, with Soljan taking up the rear. He could hear the ragged panting of Luna's breath, which somehow gave him comfort that he was not the only one struggling.

Soon however, the monotony of the trek became an unsettling rhythm that he fell into, almost like a trance. He found himself wandering through endless daydreams of his early days around the Point, when he used to explore the worn battlements with his father. Aren joined this dreamscape, vaulting over walls and laughing at the occasional dry joke that Avenir made.

Then Avenir would find himself back in cold snow, pulling the sled relentlessly, hunched over against the wind. He wondered whether he would remember this journey across the Frost in the same way.

More colorful. Or perhaps less.

His face rammed sharply into the small of Luna's back.

"Watch where you're going, you idiot." she said.

"I'm sorry Your Highness, I wasn't really looking."

"For the sake of the Seven, don't call me that."

"Fine, whatever."

Up ahead, Sen was already unfurling a tarp from inside his white sack.

"We'll make camp here. I can feel a storm coming," he said. "Runan, could you get a fire going for the food? Soljan, check around for animals. Avenir, Luna, make sure we don't die."

Avenir and Luna both laughed in response to this, but immediately stopped when they realized they had somehow both found it funny. Luna snorted and went about unfurling her own tarp. Avenir did the same.

Soon they had set up a rough tent-like structure around their individual sleds. When the others were not looking, Avenir checked on the Great Sword, bending over behind his tarp and unsheathing it slightly. The Blade still pulsed with a subdued warmth. He put it away quickly, and walked over to Sen, who was studying the map near his own sled. Runan sat nearby, blowing on a tiny pile of burning tinder he had placed in a clay basin.

"We're placing all of our trust in this map," Sen said curtly.

221

"Well, if my father is indeed as great as he was said to be, then we have nothing to worry about, right?" said Avenir.

"That's exactly what we're hoping for. Runan, how's the fire coming along?"

"Magnificent." Runan sat back on his haunches, revealing a young but hearty fire burning within the basin.

"Careful that it doesn't get too big," Sen warned. "Wouldn't want to attract any unwanted attention."

Runan nodded and turned his attention back to the fire. He was using a special type of wood cultivated by the Icesmiths, which gave off only minimal amounts of white smoke. The hope was that a Saber seeing this smoke would think it was just a puff of snow gusting in the wind rather than the marker for some human prey.

After a few minutes, Soljan returned from the nearby Frost. Luna was following behind him. Soljan slung his backpack into his makeshift tent and joined the rest of the group, who were huddled around Runan's tiny fire. A pot of boiling gruel bubbled loudly on top of the clay basin.

"I'm going to have a quick nap, if that's okay with everyone," Luna stated, half-sarcastically. "I'll take first watch tonight."

She dug beneath her tarp-tent like a Frost hare and was soon fast asleep.

"Nothing dangerous anywhere near us," said Soljan, joining the circle.

He rubbed his shoulders vigorously. The brisk cold of the air around the city walls had followed them out into the Frost.

"Just us and the snow: great news to begin with!" beamed Sen.

Avenir could not see his face clearly because of the gauze, but he knew that the man was ecstatic. They had already made it far enough so that Point Fire was just a small black rectangle on the horizon.

A certain peace had also migrated into Avenir's veins now that they were this far away from the Point. He knew the overall situation was dire, but at least it felt as if he was now a cog in a machine, not a wrench. He guessed that Sen felt the same. Being able to evade the unstable politics currently at play within the royal counsel must have been a godsend for the older Hunter.

They enjoyed the quiet for a while, eating their hot gruel. The cheap meat was surprisingly good...or perhaps it was the bitter cold that accentuated the flavors. A violent and rapidly alternating wind started to pick up while they were eating, confirming Sen's prediction about the storm.

They moved quickly, extinguishing the fire, and burying their bowls beneath one of the sleds. By this time, fresh snow had already begun to accumulate over everything in a thick layer.

"Let's hunker down," Sen barked, even his voice beginning to soften under the snowfall. "I'll see you all in the morning!"

The members of the pod all nestled beneath their tarps. Avenir pulled his hood tightly over the top of his head. He actually liked sleeping like this. All he could hear was the whipping of fabric in the wind and the mournful howling over the dunes. These sounds gradually subsided as more and more snow piled up around him.

The dull shrieking of the storm whistled like a distant kettle.

*   *   *

Avenir awoke in a small puddle of water. He cursed under his breath.

The heat from Embr caused some of the snow to melt in.

He peeled away a piece of the tarp above him to discover that he was now encased in a mushy igloo of snow and ice. He rolled over awkwardly to a more comfortable position and set to the frustrating task of digging himself out. When he finally reached fresh air, he was surprised to see that it was barely dawn. The sky contained the faintest hint of greyish light, slowly revealing the Frost below it. The rest of the pod was still asleep. Unlike his own, their tarps were all partially encased by a soft, un-melted layer of snow.

He shook the moisture out of his dunerobe, thanking its anonymous tailors for making it at least somewhat waterproof. He cursed again at Embr for getting him wet.

223

Glancing back at the horizon, he could only just make out Point Fire. It was a beautiful sight to behold. In the morning's clear conditions, the tiny dark fortress looked just like a fabled red sunrise. The subdued crimson from the heat lines within its walls were being reflected off the clouds, providing Avenir with an ominously magical spectacle.

He sat on one of the sleds for a while, taking in the scenery. A massive hand fell down on his shoulder, startling him.

"Don't worry, no Sabers here!" Sen joked loudly, without a doubt waking the rest of the pod. "Amazing isn't it? And people think being a Hunter is a tough job!"

Avenir nodded in agreement. He felt at his clothes again and was happily surprised to find that his robe was already mostly dry.

Sen laughed softly, and whispered next to Avenir's ear, "Best you quickly fix that tarp area of yours before the others wake up. It looks like you made a small fire of your own in there."

He heeded Sen's advice without another word, annoyed with himself for not thinking about it sooner.

The pod was ready within the next hour; all the tarps packed and tied back onto the sleds. Runan handed everyone some sort of dried maize for breakfast.

Avenir was intrigued at how quiet Luna had been so far. He had expected her to complain about many things – that first leg of travel, or the quality of the food – but she was completely silent now.

She must also be happy to get away from the Point. Perhaps more than any of us.

Sen gave the order to leave and they departed in single file.

The journey alternated from excruciating to effortless, as they crested and descended the dunes in the western Frost. At some point, Avenir noted that he had long passed by the furthest point he had ever traveled to. On one of their longer breaks, he left his sled in a valley and crested the largest nearby dune by himself, scanning for Point Fire on the horizon. He could no longer see the battlements, even with his

Hunter's Vision, but he could still make out the bleeding red color of the clouds above them.

A city of perpetual dawn. Or dusk.

"Do you think it would look the same if it were burning right now?"

Luna walked up besides Avenir. She removed her ice gauze, revealing her striking green eyes. They reminded Avenir of a Saber's.

He shrugged, "I don't think so. You would probably be able to see the smoke rising."

"Always so literal. Fine," she sat down on the dune. "And what about beauty. Would it be more beautiful?"

Avenir took off his ice gauze. He spent a moment thinking about her question, staring at the stained horizon.

"I don't know."

"I think it would be."

"Thousands of people would be in danger."

"Can there be beauty without danger?"

Avenir looked down at Luna, her cat-like form sitting cross-legged on the snow. He could not shake the sense of sadness he felt.

I will never come to understand her.

"Hey!" Called Runan from down in the valley. "Let's get going!"

They traveled westward for another couple of hours before being stopped by Soljan. They were at the foot of an especially magnificent dune.

"Avenir, come with me. I want to check if there are any animals near us. I need your vision."

The two of them left their sleds behind and climbed up the steep incline. The ascent took a while, but they were rewarded with an awe-inspiring view of the surrounding Frost. Even the orange haze above Point Fire seemed distant now.

"I've noticed no tracks or signs and smelled nothing so far. Can you confirm this visually?"

"Of course."

The geography at their current location was unlike anything Avenir had witnessed before. Back to the east, where Point Fire lay, the landscape undulated wildly. Dunes and valleys lay as far as he could see that way. But in the direction that they were headed, these dunes slowly receded away, eventually melting into an endless flat expanse. The area was completely devoid of all life. Avenir had an intuition that no living creature would willingly come near this area, especially Frost Flyers, which needed the cover of the dunes to survive. Even so, he made doubly sure that he could not see any signs of movement.

"We're alone," he said confidently.

"That at least confirms what I believe," agreed Soljan.

"Give me a second," said Avenir.

He pulled his bow off his back and nocked an arrow. He crouched and let it loose over the dunes towards the west. He watched it sail over the white expanse, until it buried itself soundlessly into the side of a dune.

"What was that for?" asked Soljan.

"I'm just gauging the distance. Judging by where that fell, I'd guess it's about twenty-three arrow shots to the point where the dunes stop. I think we should camp right there, near the edge – wouldn't want to sleep somewhere with no cover. It's probably going to take us two or three hours to get there."

"Hmph," grunted Soljan, impressed. "Never thought of using them like that."

They returned to the rest of the pod with the news of the impending plateau. The area was like a double-edged sword: no animal life meant relative safety, but it also meant that the environment would be essentially uninhabitable. There was no sense arguing about it, so they continued pressing further west, tugging their sleds behind them. Soon they passed Avenir's sunken arrow, which had already dipped further into the snow. Avenir collected it and tucked it back into his quiver.

"How many days did you ration us for?" Avenir called out to Sen, if only to break the hourlong silence which had ensued. Sen did not hear anything over the constant wind, so Runan responded in his stead.

"At least a month."

Avenir was not expecting an answer like that.

"A month? Does he really think we'd have to go that far?"

"Maybe, who knows? All I know is that he's determined that we find at least *some* form of helpful information to take back to the Point. Coming back emptyhanded isn't really an option."

"I think a better option in that case, would be to lie once we got back, instead of dying out here like cursed martyrs," Luna added.

"Perhaps, but let's stay optimistic for now," said Runan.

They made good time to where Avenir had suggested to make camp. As he had seen, the dunes had steadily flattened out, making the pulling of the sleds more consistent overall, much to the dismay of Runan. The older Hunter had come to enjoy waiting for the pod to descend a dune ahead of him, and then sliding down at breakneck speeds after them as he sat perched on top of his baggage. The others had tried this as well but were not as comfortable with the prospect of bailing out and having to repack everything.

Once near the edge of the dunes, they performed the same tent pitching ritual as before, while Runan readied the gruel-fire. Even Luna ate hungrily this time, tired out from the hard day of travel.

After the rest of the pod was laying snugly underneath their tarps, Avenir quietly cut off a piece of material from his own and wrapped Embr within it.

Hopefully this will let me wake up at least partially dry tomorrow.

The air was as smooth as glass that night, and Avenir could hear Sen snoring loudly from under his own tarp. Although decidedly less calming than the sound of the wind over the dunes, he was soon lulled to sleep by the man's deep-set breathing.

*   *   *

227

Avenir was delighted to find that only the outer portions of his robe were damp the next morning. He could hear Sen and Runan talking in the open just outside his tarp. He yawned loudly and crawled out from under it. The two veteran Hunters were sitting on neighboring sleds, enjoying their breakfast. They were reminiscing about some of their older Hunts and childhood activities. Soljan and Luna were nearby on the crest of a small dune. The tracker had his hand extended to the west, like he was showing her something.

"Good morning," said Avenir cheerily. He found he was in a positive mood, probably because he had managed to sleep well for what seemed like the first time in months.

"Morning, 'Nir," replied Sen heartily. He handed the young Hunter a stale slice of rye-crust and a cup of freezing water.

"So, what's the plan?" asked Avenir.

"Directly across. The 'glacier runs' on the map should be around there..." Sen pointed in a general westerly direction. "That reminds me..." He searched around in his white sack for a bit before producing another smaller bag. From it he withdrew two sets of what looked like metal chains. "For your shoes once we get there," he explained. "If a glacier is indeed an expanse of hard ice like the archives say, we should probably be properly equipped when we cross it. You wrap these around your feet – they should help with the traction."

"Amazing," exclaimed Runan.

Avenir was also impressed.

Sen really thought of everything coming out here.

"Where did you get something like this? Never seen it before."

"I had Tark make them. Custom order."

"The old blacksmith?" asked Runan.

"The one and only," smiled Sen. "He still owed me a debt from a while back. I'll give the other two theirs when they rejoin us."

Avenir returned to his sled and packed his tarp away, stashing the metal boot chains with it. Soon, the others had done the same. He noticed that Luna was also oddly cheerful this morning, asking Sen about his past Hunts and Soljan about his tracking stories.

They left shortly thereafter. The orange light above Point Fire had already disappeared far behind them.

*   *   *

The single file line jerked to a halt. For the second time since their journey began, Avenir collided with the small of Luna's back. She did not say anything this time, instead peering ahead intently. Sen was kneeling down at the head of the column, inspecting something. To Avenir's astonishment, the leader of the Hunters dipped his hand downwards...and it disappeared completely. Only then did he realize they had come to the edge of a sheer cliff of ice.

If Sen weren't constantly paying attention while we were moving, he would probably be dead right now.

"Avenir, could you come look at this?" Sen called back. "I can't see as well as I used to."

Avenir moved forward past the pod's line, and knelt behind Sen. He was now acutely aware of his footing. Luna appeared and sat beside him, looking ahead curiously. They were indeed on the edge of a cliff, but it was difficult to tell how far down it went, or even where the edge began. They were incredibly lucky that the area they were on was indeed solidly packed.

Sen motioned to Luna. "Could you shoot one of your arrows down there, maybe tie something bright onto it? Avenir, track it please. Tell me how deep this goes."

Luna went back to her sled and retrieved her bow, another new masterpiece of woodwork. She also produced a long rag of black material, which she had presumably ripped from something inside her sack. She tied it tightly to the back of the arrow and looked at Avenir to make sure he was watching carefully. She aimed the bow as far downwards as possible and let the arrow free softly, so that it would be easier to track. Avenir focused intensely on the quivering piece of fabric on the back of the shaft. It was a short journey to the bottom.

For an arrow.

229

He noticed a distinct blue shimmer where the arrow thudded into the ground, something he had never seen before.

"I think it's about two-hundred feet, give or take ten. The ground at the bottom also appears to be rock hard."

"*Lady* and gentlemen, it seems we have arrived at the glaciers!" Sen shouted loudly, almost making Avenir and Luna fall of the edge.

When he had regained his composure, Avenir asked, "How are we even supposed to get down there?"

Sen laughed and pointed at Runan. "Brother, get the pegs please. 'Nir, didn't you learn anything I taught you in the Frost? Always come prepared for a Hunt, even for things you can't foresee."

"That doesn't make any sense," said Luna incredulously.

Sen ignored her and took what he was asking for from his brother – a set of sturdy-looking long iron stakes.

"We'll camp at the bottom," he said, before jabbing one of the pegs with all his strength into the snow about five feet away from the cliff's edge.

He tested the stake by pulling on it slightly, and when he was satisfied, he jabbed another one into the ground nearby. He repeated this procedure with two more stakes, slightly further back and in line from the first two.

"Luna, you should have a length of rope in your bag. Avenir, you too. Could you get those for me?"

They did as they were told, discovering two large coils of rope buried between their other supplies. Sen looped and tied each around the sets of two stakes, one in front and one in back, and then hurled the loose ends of the ropes over the edge of the cliff.

"That's our way down!" he exclaimed proudly. He noticed Avenir and Luna's confused stares, and explained, "It should be safe. Hold onto both lengths of rope to descend. I made two, just to be cautious. Plus, we even have a safety peg for each. That sounds like four times the necessary safety to me!" He laughed loudly.

"And what of our packs? And sleds?" asked Avenir skeptically.

This seemed to him like one of the worst mistakes their pod could ever make.

"Oh, we'll have to go up and down these multiple times, carrying small amounts, of course. Runan will take down the sleds – I think that *my* combined weight with one of those could prove a bit troublesome!"

He took off his ice gauze and wiped his eyes, clearly enjoying his own joke. Luna, Soljan, and Avenir all exchanged a look of fear before Sen continued.

"'Nir, since you so helpfully gauged the distance, you can have the privilege of going first! Take only the bows with you, just so you can get used to it the first time."

At first Avenir thought that Sen was teasing him, but then he noticed the twinkle in his eyes and realized that the man was serious.

He actually thinks that he is letting me have the first bit of fun. I can see where Aren gets this sort of thing from.

There was no use in disagreeing with him so Avenir took all the bows, three in total, and approached Sen.

"How exactly does this work?"

"It should be easy. You take the ropes and hook them around your body like this" – he showed him – "and just walk backwards off the edge. Make sure you remember to put those chains on your feet. We wouldn't want you slipping!"

"Simple as that?" Avenir asked sarcastically.

"Of course!"

Avenir inhaled deeply as he did what Sen told him to. As if to ease his conscience, Sen moved to the so-called "backup" pegs and held them down with each hand. He nodded encouragement to Avenir, who lowered himself over the edge at a snail's pace. His stomach turned as he felt his back move over into nothingness. With a final effort, and a great deal of trust, he pushed the rest of his body over the edge.

The first descent was far worse than what felt like the hundreds after. Back in Point Fire, Avenir had no qualms about climbing precarious walls, or standing on the precipices of towers. But in the Frost, he found himself unwilling to take the same sorts of risks. Perhaps it had just been drilled into him at a young age by his father.

Or perhaps it's because the lives of countless others may depend on me surviving this.

Once they had gotten over their initial fear of heights, he and the others spent numerous trips going from the top edge to the bottom and back up again, as they shuttled their equipment. The base of the cliff, as Avenir had predicted, was made of pure ice, which boasted a clear azure sheen.

At many points during the day's work, Avenir, Soljan, and Luna would sit and gawk at Runan's physical prowess, who descended the cliff with ease, sleds and all.

When they were done, the last to arrive was Sen, who had to make sure that the pegs at the top were in secure enough so that they would remain there until the pod's eventual return.

By this time, it was already dusk. The light was setting behind the clouds far in the west, illuminating the cliff face behind them in pastel greys and whites. They set up camp, unfurling their tarps and nailing their sleds to the ice for fear of them sliding away in the winds. After enjoying Runan's gruel for the third time, they soon realized that sleeping on rock hard ice was not easy. Soljan was the first to think of using his white sack as a pillow, and the rest of the pod followed suit.

As he was lying uncomfortably beneath the flimsy canvas, Avenir wondered about his family.

Aren. Mother.

The hard surface beneath him constantly reminded him of the true gravity of their situation. He fell asleep thinking about the danger that was still growing in Point Fire, and the dwindling fire within the Heart.

XXVIII

Aren lay quietly on the outermost wall of the Fynn facing the Icesmith district... and the Cathedral. In the three days since Avenir's departure, he had focused all his attention on exploration and eavesdropping. But by the second day, he had already begun to get bored with it, especially since neither he nor Udar could come up with anything interesting. On the third, however, he happened to notice some of the priests rushing frantically from the Heart out towards the Cathedral. This type of behavior was nothing special – members of the Church seemed to have their own calendars and agendas – but to Aren's luck it led to something more.

For the past couple hours, he had been watching the distant Cathedral intently. He was too afraid to go closer, since there was no effective cover out in the Grey, and he would be spotted immediately. Even so, from his vantage point he could see that the priests far off in the distance appeared to be building something. Exactly *what* they were building remained a mystery. They looked to Aren like tiny red insects milling around the Cathedral – their hive. He thought of Kreymar and shuddered.

Another reason not to get too close.

He lay on the wall for another hour or two, pondering what the little ants were building. They seemed to be carrying sharp stakes and jamming them into the ground, but he could not understand what the rest of the wood they were carrying around would form.

Cabins?

"Aren!"

A muffled shout floated over the battlements from somewhere in the direction of the Fynn. Aren instinctively jumped behind a broken stone balustrade, peering over it to see who wanted him.

"Aren, where are you?" came the voice again.

He now recognized it as Udar's and shouted in response.

"I'm over here! On the wall facing the Cathedral"

"For the sake of the Seven, could you come down here?"

His voice was floating up from the street's level. Aren groaned at having to descend the high walls.

I wish I had a rope so I could do the thing that Sen taught me.

But even without a rope, he was able to reach ground level in a few minutes, finding Udar sitting on the porch of someone's home front. At the sight of Aren, Udar jumped to his feet.

"Finally!" he said, exasperated. "You've got to come see this!" He tugged at Aren's robe.

"What is it? You have to tell me first."

"It's Yob! You know, the overseer?" Udar asked excitedly.

Aren nodded.

"Yes, well he's got some sort of crowd going in the Pit." Udar lowered his voice, "I think it's about the royal family keeping secrets or something."

Aren immediately joined Udar in his excitement.

"What? Why didn't you come sooner? Let's go!"

"It's because I couldn't find you on these stupid walls-"

But Aren was already bounding down the street. Udar huffed in annoyance and jogged after him.

When they reached the portcullis to the Pit, two burly men stepped out from the shadows, bumping Aren back and blocking their path.

"Hey!" Aren yelped.

Udar immediately retreated a few feet backwards. One of the two, a muscular giant who had a sprawling mustache and grisly beard, moved forward to speak.

"I'm sorry but you cannot-" he paused, seemingly taken aback. "Aren! What are you doing here?"

It took a moment for Aren to realize who the men were.

"Julnd? Viktor? What's going on?"

Viktor, the one who had stayed back, now approached Aren as well. His head was closely shaven, and he had a beard to match Julnd's.

"There's potential for a riot in the Pit. We have orders from Sen to keep the peace near this area, so we can't let anyone go in there for now."

Aren was skeptical, "What about the royal guards? Aren't they the ones who're supposed to do that sort of thing?"

"Typically, yes. But I can assure you they've got their hands more than full right now," said Julnd gruffly, scratching at his mustache.

"In any case, no one's going in, especially children," Viktor added. "Sorry, Aren."

"Okay, okay. I get it. I'll just come back later then?"

"Of course you can. We just want to make sure everyone stays safe for now, 'specially given recent happenings. Remember, Many over the Few."

Aren shook Julnd's hand and walked back to where Udar was standing some ways back.

"What was that?" his friend asked.

"Same thing you were telling me about. They have orders not to let anyone in."

"Maybe we shouldn't go, then?" ventured Udar hesitantly.

"Are you crazy? This is exactly why we *should* go. Remember what Avenir said? If something like this gets worse, we must be the first to know."

Aren disappeared around a dark corner. A few seconds later, he poked his head back around.

"Why are you just standing there? Let's go!"

With a courageous effort, Udar moved his feet and followed Aren into the alleyway.

"Up here. I think there's a way across the upper walls," said Aren as he looked towards the battlements.

"Let's hope so," said Udar, who was already slightly out of breath.

An ancient and out-of-use heat line writhed into the corner of the alley. Aren used it as a springboard and vaulted upwards, grabbing

the top of a nearby wall with his fingertips. With unnerving ease, he pulled himself up.

"There's no way I'm doing that." Udar said softly.

"You don't have to catch the wall like I did. I'll grab your hands."

Aren lay flat on top of the wall. He dangled his arms off the edge, beckoning to Udar.

"Oh boy," breathed Udar.

The locksmith's son mimicked Aren's jump and heaved his body up towards his friend. One of Aren's hands grabbed his, but the other missed, causing Udar to swing wildly. Aren gritted his teeth as the smaller boy's body pulled at his shoulder socket.

"Grab...the other," Aren strained.

Udar managed to raise his other hand to Aren's free one. After a great deal of shuffling and grunting, Aren yanked him up. Udar rolled over on top of the wall next to him.

"Luckily, you're weirdly strong."

"Uh huh," Aren gasped.

Although I still may have underestimated that.

"I forgot how fun this is," said Udar. "Let's go!"

The locksmith's son got up onto his feet, brushed off some dirt, and marched along the wall in the direction of the Pit. Aren watched his friend leave, a surprised look on his face.

"Hey! Wait for me!"

He got up and rushed after him.

*　　　　　*　　　　　*

It was not difficult to locate the area that Udar had mentioned. Occasional shouts and jeers rang up from the streets there, breaking the silence of the dusky air.

"Careful, we can't let anyone see or hear us," Aren whispered.

In the shadows of a parapet, the two boys gazed downwards to the city below. Hundreds of people were milling about in an open courtyard lit by raised braziers. Off to the side – where the crowd was

236

its densest – stood a singular figure on a large wooden block. Aren noticed multiple contingents of royal guards at every entrance to the courtyard.

"Look, it's Yob," Udar whispered as he pointed to the man standing on the block.

Aren strained his ears, trying to hear what the overseer of the Pit was saying.

"...and that's unacceptable!"

The crowd roared in approval.

"This is *our* city as well!" Yob jabbed his finger at the ground, the jewelry on his fingers glinting in the orange light. "*Our* Point!"

The crowd erupted into applause.

Yob continued, "We cannot wait any longer! We must hold the royal family accountable for their silence! I hold King Luxus personally accountable! We experience the greatest tragedy in the history of the Point...family members killed by their brothers, wives...and they sit there in their castle claiming it was a magical farce!"

"Can you hear what he's saying?" asked Udar.

Aren raised his finger to his lips. "Shh! Let me listen."

Yob extended his hand in a gesture of accusation towards the center of the crowd.

"I don't know about *you*, but I have my own theory about what is going on..." he gave a long pause for dramatic effect. "I believe *Luna* tried to stage a rebellion against the royal throne!"

Gasps blew through the crowd like a haunting gust of wind. Yob was smiling. Aren could see his teeth glinting in the semi-darkness.

"Shocking isn't it?" Yob asked mockingly. "But who else could stage a coup besides the black sheep of the royal family? Of course, if anyone in the royal court or family is now present and disagrees with me, I charge them to have Luna make a public appearance and explain what exactly is going on in *our* city!"

At these final words, someone must have given an order to the royal guards, because they immediately swept into the courtyard. Shrieks went up from the crowd. Two of the armored men managed to make it to Yob. They restrained his arms and forcefully led him off his

wooden pulpit. As he was being pulled away, he started yelling something again. Aren struggled to make it out over the commotion.

"I charge...Luna...Two days...We will..." and with that he was gone, his voice pulled away into the throng of more royal guards.

"This is bad," Aren whispered, loud enough so that Udar could hear him over the cacophony of the streets below.

"Why? What's happened? I couldn't hear anything," hissed Udar.

The scream of a young woman pierced the general noise below. The boys both peered back over the edge, trying to get a better view of what was going on.

A girl with bright blond hair was attacking one of the royal guards. She was shrieking something about her brother. The man she was assaulting put her into a swift chokehold, attempting to subdue her. In response, a couple of nearby men tackled the guard, and the whole group clattered to the floor in a jumbled pile of armor and legs. Aren tore his eyes away from the scene.

"We should go. Now."

Udar nodded. Aren moved quickly, leaving the chaos behind and carving a path carefully over the rooftops back to the Fynn. Every now and then he checked back over his shoulder to make sure that Udar was still there. When they reached the main wall separating the two districts, Aren ducked into an abandoned watchtower. Udar fell in after him, breathing raggedly. The noise of the courtyard was far behind them now.

"Can you please tell me what happened there?" Udar begged between huffed breaths.

"Yob's trying to start something big. He was talking about blaming the royal family for what happened in the Point!"

"What does that mean?"

"I think he's called for the king to bring Luna out into the public in two days. He's accused her of starting some sort of rebellion."

Udar's eyes opened wide. "Do you think that could be true?"

"Of course not. I don't think someone like her even cares about being king...I mean queen. Also, she's not even here. I heard yesterday from Piet that she's out on a Hunt with my brother."

Aren froze.

I wasn't supposed to say that.

Luckily, Udar appeared to be lost within his own thoughts.

Aren continued, "Anyway, it'll look like the royal family is trying to hide her."

Udar's eyes snapped back to Aren's.

"What do we do then? Is there anything we *can* do?

"I don't think so. But at least we know how long we have. I think you should tell your family to hide in your secret base in two days' time. I'll also tell my mom to try and get somewhere safe in the Hunters' district. Maybe I'll ask Darch..."

Udar groaned and lay down on the cold stone. He wiped the sweat off his brow.

"Why is everything getting so... crazy?"

"I don't know," Aren replied, "But I think my brother does. And for some reason, I think he's the only one who can help."

XXIX

Avenir awoke with a horridly stiff back. He was hopelessly entangled in his white sack, and a length of rope was snaking its way across and through his legs. He struggled to get the rope off himself and lifted the tarp. It was deathly freezing outside. The cliff had blocked what little heat daylight could offer in the Frost. Avenir noticed that the ice beneath where he had slept had melted substantially. His robes were damp as usual.

Damn you, Embr.

Soljan was awake, scratching at his long grey hair which had fallen out of its bun, while he pulled the anchoring stakes out from the base of his sled.

"Morning Avenir," he whistled. "It's a little bit chilly isn't it?"

"No kidding, are the others up yet?"

"Luna is still asleep. The other two left about half an hour ago to scout out the base of this cliff. They should be back soon."

"What are they looking for?"

"No idea. Just curious I guess."

"Sounds about right."

Soon Luna was also awake, and she joined them in preparing the sleds for yet another day of travel. Her dark hair was a mess from an equally uncomfortable night. She noticed Avenir looking at her and huffed loudly as she pulled it into a tight ponytail, tucking it back into her hood.

"What do you think of this place?" she asked.

"It's amazing," came Avenir's response. "It's just like when I was exploring the battlements for the first time."

With Father.

Luna laughed. It was like the high-pitched cooing noise of a bird of prey.

"Now that's something I wish I could have done as a child. Of course, it's taboo for a member of the royal family to stoop to that level."

"I can still take you," Avenir offered carefully.

"I doubt that will happen," came the curt reply.

Just then, Sen and Runan returned, talking loudly as usual.

"Find anything interesting?" asked Soljan.

"You mean besides this beautiful cliff face?" Sen chortled. "No, nothing. Morning Luna, 'Nir."

Sen had already packed most of his sack and tarp away. He pulled the stakes out with little effort and glanced at the rest of the pod.

"Everyone almost ready? I've got a good feeling about this so-called *Castle* to the west. Maybe we'll meet our secretive voice at last."

They adopted a slightly different tactic when travelling over this new endless expanse of turquoise ice. Instead of pulling the sleds behind them, they now pushed them ahead. Sometimes, when they reached a slight decline, Runan gave his sled a powerful shove. He would then jump on the back, whooping with childlike joy as he rode its momentum over the ice.

It was not long before the rest of the pod joined him in this game. Avenir even suggested that they have a race down one of the more significant declines. Sen won this contest by a mile, his massive weight propelling him downwards at breakneck speeds. Avenir himself had come stone last, with Luna not too far ahead of him. He had managed to steal a glance at her as she careened past him, using her chained boot to gain extra speed. A wide grin had been plastered across her face, her dark ponytail trailing in the wind.

The Frost is indeed magical. The harshest place in existence, yet sometimes...

*   *   *

The air had reached a whole new level of frigidity. Ever since the cliff had disappeared from sight behind them, he could feel the moisture in his nostrils freezing with every inhalation. He wrapped his ice gauze tighter. He counted himself lucky, though, that the Great Sword at his belt still provided perpetual warmth. The others in the pod had already made numerous stops along the way to search their sacks for extra layers of clothing.

After an hour, a thick mist began to settle around them.

We must have descended a fair bit.

"Still good?" barked Sen from out front.

"Yes!" they all shouted in agreement.

"Good! Everyone, group up. We don't want to separate in these conditions."

They pulled their sleds close together, relishing the brief rest. Soljan came up with the idea of tying ropes between them. At first, Sen did not think it was necessary, but during the few minutes they were discussing it, the mist had already thickened considerably. He finally agreed, and so the rest of the pod spent some time tying ropes between the front and back of every unit.

They began moving again in a single file formation, with Avenir behind Luna, and Soljan taking up the rear. Due to the rapid decrease in visibility, they were making frustratingly slow progress.

The tracker spoke up behind him, "Avenir, how far can you see in this?"

"Not very," he responded, trying to focus on keeping his sled running straight.

"I think I may have spotted something on the right, but I don't trust my eyes in this mist."

Avenir's adrenaline levels instantly spiked. He swiveled his head rapidly, checking to the sides of their column.

"What did it look like?"

"I don't know. It might have been the mist shifting."

"Sen, did you hear that?" Avenir echoed the message to the front of the line.

He was focusing so intently on their right flank now, that he forgot to blink for a few seconds, and he could feel the cold starting to dig in at the edges of his eyes. Runan and Sen were completely obscured by the suffocating mists. He blinked repeatedly and tightened his ice gauze.

"Yes, I heard!" came the clear response from the front, "Stay sharp! Keep as close to your quarries as possible!"

All members of the pod immediately tucked their bodies tightly against their sleds. Beads of sweat were starting to form on Avenir's brow. It was incredibly itchy, but he did not dare take off the ice gauze at this moment. Even a split-second of broken sight could potentially mean his death.

One could never be too careful in the Frost. If this even is the Frost anymore-

"Avenir, movement on your left!" Luna called from in front of him.

The column of Hunters jerked to a halt. Avenir buried his body deeper into the sack at the back of sled and turned his eyes to follow Luna's warning. A swirl of mist whipped violently at the edge of his field of vision, as if something had moved away quickly. The residue of the movement was accompanied by a slew of sickening skittering and crunching sounds.

"Damn! I can't see it!" shouted Avenir, "Sen?"

"Just keep close to your sled!" Sen boomed, "Do not leave the column! And don't stop moving!"

They all started pushing again. It took every bit of Avenir's composure not to remain in place, to ready his bow. He gritted his teeth and carried on. Soljan did the same behind him.

"Red flares!" shouted Sen. "Who has the flares?"

"Here!" Luna quickly dove into her pack and tossed Runan a cylindrical vessel.

This time Avenir saw the movement clearly. A lower section of the mist not five paces away from him briefly gave way to reveal a hardened and spiked appendage which was jammed into the ice. The appendage dislodged with a crunch and disappeared.

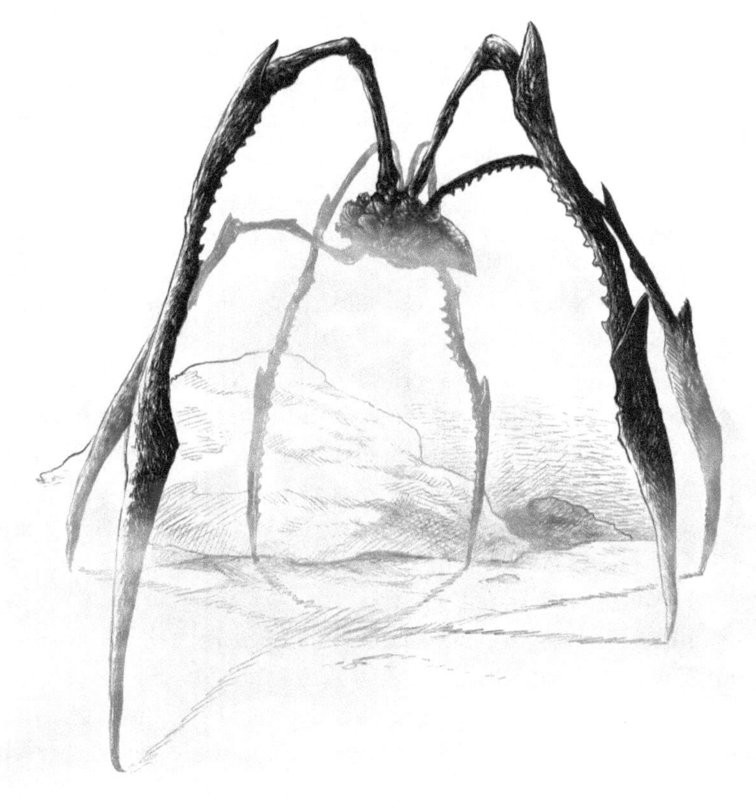

"What in the name..." Avenir breathed.

"It's like a giant... spider!" Luna shouted, fear rising in her voice.

"It's okay!" Sen shouted in return, though his voice now also carried a hint of fear. "We just need the flares. They are afraid of fire! Runan! Use them!"

There was a wet crunch behind Avenir, followed by Soljan's blood-curdling scream. Avenir looked back to see a spider-like appendage stabbed cleanly through the man's calf. It looked just like the chitin-plated leg of an insect. A sharpened toe was now wedged firmly into the ice on the other side of Soljan's flesh. The tracker was frantically clawing at his limb, but to no avail.

Avenir's hearing became muffled from the adrenaline. Sen was yelling something out in front, but he could not make sense of it.

The insect-leg started to retract. Soljan's muffled screaming intensified. At this point, Avenir noticed the lines of grotesque fishhook-like barbs along the monstrosity's limb. Some of these had caught fast in Soljan's calf, or perhaps his bone, and were pulling him upwards. Avenir traced his eyes to where the leg began. He could feel his pulse accelerating as he saw that the creature itself was likely over fifteen feet tall.

Runan must have lit the first flare because the whole area around them became bathed in a red tinge. The front side of the creature, now illuminated in the glow, stirred a deep terror in Avenir's mind. It was indeed gruesomely tall, twenty feet at least, and appeared to be a grossly elongated spider.

The appendage jammed through Soljan's leg was one of many; the other ones were held firmly in the ice by their spiky toes. The thorax of the creature was a mess of bile and sharp fangs, all gnashing silently in anticipation for the upcoming meal. And now, at the edges of Avenir's peripheral vision, multiple numbers of these demons were slinking away from the light.

They were clearly startled by the flare, but the one with Soljan on its leg refused to give up its prey that easily. It tried backing away from the light while pulling its human quarry along with it. Soljan's body was being held upside down at this point. He stopped batting at his calf, turning instead to grab at his sled. He managed to grip a segment of the white sack. White-knuckled, he held onto the fabric for dear life, screaming maniacally. Finally, Soljan seemed to notice that Avenir was standing right behind his sled.

"Help. *Help!*" he gargled painfully.

This snapped Avenir out of his momentary daze. He moved instinctively, opening his dunerobe, feeling for the hilt of Embr. He found it almost too easily – the crystal-lined leather covering the grip had burnt off again. Somehow, he had not felt this.

The touch of cool stone.

He could feel the tiny red thorns begin to emerge from the sword and dig themselves into his skin. But he did not care. His mind was elsewhere.

He vaulted up and onto Soljan's sled, standing over where the tracker was still clinging onto the sack with all his might. The monstrosity was now fully lit by an intense orange-white glow. The new light was coming directly from the Great Sword. It was as if the sun had finally revealed itself from behind the clouds over the Frost.

The creature screamed in an unholy register, and its remaining legs tensed to jump. Avenir brought the Great Sword in a horizontal arc across the spiky limb embedded in Soljan's calf. The fiery Weapon cleaved the insect being's leg easily. The stump smoldered loudly and the aroma of burning flesh filled the air.

Now free, Soljan fell back down to the ground, clutching at his calf, which still contained a severed segment of the fish-hooked appendage.

The spider creature jumped away, its remaining toe spikes leaving the ice with a loud *POP.* Its body disappeared into the mists. The other monstrosities were already long gone.

Avenir gasped for air. His chest was burning intensely. He tried to let go of Embr, but it remained stuck, the thorny barbs embedded in his hand. He looked down. He was bleeding, some of it staining his dunerobe up to his elbow. His vision began to blur, and he stumbled backwards off the Sled and onto something soft. He lost consciousness to the sound of Soljan's whimpering.

*　　　　　*　　　　　*

Red eyes. Watching me. Watching all of us. Telling me what to do.

A harsh bump of the sled woke Avenir from a restless sleep. He remained motionless, taking a few seconds to adjust. He was on top of one of the white sacks. Soothing mist flowed around him. Sen was grunting just ahead, pulling him along.

Avenir sat up, trying not to lose his balance on the sled. The rest of the pod was still moving in single file. Runan was directly behind him, pulling Soljan in a similar manner. The tracker was fast asleep...or unconscious. His leg was now wrapped in a thick swathe of blood-clotted bandages.

At the far rear, Luna was raising one of the flares as she pulled her sled. The entire area surrounding them was still bathed in the same eerie red light. Avenir rolled off the sled sideways, landing heavily on the ice. He struggled to his feet. Sen immediately stopped and turned around.

"'Nir! You're awake! Thank the Seven."

Luna and Runan stopped their sleds. Avenir's hand fell to his belt. The Great Sword was no longer there.

"Where's the Sword? Sen, *where's the Sword?*"

He could feel Luna's cold gaze boring into his back.

Sen raised his hands, "Whoa, calm down 'Nir. We're safe now. Soljan's okay as well, relatively speaking."

Avenir was now fully awake.

"I need to see the Sword. Please."

"What even *IS* the Sword, Avenir?" Luna snapped.

Avenir could sense the hatred and disgust in her voice, but he ignored her.

Sen lowered his hands. "Yes, okay, okay. It's right here. Took a damned effort to get it back into its sheath without burning myself."

Sen reached over to the other side of the sled and unhooked the crystal-lined scabbard. He handed it to Avenir, who snatched it away quickly. Before the veteran Hunter could react, Avenir had drawn Embr. It was now pointed at Sen's throat.

No sooner had Avenir raised the weapon than it began humming again. Angry flames licked around the blade's silver edges.

Luna and Runan reacted instantly. The princess drew her bow and nocked an arrow. Sen's brother whipped out his own Shard at a terrifying speed. Both weapons were now trained on Avenir.

"Whoa, whoa..." Sen spoke quietly, carefully. "What is the meaning of this?"

"You." Avenir stated with a strange sense of calmness. He could feel the Sword's hidden power holding him steady. Little thorns pricked at his hand, begging to be let inside his skin. "You lied to us."

"Oh?" asked Sen, quite surprised. "What do you mean by that?"

The massive man did not move. He could sense that the young man in front of him possessed the will to kill. Avenir thought very carefully about the phrasing of his next words.

I have to convince the others as well, or I'm dead.

"Remember what I told you? You said that my father left alone that night, all those years ago. I couldn't believe that a Hunter as good as you would let that happen, especially in the Frost. But I was willing to give you the benefit of the doubt. Everyone makes mistakes, even you..." Avenir heard Luna's bowstring being pulled taut. He continued, "But then we reached that cliff. And those glaciers. Things *you said* that no one besides my father has ever known to exist. Yet *you* came fully prepared...the boot spikes, the ropes for the cliff...enough for me to believe that it was no coincidence."

Sen's frown had deepened. Avenir knew that Runan and Luna could have killed him by now.

But they haven't...yet.

He was determined to see this through.

"And now, when those *demons* attacked. You knew exactly how to deal with them. You knew that they were afraid of flares. Don't tell me this was all just *by accident.*"

The pod was deadly silent. Even the slowly swirling mist seemed like a deafening typhoon in comparison.

Finally, Sen spoke, as something changed in his expression.

"Yes, 'Nir. I am sorry."

XXX

It was dusk, and Aren was leading his mother around the inner edge of the Pit. As he had told Udar he would, he had urged her to take refuge in the Hunters' district. But before doing this, he had spoken to Darch, the barman and old friend of his father, to see if she could spend a night or two in the tavern loft. At first the man had just scratched at his bushy eyebrows and refused Aren's request. But eventually, after Aren's incessant badgering, and a considerable amount of Avenir's stored up Blood, the man caved in to his greed.

"Fine, fine," Darch had said, "If your mother does agree to this for whatever reason, I accept."

As he could have predicted, convincing his mother was a far harder task than bribing Darch. She was finally swayed by Aren's half-truth that Avenir had told him to do this.

"And it's only for a night or two. Avenir was really worried about it, Mom."

Before he and his mother left, Aren had paid a quick visit to Udar's house. After the fifth knock, his friend finally answered the door.

"What is it? We're getting ready to go to the basement," said Udar.

"Good, I just wanted to make sure."

"Hey, Aren."

"Yeah?"

"I'm scared."

"Me too, but I guess that's why we're doing this."

As Aren and his mother traversed the edge of the Pit, they discovered the entire area to be a ghost town. Commerce, trade, and all social enterprises had come to a standstill in the city. The occasional lone person would lower their head and walk past them quickly. They had passed too many locked doors to count.

They moved through the portcullis into the Hunters' district. Immediately, they found themselves surrounded by far more people, most of them Hunters, and all of them heavily armed. Aren approached the nearest group, much to the dismay of his mother.

"What's going on here?" he asked nonchalantly.

A tough-looking woman with a bow slung over her shoulder turned to him, smiling when she recognized him.

"Aren? What a surprise! Are you–" the woman noticed his mother trailing behind him, "Hello, Sylis, what brings you here?"

Sylis responded curtly, "Evening, Marin. Aren's brought me here to stay a couple nights. Apparently there's been some violent stirrings in the Pit?"

The woman smiled a yellow grin.

"Wow! Talk about cautious. I thought that was always more of a 'Nir thing."

"It *was* 'Nir's idea," exclaimed Sylis proudly, "but he's out right now."

"Out? Where to? Surely not on a *Hunt*? These are indeed troubling times." She nodded at her bow. "As you can see, most of us are guarding the entrance to the Hunters'."

"Sorry, we really have to go, already late!" Aren yanked his mother away from Marin. He waved to the bow-wielding woman and pushed his mother into an alleyway. "Mom! No one is supposed to know!"

"Oh, stop being so harsh. Sorry, I forgot."

To avoid further contact with anyone, Aren led her through back alleys and hidden walkways until they arrived at Darch's tavern. Unlike the establishments in the other districts, there was still a substantial amount of activity around this one.

"Sylis! Aren!" The barman pushed through a group of people to welcome the duo. "I've been expecting you. At that price, I'll be sure to have you living in Loft Luxury!"

He laughed to himself and retrieved two tankards of ale for them. After a disapproving look from Sylis, he nodded guiltily and returned them back to the counter. He then disappeared behind a nearby group, responding to a call for another round of drinks.

"Aren, you *paid* for this?" Sylis asked, stunned.

"Don't worry, it wasn't that much," he lied. "You should go check out what the loft looks like."

"And you haven't *seen* it?"

Aren could tell his mother was getting angry, so he added, "I have to go check on something in the district really quick. I'll be right back."

"You better be, young man," said Sylis in a threatening tone. As Aren turned to leave, she added, "Please, be safe."

Aren left the tavern and when he was sure no one was looking, darted into the shadows behind the building. From there he used an old sewage shaft to reach the top of a nearby wall. He realized he was not high enough, and swiftly vaulted over a few stone blocks up to a better vantage point.

"Now where is Sen's...? There!"

He spotted Sen's cabin – and office – not too far away. It was a small distance off towards the edge of the city walls. Aren moved like a cat, creeping and jumping between outcrops and slanted slabs, until he was twenty feet above Sen's office roof. Without a moment's hesitation, he launched himself from his perch. He rolled on impact with the dark slabs of the roof, making no sound.

After stopping his momentum, he crawled to the front of the building. Two men were stationed outside the entrance. Pursing his lips in frustration, he skirted around the edge, looking for another potential entry point.

I need to get in. To figure out what is really happening.

He found what he was looking for: an open skylight window.

Sen must really love the cold of the Hunters' district.

It was set high up on the northern wall of the building, but it would be possible to enter through it if he swung off the top of the roof.

He did just that, taking the risk that the fall would be land-able once he got through the opening. As he cleared the frame's edges, he had a split second to gauge what lay below him. His heart jumped as he realized that he would likely be landing on top of Sen's desk, which was cluttered with ink pots and quills. He attempted to roll again as he landed, and his foot brushed one of the items.

Time froze as a metal inkpot wandered towards the edge of the table. Aren recovered from his roll – *thank the Seven that this table is so big* – and desperately dove at the pot as it began to fall. His hand closed around it and he landed with a very painful, although silent, thud on the floor's flagstones. He lay there momentarily, thinking about whether this was a good idea, and if he might have cracked a few ribs.

Regaining his breath, he glanced around the room. The four massive statues he had climbed on as a toddler towered in each corner. The two at the entrance looked like Hunters. They were in the form of a hardened looking man and woman, with real swords gripped in their stony hands.

The guards would never let me play with those...

The two statues at the back of the room were towering Sabers, frozen mid-roar. The giant central desk and its accompanying chairs completed the rest of the cavernous office.

"Alright, let's find out what's going on," Aren whispered to himself.

He got up and put the inkpot back on the edge of the table. Opening all the drawers in the desk, he quickly rifled through everything. Most of the clutter was either payment bills, or debts related to the Hunters' Association.

There must be something I'm missing.

He racked his brain, imagining where Sen would hide important documents...or secrets.

What does he know that no one else knows?

"What can he *do* that no one else can? Aren mumbled to himself silently.

He pictured Sen in his mind. Aren almost laughed out loud.

Move heavy things.

He looked at the enormous Saber statues in puzzlement.

Now how in the name of the Seven am I going to move one of those?

He scanned around the room for anything that could act like a lever. The swords carried by the Hunter statues immediately caught his eye.

Silly Sen, it's almost like you wanted me to find something...Or maybe these are here in case you pulled out your back.

He wrenched one of the swords from its owner's cold hands. It came away surprisingly easily, as if it had been moved many times. The oversized weapon was ridiculously heavy.

"And there we go." He grabbed one of the empty ink pots. "This better be strong enough," he mumbled to himself.

He set up a makeshift lever system, carefully balancing the sword on the metal ink pot, and inserting the flat of the blade underneath the left-hand Saber statue. He pushed down with all his might on the hilt. Slowly, the statue tilted over onto its edge. For a brief and terrifying moment, Aren thought that the whole thing was going to crash over, but the top of the Saber leaned over slowly to softly rest against the stone wall on the other side. There was absolutely nothing beneath the statue.

Of course, always unlucky.

After painstakingly letting the Saber return to its upright position, which was much harder than he had anticipated, he moved across the room and performed the same maneuver on the other statue. He gasped as the statue tilted. A single unassuming and neatly folded sheet of paper lay below it. He gingerly reached under the stonework, wary that it might accidentally fall and crush his arm.

After making sure that the statue was back in its original place, he sat down in one of the chairs and opened the letter.

Bring Him. Make Sure He has IT. Many over the Few.

Aren scratched his head in confusion. He was sure that this message meant something extremely important – *why else would Sen go through the trouble of hiding it?* – but try as he might, he could not decipher it.

He spent a few more minutes exploring the office, even tilting over the Hunter statues with their own swords, but ultimately came up empty-handed. Deciding he had already spent too long searching, he committed the words of the letter to memory and returned it to its original place. He placed the two chairs in a stack on top of the desk.

I'm sure Sen wouldn't mind this...

Aren clambered up the mound of furniture and jumped up to grab the windowsill, toppling the chair-tower back to the ground in the process. He peered outside, and once he was sure the coast was clear, let himself down from the ledge.

XXXI

"**I** can explain," Sen repeated softly.

Somehow it was still a loud phrase to Avenir's ears. The massive man glanced at the other members in his chosen pod. Embr was still pointed at his throat. The heat from the blade was causing rivulets of sweat to stream down his neck. Luna's arrow was now trained on Sen's chest. Runan, unsure of what was happening, lowered his Shard, but kept it at the ready. Soljan groaned painfully in his sleep.

"Please, Sen."

Avenir maintained a firm grip on the Great Sword. Thankfully, the thorns had not yet broken his skin. He could feel them pressing like hungry needles against his palm. Somehow, he had managed to will them into stagnation for the time being.

"Yes, it's true," Sen spoke, a sense of deep sadness in his voice. "I have been here before."

Runan sheathed his Shard. "Tell us then, brother."

"Avenir, you can lower that...*thing*. Don't worry, I won't let him do anything," Luna called out from behind him.

Somewhat relieved, Avenir lowered the Great Sword. He could feel the little red thorns retracting, as if they were disappointed. He did not sheathe the Weapon, keeping it ready at his side.

"Thank you, 'Nir. I'm sorry I didn't tell you all sooner, I wanted to wait until we reached the Castle. I have never seen the Tall Ones..." he nodded at the mist around them, "...out this far."

"What even is this *Castle*? And what in the name of the Seven were those demons?" asked Avenir, almost retching at the memory of the spider-creatures.

"The Castle is the last place I saw your father...The last place I saw Borea. I think those creatures are simply...the surviving inhabitants of this western land."

Avenir gulped. He knew that his father would somehow have a part in this.

It seems I can never escape his presence.

"Yes, I lied," Sen admitted. "And I have been lying for many years. To you and to everyone. But you must understand, I believed that telling the truth would have made things worse."

"Then stop avoiding it. Tell us the truth. Now."

Sen sighed, as if finally giving up. "We built it ourselves, Borea and I. The *Castle* on his map. We wanted to venture out further than ever before and we needed a safehouse...Of course, knowing our Hunters' rules forbade something like that, we did it in secrecy. Eventually we reached a place not too far from where we stand now, where the Darkness begins. The Darkness, as its name suggests, is a formless black shape that lies over the ice. It writhes and struggles as if alive. We built a camp near that edge, not daring to enter its embrace." Sen laughed nervously. "It was unusually dark over the ice, and we were lucky enough to have a burning torch with us the first time we encountered the Tall-Ones...or I would not be speaking to you right now. As you saw, they are terrifying creatures, and become more numerous the closer one gets to the Darkness. But they are harmless once you take advantage of their fear."

Soljan moaned, sending a chill down Avenir's spine.

Sen kept Avenir's gaze. "We returned to the camp site many times, and eventually it became what Borea fondly called his '*Castle.*' In reality it is far from anything of the sort. There, we studied the Darkness a great deal, but never entered it. There was no reason to risk our lives. However, one day in my office, Borea told me that he had experienced a special 'dream.' 'Embr spoke to me!' he said. At first, I thought the whole situation was ridiculous...and then I saw the slight scorch marks on his face and hands – and I knew he had just come from the Inner Sanctum. He told me what the Great Sword had said in his dream: 'It's *alive*, just as the legends say. It's a *god*, sleeping at the heart of our city! It prophesized that one of the Novari bloodline will be chosen as its heir.'"

With that, Sen gazed with knowing sadness at the young Hunter before him. Avenir dropped the Great Sword onto the ice. He fell back on the sled behind him, stunned. Sen looked at the young Hunter, his eyes full of pity.

"I am sorry, 'Nir, but the Sword seems to have been awakened by a Novari, as Borea predicted."

Avenir struggled to find his voice, "...Tell me the rest."

"Very well," Sen leaned back on his own sled, still wary of Luna's bow. "After this dream, Borea lost interest in the Darkness out there" – he motioned towards the west – "and turned his focus to the Heart. We would still occasionally come to visit the *Castle*, but he quickly grew impatient, and always asked to return to the Point. During those days, he became obsessed with the Great Sword and the gift he believed it would bestow upon him. He joined the Church of Embr and visited the Inner Sanctum often, hoping for Embr to finally accept *him*, the 'Chosen Novari.' I tried advising him many times to let it go, to let fate decide his path, but he wouldn't listen. He became restless. His anxiety and obsession grew with each day that passed." Sen looked at Avenir. "I'm sure you can recall how many times he showed you around the Heart when you were a child."

Avenir did not respond and the veteran Hunter continued.

"Finally, after a few years, he had had enough. His impatience got the better of him. He asked me to join him in an excursion to the Castle, despite months of us not having done so. I was worried for him, but I thought the journey would help take his mind off the Great Sword's prophecy. That first night, when we were at the Castle, he told me that he was going to enter the Darkness. I firmly objected, of course, but again he wouldn't listen. He just started walking into it... and I didn't follow him."

Avenir noticed tears welling up in Sen's weathered eyes. He buried his face in his hands.

"...I was telling the truth, 'Nir! Leaving Borea to go alone was my greatest failure as a Hunter. I was afraid. Afraid of the Darkness. I waited there for three days. *Three* damned days. On the third – as you heard me say at the royal council – I felt that surge of Evil. I ran all the way back to the Point.”

“So why are we here then?” Luna’s sharp voice cut through the air. She had lowered her bow slightly, but still stood ready to kill at a second’s notice.

Sen wiped his eyes. “A year after Borea’s disappearance, I received a sign. It was no ordinary message. I left a loose sheet of paper on my desk and when I had returned, the words were written on it, clear as day. I thought I had seen one of the guards near my office do it, but he denied everything.”

“What words?” Luna asked.

“‘It is me, Borea.’”

“Bullshit, Sen.” It was the first time Luna had referred to the massive man by his first name.

“You can choose not to believe me if you want to. But after seeing *that*, the *Heart* of Point Fire, in Avenir’s hands,” Sen nodded towards the Great Sword lying on the ice, “Why wouldn’t you?”

“Was that the only note you received?” asked Avenir. He had gotten back to his feet.

“No. I’ve had dozens appear on my desk over the past six years, insisting that the prophecy was still yet to pass...that Borea had found a solution to what he called the ‘Final Question.’ I caught one of my guards writing one of the letters once, but he still vehemently denied it; said he couldn’t remember a thing. I didn’t want to believe it was Borea. Wanted to believe that my guys were just pulling some twisted joke on me...but I couldn’t deny the content of the messages. It could be no one else but him. The final message was: ‘Bring him. Make sure he has it. Many over the Few.’ I knew then that Embr had chosen an heir at last...after ten long years. I organized a team to move west, something especially necessary after what you heard in the banquet hall and what had happened in the Point. I would have postponed the journey until either you or Aren made the Great Sword’s decision known to me. Of course, I had no idea which one of you Embr had chosen. And then...*you* came.”

"Aren?" Avenir asked angrily, "Tell me you wouldn't have brought him here."

"I've trained him well. I've been preparing for this journey a long time, my boy."

Avenir screamed and kicked Embr away over the ice, where it stopped and sizzled softly. Sen got up from his sled and moved towards Avenir. Luna immediately raised her bow again.

Sen raised his hands. "What do you take me for? I don't want to hurt anyone here. There's no turning back, anyhow."

The veteran Hunter put his arms around Avenir.

"I'm sorry 'Nir. I wish none of this had ever happened, but you must see that I had no choice."

Avenir buried his face in the man's dunerobe, trying not to cry. He was searching for something, any little piece of rhetoric that he could use against Sen's account, but he could not find any. He knew that if Sen were indeed telling the truth, he would have done the same.

"I believe you," Avenir said, straining against the tears. "Let's go then. I want to find him. I'm *going* to find him in this Darkness."

"I knew you would understand," said Sen, hugging Avenir tightly.

"Wait just a moment!" shouted Luna. "Do you really expect *us*," she nodded at Soljan and Runan, "to follow you on this idiotic quest? Even if we did believe you, why would we risk our lives over this?"

"I believe my brother," said Runan, "and if what he's saying is true, then Point Fire needs us to figure this out." He looked at her with a mild sense of disdain. "What about you, Luna? Don't you want a chance to do something no one in Point Fire has ever conceived of? Or perhaps you would like to return to the comfort of the royal palace?"

These words struck a chord with her, and she slung her bow back over her shoulder. With a fleeting look at the sizzling Sword on the ice, she spoke.

"...No. Let's just get it over with."

*　　　　*　　　　*

As Sen had promised, he led them towards the Castle. It was an arduous journey over the ice, lit by the ever-present flares which Luna held above her head. Every now and then, they would catch a glimpse of a Tall One in the distance, which usually quickly fled from the red glow. When the subdued light of dawn first revealed itself, only then did Avenir suddenly realize that they had been traveling throughout the night.

The place appeared abruptly out of the mist, a worn-down entanglement of tents and ropes. At the center of the sprawl, a single large canvas shelter seemed to have uniquely survived the elements. They pulled their sleds off to the side, anchoring them to the ice. The Darkness that Sen had described, the mystery he had spoken so fearfully of, was nowhere to be seen. The pure ice beneath their boots stretched out as far behind the campsite as one could imagine.

"The Darkness is gone...where are you Borea?" Sen breathed.

The massive Hunter drew his Shard and motioned for the rest of his pod to do the same. Luna perched herself on top of a sled near Soljan's, training her bow on the encampment. Avenir followed Sen forwards, Embr in hand, with Runan bringing up the rear.

When they were closer, Sen assumed a half-crouch position and crept towards the central tent. The Castle seemed devoid of all life. The windless air settled around them like a blanket. Avenir could tell that Sen was focusing all his attention on that one lone tent. The single surviving structure this far out in the Frost.

A canvas flap covered up the entrance to this shelter, and as the group approached, Avenir noticed that torchlight was shining through the gap beneath it. Sen saw it too and tightened his grip on his Shard. He glanced back towards Avenir. His ice gauze was off, and for the first time in his life, Avenir could tell that the veteran Hunter was consumed by fear.

Then, a voice called out, "Sen, my old friend. Why are you afraid? Come in – I have been waiting for you."

Father.

XXXII

Aren was so tense that he had almost forgotten to eat breakfast. His mother was still fast asleep in the loft. He soon found Darch setting up the bar downstairs, and was successful in begging the man for food. After eating the measly portion of oatmeal that the tavernkeep had coughed up, he rushed outside and over towards the Fynn. He wanted to make sure that Udar and his family were locked away safely.

It was quick work sneaking across the fortress walls. The Point had once again become eerily silent, just as it had been after that wave of... *Whatever that was.* The only citizens who were brave enough to walk the streets were seasoned Hunters or members of the royal guard.

Word must have gotten out about Yob's challenge. The two days have already passed. People can sense something terrible is going to happen again...

Aren reached the section of the fortress that belonged to Udar's family and tried to get a look in through its high-set windows. He could not tell if there was something blocking them or if it was just really dark inside, but he felt relieved.

That must mean they're all in the secret base, or at least somewhere underground. Good.

*   *   *

The muffled light was rising over the horizon, and Aren was running out of time. He needed to get back to the vantage point over the Pit's royal courtyard before too many people assembled there. The last thing he wanted was for someone to spot him and come looking.

He managed to creep, undetected, into the same lookout location as before. He looked downwards from the shadow of the

parapet. Far below in the courtyard, men who looked like Yob's lackeys were setting up another wooden pedestal. In front of this, a small crowd had already begun to form, hopeful that the landlord of the Pit would be able to provide the answers to their questions.

*   *   *

Aren was woken from his nap by a raucous roar of approval from the crowd. He flinched instinctively, ducking away from the fortress's edge. When he was sure that the coast was clear, he peered carefully back over the courtyard. The crowd had increased in size tenfold – it was now far larger than the one he had seen a few days ago with Udar.

A great number of royal guards was also present. Their sets of armor, colored in blacks and oranges, lined every entrance to the courtyard.

They clearly came prepared for the worst.

Aren scanned the area until he found the reason for the increase in energy. Yob had arrived and was being escorted by a band of heavily armed men through the far edge of the crowd. The men were clearly unaffiliated with the royal family.

Hired Hunters, perhaps?

The landlord ascended the now completed wooden platform and raised his hands to the crowd. He quickly waved away the initial round of cheering. After enough silence fell, he spoke up, loud enough so that his voice rang off the walls at the back of the plaza.

"The fact that all of you came back here, instead of hiding safely with your families, tells me something." He laced his jeweled fingers over his chest. "It tells me that I am not alone in my suspicion!"

Various cries of "YES!" and "Of Course!" danced around the courtyard. Yob motioned for silence.

"This is a clear message to the royal family that the people of Point Fire deserve to know more. To know what is truly going on...and with that, there is nothing more to say. I summon Luna, daughter of our King, Luxus II, to explain herself!"

264

With that, he gestured openly towards the crowd, as if Luna were standing amongst them. Pure soundlessness smothered the courtyard – a miracle given how many citizens were present. Not a single person dared to make a noise. Even at this distance, Aren could see a triumphant grin working its way across Yob's face.

"YOU SEE?"

The harsh sound of his voice made multiple people jump in surprise. Murmurs began to stir like a hive of angry bees.

"As I could have guessed, the royal family has refused to give up the truth!" he proclaimed proudly. "However, I also refuse to give up! I urge *any* member of the royal family that is present – *even a guard, by the Seven* – to say anything on behalf of the leaders of our kingdom. Why have the storms been getting worse? Why have so many people died and suffered seemingly without reason? And why have you kept silent?"

Again, a painful silence fell over the crowd. Like the rest of them, Aren waited in apprehension. Finally, one of the men clad in royal black armor buckled under the pressure and spoke up. His voice was clear, and calming to the ear.

"I am Justar, captain of the royal guard! I bid you to hear my case!"

The sustained silence of the crowd begged him to continue.

"I am a military official, and I once took an oath to prevent me from furthering my own agenda above that of the royal family. During the first few years under this oath, I struggled with my thoughts daily, questioning the idea of serving a higher power without regard for personal ethics. I still believe this is an important question. However, I also believe that I have come to the answer. I discovered that my personal ethics are not always trustworthy! Not only this, I discovered that there is only one true moral code in Point Fire...survival! *This* is why I am at peace with my occupation, not because it is good, but because it helps us all *survive.*"

"And what of the ones who died? We demand an explanation!" a man's voice rang out.

Before the roars of agreement could get any louder, Justar spoke again, this time shouting to be heard. Most of his sentence was cut off by the white noise of the crowd.

"....to listen!"

The people quieted down slightly.

"Have you all not learned the history of this city? We are alone! Have you ever truly thought about this fact? The only thing keeping us from icy oblivion is a simple stone wall, and the *royal family's* government and protection! Rest assured, the family is working tirelessly to understand and to fix the recent events in Point Fire. This is precisely the reason why there are so many guards here! It is for your safety and your safety alone!"

Aren saw that some members of the crowd were nodding their heads. People near the entrance of the courtyard had already begun filtering out into the rest of the Pit, satisfied with the answer that the captain of the guard had given.

"Wait!" Yob's voice rang out again, a slight hint of desperation around its edges. "Justar – you say your name was?" He nodded towards the guard. "That was a good speech indeed, but I believe that I – as well as many others – would like to hear something similar from an *actual* member of the royal family. This is not meant as a sign of disrespect towards you, but rather a sign of...respect for the royalty. As you said, we can thank their government for our safety. Surely a member of this government can make time for an explanation to this crowd?"

The captain motioned in the direction of the Heart. "Yes, as I said, the royal family is working tirelessly towards answers, and perhaps solutions, to recent events. It is only—"

Justar stopped speaking, aghast. Aren traced the captain's gaze to find that Luxus II — *the king himself!* — was slowly ascending the stairs to Yob's raised platform. The king was not wearing his customary royal garb, donning instead the clothes of a commoner.

Had he been in the crowd this whole time?

Yob did not even notice the man until a few moments later, when the king was practically standing beside him. The landlord bowed deeply, ashamed.

"Your Majesty," Yob said as he resumed an upright posture. "Thank you for making an appearance. I'd only hoped you had come at an earlier time."

"Indeed, Yob," the king was addressing both the man in front of him as well as the crowd, "but I do believe Justar has made a fine case. However, as you – and many others have requested – I will tell you all the truth about what is happening, and what has happened, in our City." The king sighed deeply before speaking his next words. "We have absolutely no idea...and my daughter Luna has disappeared from the Point altogether."

XXXIII

The sound of his father's voice froze Avenir in his tracks. As if a dam wall had broken, memories of his childhood washed over him.

Those first few Hunts. Dinners at home. Visiting the Inner Sanctum.

He had not heard that voice in so long, it felt like he had almost forgotten it. But now all its detail came rushing back to him, and with a painful and sinking realization, he now knew why the disembodied voice he had heard from underneath the royal chamber had sounded so familiar.

How had I not recognized it instantly?

Sen was having a similar reaction. But before either of them could move towards the tent, the flap was brushed aside, and there he stood. Borea smiled and opened his arms in a sign of welcome.

He was exactly as Avenir remembered him. A ponytail of curly brown hair fell roughly behind his neck. He had suggested such a hairstyle to Avenir many times, who had always preferred to keep his short. His father was clean-shaven – as always – and his green eyes were piercing, even at this distance.

"Avenir. So, it chose you."

Borea whispered this, but Avenir heard it as if it had been screamed. The Great Sword pulsed in response. Borea's eyes snapped onto the Sword in Avenir's hand. Because of his Hunter's Vision, Avenir could easily detect the fear and greed in his father's eyes.

Something is wrong. Very wrong. And Father has never called me by my full name.

Sen had worked up the courage to approach his old friend and was staggering towards him. Embr burned fiercely in Avenir's grip.

"Avenir? What is happen-" Luna began behind him.

"SEN! GET AWAY FROM HIM, THAT ISN'T MY-"

Sen was about halfway towards Borea, one hand outstretched in a gesture of happiness, when it happened. Borea raised his right hand to the grey sky above and closed it into a fist. For a moment, his father's form changed, becoming a painter's rendition of himself, a watercolor image composed of only blacks and greys. In the next instant, a circular wave of formless shadow pulsed outwards from his figure. The wave passed through Sen, who disappeared behind its dark boundary. It hurtled at lightning speed towards Avenir. Closing his eyes, he braced instinctively against the impending wave, feeling the thorns on the hilt of Embr digging deeply into his palm.

The darkness passed through him, accompanied by an unthinkably high-pitched whine: the same one he had experienced with Soljan on the Hunt. He was startled to feel no physical force. Avenir was just beginning to open his eyes again when he was hit by a blistering assault of mental erosion. Fear, regret, hatred...and an unshakable sense of impending doom rocked his mind like the ragged winds of a Frost Storm. He opened his mouth, gasping for air, but his lungs refused to work. He had never imagined that such a state of despair could be possible.

This jarring of his psyche was so powerful that he found his body frozen in time. It was like experiencing utter terror, sleep paralysis, and crippling humiliation all at once. Although his eyes remained open, he had become all but blind. Blue flashes and black shadows flickered across his vision like agile demons, as if they were afraid of remaining still and being caught by his gaze.

Slowly, he became aware of a single powerful presence in this realm of despair.

No, there are... Two.

One of these presences existed near the tent right where his father had been standing. The other one was much closer... at his own right hand.

Some physical sensation had returned to this part of his body and he could once again feel the Great Sword's tiny thorns digging into his flesh. As the thorns dug ever deeper, his mind began to clear. It was

a curious sensation – having the mental pain fade away only to become more aware of the physical pressure in his hand.

Within seconds, the crimson thorns had burrowed far enough to bring him out of the psychological stupor. The colors in his eyes faded away, and he found himself back in the Frost. His father was kneeling besides Sen, who had crumpled downwards onto the ice. His hand was placed on the large man's shoulder, as if he were paying his respects. It was then that Avenir realized that his own knees were also buried in the snow.

He quickly glanced behind to where the others had been. Luna had toppled off the sled and appeared to be frozen in the fetal position. Her bow lay haphazardly off to the side. Runan sat, crouching, beside one of the sleds. Avenir was about to call out to him when he realized that he, too, was frozen in place. Soljan still lay on top of his sled, although his painful whimpers had now turned to silence.

His father stood up and turned to Avenir, apparently surprised to find that he was still conscious. A strong wind had begun to stir, and flakes of snow whirled upwards towards the skies.

"Of course you resisted it...you have the Great Sword with you," he said, almost sadly.

With a desperate effort, Avenir forced himself to his feet. His mind was still recovering from the shadow-wave. He tried to ask his father a question, but all that came out was a strained gasp.

"I know how it feels, Avenir," said Borea, the use of his full name sending chills down Avenir's spine. "It is Dark. Powerful." Borea took a few steps towards his son before speaking again, "But the longer you experience it, the more you understand that it is a necessary part of life. The other side...the side that is often forgotten, avoided."

Avenir attempted a response but managed only a croak.

I am too weak. Embr, please help me.

His father continued, "I wanted to make this as quick and painless as possible...my son. If you had been in my position, you would have come to the same conclusion. All that matters is that *one* person succeeds in their mission...and that person happens to be me."

Embr's claws were now deeply embedded inside Avenir's flesh, perhaps even his bones. He could feel the Blade itself vibrate in anticipation. The frequencies were somehow entering his bloodstream, revitalizing his body. A pleasant warmth was making its way up his right arm and across his torso. The warmth seemed to be bringing his senses back to normality. Finally, Avenir found himself able to speak, as the warmth passed over his lungs. It was a single word, packed with confusion, grief, and anger.

"What?"

Borea sighed deeply, and it appeared for a moment as if the legendary Hunter were about to cry. He clenched his fists and collected himself.

"There is no use in delaying this," Borea raised his hand like before, as if to issue another command. He then paused, hesitating, "No. You deserve at least some explanation, so you can survive in some modicum of peace after I have left."

Avenir had not moved yet, but the warmth had almost spread to every part of his body, save his head. He kept his eyes trained on his father. As the heat reached the base of his skull, he could sense a furious rage building within him. Borea spoke.

"Avenir, can you remember the Inner Sanctum clearly? I have not been there for many years, of course, but I can still see the words on those six plaques."

Avenir struggled to concentrate on the words coming from Borea's mouth. The warmth had now consumed his entire body. All aspects of the environment surrounding him had now taken on a red tinge. The outlines of objects had become clearer, more defined. He felt as if the precision of his Hunter's Vision had been multiplied a hundredfold. He could even make out the creases tracing outwards from the corners of his father's mouth as he spoke...he could see the individual particles of water vapor leaving his lungs.

Borea sensed the change in his son and surveyed the area around them. It was now bathed in a soft glow of orange light. The origin of this light was coming from Avenir. His father allowed himself a sad smile.

"So, this is the true power of Embr...I'm not sure if you can hear me right now, Avenir, but I can tell you with conviction that it is *all* true. The Weapons of The Seven exist. Those plaques are all true, and you are in possession of one of those Weapons right now. As am I." Borea made a motion towards his chest. "They are all different, and all necessary for Existence as we know it. Embr is the Great Weapon of Fire – the first instrument of hope...and anger. The one I wield is more concerned with...knowledge, and..." he paused, deciding on which word to use, "...entropy."

He waited for a response from Avenir, which did not come. His son had sunk to his knees once more. The power coursing through him was too much, his senses too acute, the world too detailed. He tried to let go of the Sword – anything to ease his current state of hypersensitivity – but it remained firmly stuck to his palm.

Borea regarded his son with pity. "As you can see and feel, these Weapons are not of this world. It is too much for you to withstand now. It took me many years of training" – Avenir gasped in pain as his father continued – "and I have had a long time to become accustomed to these powers. The ones *my* Weapon gives, I mean. I can now use them at will." He raised his hand slightly, a dark aura hazily emanating from it. "You have seen my waves. It is what I just used to incapacitate these Hunters around us. They have many purposes, including mental control and...surveillance. As you heard beneath the king's banquet hall, I can also project information over great distances. Quite useful, might I add, since sending mere information does not carry the risk of people going berserk beyond my control, like Soljan and so many others in Point Fire did. However, sending information does spread a good deal of my Weapon's Darkness."

Borea inhaled deeply, and he lowered his hand before speaking again.

"When you removed Embr from that Inner Sanctum, I was finally able to send a wave into Point Fire, and beyond. Yes, Avenir...*Beyond*. Those heat lines were acting like a defensive grid of sorts, but with their power source gone..."

Borea paused again, gauging whether Avenir was still conscious. His son was still breathing, albeit raggedly, as he swayed to and fro on his knees.

He continued, "The Waves allow me to see things far beyond your world. They are my eyes and ears into the rest of this realm. As you may have noticed," he motioned towards the rest of Avenir's pod, who were still frozen in mental agony, "they can have adverse effects, especially on those with impure or fragile minds, or those not fortunate enough to be under the protection of Embr. I am well aware that many perished in the Point after I used the first wave. But I had to test its effects. I had to know how far it can be pushed. Know the extent of the control it gives me over others...I cannot allow the well-being of people to slow my progress. It is too late for that."

Avenir groaned and stood up. Somehow, he had managed to subdue some of the warmth that was begging to consume every fiber of his being. Borea took a step back, keeping a safe distance. Avenir spoke again, only managing another singular word.

"Why?"

"Why?" Borea repeated, as if the answer were obvious. "You ask why I no longer care about the welfare of those in Point Fire, or the pain of others? The answer is simple: none of it matters in the grander scheme of things. I know you have read the plaques. These Weapons were never meant to *be* in our reality. They must be returned to their original status – as the instruments of the Seven. The Seven are, of course, those entities trapped in the Weapons I speak of. They cannot exit the weapons in their current state because they were never meant to *exist* here. Yet, I believe that if I can acquire all seven, their combined power will be great enough to open a gate to the Pinnacle of Existence. There, the Seven Masters can finally be released. They will slay the Blacksmith and return to their former Council, and thus restore the sanctity of the Knotted Rope. If this future does not occur, Existence itself will unravel and disappear as if it had never been there before. No more past, and no more future. A void so pure not even Darkness can exist there"

Borea gazed through Avenir, as if aloof.

"The path I am on is inevitable. By some cruel trick of fate, we both happened to be born in this particular time. For thousands of years, the Weapons – and the Masters enslaved within them – have been crying out. Crying out to return to their Council. Crying out for revenge. You must remember the inscription: 'The Weapons fell to the realm of mortals.' That is *our* realm, Avenir. Eons ago, Embr was discovered, and it was used to create a shining city on a lake. A place of hope and brilliance. And just *look* at this place now."

Borea gestured in a circle before speaking again.

"It is Dark. It is cold. You would not understand what these things mean because you have lived here all your life. This wasteland is the limit of your horizon. But my Weapon allows me to see what lies beyond. What exists beyond."

His father turned around to face the great expanse of ice that lay beyond the Castle. His hair flowed quietly in the blowing winds. Avenir held his father's back in his gaze. The rage within him was still building with no foreseeable end. The control of his body was slowly returning.

Just a few more minutes.

"Do you know how the Frost came to be?" Borea asked, his back still turned. "It is a mistake. An oversight. Imagine this: a farmer breeds his livestock, and cultivates lush fields for them to graze in. Everything is in perfect order under his supervision. Elsewhere, a treasury keeper feels proud that his accounts are in order. He makes sure to tally everything, day and night. Then, one day, both of them simply disappear. Of course, for days, weeks, and even months, the livestock will still be sated, and the accounts may be preserved. But as time passes, things fall out of order. Numbers go missing. Weeds and signs of erosion begin to appear in the fields..." he turned back to Avenir, "Such is the nature of the Frost. It is what happens when gods vanish. It is an indication that the Knotted Rope is unraveling. I am sure you have noticed the Frost getting colder, the storms getting worse. These things are mere *snowflakes* in comparison to the true storm which follows. The fabric of reality is coming apart. It always has been, ever since the Council of Seven was betrayed. In time, and if left unchecked...." Borea trailed off.

"Why tell me this? What does it even mean?"

Avenir found he could almost speak normally. He had managed to control the sense of warmth focused around his face. The rest of his body, however, still burned with a form of primal rage. It took all his willpower just to force it into stagnation. Part of him wanted to rip his father to pieces, but he needed to hear what the man had to say.

I want to still believe you're there, Father.

Borea paused for a moment, as if deciding on the correct response. Avenir sensed that these would be his parting words. Where the man wanted to go after speaking them, he could not bring himself to understand.

"For you, it does not mean anything. Avenir, you must understand, I have spent seven years grappling with these ideas, and the knowledge my Weapon – and its Master – have granted me. It has shown me the path to salvation. Not just for Point Fire, but for all of existence. I only tell you these things to ease your passing in this life. Only *one* mortal soul can save this reality, by bringing all Seven Masters back together, and allowing them to retake their celestial thrones. *I* am that mortal, and the only thing that has slowed my progress was Embr itself. You see, Avenir, it is only after one of the Great Weapons has chosen its bearer, that another human can reclaim and wield it. Thus, I have been patiently waiting here...waiting for the moment Embr made its decision." Borea closed his eyes, "I have seen it in my dreams, seen the final battle against the one who betrayed them, the Masters. At that time, all else will have crumbled to dust. Perhaps once the Masters have been returned to their rightful place, we will all be transported back to a time before the Cold, before the Darkness, before I left Point Fire, before you found Embr, before anything. It will be as if the Great Weapons had never existed, and we will be able to carry on with our lives, oblivious to the disaster which was averted in the future of our past. Perhaps the city will shine once again." He raised his hand menacingly. "But this is just a hope, nothing more. If that ideal future is impossible, then so be it. The alternative to it is my total failure, and the complete and utter destruction...of everything."

That cannot be true.

Borea lowered his hand. Avenir did not know whether he had spoken those words, or if Embr had spoken them through him. Borea's face turned cold, his eyes betraying a dark sense of fear and anger.

"It is, Master of Fire. I tried to reason against it for so long, but to no avail. I have been trapped here, at the edge of the Frost, for seven long years. The price of accepting and wielding my weapon is *imprisonment*. But I believe having Embr in my possession will allow me to be free once more. I just wanted..." Borea trailed off. A tear froze on his cheek. He closed his eyes as he spoke again, "No. I must begin, before you gain more control."

He closed his raised hand, and before Avenir could react, Luna and Runan dashed up behind him, each of them seizing one of his arms. Their eyes were clouded by a dark blue haze and their hands sizzled as they met the fabric of his brightly flaring dunerobe. He looked at Luna, stunned. Her face was blank and showed no signs of pain.

Borea was now standing right before him. Avenir tried to escape the grip of his fellow pod members, but they held on with an otherworldly determination and force.

EMBR!

Instinctively, he called upon the powers of the Great Sword again. He could immediately feel the warmth flowing from the hilt and making its way through the thorns and into his bloodstream. The sound of Luna and Runan's sizzling flesh became louder. Borea spoke. He was so close that Avenir could feel his breath. Only now could Avenir see the clear remnants of burn marks on his father's visage.

"I am sorry, Avenir. You would have done the same."

Borea placed his hand on his son's chest and closed his eyes. Avenir screamed as another mental barrage, far more powerful than before, invaded his thoughts. A dense and powerful wave of shadows emanated outwards from Borea's body.

This time, other feelings had been added to the senses of despair and doom. Desire, loss. It was as if a floodgate of destructive information had been opened inside his mind. His vision flickered and swayed in brilliant auras. He could feel the warmth slowly draining from his body.

The retraction of heat began near his head. It was as if the warmth itself was being sucked back into the Great Sword at his right hand. As the last of it left his torso, his senses became painfully aware of the Frost's cold once again.

The stormfront had reached them. Snow was already gathering steadily on his eyebrows and in his hair. As their final act, the thorns painfully retracted from his flesh. The sizzling came to halt. Borea gingerly slipped Embr from Avenir's weak grip. He stepped back and opened his hand again. Both Hunters let go of Avenir's arms, as he slumped to the ground, defeated. Luna and Runan soon followed suit.

Borea turned the Great Sword over in his hands, admiring its ancient craftsmanship. Snowflakes melted softly over the gleaming silver Blade. A faint lining of glowing orange persisted around the edge. He smiled: an expression perhaps borne out of relief.

"The journey to our salvation can finally begin."

"Borea..." a strained voice called out the Hunter's name.

Avenir, struggling to come back to his senses, raised his head. It was Sen that had spoken. Borea laughed, more out of astonishment than cruelty.

"Sen!" He strode over to the massive Hunter, who had managed to make it back onto one knee. "Who knew that your will would be strong enough to oppose that of a god?"

"Borea...What...What are you doing? It's me! That is...that is *your son!*"

Borea looked at Sen coldly. "You must have still been gone while I was explaining this to Avenir. I cannot waste any more time, so I will show you through my own eyes."

He placed his hand on Sen's forehead and closed his own eyes, as he had done with Avenir. Sen groaned pitifully and almost lost his balance. His father's old friend staggered, as he bore witness to whatever

horror he was being shown. After a handful of seconds, Borea opened his eyes once more, bringing Sen's groaning to a halt. To Avenir's astonishment, Sen stood upright, seemingly oblivious to the pain he had just experienced.

The wind of the storm was now reaching dangerous speeds, and Avenir could barely make out the shapes of the two men through the snowfall, let alone hear what they were saying. Sen's voice came in snippets through the storm's winds, loud as ever.

"I am sorry... I will...Luck."

Borea appeared to be nodding. It was a solemn motion – that of a friend saying goodbye for the last time.

"...over the Few..."

Then, it seemed as if Borea himself had become a roaring fire. For a moment, he appeared to be struggling with the Great Sword, almost faltering as he forced it to bend to his will. The fire dimmed slightly, and Avenir's father rose once again. Sen raised his hand, both to shield himself from the heat, and to wave goodbye. In response, Borea sprinted away in the direction of Point Fire at an otherworldly pace, his footsteps melting the ice beneath him. Embr glowed brightly in his grasp.

Sen approached through the blizzard. Avenir sat back onto the hard ice, struggling both to understand what had happened and to regain control of his body.

"I guess that's the end of our tale, Avenir," began Sen.

He is saying my full name, just like my Father. Please Sen, tell me you're still there.

"How can you say that?" Avenir breathed. "What just happened?"

"I think we were just lucky – or unlucky – to have been chosen as variables impacting the fate of our reality. Now our part is done. Borea has shown me the truth. Nothing *we* do matters anymore." His expression was deadly serious.

"And what of the Point? Of everything we've worked to protect? Everything *you've* worked to protect?"

"All of that is mere dust on the fabric of reality. If that fabric is unraveled, as it *will* be if Borea fails to bring the Council back, everything will disappear. It is as Borea told you. We must believe in his quest against the Blacksmith...allow him to return the Seven to their divine council. If his mission fails–"

Avenir interrupted him, standing up, his legs aching severely, "How can you say that? What makes you believe him?"

"You cannot understand, Avenir. I have seen it with my own eyes. The destruction and horrifying death of everything – everyone – in Point Fire...and *beyond*. Imagine you could witness the future. If you knew that just around the corner, fate might end all existence as you knew it, would you still have the will to resist?"

Avenir stared at Sen incredulously.

Is this the same Sen, the one who took Aren under his wing?

"You would leave everyone to die now, just because they have been chosen to perish at a later time? That is not what living means! We *know* that death is inevitable, yet we still value life! We can't give up now! We have to go back, find out what's truly going on. Stop my father – or *whoever* that man was – if we have to. Many over the Few!"

Sen laughed dryly. "Yes, Avenir, Many over the Few. That is the code which Borea has followed throughout his life, even now. You still do not understand. It is not death that has been ordained for everyone if he fails to return the Weapons. It is erasure. Complete elimination. Something beyond Darkness. *That* is why there is nothing we can do. *That* is why any life has no meaning...unless he succeeds."

Avenir could feel tears forming in his eyes. He had come so close to reaching an answer to all his questions, only to discover that there was never a comprehensible question to begin with.

If everything is bound to disappear anyway, could Sen, and my father, be right?

*

But, for some reason, Avenir could not bring himself to believe what he had heard. The lingering residue of Embr's warmth remained

279

inside him. It was a reassuring warmth, one that did not even so much as hint at the eventual destruction of reality. In fact, just as his father had explained, there was another emotion besides anger, one that had come with Embr's coursing warmth...Hope.

The Masters are all just smaller parts of a single whole. They are incomplete without each other. This could mean that my father's weapon may have given him incomplete information. The unseen and unnamed Weapon of the Seventh Master. Entropy, Chaos, Darkness.

He also knew that the man who had spoken to him had not been his father, or at least was not the same man he had once been. The man who spoke was a being enslaved by finality and fate.

I still remember you as you once were, Father. Excited by the unknown. Adventurous. Kind. Free. I refuse to forget that.

A faint flame glimmered in the deepest recesses of Avenir's heart. As his father had said, perhaps the Avenir of *old* would have done the same...given in to the law of fate. But what his father did not understand was that Avenir had spent seven long years without him. Protecting his mother...and caring for Aren. He could not let them down now.

"Sen, I cannot give up," he said abruptly. "I hope you understand. I'm going back to the Point. It needs us."

He turned back to the sleds. Luna and Runan still lay unconscious on the ice. Their bodies were already being covered by the snowfall. He brushed the flakes off their robes and began pulling them onto the sleds.

"I will not let you go, Avenir," came Sen's voice. "We must not interfere with Borea's quest. As I have said, all that matters now is that he succeeds, nothing else. I will not let you stand in his way. That was my promise."

Avenir turned to face his mentor.

"What are you going to do Sen, *kill* me? After all you've done for me? For Aren?"

Avenir could not believe what he was hearing. For a moment, Sen looked saddened. He then shook his head, as if remembering something. The veteran Hunter's eyes had become clouded. A dark blue mist seemed to be emanating from within his pupils.

"Perhaps, Avenir. What do you say to one last Hunter's Game? One between you and me. Just like the ones you enjoy with your brother. We will let fate decide what is meant to be. I'll give you a head start. After that, I won't hesitate...to kill you."

"Sen?"

Tears in his own eyes, Avenir searched the Hunter's for any signs of hesitation. He was met with the cold stare of a man charmed by fate.

Avenir turned and ran.

XXXIV

The crowd gasped in shock at the king's words. He had confirmed the worst of their fears – that even the royal family was helpless. So helpless, in fact, that they could not keep track of their own members. Aren watched in frightened apprehension as the crowd's jeers grew louder.

Yob was clearly disturbed by the news, but he managed to retain his composure and raised two hands to the crowd. Minutes passed before a relative degree of silence was achieved once more.

"Your Majesty," Yob said, struggling to be heard over the noise of the crowd, "that appears to be dreadful news! Are there any words of assurance you can give the people of Point Fire?"

The king nodded gravely. "Yes, of course. But it is also important that we–"

Aren was the first to see it coming. Again. A faint dark shadow was engulfing the battlements from behind where the two men stood on the raised platform. And then it had already passed over them, and they crumpled onto the wood immediately. People in the crowd fell to the ground in unison as the shadow eclipsed them. A wave of bodies falling. It was a horrifying sight to witness. And Aren knew it would soon be upon him. He closed his eyes and prayed to the Seven.

*   *   *

Kreymar opened his eyes.

"It has passed."

He was sitting cross-legged at the center of a charcoal circle in the Cathedral's worship hall. The rest of the pews in the cavernous chamber had been stripped away, the wood taken elsewhere. All

282

around him, hundreds of priests sat within similar circles. They had all opened their eyes when Kreymar spoke. As the wave had passed over the congregation, a few of them had remained frozen in place, their faces contorted in mental anguish.

"Ready yourselves. Now!" came Kreymar's harsh command. All priests stood to attention. Kreymar gave his next orders, "Kill those who are frozen as quickly as possible. They were not able to resist the effects of the Darkness. They will soon reawaken, consumed by evil forces, as has happened before. The rest of you, take your positions at the battlements."

The young leader of the Church of Embr got to his feet and straightened his crimson robes. His fingers glanced over the light chain mail he had donned beneath the fabric. He strode confidently down the long corridor leading to the entrance of the Cathedral. Swarms of other priests were now milling about him, carrying weapons and slats of wood. He did not blink an eye as a group of them carried the dead body of one who had been frozen past him.

"Such is the price of harboring an impure mind..." he muttered to himself.

He absent-mindedly scratched at the stump that remained of his left arm. A hand fell on Kreymar's other shoulder, slowing him down. Kreymar swiveled around and was greeted by the yellow-toothed priest who had brought Avenir to the Cathedral.

"What is it, Quarrth?" he asked curtly.

"Master Kreymar, I just wanted to know if Embr has again blessed us with its wisdom."

The man eyed the newly formed and blackened scars on Kreymar's face with interest. They continued down the tunnel.

"No, my brother. It is as before. The Great Sword has informed us of the battle to come, and we are to defend this place from any who may attempt to enter. It does not matter if it be your mother, brother, or an old friend. They could all be tainted by darkness."

The two crimson-robed men reached the end of the tunnel and exited the spire to the outdoors. Before them lay a terrifying sight. Row upon row of wooden barricades and reinforced battlements stood in

concentric circles around the Cathedral. Heavily armed priests manned every inch of the newly constructed timber fortress. Orders were being passed around as the priests made last-minute adjustments to the walls, as well as their weapons.

Many of these crimson-robed figures had only recently been inducted into the Church. Usually, the process of induction would be long and arduous: the indication of a lifelong commitment. Kreymar had been forced to make significant exceptions to this requirement as of late. All that mattered was that that he could raise a formidable army and raise it quickly...exactly to Embr's specifications.

He gazed beyond this fortress, past the expanse of barren desolation that people called the Grey. In the distance lay Point Fire, the age-old bastion of warmth. It stood there silently, foreboding even. Kreymar understood that this silence would soon come to an end.

Starting just over a week prior, Kreymar had found himself the recipient of multiple messages from the Great Sword itself. He had been alone in the Inner Sanctum when the fire that Embr had left behind flared up with new knowledge. He knew that Avenir carried the Great Sword with him, likely far out in the Frost, but it seemed that Embr was able to send messages back to its place of origin, its home.

The initial utterances were repeats of themselves, as if the Weapon were searching for someone who would listen. Kreymar had made himself known by meditating next to the fire, and Embr began to convey further messages. They had been almost fearful in nature, something that had never occurred to Kreymar as being possible. The previous signals from Embr – *Darkness. West. Damnation. Seven Years* – had been straight to the point and emotionless. The ones that Kreymar had been blessed to receive were now urgent, even frantic:

Defend. Cathedral. Army. Pure of Mind. Charred Circle.

He raised his hand to his face. It was now severely disfigured on its left side: collateral damage from Embr's messages. His overall physique had now become grotesque, even harrowing. Anyone who viewed Kreymar from his right side would simply see the man as the vainly perfect leader he had once been. The left side of his body told a different, more frightening, story.

The time has come for us to prove our worth to our god.

"The weapons from the Icesmiths were indeed a godsend. We would not have been able to sufficiently arm ourselves otherwise," said Quarrth, gazing upon Kreymar's horrific burns with admiration. "Your recruitment of new brothers was also...marvelously efficient."

"Of course, Brother. Ties run deep between our Church and the Icesmith elders. We are, after all, the only ones to live out here in the Grey."

"Indeed."

"I need you at the frontlines, Quarrth. Your role is to guide the new brothers in combat. They will look up to you." Kreymar placed a hand on the priest's shoulder, urging him to tend to his duties.

"Thank you, Master Kreymar. It is an honor."

"Now go. I expect it won't be long before they come."

*   *   *

Aren found himself back in his home. He was sitting at the dinner table with Avenir. His mother and father sat across from him. Warm hare stew lay steaming on the table. Egg yolk was melting slowly over the top of the meat. The sight of this rare delicacy caused his mouth to water. His mother said a brief thanks to the Seven, and they began eating. They ate in silence, enjoying the time together. His father was the first to speak, and he outlined the details of the previous day's Hunt. He had caught two Frost Flyers, and Aren gasped in awe, memorizing every detail of his description.

Then, during the middle of his father's explanation, the man suddenly crumbled to dust. The fine powder swirled around the kitchen, caking the table and the food on top of it in a darkly colored layer. Aren's mother continued eating as if nothing had happened, spooning the dusty stew into her mouth. Avenir, however, let out a yelp of fear and reached out to where their father had been. His hand passed through the air, groping at nothing. As his brother reached out, he too vanished into dust. Now it was only Aren who was grasping at the particles glinting in the light. His mother finally stopped eating.

"You see, Aren. This is what the Point does to our family," she said, stew falling out of her mouth.

"I...I don't understand," Aren stammered.

"This city is a prison. A ghastly prison..." she started sobbing.

"Please don't cry, Mom... Mom?"

Sylis stopped sobbing as the house around Aren fell away into blackness. All that remained was the kitchen table, and his mother bent forward over it with her face in her hands.

"It's at the Church, Aren," she said, her voice muffled.

"What?"

"The Cathedral, the one across the Grey. You must know it."

His mother raised her head. Her face was emotionless, cold. Something about it made Aren want to look away, but he found his gaze was locked in hers. Her eyes twisted cruelly.

This isn't my mother, it's something else.

"You must take the Cathedral," she continued, louder. There was a malicious bite to her tone. "No one can stand in your way. It is the only way to free us."

She grinned widely. The rest of her facial features distorted outwards in a horrifying elongation.

Aren felt a crushing weight descend on him. He spun off his chair and downwards into the blackness, falling faster and faster. The acceleration of the descent was nauseating. As he fell, another, heavier weight descended onto his mind. It squeezed his thoughts as they struggled to rise from under the surface of a black lake. Anger, desolation, and fear exploded in every fiber of his being. It felt as if there was another power attempting to take hold of his body.

Aren struggled against these feelings, fighting desperately for the control of his mind. Then, when he had finally reached the center of this storm of darkness, and as he cried out with all his might against it, it all vanished, as if it had never begun.

*　　　　*　　　　*

Aren shot upright, sweating profusely. He groped around where he sat, trying to regain a handhold on reality. Eventually, the residual fear from the dream subsided, and he realized he was still sitting on the ledge overlooking the courtyard.

I survived it...whatever that was.

Still dazed, he peered over the ledge, expecting the worst. The crowd below was frozen in place. Some members were curled into balls, others were standing upright, just like the mimes sometimes did around the Circle. It was a few seconds longer before the king, and Yob, were the first of the people below to break out of their trance-like state. King Luxus II sputtered loudly and coughed. He slowly stood up, attempting to take in his surroundings. He placed a quivering hand on his chest, making sure that he was indeed still alive. Yob had also managed to get up into a kneeling position.

"What has happened? Yob?" the king said, his tone quivering.

Aren could scarcely hear him, but the absolute silence of the rest of the city carried his voice over the still air.

"Yob?" the king croaked again.

"The Cathedral," Yob gurgled in response. "We have to take it. They are hiding something there."

Other members of the crowd had now managed to wake up from their stasis, and the occasional groan filled the quiet air between the fortress's walls.

"You had the same dream?" the king questioned, stunned. "I wonder what it means? We should send a royal party out to the Cathedral at once. Perhaps they can give us some answers."

"No." spat Yob. "He said we must *take* it. No more questions. The time for action is *now*. We can no longer wait while they connive out there across the Grey."

"Yob, listen to yourself. Have you gone mad?" A look of genuine confusion was splayed across the king's features.

"Are you trying to stop this? You cannot. I will not allow you. I will have *his* army ready soon. They," he motioned to the crowd, "and

many others will join the cause. Perhaps your precious Luna is hiding there as well, in the dark corners of that forsaken spire."

"Yob, please, now is not the time to-"

The king doubled backwards. A dagger was buried deep in his chest. Yob looked at his own hands in astonishment. The king fell off the wooden palisade onto the hard cobblestones, clutching desperately at his robes and choking on blood. Yob turned, ignoring him, and faced the crowd. Many of them had seen what had happened, and a slow clap began, as more and more people joined in their applause.

"You see!" shouted Yob, after the applause had stopped. He addressed the king's lifeless body, "They too know what must be done!"

Aren fell away from the ledge, reeling from what he had just witnessed. As he had watched the king dying in the courtyard, he realized that Point Fire as he knew it had come to an end.

Mom.

He vaulted over the low concrete ledge next to him, running in the direction of the Hunters' district. Cries and shouts were beginning to echo upwards all around him.

I must hurry.

Sweat was streaming down his skin underneath the dunerobe, despite the current frigid temperature. As he ducked beneath stone slats and flying buttresses, he noticed the first few snowflakes beginning to fall. It would not be long before Point Fire was engulfed by another Frost Storm. The stonework flew by in a blur as Aren sprinted across the rooftops.

By the time he reached an area overlooking the tavern, he was breathing raggedly, the harsh cold burning at the deepest parts of his lungs. Thankfully, there were not many people in the area.

Or perhaps they're still frozen like the others.

The people that *were* there - who looked like Hunters for the most part - were shambling towards where Aren had come from. They seemed dazed, as if daydreaming. Some were shaking their heads in an attempt to clear their minds.

When the coast was clear, Aren descended the fortifications quickly and ducked through the tavern's back door. It was empty inside.

Darch was nowhere to be found. Fearing the worst, Aren rushed upstairs to the loft.

He found his mother sitting on the side of the simple bed, her head in her hands. She looked up as he entered, a dazed expression on her face.

"A...Aren?"

"Mom!" Aren ran over and embraced her. "Mom...the king...he, he's *dead!* Yob...He killed him!"

"Hmm?" Sylis grunted, as if still half asleep. "Oh."

Aren took a step back to get a better look at his mother's face. It was devoid of emotion. Her eyes had adopted a horrifying, clouded shade of blue.

Sylis spoke again, "It's okay. We just have to get to the Cathedral. That will fix everything."

"No, mom!" Aren's heart was racing. "I think that's all a lie! It's something bad...it's telling people what to do!"

Sylis got up from the bed and walked past Aren towards the door. In desperation, Aren grabbed her sleeve. With lightning speed, Sylis turned around and slapped Aren as hard as she could. The pain and shock sent Aren flying backwards. He landed with a clatter in the corner of the loft. Sylis turned and continued through the door. Aren was trying his best to suppress the urge to cry.

That can wait. I need to do something, now!

He had landed in a pile of tools and ropes. Without a second thought, he grabbed one of the lengths of rope and sprinted out through the loft door. Outside, his mother was busy making her way down the stairs. She either did not notice or paid no attention to him. He tailed her quietly. When she reached the bottom, Aren pounced.

Sylis yelped as the young boy charged into her back. After she fell, Aren used his legs to hold her torso on the ground – one of Sen's many techniques – while he struggled to bind her ankles together. Sylis began screaming, flailing wildly.

"I'm sorry, I'm sorry, I'm sorry!" Aren jabbered as he went about securing the knots around his mother's legs. He finally tied the last loop and rolled off of her.

"How DARE you!" his mother shouted.

She tried to get up and tripped awkwardly into the nearby bar counter, sending a couple of glasses flying. They shattered loudly against the tavern floor. Aren was already racing upstairs again, getting another length of rope.

When he returned downstairs, he found his mother hopping towards the tavern door, seemingly oblivious to the scuffle that had just taken place. Aren tackled her again, causing both of them to land sideways on the ground. It was a gut-wrenching ordeal, but eventually he managed to grab and tie her hands behind her back. At this point, she was shouting a barrage of profanities. Aren could feel the tears rolling down his cheeks. He ripped a piece of his dunerobe off and gagged her. She squirmed around on the floor like an injured worm.

"I'm sorry, Mom. I'm so sorry," Aren apologized.

He felt terrible, but he did not know what else to do. Half-closing his eyes, he dragged her to one of the storage cupboards behind the bar, wincing at her muffled screams. After rolling her inside and making sure that there were no objects there with which she could untie or hurt herself, he closed the door behind him and locked it. He slipped the key into his dunerobe pocket, and sank to the floor, sobbing loudly.

The door to the tavern crashed open, almost ripping off its hinges. Instinctively, Aren ducked behind the bar counter. He looked around the edge, trying to stifle his sniffing. The hulking frame of Piet stood in the doorway.

If he's also gone mad, I'm done for.

Piet shouted into the empty tavern.

"AREN? SYLIS? WHERE'RE YOU?"

Avenir staggered through the stretches of deep snow that had already begun to form over the ice. The storm was now in full swing, and the flakes whipped at the corners of his eyes through the ice gauze. He did not know how far Sen was behind him, or if the Hunter was even following him.

They've all gone crazy. All of them.

His body felt like lead. His mind felt worse. It was as if he was wandering through some sort of lucid dream. He did not even know if he was truly controlling his movements. It took almost all his mental strength to find the will just to carry on.

His boot caught in a particularly deep trench of fresh snowfall and he collapsed forwards. The blizzard had become so dense that it was already difficult to tell the ground from the air above it. With a soundless puff, he found himself face first in the snow. He was now acutely aware of the true cold of the Frost.

I must have gotten used to having Embr's warmth.

"Av ..eni..r"

The sound of Sen calling his name floated towards him on the ragged winds.

He knows I can't beat him. Why else would he be calling to me?

Avenir knew that he would never be able to defeat Sen in hand-to-hand combat. The man was a monster. Plus, Avenir did not even think he would be mentally capable of hurting the man who helped raise him, and Aren, for so many years.

But the old Sen is gone. Like Father.

Avenir groaned deeply and pulled himself up.

Right now, it's me or him.

He removed his Shard from his belt. He wished he had his father's old bow. It was still lying near the sleds where Runan, Soljan and Luna were all unconscious. At least then he would be able to try to take down, or at least incapacitate Sen from a far safer distance. Shards were meant for last-minute, desperate, close quarters combat.

The worst scenario possible for me right now.

Avenir tried to move as fast as possible away from where Sen's voice had come from.

I have to buy more time...think of something! Or maybe I'll get lucky and find some form of rock or ice formation I can hide in.

The temperature dropped suddenly, and the wind became more erratic. The eye of the storm was nearing. Although the storm was not as severe as the one he and Aren had faced all those months ago, the freezing pain only the Frost could deliver was working its way through his skin.

Avenir stopped moving. He suddenly knew what to do.

*   *   *

Sen cut a path through the Frost Storm. Every few steps he would stop, crouch, and take a moment to scan his surroundings. The eye of the storm was almost upon him, and the snow was coming down in diagonal sheets. If he had not had his soft-sole boots on, he would already have sunken down to his knees.

"Avenir!" he called out loudly. "I know this is a Hunt game, but don't go dying on me before fate decides it!"

He stood up again and resumed his pace. He knew that Avenir could not have gotten far. Moving through this flurry would take a great toll on anyone, no matter their strength. And Sen very much believed in his own strength.

A few steps later, something caught his eye. Half-buried in the layers of snow that were perpetually forming underfoot was a piece of Avenir's dunerobe. Sen immediately dropped to a low crouch.

Although he was confident enough to call out to Avenir from a safe distance, he knew that the young man was still a capable Hunter. Any small lapse in concentration – especially at close range – could cost him his life. The thought of dying, however, no longer struck fear into Sen's heart.

He *was* surprised, though, to find that he was not the least bit hesitant, worried, or even sad that he would end up killing Avenir. The dream that Borea had shown him had eliminated most of his cares in the world. He had experienced Borea's vision as a lifetime. He had seen what would happen to Point Fire in the coming years, and what Borea believed would happen if he did not succeed in his quest. The latter drove daggers of terror into Sen's soul, far deeper than the fear of death ever could.

Point Fire's end was inevitable. Regardless of whether Borea failed or not, it was unreasonable to assume that he could accrue the remaining five weapons fast enough in order to prevent the temporary destruction of Point Fire. The city would eventually succumb to the elements. Every last man, woman, and child would eventually be wiped out by the ever-worsening storms, with no heat source to save them. The only hope was that Borea's success had the potential to revert the catastrophe once it had passed.

The Hunters' mantra – *Many over the Few* – was now meaningless in the face of this eventual death. Sen felt strangely at ease risking his life now. The shadow of an inescapable fate had changed him forever.

He straightened from his crouching position and moved forward carefully, holding his Shard up in a defensive stance. He was well aware that the scrap of dunerobe could have been a last-ditch effort from Avenir to try to confuse him. He was not about to let that happen.

It was extremely difficult to see through the snowfall at this point, and Sen knew that if he moved slowly it would be almost impossible to detect him. His veteran's dunerobe merged perfectly with the whites and greys around him.

The cold had finally reached its tipping point. Even Sen, who was renowned for his ability to steel himself against most of the Frost's temperature ranges, felt the beginnings of pain creeping into his extremities. Rather than cause him fear, this pain kindled a deep sense of excitement within him. To brave death out in the Frost. To Hunt. These things would always make him content, and right now he was experiencing both of them in their most potent form.

He found himself fantasizing about the death-defying Hunts he would organize when he got back to Point Fire. It was liberating to no longer care about wellbeing, neither his own nor that of others. He would commission expeditions further than ever before, testing the absolute limits of his Hunters. Seeing who truly deserved to be a survivor of the Frost.

What does it matter if they die? We're all dead anyway.

Sen froze. A particular feeling shot through his nerves. A feeling he had not experienced since his early days as a Hunter. It was the feeling of impending death, one which slows time to a crawl and makes a heart turn to stone. The feeling originated at his right ankle. Wrapped around it was a gloved hand, protruding from the newly fallen snow.

What happened next occurred in the blink of an eye. Avenir pulled his body with all his might out of the snow, using Sen's boot as a handhold. With his other hand, and with the slightest hesitation, he stabbed upwards with his Shard. The tip of the weapon caught Sen just below his ribs. Avenir summoned his remaining strength, driving the Shard as far as possible. Sen shoved him hard, backpedaling away. Avenir fell into the snow, trying to keep his concentration on his adversary. The Shard did not stay lodged in Sen's body for long. It quietly slipped out from under his dunerobe and disappeared silently into the snow. A cascade of crimson followed close behind.

Sen ripped his ice gauze off and placed a hand under his dunerobe, trying to staunch the flow of blood. He stared at Avenir, who was now feverishly trying to get back to his feet. The upper layer of powder made it extremely difficult to regain balance.

"You..." Sen sputtered.

The part of his dunerobe where his hand was had now turned a dark shade of maroon. It was a fatal wound.

Avenir finally made it back onto his feet. Wet snow was dripping down his back inside his dunerobe. He knew he should be freezing, but his current adrenaline levels were too high to allow that.

Sen fell to his knees and dropped his own Shard. It sank beneath the powder.

"Ah yes," he mused, far away. "That was something I taught our Aren. How silly of me to forget."

Without another word, he crumbled face first into the snow.

The adrenaline was beginning to wear off and Avenir knew he had to make it back to the Castle before it was too late. The new snowfall had already begun to cover the veteran Hunter, the bloodstains where Avenir's Shard had fallen disappearing in an instant. He moved over to where Sen lay. Closing his tear-filled eyes, he placed a hand on the massive man's back. Feeling the man's broad shoulders under his fingers caused a well of sadness to be opened within him. For a few moments, he sobbed intensely.

I promise Sen. I will fix this. Maybe one day, as my father said, it will be as if none of this had ever happened.

He retrieved Sen's Shard from where it had fallen and tucked it into his belt. Sen's family crest – a closed fist – caught Avenir's eye as he sheathed it. A deep sense of regret swelled in his chest. He did not even attempt to look for his own Shard.

I never want to see it again.

He started pushing towards the direction that Sen had come from. Behind him, his mentor's massive body vanished noiselessly beneath the icy tears of the Frost, almost as if the man himself had always been as silent as the snow falling around him.

Thank you, Sen, for teaching me how to be a true Hunter.

XXXVI

Avenir gasped in relief as the rough outlines of the Castle came into view. Even though he was barely fifteen feet away, it had almost escaped his vision. He was at the brink of unconsciousness. The last few minutes of movement had felt like walking through honey. Worse still, a strange warm sensation was flowing through his body: a sure sign of impending hypothermia and...death.

The sleds that his pod members had pulled all this way were almost completely submerged beneath the flurries. He noticed that Soljan was no longer tied on top of one. Runan and Luna were nowhere to be seen.

Doesn't...matter...get...inside.

He willed his legs back into motion. Struggling to breathe, he made his way towards the one large tent from where his father had first made his appearance. His body finally gave out. He collapsed into the snow, arms outstretched, moaning for someone to come save him. Everything had gone quiet.

...Just as Mother said it would...

As he fell into darkness, he saw a white figure emerging from the tent, weapon drawn.

*　　　　　*　　　　　*

Avenir was soothed out of a nightmare by a wonderful sense of warmth, far different to the deadly one he had felt before passing out. He slowly woke up and discovered that he was face to face with Luna. Her green eyes, neutral at first, turned to their usual scowl of contempt when she sensed that he was awake. It was a few seconds before he realized what was happening. They were both naked, bundled up inside a single dunerobe. She had been using her body heat to keep him alive. A small fire crackled close by.

Avenir sputtered gibberish and attempted to wriggle out of the robe. He only succeeded in elbowing Luna painfully beneath her breasts and scraping his back against some hard object.

"Stop that, you buffoon!" Luna yelled.

Avenir stopped moving and watched Luna carefully slither out of the dunerobe. He turned away as she put on spare clothing. They were inside the large tent at the center of the Castle. It was completely bare save for a simple wooden desk that Luna had pushed off to the side. A couple piles of supplies were packed into the corner. Next to these supplies lay two bodies – the other Hunters.

Still in the dunerobe, Avenir struggled upright.

His first words came out awkwardly, "Luna...Thanks. I don't know if I'd have made it without your help," he turned away again. "Soljan, Runan? Are they alive?"

Luna finished dressing and huffed loudly.

"Yes, unfortunately...I mean, Soljan has been out cold this whole time since those things attacked us. But Runan–"

"What? What happened? What do you mean unfortunately?" It hurt Avenir's throat to speak.

Avenir struggled over to where the bodies lay. Soljan still appeared to be unconscious, trapped in whatever fever dream he was experiencing. Runan was also unconscious, but his legs and arms were bound together, and there was a cloth gag in his mouth. A tender purple lump was growing on his left temple.

"Luna," Avenir started, still naked beneath the new dunerobe, "what happened here?"

She walked over and gave Runan a painful-looking boot to the ribs.

Before Avenir could react, she said, "He went absolutely raving mad. Tried to kill me. I think we were both trapped in some dream. Mine was terrible: something about returning to the Point, attacking the Cathedral." She knelt next to the unconscious Hunter, looking at him with disdain. "Anyway, when we came to, he went on and on about that

297

damned spire. It was like he forgot what just happened with your…father. He was about to run off into the Frost alone, so I tried to stop him from leaving. That's when he attacked me. Went all-out, mind you. I managed to smash his head with a canister from one of the sleds. He's also out cold." She stood up again, shrugging, "I couldn't just leave him out there to die in the storm. And then you came along, half-dead. And where's Sen? Where's your father?"

Avenir noticed that Luna had medical wrappings and bandages around her hands.

From the burning earlier. It seems she can't remember anything. Although I guess there's no use in keeping anything from her anymore.

"Sen's…Sen's dead…I killed him. And that wasn't my father. He's become something else." He could feel the tears coming back.

"You *killed* Sen?" Luna laughed curtly. "Avenir, this is no time to joke."

Avenir did not respond, and when she saw the look on his face, she turned away, both frightened and aghast.

"H…How did it happen?" she asked softly.

Avenir shook his head. "It sounds like it was the same deal with Runan. That thing pretending to be my father did something to Sen and he just became…cold. He tried to Hunt me down in the Frost, like I was just another Flyer. There was nothing else I could do."

After changing back into his old clothes, which were still uncomfortably damp, Avenir explained to Luna what had happened, down to every last detail. He told her everything, from his encounters within the Cathedral and the Inner Sanctum, to what Borea had told him. Luna sat silently as she listened. The small fire she had made heated her face as the coals burned brightly. It was not too long ago that she would have thought these stories to be insane, but like Avenir, recent events had forced her to reconsider what she thought was possible. Avenir finished talking, and they sat quietly for a bit. Luna fiddled with the wraps around her hands.

"What now?" she asked.

"We have to go back. If people like Sen and Runan were affected in this way by my fath..." he trailed off, "...by Borea's wave, I can only imagine what is happening back in the Point right now. Every second we waste–"

"Then let us get ready," she cut him off.

Luna stood up and began checking her equipment and tools – items she must have brought in from her sled.

"How?" Avenir asked. He felt completely exhausted. "There's the storm outside. And the matter of the two," he nodded towards the bodies, "over there."

Luna laughed. "The storm passed a long time ago. You were out for a few hours. We can pile these two on the sleds, like Soljan was before. Hopefully if Runan wakes up, he won't try to slit our throats."

Avenir blushed again at the thought of what Luna had done for him during those hours. Luckily for him, the hood of his dunerobe was now obscuring most of his face. He nodded in agreement with her proposal.

After digging their sleds out from underneath the newly fallen snow, they were ready to leave. With considerable effort, Runan had been strapped onto Avenir's sled, and Soljan to Luna's. Outside the tent, the landscape around the Castle had been completely transformed. A thick layer of whiteness had descended on everything, covering almost all the other run-down tents. Even getting out of their own shelter had been a struggle, requiring a significant amount of shoveling before it was possible to exit.

"You ready?" called Luna, her voice muffled behind a piece of fabric she had pulled over her mouth. The temperature was still frigid.

"I don't know," Avenir said as he turned to Luna, who waited impatiently behind her sled. "I wonder what would happen if we didn't go back at all. I mean, even if we did make it, do you think we'd be able to change anything? What if we are really too insignificant to make a difference...to change fate?"

Luna coughed in exasperation. Avenir watched her breath seep out from the fabric in a soft cloud of crystals.

"I can tell you right now that we are *fated* to die if we stay here any longer," she snapped.

Avenir laughed dryly. "I suppose that's one way to look at it."

XXXVII

Thankfully, Piet had also remained unaffected by the communal nightmare. Aren could not feel relieved enough when he had heard the large man continue to call into the tavern,

"Aren? Somthin *scary's* happenin...You here?"

At that moment, Aren had known that it was still good old Piet. After waving the man inside, Aren explained what had happened to his mother and where she was, fighting the urge to begin crying again. In response, Piet moved over to the closet behind the bar. Aren pulled him back immediately, shaking his head.

"She should stay there, Piet. At least until we know what's going on, and how long it's going to last for."

"Ye sure? Maybe I could talk sum sense inta her."

"No, I think it's too late for that."

Aren steered him away from the closet, nervous that he would attempt to talk to his mother.

"What happened to you?" Aren asked. "You said something scary is going on, so something bad must have happened on your side as well."

"Terribl'!"

"What? Tell me."

"It's Viktor and Julnd. They gon' mad! Aft'r we all got sick they were ravin about stormin the Cathedral...I tried stoppin them, and they attacked me!"

It took Aren a moment to figure out what Piet had meant by "got sick."

"The same 'sick' thing happened to me too," he said. "It almost got me. Where are they now? Where did they go?"

"I was lucky te make up sumthin about joinin them, and they stopped tryna kill me. They ran off sumwhere, maybe to the Pit."

"I have to go see what's going on."

Piet frowned and shook his head. "You outta stay here. Pretect yer mum. Besides, s'dangerous out ther'. No use goin out I think."

Aren eyed the locked door behind the bar counter. "I think she'll be safe here. We *have* to get outside and look around. Something even worse could be happening. Piet, I think you should go and find every Hunter that still seems normal and bring them back here."

"Sen'll take care of things like that."

"Sen isn't here anymore, remember?"

Piet raised his eyebrows as if Aren had told him a compelling secret. He then shook his head again.

"Sorry, Aren. I fergot. Must've been the crazy stuff that happen'd with the guys outside that got me 'ead screwed loose." The bulk of a man stood up, his hair scraping the ceiling. "But I think 's a good idea. Get everyon' that's right in the 'ead back here. See if we can make a plan te help th'others. Aren... be careful. Come right back 'ere and let me know if anythin's lookin bad."

Piet left, squeezing through the doorframe awkwardly. After working up the courage to leave his mother by herself, Aren followed him outside. As he left the tavern, he turned north.

I need to get to the Keep.

The portion of the castle where the royal family resided was the most elevated location in Point Fire.

If I could get somewhere high up, maybe I can make sense of what's happening.

Aren kept off the streets as much as possible. He skirted the fortress walls and ledges, constantly aiming for the ever-glowing ball of orange light that marked the Keep's location.

The scene playing out at ground-level was almost mesmerizing. Shattered gourds of Blood lay strewn about the cobblestones. Here and there a stray article of clothing or a half-broken object lay trampled. What people he did manage to see were always shambling in one of two directions – either towards or away from the Pit.

Not good.

Soon, the magnificent view of the Circle greeted Aren. Except it was not nearly as magnificent as it used to be. The storefronts, taverns, and stalls were all empty. Most of them had their contents splayed out over the ground. The entertainers were gone. Houses of pleasure and gambling were shut. Candles were blown out in every apartment, in every segment of the fortress. There were a few people near the center of the Circle, but the large majority of them sat kneeling. They faced the bright orange of the Heart and the bridges crossing above it, hands clasped in a last-ditch gesture of hopeful prayer to the forgotten god beneath the city.

Aren clambered down a nearby wall, using scathing-hot pipes for handholds, and ducked through the portcullis into the Circle. The conspicuous lack of people in an area that was usually overcrowded made him feel like he was constantly being watched. Before the paranoia could get to him, he sprinted towards the center, in the direction of one of the black bridges.

The density of the small crowd of people praying on their knees increased the closer he got to the glow of the central heat lines. They ignored him as he ran. Even so, their silent beseeching made him feel uncomfortable.

They think it's the end of the world.

Aren was not surprised to notice an absence of royal guards around the entrance to the bridge, or even on it for that matter. It was a surreal experience, being allowed to run across the entire span of the crossing freely, feeling the heat increase in intensity as he approached the Keep.

The royal palace itself stood dark and apathetic against the pulsing of the fire below. This image had once filled Aren with awe and inspiration. However, the recent pandemonium across the city had transformed the sight into something ghastly. Something evil.

Like I'm running straight towards a kingdom of the dead.

He soon reached the end of the bridge and the base of the Keep. Off to his left lay the trapdoor that led to the Heart. Not so long ago, his brother had descended those steps with him.

'Nir, where are you.?

Twenty feet in front of him, at the giant doors which led to the interior of the Keep's dome, stood the only royal guards he had seen so far. There were five of them in total, and they were standing in a strict arrowhead formation. He noticed a few other guards far off in the distance, some way along the rotund base of the towering palace.

"Hey!" Aren called out to them. "What's happening? Does the prince know?"

The man who had been at the front of the formation stepped forward and raised his sword as a warning. He lowered the tip slightly when he realized that Aren was just a child.

He called out in response, "Go home! The city is too dangerous!"

"I know, and that's why I can't!" Aren shouted back. "I saw what happened in the Pit square! Does Prince Luxus know?"

Aren got ready to run, just in case the guard decided to give chase.

"Of course he knows!"

The soldier moved forward aggressively, attempting to scare him off. Aren called his bluff and did not move. The soldier came to a halt and seemed stunned for a moment.

"Aren...Novari? That's your name isn't it?" he asked bluntly.

Aren nodded. He noticed for the first time that the soldier's armor was splattered with the dark crimson of dried blood. His sword was too. The man took off his helmet. It was Justar, the captain of the royal guard. The man who had the courage to speak to Yob.

"I've heard about you, Aren... you and your brother. The 'New Hunters,' I've noticed some people call you two. Anyway..." he trailed off, his gaze far away. "Yes, Luxus III knows. He is our new king now. The question is, my young friend, how do *you* know?"

The man's patchwork of scars marred a face which may have once been handsome. Years of stressful service had pulled the color out of his hair, leaving it wispy and silver.

"I saw it myself. I saw Yob kill the king. I was up on the walls."

Justar raised his eyebrows. A deep gash was cut across one of them. He turned around for a brief moment, making sure that his men were still in formation and that no one had attempted to approach the Keep gates. He turned back to Aren.

"So why are you here then?" he said gruffly. "You know that Point Fire is on the verge of collapse. Most people, Yob being the first, have gone completely insane. Inside the royal house as well. I was lucky just to make it out of the courtyard alive." He glanced towards his bloody sword. "Others weren't."

Aren could tell that Justar wanted him gone, but he could not leave without getting more information.

"So, what are you defending?" Aren started again. "And what about the Cathedral? My Mo–" he stopped, choosing different words, "Some of the people that went crazy were talking about going to the Cathedral."

Justar looked deep into Aren's eyes, assessing him. He redonned his helmet.

"My duty is to the royal family. I will protect them above all else. King Luxus and the other officials who managed to retain their sanity are inside, attempting to come up with a plan to save this city. As for the Cathedral..." Justar brushed a bit of crusted blood off his armor. "Yob is raising an army in the Pit. I can only guess that he plans to march through the Fynn, across the Grey, and assault that black Spire for some inane reason. My orders are to defend the Keep and the Keep alone. The remaining royal guards are positioned as such around the palace. If Yob's madness leads to his own destruction at the hands of the priests, then so be it. As long as the Keep stands, Point Fire will survive."

Justar turned to leave.

"Wait!" Aren shouted. "What do you mean 'destruction at the hands of the priests'?"

Justar stopped but did not turn to face the boy.

"My men have informed me that the Church of Embr may have raised an army of their own. Be safe, Aren."

He began to move away again, when Aren interrupted him a second time.

"I want to climb the walls of the Keep. I want to see what's going on...from above."

This time Justar did turn around.

"Ridiculous. Just because I know who you are, do you really think I'd let you do something like that, something that runs directly against my orders?"

"It's not against your orders," Aren pleaded. "If I see anything interesting up there, I'll come right back down and tell you about it. You could then tell the prince – I mean king – what I saw. I'm sure he'd like some help. It's not like anyone else is crazy enough to climb to the top of this thing."

Aren knew that the structure of the Keep was unique in that it was impossible to enter, or exit, the building anywhere except on the ground floor. Theoretically, the only way to ever reach the top would be to scale it from the outside.

Justar did not respond and walked back to his post. He waved his hand dismissively towards the Keep's walls. Despite all that was going on, Aren could not help but feel childish excitement.

This is a once-in-a-lifetime climb.

Aren watched Justar rejoin his squad. He then glanced at the highest point of the Keep, a windowless and imposing smokestack that poked at the dim skies above. The bottoms of the clouds were reflecting the orange glow from the heat lines, bright as ever.

I just have to hope that I can find some answers up there.

Justar was talking to his soldiers, likely telling them to ignore the small boy who would soon be scaling the palace. The captain finally nodded in Aren's direction, then returned his gaze out over the bridges.

Aren wasted no time in searching for an appropriate place to begin his ascent. He spotted a small ridged gutter inlaid into the dark dome.

As good a place as any.

He traced the gutter upwards to its terminating point, just below an assortment of flying buttresses. Most of the palace was built from large stone bricks. The gaps between the stone chunks were deep, but small. However, they would still be large enough for Aren to squeeze his tiny fingertips into.

Without delaying further, he scurried up the gutter, gripping the sides of the rusting metal. He had not even broken a sweat by the time he reached the bottom of the lowest buttress. Making sure one of his hands was gripping part of the ledge above tightly, he looked down and took a deep breath. He was already around eighty feet off the ground. Justar and his soldiers seemed far smaller. Aren made a silent promise to himself not to look down again until he reached the top.

Over the course of the next twenty minutes, Aren carefully ascended the walls and structures of the Keep. His fingers were beginning to hurt, having been wedged between so many layers of stone. He consciously chose to ignore this pain.

I can't think about anything else but getting there.

He forced himself to enter a trance-like state, only focusing on the next handhold, the next crack, the next buttress. He somehow managed the self-control not to glance down, but he could feel the altitude increasing just from the strength of the wind.

Before he knew it, his hand crested the ledge to a small flattened plateau, right below the final smokestack. He pulled himself over the edge, and lay on his back for a moment, resting his arms. He was not certain if it was an illusion, but the clouds appeared far closer. The orange light reflecting from within them gave the impression that they were in fact large puffs of smoke, obscuring some great fire in the heavens above. Aren finally found that he could not resist the urge, and he crawled back to the edge of the plateau to take a peek at the world below.

The sight was vertigo-inducing. Justar's contingent of soldiers were now just black specks at the base of the building. He could see across the entirety of the Circle, as well as the parts of the city beyond it on all adjacent sides. Though the view was breathtaking, he found himself disappointed that he was not able to see the Point in its full invigorating glory when ample crowds still roamed the streets.

This height was one Aren had never been able to reach before, but he still was not high up enough to have a clear line of sight into the Pit's courtyard, or across the Grey to the north. He could, however, see far more clearly the direction that many people in the Circle and its neighboring areas were taking. As he had guessed before, there were two obvious streams of traffic. One moved towards the Pit, and one moved away from the Pit.

They're all going through the Courtyard.

The Grey, and the area around the Cathedral, was still a mystery. He needed to gather more information.

And there's only one way to do that.

Taking a final deep breath, he got to his feet and moved his eyes back to the smokestack. At its pinnacle, a steady but weak stream of black smoke billowed upwards. The stones that made up this final tower were far more neatly packed, and the cracks between them were barely big enough for even Aren's fingers to fit into. He found himself wondering if this would be the last time he'd ever be able to climb it. He closed his eyes and took a few moments to get back into his climbing trance.

Try to forget about everything that's happening. None of it matters if you make a mistake doing this.

Snapping his eyes back open, he placed his fingertips into the first available crack at the smokestack's base.

About halfway up the tower, the winds really began to pick up.

They must be blowing over from the lake. This high up there's nothing to stop them.

Aren swore under his breath, angry at himself for not bringing something to cover his eyes with. The snappy cold winds made it painfully difficult to keep them open for more than a few seconds. His ascent dropped to a snail's pace, with him having to stop every few cracks to let his eyes fall shut, relishing the break from the blistering gusts.

When he was thirty feet from the top, the gusts had become so cold that he could no longer keep his eyes open for more than a split

second. Tears ran down and froze on his cheeks as his body tried to cope with the dry, icy winds. He did not dare wipe them away, for fear of losing his precarious grip.

What do I do? I'm so close, but I can barely see anything.

He had to get to the absolute top.

Once I get there, I could sit on the ledge and use my hands as a shield from the wind. Until then, I guess I'll have to do with climbing blind.

Concentrating intensely on his sense of touch, Aren inched one hand after the other up the stone bricks, constantly feeling for the next handhold. Once his fingertips slipped into one, he pulled his way further upwards. Finally, he felt the stonework disappear into nothingness. Exhilaration and relief flooded through his body.

I made it! The first person in history to climb the Keep!

With a heroic effort, he pulled himself up and onto the circular ridge of the giant smokestack. At last he could open his eyes, shielding them from the buffeting winds with both of his hands. He pulled his hood as low as possible. Luckily, the ridge was wide enough so that he was still far away from the smoke rising from the center of the column.

Otherwise this entire climb would have been useless.

He turned around, dangling his legs over the edge. The view itself was terrifying. He could see the entirety of Point Fire – all the way from the eastern edge with its wind breakers hugging the lake, to the dark western wall which stood stubbornly against the Frost. He moved his gaze over the Pit, still shielding his eyes from the incessant winds. He scanned the streets there, searching for any areas of interest. Soon Aren grew frustrated, wondering why he could not pinpoint the exact location of the Courtyard.

The cobblestones there are light colored, so why can't I see it? Maybe if I follow where the people are going from the Circle...

He shifted his attention onto one of the tiny dots moving away from the Circle's gates. The dot joined a few others, and eventually joined a larger stream flowing through the city streets. He traced this river of distant people until...

309

Aren gasped, and it finally dawned on him why he could not visualize the courtyard: it was covered, quite literally, with thousands of people. There were so many dots in fact, that they seemed to spill outwards from where Aren now assumed the courtyard was located, filling in all of the adjacent streets.

He noticed something else too: a steady stream of these dots was moving out from the northern portion of the Courtyard off in the direction of the Grey. He traced the stream carefully. As it reached the northernmost gateways of the city proper – the ones that led out onto the Grey itself – the stream splintered outwards...into what seemed to be perfect lines. Aren's heart skipped a beat when he realized what was happening.

They're forming ranks. It really is an army!

Even further to the north stood an unspeakable sight. Aren now realized what the priests had been building.

Row upon row of wooden battlements stood against the ice, far across the Grey from where the dots were forming lines. Roughly erected towers had been added to the battlements, which Aren guessed were vantage points for archers. Certain areas had been reinforced with what appeared to be piles of stones. It was almost too far for Aren to see, but he could just make out the streams of red dots scurrying around the makeshift wooden fortifications. The layout of these defenses was clearly built with a simple goal in mind – to allow absolutely no one near the Cathedral.

The battlements formed a trifecta of concentric, fortified circles around the obelisk-like building. It was almost as if the Cathedral had become a smaller Keep in its own small version of Point Fire.

The outermost layer of defenses was low, and crudely constructed. It also contained the highest density of the stone piles. None of the red dots moved outside this ring.

It's the first line of defense. The outer wall.

A few of the dots milled around between the outer and middle lines. The central line of fortifications was enormous, and was also the one which housed the archer towers. As the attackers would presumably be struggling to get over the outer line of defenses, they would make easy pickings for the incoming arrows.

The final, inner circle looked much like the outermost one.

The last line.

The large majority of the red dots existed in the space between the inner and middle circles. It was an impressive display of defensive strategy, reminding Aren of all the times he had seen similar layouts in his school's dated history textbooks.

I have to tell Justar. People are going to be massacred. The royal family needs to hear about this.

Aren doubted that anyone else had had the time, or the vantage point, to have discovered what was currently happening at the far northern outskirts of the city. All of the royal guards had been recalled to protect the Keep, so the information available to the royal family must have been greatly restricted.

I might be the only one who knows.

Before preparing himself for the dangerous descent, Aren gazed out over the Frost. It was a melancholic sight. Memories of playing Hunt Games with his brother filled his mind. Other memories rose up as well. Faded ones of his father. The sight of Avenir leaving their home...

*

Aren squinted. Something was shining out over the snow at the edge of the horizon. Even at this distance, it looked like a bright orange, or perhaps red, beacon against the Frost. He rubbed his eyes, making sure it was not a trick of the light...or the wind. Sure enough, something bright shone out from far away.

It's coming...closer.

He was not sure why, but a faint tinge of fear began to kindle itself deep within him. He shook his head and dragged his eyes away from the light.

Just concentrate on getting down.

311

After a last glance at the approaching light, he closed his eyes again and slowly lowered himself over the edge, deftly probing for a suitable foothold.

XXXVIII

Avenir gulped down a piece of tough hare meat. It was raw, but he still relished the taste of it as it slid down his throat. Luna did the same, as she perched on her sled like a ravenous crow. It was a few more seconds before Avenir spoke up.

"Okay, that's enough rest. We have to keep moving."

He threw the remaining scraps of fur off into the Frost and began pushing his sled once more. Luna followed suit, not bothering to say anything. Soljan and Runan still lay unconscious on top of their sleds, slowing their progress. Avenir and Luna had both almost reached the limits of their endurance, but somehow, it felt as if the limit itself always lay just out of reach.

Eventually, moving forward becomes natural. A simple requirement of staying alive.

They pressed forward in a silent single file, the ice around them illuminated by one of Sen's remaining flares. They dared not risk attracting the Tall Ones again. Sometimes they would see a flash of movement in the distance, and their adrenaline would kick in momentarily, making them forget their exhaustion.

The daze of the red glow gave their journey an otherworldly flavor. At some points, Avenir could have sworn that they were already dead, and this was simply the next pilgrimage to whatever heaven – or hell – lay in store for them.

*   *   *

"Look," said Luna.

Avenir tiredly raised his head.

Had I almost fallen asleep?

313

When he saw what lay before them, both hope and despair filled his heart. They had finally reached the cliff face which Sen had helped them descend. The ropes they had used still hung against the wall of ice, silently waiting for their eventual return.

"I should be happy...but–" Avenir started, exhausted.

"I know," said Luna, coming to a stop at the base of the cliff. "How in the name of the Seven are we going to get from here" – she looked with contempt at her fallen companions, then at the ropes – "to up there?"

As if in response to this question, Runan began sputtering loudly. Avenir rushed over and grabbed his head.

"Runan! Are you okay?"

He moved the older Hunter to a more upright position, where the man continued to cough wretchedly. Runan opened his eyes a crack. He jerked awake violently, grabbing Avenir's collar in a fierce grip. His eyes were wild, confused. He attempted to pull Avenir to the ground.

"It's okay!" Avenir tried to calm him down, at the same time attempting to avoid being throttled. "You're okay, Runan!"

After a few more seconds of wild thrashing, the man seemed to come to his senses. He looked around, some of the color returning to his weathered face.

"Where am I? What happened?" he sputtered.

He let go of Avenir and rolled off the sled, landing with a soft thud on the ground. He got up, struggling. It took a decent while for him to truly realize where they were, and a bit longer for Avenir to explain their current situation.

And then, the inevitable question came, "Where's Sen?"

A shameful heat spread across Avenir's back. He did not want to lie to Runan about what had happened, but they could not afford another setback when they were this desperate.

"My...father killed him. He died out in the Frost while you were unconscious."

Runan sank to his knees.

"Sen..." he sobbed quietly.

Avenir took a quick glance at Luna. Her face betrayed no emotion, but she seemed to agree with what he had told the older Hunter.

I'm sorry, Runan.

"I know. It's terrible. I don't know what my father has become. This is why we're heading back. We have to make this right."

Runan cried quietly for a few minutes.

Then, he stood up abruptly as he wiped his eyes. "I will never forgive the man who killed my brother. I *will* avenge his death, even if it kills me!"

Avenir avoided eye contact with him and pretended to make sure the ropes on his sled were fixed securely.

With Runan's help, they were able to scale the cliff. The pace was painstakingly slow, but eventually they managed to haul the two the sleds and their contents, as well as Soljan, over the upper edge. Though fatigued, Runan had managed to preserve at least some of his inhuman agility.

"I think we could make it back in a day, if we push hard," said Avenir.

"Yes, three people for two sleds," agreed Runan. "I can pull one for the first leg. I feel guilty for you having to work so hard to save me."

"It's okay," Avenir studied Runan, who still seemed a little bit worse for wear. "You can take the second shift."

"Thank you. I owe you two my life."

In his recap of the events that had transpired, Avenir had also chosen to omit the fact that Luna was the one responsible for Runan's recent unconsciousness and head injury. Luna had not said anything either. The older Hunter had shuddered when Avenir mentioned the time limit set on Point Fire's lifetime. However, he was less bothered than Avenir thought he would be.

All that's left on his mind is revenge.

Soljan lay on the sled silently. He had become far quieter in his breathing, and this made Avenir both relieved for him and worried for his health. The man no longer appeared to be in great pain, but this change might have been an indication that his condition was deteriorating.

"We need to move faster," Avenir said emotionlessly to the other two Hunters.

XXXIX

Kreymar adjusted the chainmail underneath his crimson robes. He was sitting in his private room, a third of the way up the spiraling tower of apartments in the Cathedral. Opposite him, a small circular frosted window was set into the dark stonework. From this viewpoint, he gazed back over the Grey towards the distant walls of Point Fire. Right below him, the masses of priests – Elders and new recruits – scurried around the battlements, their own crimson robes flowing in the icy winds. The time of Embr's prophecy had finally come to fruition – the priests below could sense it too.

Following Kreymar's orders, they had begun to assume their battle positions. Kreymar had spent the entirety of the Church of Embr's treasury in order to finance this army. The hundreds of newly purchased bows and spears, and the men who wielded them, were now falling into ranks behind the central circle of fortifications. As many as possible had already moved into the towers, which were evenly spaced among the wooden palisade.

The new recruits had been armed with the spears, which were all painted a dull red. These men – most of them barely twenty years of age – were packed between the inner and outer walls.

The first, and hopefully last, line of defense.

Kreymar could not see the final cohort of men in his army – the older priests, people Kreymar had known his whole life – from this angle, because they were right at the base of the Cathedral, behind the final circular wall.

Out over the Grey, the cursed army of Point Fire was growing steadily. Kreymar watched in stoic curiosity as the number of lines in the distance increased. He assumed that ordinary citizens, and perhaps even children, would be a part of them.

But it does not matter. We will kill them all. Such is the will of Embr.

He had only managed to muster just over one thousand soldier-priests for this inevitable battle. The force he and his Brothers were facing would severely outnumber them.

How many more do they have? Five thousand. Ten thousand?

Kreymar closed his eyes as he stood up, scraping his chair backwards on the hard floor.

Embr, protect us.

He raised his hood over his head as he left his room and descended downwards to his army below.

*　　　　　*　　　　　*

After descending the Keep's walls, Aren relayed the information to Justar immediately. The captain took a deep interest in the description of the army forming to the north and ordered one of his soldiers to further relay the information to the newly crowned king. Much to Aren's frustration, however, Justar mentioned his doubt that this would change the king's current strategy of solely defending the Keep.

"It's too risky to leave this place unguarded," said the captain. "And even if we *could* send a detachment of royal guards to attempt to stop what you said looks like an organized army, we would be severely outnumbered. If their minds are indeed set on blood, there is nothing we can feasibly do."

*　　　　　*　　　　　*

Aren bashed on Udar's door. "Udar, are you in there? Are you okay?"

He feared the worst.

Had Udar's parents also...? Or Udar himself?

"Udar! Let me in! This part of the city is safe, at least for now!"

318

To Aren's astonishment, he heard multiple bolts and latches unlock. The door swung open, revealing Udar's tear-stained face. The boy rushed over and hugged Aren, almost crushing him. He started to cry profusely.

"Udar, stop! What's happened? Hey!"

Aren pushed Udar off of him, trying to get a better look into their home.

Is someone dangerous inside?

"Was there a break-in?"

Udar shook his head miserably, "It's my mother and father. They've gone crazy!"

Aren could immediately guess what Udar meant and looked inside for signs of his friend's parents.

"You mustn't let them out!"

"I didn't...I didn't!" Udar moaned. "They're locked in the basement!"

Aren moved past him through the doorway.

"Aren, what do I do?" Udar whined as he followed him in.

The inside of Udar's place was simple and homey. Right adjacent to a small entrance foyer was the kitchen - similar in layout to Aren's house - except this one was outfitted with all the very best stoves and cookers. Rows and rows of spices and ingredients lined the walls, stretching almost to the ceiling. Aren had a hunch about where Udar's slight chubbiness came from.

At the back of their home, past two bedrooms, lay a trapdoor. It was partially obscured by a long and heavy table, which Udar had presumably pushed over it.

"They're under there," Udar quivered.

Aren moved closer and crouched next to it. He could hear a distant banging coming from beneath the trapdoor. He slid his head underneath the piece of furniture and put an ear to the wood.

He listened to the muffled ring of a man's voice yelling. It even sounded like there was another door far below that the man was behind. Occasionally, a higher-pitched voice would join in with the man's cries.

"How far does this go down? Can they get out?" Aren asked.

"There's a ladder that goes about thirty feet. And another door at the bottom of that." Udar sniffed. He had almost managed to collect himself. "They tried to leave earlier, even though I told them it was too dangerous to go. They kept saying something about going to the Cathedral. I took the key and tried to make them stay. My father hit me," Udar wiped a final tear from his eye, "but I somehow opened the door and got out. I locked them in. Do you think they'll get hurt?"

Aren scooted out from where he had been listening,

"No, I don't think so. You were really lucky. You should see what's going on out there...If your parents had managed to escape, I think they would be in some kind of weird army right now."

Udar's eyes widened. "*Army?* What? But do you think I can just leave them down there?"

"Yeah, an army. I saw thousands of dreaming people going to join it. They're gathering right on the northern edge of the Point and are probably going to attack the Cathedral." Aren's brow furrowed. "I think you can leave your folks down there though. I had to do a similar thing with my mom," he shook his head, thinking hard, "but right now, you have to come with me. I need to show you something."

*   *   *

"So past that trapdoor was your secret base?" Aren asked as he guided Udar across the rooftops and balustrades in the direction of Point Fire's western wall.

"Yeah," Udar sighed. He was severely worried about his parents. The tears were still fresh on his red cheeks.

Aren had insisted that he keep them in the basement for the time being. To Udar, it seemed like the young Hunter understood at least a little bit of what was going on, which was far more than most people, and he had done as his friend had suggested. Plus, Udar's family would have been in great danger if it were not for Aren's advice to begin with.

"Why are we going towards the Frost?" asked Udar.

320

Aren stopped, balancing on a particularly smooth piece of stone. "I saw something weird when I was looking down from the top of the Keep."

"When you were *what?*" Udar's eyes looked they were about to pop out of his head.

"Oh yeah, I forgot to tell you. I climbed all the way to the top of the Keep so I could see what's happening everywhere. It looked like some kind of light was coming towards the Point from the Frost."

"Aren. You're an idiot," Udar said incredulously.

Aren laughed dryly and hopped off the stone outcropping.

The two of them pushed at a steady pace over the streets and alleyways of the city. The entire metropolis was now eerily quiet, and the tension in the air was somehow far worse than before. The two opposite-moving streams of people had completely disappeared from the roads below. Lights were still on in a few of the homes, but these homes were also abandoned. It was an eerie paradox: the places with no lights on were where the remaining sane people in Point Fire hid, cowering from the unknown.

Eventually they arrived back at the Circle on its eastern side. The number of people praying had increased greatly. Every few feet or so, the two boys would pass by yet another person kneeling in silence. They gave them all wide berths.

"I can't believe you climbed that thing," Udar muttered under his breath as he gazed up at the distant smokestack.

Once across the Circle, Aren lead them on an ascent up the imposing dividing wall between the North and South sides. As they crested the top, Aren looked out in the direction of the Frost. From where they were now, right adjacent to the Circle, it was a straight shot to the outer wall. The endless stretch of fortifications created an elevated stone highway towards the icy wilderness beyond. A large heat line ran along its entire length.

"You ready for a run?" Aren teased.

Udar nodded and they set off at a fast pace together, the residential segments of the castle-city falling away behind them to make room for more rural areas, and eventually open fields of near-wilting crops. Although they were both fearful of leaving their parents so far behind, locked away in their respective prisons, an invisible weight lifted off of their shoulders as they put distance between themselves and the Pit, and the silent grievers of the Circle.

Soon they had traveled far enough that places of residence were few and far between. The only structures this far out were buildings that looked like large blocks – some of them indoor chicken coops – and the occasional grey barn. They spotted a couple of emaciated-looking cattle and a farmer guiding them into a nearby fortification. Out here, one could easily forget that an entire army was being formed at the northern edge of the Point.

The raised outer wall of the city was now far closer. It was not much longer before Aren and Udar reached this elevated segment. They clambered upwards, fingers slipping over the frigid rock. Udar was surprised to catch himself smiling – there was no way he would have been able to do something like this in the past. Although Aren had indeed introduced significant danger into his life, he could not argue that the wild boy had also honed his endurance to an amazing standard.

As he climbed, Aren looked down at the hundreds upon hundreds of copper portcullises dotting the outer wall. Doors that he and his brother had gone through using his father's old Hunter's key. It felt like everything he saw was now reminding him of Avenir.

"Hurry up, Aren! Come look! There *is* something out there!" Udar called from the top of the walls.

Aren almost jumped from the shock that Udar had beaten him to their goal. He tore his eyes away from the copper doors and scrambled up to join Udar.

Sure enough, what Aren had seen from the precipice of the Keep had not been an illusion. A glowing orange beacon was shining far away over the Frost. But it was much closer than when he had first seen it from the top of the Keep's smokestack.

"It's the same color as the heat lines!" Udar exclaimed. "What do you think it is?"

"Hey, you're right. I didn't even think about that," Aren sank down to his haunches and squinted his eyes again. "I don't like it. Something about it...I can't put my finger on it."

They sat in silence, studying the strange light. At any other time in Point Fire's history, a sighting like this could even have been cause for celebration. The idea of life outside the walls would spark a new hope for humanity. But with the recent and terrible occurrences, it made Aren and Udar tremble. It was like they were watching the glow of a final dusk.

Tens of minutes passed, and suddenly the light appeared much closer.

Whatever this thing is, it's moving at a ridiculous speed.

Aren did not have any type of telescope with him, so he strained to see what lay within the inferno of orange light. He could just make out what appeared to be rapid and repetitive movement.

"I can't see what it is," he said to Udar. "Can you?"

"It looks like... a person!" his friend stuttered.

"*What?*" Aren turned to Udar, making sure that his friend was not joking.

"A person. See – it looks like a person running!" Udar was pointing frantically towards the approaching light.

Aren tried to understand what he was talking about...

It IS a person.

Aren could now see the movement for what it was – the rhythmic pumping of arms and legs.

"By the Seven," Aren whispered.

*   *   *

Soon the person was close enough that they could see his outline. Whoever it was, they were sprinting at a blistering pace.

A terrible, inhuman pace.

323

Aren could now also see that held backwards in the person's right hand was a white-hot flaming Sword. The tip of this Sword was streaking above the surface of the snow, causing geysers of steam to burst upwards. Enormous orange flames fanned out in all directions from the Blade, occasionally utterly engulfing the person that was wielding it.

Aren and Udar lowered themselves behind the jutting fortifications at the top of the outer wall, peeking out with only the tops of their heads. They did not want to be seen by whoever, or whatever, that was.

"What is that... monster?" Udar shivered.

Aren did not answer; his eyes were glued to the person running, who he could now clearly see was a man.

Had Avenir witnessed this? Is this even a human? Is it a god?

And then the man was not far away anymore, and Aren and Udar could begin to feel the staggering heat emanating from him. They also began to sense something else – a dark and unseen feeling of fear. It was terribly similar to what Aren had experienced after the wave of shadows first hit him.

As the man approached the outer wall, the two boys ducked for cover, but not before Aren saw him jump at least twenty feet into the air, wedging the Sword into the icy stones of the outer fortifications. Udar closed his eyes, sweating profusely.

Aren wanted to do the same. The strange sense of fear had grown stronger. It felt like a hidden pressure coming from the inside of his chest. He forced himself to keep his eyes open.

In the next split-second, he saw the man vault over the top of the wall as if it were nothing, not one hundred feet from where he and Udar hid. The blazing inferno surrounding him scorched their clothes and hair. And then he was gone, moving across the North Side of Point Fire.

Aren immediately got up and rushed to look over towards the center of the city. The man had already almost made it one third of the way back to the Circle.

"Aren, what...what..." Udar stammered, not able to find the words to describe what they had just seen.

"I...I don't know," Aren gasped, equally struck, "but I think I know where he's going."

XL

Kreymar stood in one of the archer's towers lining his fortifications. He watched silently as the bright orange light appeared over the western edge of Point Fire. In response, he knelt in the charred circle he had readied, and closed his eyes in prayer.

Embr, help us. Reveal to me what must be done.

A burst of flame erupted from the already-damaged side of his face. For a split second, the orange light moving across the edge of Point Fire flared up intensely. The nearby priests rushed over to help Kreymar, who raised his hand, commanding them to stop. Kreymar gritted his teeth, his eyes still closed. A few seconds later, he stood up, yet another scar added to his visage.

"Embr has given us our final message."

The other priests bowed their heads at the mention of the Great Sword.

"The bearer of Darkness has arrived," beseeched Kreymar as he waved his hand in the direction of the army across the Grey. "He will wait until we are weak before he joins the battle. He does not wish to unnecessarily risk his own life. It is for this reason that we cannot, we *must not,* allow them to break our defenses. If we do, it will be the beginning of the end of Point Fire." Kreymar closed his eyes one final time, hardening his will for the fight to come. "To your stations, my Brothers. Do not falter."

"Yes, Your Holiness."

Most of the other priests near him – the soon-to-be commanders of various regions around the makeshift battlements – all stepped out from the tower and descended the flight of wooden slats to the ice below. Kreymar was still tracking the movement of the orange light. It had almost reached the location where Point Fire's summoned army stood waiting.

Who is behind all of this? Who is the 'He' you speak of?

A dark red helmet with an obsidian torch affixed to its top rested on a small desk off to the side of the tower. He scooped it into his arms. Pushing past the archers stationed within the structure, he quickly ascended a ladder to a trapdoor in the ceiling, opened it, and climbed to stand on the very top of the rickety building. The rest of his army was in position, lining the walls surrounding the Cathedral.

The head priest produced an ornate tinderbox from his robe and proceeded to light the helmet's torch. It sprung to life, the flame adopting an otherworldly shape. He raised the helmet with his good arm and let it fall over his head, covering the many scars he now bore. He could feel it: this was the defining moment of his life. Nothing else mattered. All the men below turned to face the one with the burning torch on his helmet. Those on the opposite end of the defensive circle listened intently.

"THIS IS NOT A BATTLE FOR YOUR LIVES!" Kreymar boomed from the archer tower, his crimson cloak billowing in the icy winds that wafted upwards. "THIS IS A BATTLE FOR YOUR VERY *WAY* OF LIFE. IT IS FOR ALL THOSE IN POINT FIRE, WHO *FEAR* FOR THEIR LIVES. WHEN THIS IS DONE, THE CHURCH OF EMBR WILL BE REMEMBERED AS THE SAVIOR WHICH DELIVERED THIS CITY FROM OBLIVION. THIS CITY, THIS LAST BASTION OF HUMANITY, WILL NOT FALL TO EVIL!"

With his last words, Kreymar unsheathed a vicious obsidian-black scimitar. He pulled a small vial from his pocket and poured its contents over the sword's blade. He raised the weapon to the torch burning on top of his helmet. The blade caught alight instantly, burning in a brilliant orange. He raised it triumphantly.

Every single priest responded with a thunderous roar. The young men who lined the outer palisade raised their spears, the shafts shaking in the blustering winds. The sound of the priests' roar was terrifying, shaking the very foundations of the Cathedral itself.

Intermixed with this sound was the clink and rattle of their armor and weaponry, as they moved to their final defensive positions. Multitudes armed with bows were feverishly filing into the other towers.

Soon, a calm silence fell over the army below the Cathedral. The orange light had finally reached the force across the Grey. The silence entered a crescendo and intensified towards a deafening stillness. Then, softly, almost like a distant heartbeat, the sound of a uniform march crept through the air.

They are coming.

*　　　　　　*　　　　　　*

Soljan yelled loudly as he woke up, emerging from the longest and most terrible nightmare of his life. Avenir immediately rushed to aid him.

"Aghhh!" the tracker groaned.

He took one glance at his leg – mangled and wrapped in bandages – before retching loudly. Luna and Runan were soon at his side as well. Soljan finally noticed his surroundings, and the worried faces of his pod members. He smiled a pained grin.

"What did I miss?" he croaked weakly.

The other pod members could not help but burst into nervous laughter.

*　　　　　　*　　　　　　*

Aren and Udar were sprinting back over the raised stone highway towards the Circle. They had both agreed that they absolutely needed to see what was happening in the Grey. They also wanted to witness the Man on Fire a second time, even though the thought of him turned their blood to ice. Cold winds had already started whipping at their hands and face as they ran. The ground was shaking, and it was as if the city itself was trembling to a rhythmic beat.

*　　　　　　*　　　　　　*

The distant heartbeat of the march had escalated into a deafening pounding. The army was much closer now, and Kreymar could begin to make out individual people. Women wearing dresses, blacksmiths in their work aprons, even teenagers. All of these people were in the front line of the attacking force. The enemy's armaments were also highly varied – some carried pikes, others shortswords, and a few even wielded daggers or pitchforks. At the back of the army, the static orange light glowed ever-steadily.

The advancing force marched in perfect step. It was an inhuman motion, as if all their minds and bodies were united perfectly. As a result, each step of their advance sent small shockwaves outwards to the Cathedral. But this was the only sound Kreymar could hear. The army itself was silent. Not a single voice filled the air.

"HOLD NOTHING BACK," Kreymar bellowed from his vantage point. "DO NOT SEE THEM AS PEOPLE. THEY HAVE BEEN CONSUMED BY DARKNESS."

The rows of young priests sank into a tight formation behind the outer spiked palisade. They stood shoulder to shoulder, holding their spears upwards at a slight angle just behind the splintered wall.

Kreymar studied the incoming force carefully. It seemed they had no intention of encircling the Cathedral. They were going to attack it head on, from the direction of the city.

They will try to force a weak point in the defenses.

"GET AS MANY MEN AS POSSIBLE TO FACE THEM. IF YOU ARE NOT ON THE SIDE DIRECTLY ACROSS FROM THE POINT, GET THERE NOW." Kreymar opened the trapdoor, and motioned to two of the archers below. "You two, see that this is done. I want ninety percent of our men on the side facing the enemy. They are planning to punch through in one area" – he pointed towards the door – "Go!" He slammed the trapdoor shut as the two priest-archers scurried down the slats. He faced his army again, calling out to them, "WE MUST FIGHT THEM HEAD ON. DO NOT LEAVE THIS NEW POST UNLESS THE ORDER IS GIVEN."

It took only a moment for Kreymar's orders to spread. Soon, swaths of red bodies were pouring from the other locations in the defensive circle towards the segment facing the incoming army. An additional platoon of priest-archers was now ascending the slats towards the tower that Kreymar stood on. The army of Point Fire was almost in range.

"ARCHERS READY. SEND THE SIGNALS."

Kreymar could hear the sound of arrows being drawn and bowstrings being pulled taut below him. On either side of the tower, one of the many priest-archers lit a large hanging brazier. Soon, all of the other towers had lit braziers of their own, an indication that the archers within were ready to fire.

The incoming army marched forwards mechanically, its uniform step like the beating of a death drum. Kreymar could now make out individual faces among the thousands that approached. His heart sank when he saw a young boy carrying a sharp piece of scrap metal. He closed his eyes.

It must be done.

"FIRE!"

A tremendous cascade of plucking noises echoed out from beneath him. Within a heartbeat, the sky was filled with a shower of flaming specks. These specks were joined by hundreds of others spewing out from the towers. It was like the clouds had opened and it was raining in bright lights.

The orange blanket descended in slow motion upon the approaching army. The sound of its impact was drowned out by the incessant march, but the effects were clear. Bodies began falling like heavy snowflakes. With some form of morbid curiosity, Kreymar tried to keep track of the young boy he had seen marching earlier. Part of him wanted this boy to survive...for him to somehow avoid his fate and escape the falling arrows. But he could not find him anymore. The boy had been lost in a sea of death. No shouts of anguish or pain reached Kreymar's ears. The army approached steadily, as mute as before.

The attackers picked up their marching pace. It was a harrowing sight, seeing every person perfectly increase their speed in unison.

"RELOAD AND FIRE."

Another barrage of arrows illuminated the sky. This time, the volley was slightly overshot – the army was approaching faster than expected.

"AGAIN."

Suddenly, Kreymar found himself blinded. The stationary orange light at the rear of the approaching army had flared up to a brightness far eclipsing that of the Inner Sanctum. He could hear the startled cries of the priests beneath him. His vision had been completely whited out from the flash, but nearby outlines were already beginning to reappear.

"RELOAD!" He bellowed again. "DO NOT LET THEM ADVANCE SO EASILY."

The third volley of arrows was delayed enough so that by the time it was let loose, the approaching army was no more than one hundred feet away from the outer line of fortifications. Due to the close proximity of the approaching horde, the angle the arrows took was negative, flying downwards from the towers. The younger spear-wielding priests ducked as the sheets of orange flew over their heads, peppering those across from them.

Then Kreymar heard a distant, but powerful, voice. It was much like the one he had heard when receiving the messages from Embr, but even clearer, Darker.

Go.

Instantly, the army of Point Fire began to sprint forwards, still in perfect time. Each step of the oncoming force rattled the foundations of the towers and the palisades. The walls surrounding the Cathedral shook with each motion of the advancing army.

"FIRE AT WILL!" bellowed Kreymar, desperation creeping into his tone.

The army crashed into the outer wooden palisade like a tidal wave. The force of the impact was so devastating that some of the outward-facing spikes instantly snapped. Kreymar could see bodies being thrown off the fortifications at wild angles. The way the people had simply launched themselves into the spikes with no regard for their own lives sent chills down his spine.

Surprisingly, many of the young new recruits seemed to possess strong resolve, and instantly went to work with their spears on the gaps in the palisade. They stabbed mercilessly, skewering those who had managed to get through the defenses. Rivulets of dark blood were already being absorbed by the snow below their feet.

All along the rest of the line, where most of the outer wall was still intact, the terrified priests frantically did their best to slow the push of the army before them.

The horde of attackers kept sprinting forwards, the might of the thousands behind them forcing the forerunners to their deaths, gored on either the spikes or the spears of the priests. The occasional burning arrow flew through the air into the masses of people attacking, as the archers started regaining their eyesight and bearings. With a terrible realization, Kreymar saw that the entire outer wall would soon fall. It was like trying to hold back an unstoppable wave with a wrought iron fence.

Some of the younger priests had already fallen, slain by an assortment of knives, pitchforks, and spears. The instant they fell, they were replaced by another crimson-robed priest stabbing furiously at whoever killed their Brother.

The area where the opposing army had made its initial impact was now devastated by torn bodies and broken wood. The enemy forces ignored this, trampling over the masses of the dead in their mindless quest to push through. The corpses of women, children, men, and the elderly piled up beneath the feet of the attackers. Within seconds, other areas on the outer circle had adopted a similar ghastly appearance.

How does one stop something this evil? This terrifying?

"FALL BACK TO THE CENTRAL WALLS."

The priests below Kreymar poured a powdered blue crystal into the two braziers. The flames flared up and turned a deep green. It took only a few seconds for the priests outside of the central walls to notice the change in the light's color behind them. They immediately turned and began running towards the central fortifications. Some of them stayed behind, stabbing without cease, their minds consumed by battle rage. These priests were trampled within mere moments.

Kreymar watched with building terror as the remainder of his young troops who had not been trampled or maimed ran frantically back towards him. Behind them, the army of Point Fire pushed up and over the wooden palisade. It was like a dam wall finally breaking. The outer defenses were no more. Behind this sea of humans, the orange light still shone brightly.

"ARCHERS. READY AGAIN TO FIRE AT WILL."

This time, the priests below Kreymar poured a white powder into the braziers, and the flames resumed their natural color once again. The archers in all the other towers repeated this signal, and soon a ring of orange fires surrounded the Cathedral.

The retreating priests had almost reached the central ring of fortifications. Heavy wooden doors were being pulled open as the men ran for their lives towards them. Behind their backs, an unending swarm of people pursued them, the corpses of the slain disappearing beneath their feet.

How many have I cut down? One thousand? Two thousand? And still they charge.

As the first of the retreating young priests filtered back through the doors and behind the central line of large wooden walls, another volley of arrows was released from the tower beneath Kreymar. The approaching mass was only a stone's throw away, and the arrows pierced into them directly. The first row of oncoming people fell away like a curtain and were instantly trampled by those behind them.

"CLOSE THE GATES. KEEP FIRING."

Kreymar need not have shouted this last order. The wooden doors were already being closed, the priests operating them pulling the mechanisms in a frenzy. Some of the younger priests were going to be locked out, and they screamed at their Brothers inside the walls to slow their operation. Their pleas fell on deaf ears, and the doors slammed shut. The ones who had arrived too late banged their fists and heads deliriously on the thick wood.

Then the wave of attackers hit them from behind, not as any normal army would, but truly as a *wave*. Although some of the abandoned priests were stabbed or bludgeoned to death, the vast majority were simply crushed by the brutal force of the horde.

As the army impacted the walls again, this time right beneath him, the tower Kreymar was standing on shook violently, almost collapsing. The attacking army pushed forth relentlessly, the frontrunners still being crushed from behind. Bodies were piling up against the bottom of the walls. It was then that Kreymar realized that there was nothing that could have feasibly prepared him for this type of onslaught.

How can mere mortals stop something like this?

He regained his balance, dropping to a crouching position to prevent being thrown off the side of the tower.

"OIL, OIL!" he shouted, desperation now taking over his voice.

The priests in the tower below poured a different white powder into the braziers, and the flames turned neon red. The rest of the archers were now firing arrows as fast as they could into the attackers right below them. But after each projectile felled someone, another was right behind them to take their place.

In response to the new signal, the veteran priests lining the expansive central walls, as well as the recruits who had made it back from the outer palisade alive, began dumping vats of oil onto the masses below them.

The steaming black liquid hissed as it hit the flesh of those underneath. More bodies fell, adding to a grim heap of the recently deceased. No screams of fear or pain accompanied their demise. It was like they were all hypnotized, oblivious to the reality of their doom.

The priests continually poured the vats over the edge of the walls. The flaming arrows which were being launched into the fray ignited the oil in patches, adding to the levels of destruction at the base of the walls. A nightmarish pile of burning bodies grew beneath him, over which the rest of the army continually climbed. It had turned into a scene straight from hell.

The orange light had approached steadily behind the army and was now emanating its rays just out of range of arrow fire. Kreymar managed to tear his eyes away from the carnage below as he squinted towards the light.

It's a...man!

He almost dropped his sword from the shock of the realization.

"A commander of light, hiding in the rear," Kreymar mumbled to himself. He spat on the roof of the tower. "Shameful."

The pile was still ascending up against the outer edge of the central walls as more people fell, and more attackers trampled over them.

Countless *thousands dead, and they aren't stopping.*

Kreymar stole a quick glance at the rest of the oncoming army: the ones still waiting to trample over their fallen comrades. He estimated the remaining number at around five thousand.

With a deepening feeling of horror, he watched as the pile slowly crept up the height of the wooden fortifications. Another few minutes and they would be over the top.

We need to stop them. Here.

"BROTHERS. HOLD THEM BACK. USE SPEARS OVER THE EDGE. PUSH THEM DOWN."

Most of the defending priests could not hear his orders over the cacophony of battle, which was made even worse by their own cries of fear. The attackers remained ever silent. However, the nearest priests to Kreymar, adjacent to the sides of the tower, called for their spears and began stabbing downwards. The people below were now in range of these melee weapons, and the priests skewered them without faltering. Some of the other Brothers adorning the central walls were now using their spears as makeshift levers, attempting to pry the growing pile of bodies away from the tops of the walls. Their terror fueled their muscles with a seemingly endless supply of adrenaline. Anything to stop this mindless onslaught.

This savage and brutal work carried on for what seemed like an eternity. But the endurance of every man defending the walls was slowly sapping away against the near endless ocean of bodies. Kreymar and his crimson army barely noticed that night had already fallen...and had in fact almost passed them by.

The trapdoor flew open at Kreymar's feet and a priest stuck his head through the opening, pure terror in the young man's eyes.

"We're out of arrows!"

Kreymar looked down at the priest, then back below the tower, where the corpse pile had just about reached the top of the walls. Members of the assaulting army were clambering over this mountain of the dead feverishly.

"Fall back...we have to fall back," Kreymar repeated, finally coming to terms with the situation at hand. "FALL BACK!"

The other priest immediately disappeared back through the trapdoor. The braziers hanging off the edge were extinguished. Almost instantly, the rest of the crimson army began their retreat. By the time every brazier had been extinguished, the vast majority of Kreymar's force was already running for the final line of defenses: a spiked wooden palisade identical to the first.

Kreymar followed suit, dropping beneath the trapdoor. Before he left the tower, he glanced back towards the man of light. He was much closer now, but Kreymar still could not make out his facial features. The orange glare was far too intense. Yet, he could now tell that the glow was not coming from the man himself. It originated from a point where his right hand would be.

The sound of wood splintering nearby brought Kreymar back to reality. He ran down the slats, joining the rest of the priests in their retreat.

*   *   *

Aren and Udar felt sick. They had been watching from the dividing wall between the North Side and the Icesmith's districts when the central defenses around the Cathedral had been broken. Although they were still quite a distance from the Cathedral itself, they were close enough to see the armies of red and dark dots colliding with each other. Though impossible to see it clearly, they imagined people being crushed and trampled, and multitudes being killed with an assortment of bladed weaponry. The cries of fear from the priests carried all the way across Point Fire: a symphony of wailing. They dared not go any closer.

"Aren, what do we do? What *can* we do? There could be people we *know* there!" Udar said, aghast.

Aren leaned against a nearby wall. He could not take his eyes off the distant carnage that unfolded before them. He watched as countless dots scaled the central circle of fortifications, moving over a newly forming mountain. The Man on Fire – his bright glare surrounding him like a burning haze – had remained at the very rear of the attackers. Aren and Udar had soon realized that this man was the true commander of the army. Yob had merely been a placeholder, a person who would prepare for the arrival of whoever this demon was.

Aren sighed. "I don't think we can do anything. This is too much. It's too evil. I just hope that Mom is safe..."

Aren started to sob. He slouched downwards against the stone wall and placed his head in his hands.

Dad... 'Nir... anyone! Why aren't you here to help us?

Udar placed an arm over Aren's shoulders. He began to cry too.

*   *   *

Avenir had taken point, with Luna and Runan pulling the sleds behind him. Soljan, with his gored leg, still sat on top of the sled that Runan was handling. He was hard at work mixing healing salves using

338

the various ingredients in his tracker's pouch. Avenir was wielding his father's short bow again, scouting the dunes ahead.

There was a moment during their travels in which he felt that he should destroy it, his father's old weapon. The thought of what his father had become still made him queasy. Yet, he still loved something about the thing. It had been with him for so many years. So many Hunts and adventures. Finally, he had convinced himself that this weapon was a gift from his *real* father. It was a reminder of who he once was, and what Avenir should never become.

He kept his head low as he ascended the next dune. The last thing any of them wanted now was to be spotted by a Saber, or a startled Frost Flyer.

Instead, what he saw when he crested the top sprouted a blossom of hope deep within his heart. There, far in the distance, lay the dark walls and orange glow of Point Fire. A dark silhouette against the faded dawn.

We made it.

Avenir turned back to his remaining pod members, who were struggling to get their sleds up the hill.

"We made it! I can see the Point!"

Luna stopped pulling. She did not respond, instead rifling through the contents on top of the sled. She seemed satisfied once she had retrieved her weapons, as well as a few rations of food and a gourd of water. She looked up at Avenir, who was staring at her curiously.

"Do you know what that means?" she asked rhetorically.

Not waiting for a response, she violently kicked the sled, sending it tumbling down the slope. Vials, skins, and scraps of tarp spilled all over the snow.

"...and that's the last time I'm ever touching one of those. Sleds can all go to hell!"

Avenir laughed so hard his ribs hurt. Soljan and Runan joined in. At first Luna was annoyed that they were making fun of her genuine anger. But soon, an unstoppable smile began to creep its way across her face, which was turning a bright red underneath her ice gauze.

Avenir managed to stop laughing – probably because of his extreme fatigue and the pain in his chest – and he turned again to study the outlines of Point Fire. He had never been so relieved to see those dark walls.

Then he noticed a bright glow – brighter than the usual one given off by the heat lines underneath the Keep – off towards the northernmost segment of the city. He strained his eyes, pushing his Hunter's Vision to its limits. He could just make out multiple trails of smoke rising from the location of the glow.

It's near the Cathedral.

And then, with terrifying realization:

Luna and Runan's dreams about the Cathedral…That's where father must have gone.

"Hey," he said, trying to grab the attention of his friends, who were still laughing loudly. "HEY!"

Soljan rubbed tears from his eyes, "What is it Avenir? Something nearby?"

"It's the Point. It's burning near the Cathedral. I think something horrible is happening there. My father–"

"Then let's go," interrupted Runan. "I cannot wait to see him again. This time, I'll make sure he doesn't escape."

Runan pushed past Avenir, bow over his shoulder, with Soljan on top of the sled in front.

"Wai–" Avenir started.

But the large Hunter was already guiding the sled down the other side of the dune in a rapidly accelerating slide, Soljan holding on for dear life. Avenir turned to Luna, searching her for a response. She nodded.

"Let's just get back alive…all of us."

Avenir nodded in agreement and jumped over the edge of the dune after a running start. He landed on the small of his back softly and began picking up speed. Luna did the same behind him. The wind whipped at their ice gauzes as they slid, their bodies soon reaching a blinding pace down the back of the mountainous dune. Their *Breaths* kicked up high and far behind them.

*   *   *

"WE CANNOT LET THEM ENTER. SUCH IS THE WILL OF EMBR!" screamed Kreymar, his torch-helmet flickering in the winds encircling the wooden tower.

The last of the priests raised their spears in a haphazard phalanx-like formation. There were still a good number of able-bodied men capable of defending the Cathedral.

Fighting for their very sanity.

The line of spears stretched almost one-half of the circumference of the inner boundary. By now, all the priests who had previously been stationed on the other segments were in this final location. They would make one last attempt to stop the incoming horde as they continued to approach head on, or die trying.

A few hundred of the attackers had already made it over the central fortifications and were barreling towards their location. Even more followed, still unseen behind the walls.

"HOLD YOUR SPEARS STEADY. DO NOT LET THEM PASS."

The circumference of the final defenses was now small enough so that Kreymar's voice could be heard clearly by all those around him. The head priest pointed his dark sword at the oncoming force.

"LET THEM FEEL THE WRATH OF EMBR!"

The first wave of silent attackers was upon them. Most of them instantly impaled themselves on the stakes. Some of the citizens of Point Fire were lucky, and by pure chance managed to avoid the first row of wooden spikes, even with the pressure of hundreds behind them. The nearest priests to these forerunners viciously stabbed and slashed at their chests and throats. Sprays of blood exploded at horrific angles, bathing all those around them in a red haze. Most of the priests, even the veterans who had the privilege of staying near the rear since the entire ordeal started, were now soaked in the blood of their Brothers, and the slain citizens of Point Fire. The entire area had entered the realm of nightmares, as the snow underfoot slowly turned to a red-tinged sludge.

Kreymar himself swung his scimitar wildly, doing his best to keep the onslaught at bay. The people attacking were by no means soldiers. They would occasionally swing whatever weapon they were wielding and hit their mark with blank expressions, but for the most part they were easy pickings for the determined priests. They did, however, possess near endless numbers. Already the cracks were beginning to form in his last circle of defenses. Priests began falling around Kreymar. There was no way that they would be able to hold the line for much longer.

Kreymar doubled back, calling for a handful of nearby priests to follow him. A group of other red-robed men instantly filled the gap they left behind, doing their best to halt the progress of the incoming army as it barged through the last remaining wooden spikes.

He swiftly led this small detachment of priests back to the black gates of the Cathedral. The two massive obsidian colored doors loomed in front of him, bearing their intricate carvings of the Inner Sanctum. He pulled the still-lit torch from his helmet and placed the naked flame above the location of the fifth plaque, where Embr would have been. The doors groaned as they swung open, and he ushered in the other priests fortunate enough to have accompanied him. Kreymar threw his helmet to the wayside and instructed the men to close and lock the doors.

They followed this instruction without hesitation, but not before a particularly aggressive attacker managed to burst through the opening. It was a young man in his early twenties, wielding a small hand-axe. His eyes were dull and glazed over in a blue haze.

Before he could take another step, Kreymar cut him down with his blade in a wide sweeping arc. The man fell sideways, the open gash in his torso spurting. As the unfortunate youth lay dying on the cold floor, the other priests finally managed to close the doors again.

"Break the opening mechanism," Kreymar ordered, tossing a key to the nearest cloaked man.

The priest hesitated for a moment. There were five of them in total that had made it back inside with Kreymar.

"DO IT NOW!"

The priest holding the key jumped into action, unlocking – fumbling a bit – and entering a tiny room just off to the right of the obsidian doors. The other remaining priests followed. A few seconds later, the screeching sound of metal slamming on metal echoed throughout the Cathedral. Then, a dull crunch followed as the men inside the room lay waste to the machinery controlling the doors.

The muffled sounds of the ongoing battle raged on. Kreymar closed his eyes as he listened to the dying screams of his priests and the dull thuds of thousands of feet trampling over snow, all in that terrifyingly steady rhythm. The priests emerged again from the side room. One stepped forward, his face obscured by a bloody hood.

"Your Holiness...what do we do now?" The fear in his voice was almost palpable.

Keeping his eyes shut, Kreymar sighed and sat cross-legged on the ground, facing the doors. He placed his dark scimitar carefully on the ground. He ran his hand through his hair, pulling drying and clotted blood out from the long black strands.

"Nothing," he whispered. "We can do nothing, Brother. We wait...and we pray to Embr that they cannot enter."

Two priests fell to their knees, defeated. One of them began pulling his own hairs out in anguish. Kreymar ignored them.

Perhaps only fate can decide what will happen next.

He heard the footsteps of the other ones fading away in the direction of the apartments.

Cowards.

Kreymar sat like this, eyes closed, listening to the sounds outside for a long time. The muffled screams approached ever nearer, until they seemed to be coming from right outside the doors. The banging of hands on the metal confirmed this. His Brothers were calling for help from outside, but Kreymar did not move. He could not risk the man of light entering.

Soon their voices were no more. The rhythmic thudding of footsteps continued for a few seconds, and then came to an abrupt halt. The silence that followed was frightening. It was as if all movement had stopped outside the Cathedral. He imagined an entire army – thousands of people – quietly standing behind the doors. In a brief moment of peace, Kreymar believed that this nightmare may have come to an end.

He was pulled from this wonderful fantasy by an otherworldly sound. It was sharp, like a kettle boiling...and it was getting louder. Suddenly, he was aware of a significant amount of heat on his face. He opened his eyes.

In a small concentrated area, the great doors were glowing a bright red, like the coals of a blacksmith's forge. Steam and smoke erupted ferociously from this location. Between the clouds that billowed forth, he saw the tip of a sword emerge. It cut through the thick metal like it was butter. And then, the terrible, soul-shattering revelation:

Embr.

*   *   *

Borea finished cutting a square through the doors of the Cathedral. He kicked forwards and watched with satisfaction as the metal fell away into the spire's interior. All around him, the citizens of Point Fire who had survived the assault stood static, their eyes and minds frozen in place. Some part of him had almost felt pity for them, especially when he had seen so many children fall.

He willed the nearest five citizens through the now-open doorway, in case of a potential ambush. They obeyed instantly, running trance-like through the smoking opening. He waited a couple of seconds, and when no further noise came, he stepped through.

Inside, he found Kreymar sitting cross-legged, staring blankly at the Sword in his hand. A dark and bloodied curved weapon lay within reach of the head of the Church of Embr, but the man made no attempt to pick it up.

For the second time in so long, Borea felt a deep sense of sadness. He walked over to the defeated priest and knelt in front of him, spinning the tip of Embr's blade on the cold ground. It sizzled and cut downwards slightly into the rock. Blood was pouring out of Borea's hand where the thorns had just retracted. Kreymar said nothing, his eyes fixated on Embr's glowing shaft. Borea put his non-bloodied hand on the man's shoulder before standing up.

"Little Kreymar. You were so much younger when I last saw you. Look at you now." Borea eyed his missing arm, his scorched face.

There was a genuine sadness in his voice. He raised Embr again so that Kreymar could see it clearly.

"Embr. *The Sword Cloaked in Fire.*" Borea said these words mockingly.

He then frowned when he saw the trails of hot blood dripping off his own arm. He shook some of it off, spattering the liquid over the ground.

He looked Kreymar dead in the eyes and continued, "It seems the Master within this Weapon has been communicating with you in a desperate attempt to stop me. It's surprising isn't it, how even the Masters can disagree amongst each other? They're like wild animals, bickering away inside their cages. It's a shame that all of humanity will have to rely on them to ultimately save us. But it didn't matter what the Master of Fire told you, because I could see everything. I saw you preparing your army, Kreymar. And thus," he motioned towards the still-smoking hole in the door, "I had to prepare my own." Borea sheathed the Great Sword in a crystal-lined scabbard. "I was like you once, Kreymar. I believed in what the Church of Embr taught. That this Weapon itself was a deity worthy of devotion. That it is the sole reason we have survived all these millennia, a tool which provides warmth. I do not disagree with the latter. But that is all it is. This thing," he touched the scabbard, "is just that: a tool, nothing more, nothing less. It may house the soul of a god, but until that god is set free, it is merely a means to be used towards an end. The end *I* have in mind is the salvation of all reality. The Masters inside the weapons may disagree on the specifics as to how this will be achieved, but I do not care. For now, two of them are under my control."

Kreymar said nothing. He continued staring blankly at the scabbard. Borea unsheathed the Sword again. The shaft began to glow white-hot. He placed the Blade's edge on the priest's shoulder. It seared the robes instantly, as well as the skin beneath them.

"What a tragic end. Defeated by the very thing you believed in," he said quietly.

Borea raised the Great Sword as if he were about to kill the man sitting on the ground. But then he lifted the weapon away and strode determinedly past him. Kreymar remained there, unmoving.

XLI

Dawn had fully arrived by the time Avenir and the others finally reached the copper portcullises lining the North Side. Runan produced a key and turned it in the large metal lock. They were all exhausted. It was a feat in of itself just to remain standing. They moved in and swung the interior door open, which greeted them with a view of a small, barren farmland.

"Home," Runan breathed.

He pushed the sled – Soljan still sitting on top – through the entrance.

"Runan, could you take him to the Hunters' district?"

"One step ahead of you, 'Nir. I also want to make sure word of what happened to Sen gets out. After that, I will be going to the Cathedral. I don't care who gets in my way. I will find the man who killed my brother."

"Be careful," Luna chimed in, trying her best not to glance at Avenir.

Avenir was too tired to be affected by the memory of Sen at this point. Every step he took felt hallucinogenic.

But I have to get there. I have to know.

"I'm going towards where that light was." He looked to the northeast, over the Grey. "I need to see what's happening."

Just recently, as they were approaching the outer walls of the city, Avenir had noticed the orange glow was already disappearing.

"I'm coming with you," said Luna. "I'm sure Runan will be fine by himself."

"Of course. We'll meet again later." The words coming from Runan were curt. Even the veteran Hunter had reached the limit of his endurance.

Runan began pushing Soljan southeast, towards the Hunters' district, while Avenir and Luna moved in a northerly direction. The Point was a ghost town. As they traveled inwards in the general direction of the Cathedral, the roads and agricultural areas remained abandoned. Almost all the candles, torches, and other sources of light jutting from the stonework had been extinguished within the multitudes of forts and castles.

"Avenir..." Luna started, as they made their way through a silent network of winding streets near the intersection of the North Side and the Grey.

"I know," he replied. "It's worse than we could have ever imagined."

He wanted to knock on a door, just to make sure that the people inside were okay, but he knew deep down that he did not have the time. They needed to get to where that light had been.

It was probably Embr. Please, tell me it's not too late.

After the next turn, they found themselves in front of a small wrought iron gate. Beyond the gate lay the Grey. The black spire of the Cathedral stood silhouetted against the whiteness on the horizon. Luna vaulted over the gate first and was already striding out over the ice, bow in her hand, when she turned and noticed that Avenir appeared to be frozen, still behind the iron bars.

"Hey! HEY! Don't tell me it happened again." There was a note of sincere fear in her voice.

A single tear rolled down Avenir's cheek. It landed silently on the snow beside his boot.

"So many."

"What is it? What happened?"

His tears were now streaming.

"What have you done?" He struggled to speak further. "Luna, you might want to stay here. It's far away, so you can't see it yet."

"Damn it, Avenir. Tell me what it is!"

"Something no one should ever witness."

He pulled himself over the gate, wiping his eyes. He walked past her, not daring to look at her.

"I'm warning you. You don't want to follow me."

"Well, it doesn't matter what you say. I'm the daughter of the king. I've come this far, and I am not stopping here."

He ignored her and carried on walking towards the Cathedral. Luna breathed in exasperation and followed Avenir, not yet understanding the true nature of the horror which awaited them.

*   *   *

It was a sea of red. The bodies of thousands of people lay mangled and forgotten, strewn across the snow in multitudes beyond comprehension. Edged weapons jutted outwards at evil angles, both from the snow and from the ocean of bodies. Most of the corpses were yet untouched by blades, instead having met their fate underneath the boots of their comrades.

It smelled wet, just like the stench of waste being thrown out in the backstreets. The bodies of children, merchants, Hunters...entire families, lay in piles up against what remained of the wooden fortifications.

Luna was retching loudly. She could not walk forwards anymore. Avenir stopped and waited for her to recover. He knelt down and picked up some of the snow in his glove. It was dark red. He crushed it in his hand, watching it fall to join more redness below. The indescribable sadness he had felt when he first saw this from afar was being replaced by something far darker.

How could you?

Luna tapped him weakly on his shoulder. He started walking again. They reached the outer circle of the ruined defenses. The eyes of the countless people who had died watched them in silence. Some arrows still smoldered on the inside and on top of their targets, creating a lingering smell of singed meat that plagued the air.

There was no way past the first layer of broken defenses that did not involve stepping on the corpses of the dead. But Avenir was beyond caring. He moved over them as if they did not exist. Past the

349

young men impaled on the spikes, past the women, some of them still clinging onto life by a thread, gasping for air.

Luna could not do it. She leaned against the nearest upright spike and vomited. The spike itself was covered with spatters of dried blood. A woman missing an arm lay face down in the snow next to it.

The view of the central defenses was equally, if not more, harrowing. A mountain of bodies, hundreds strong, was stacked up against the thick wooden walls. Avenir approached it over the brief stretch of land between the outer and central defenses. The snow underfoot was now wholly crimson. Everywhere, steam rose up out of the ground and from between the bodies in their piles.

Your lives will not go to waste.

He climbed up the pile of corpses. It chilled him every time his boot came down on part of someone that he may have seen before, or his glove reached to pull himself up using a spear imbedded in a young man's torso. Thankfully, he soon reached the top of the pile, and he vaulted over the edge of the wall onto the platform behind it. He could now see beyond the third and final layer of defenses, and it offered him a nightmarish vision.

There, standing like inert mannequins, stood what remained of the army that had attacked. They waited silently, the icy breeze of the winds circling around their shoulders. There were probably well over a thousand people just standing there, rooted to the cold ground. Avenir could not imagine what the original force had looked like.

As he got closer to the Cathedral, the frequency of crimson-robed bodies increased exponentially. The number of dead citizens was staggering. He reached the beginnings of the final inner palisade. Hundreds more innocent people had been gored on the tips of the stakes and spears here. Luna was far behind him now. She had not even scaled the first pile of bodies yet, and probably never would. These people were her family's subjects, their responsibility. The residents of the Keep had indeed failed them all.

Avenir walked between the citizens who were still standing. They all stared forwards blankly, their arms hanging by their sides as they faced the Cathedral, like they were waiting for something. The door to the obsidian structure was cut open...still smoking.

Embr. I know you're close.

Avenir stepped through the smoke, rage building in his heart. The familiar smell of singed flesh filled his nostrils. Kreymar was kneeling inside the building, not twenty feet away, his eyes blank. He was staring out through the doors of the Cathedral. Avenir crept over and examined him, noticing a fresh burn wound on his shoulder. He shook his other shoulder slightly in an attempt to wake him from whatever daze he was in.

Kreymar mumbled something unintelligible.

"What?" said Avenir, moving his head closer so that he could hear him better.

"*Embr, Embr, Embr...*" Kreymar whispered softly. He continued repeating the name, over and over.

It was no use. There was no getting through to him. Avenir could not bear to look at the man's disfigured face any longer. He stood up and stepped past the priest.

"WHERE ARE YOU?" Avenir called out into the empty spire, his voice filled with rage.

The sound echoed down the corridor to the worship hall and up into the heights of the apartments. No one responded. He was about to call again when a terrified priest stuck his head through the crimson curtains leading to the tunnel marked "Worship."

"You, y...you there. How did you get here?" his voice was weak, wounded.

"Tell me. Where did he go?" It was a cold question.

The priest understood what Avenir meant and nodded towards the third and rightmost tunnel – the one marked "Caverns."

That was enough for Avenir. He ran off in the direction the priest had indicated, down the tunnel, and down the torch-lined stone staircase. Although he had never been in the Caverns before, he knew of the rumors detailing their frigid temperatures. Lessons he had learned about them all those years ago cycled through his mind.

And Father, forbidding me to come here.

His footsteps echoed loudly as he descended the stairs. If his father were indeed down there, he would be able to hear him approaching. But Avenir did not care.

Reaching a set of crimson curtains at the bottom of the long descent, he stopped for a moment, listening out over the silence in the adjacent area. There was no indication of movement. The air around him was warm...pleasant.

Embr?

Avenir gripped Sen's Shard tightly in his hand and brushed the curtain aside.

He was greeted by a wave of heat and a brilliant blue light, both of which filled the cavern. In all his years of exploring the city, he had never seen anything quite like this.

Why was I never allowed here?

As he had grown older, Avenir had lost interest in the Caverns, and the Cathedral in general, focusing his need to explore on the Frost. He now hated himself for not exploring this place further once his father had left.

Aren has always liked the city more than what lies outside the walls. I wonder if he's been here before.

He gazed across the azure chamber. The curtains opened onto a raised platform, so he had a view of the entire area. The first thing that drew his attention was a circle of chairs and piles of books near the back of the cavern. And there, some ways behind the scattered furniture and writings, walked his father. He was strolling down the length of the back of the chamber, a scroll in one hand and Embr in the other. The wall next to him was flat...turquoise...otherworldly. Embr was glowing a dull orange. Yet, Avenir sensed that the heat in this place was not coming from the Great Sword alone.

It did not appear as if his father had heard Avenir approaching.

He's too absorbed in whatever he's doing.

Borea did not notice Avenir enter as he stepped past the crimson curtains. Avenir crouched low and began to descend one of the dark stone stairways leading to the ground below. He was gripping

Sen's Shard so tightly that his knuckles hurt. His eyes were glued to Borea's back as he traced the tip of Embr along the azure wall.

How could you have done something like this?

Borea stopped suddenly, and Avenir froze. His father seemed to be studying something in the scroll he was holding. He then looked up and made his way further along the cave wall. Avenir crept forward. He still had his father's bow around his back, but he wanted to do this personally.

To use Sen's weapon.

The thought of the massive Hunter made Avenir's rage all the more poignant. His father moved his head closer to the azure wall, inspecting it closely. Avenir began moving again. He reached the ground, an uneven rocky sprawl, and focused on moving as silently as possible towards his father. Borea dropped the scroll and assumed a two-handed stance in front of the azure wall.

Avenir had now made it to the edge of the chair circle. If he sprinted from this location, he could make it to his father in a matter of seconds. He hesitated for a moment. Even though furious rage burned within him at the monster standing near the walls, the man still resembled his father. He felt his grip weaken on Sen's Shard.

If I kill him now, will I have become just like him?

"You see, Avenir," Borea said, still facing the wall as he raised the Great Sword over his head. "This is why it must be *me* who completes this duty. It must be someone who doesn't hesitate...even when the act is truly terrible."

Borea swung Embr downwards towards the back wall of the cavern. To Avenir it all occurred in slow motion, and all he could do was watch in horror. A stripe of brilliant fire trailed behind the tip as the Great Sword collided with the wall. Upon impact, a blindingly bright shower of sparks and flames erupted from the smooth barrier. A deep *CRACK* rang out, loud enough to make Avenir's bones vibrate. The heat wave from the strike knocked Avenir off his feet, and he flew backwards through the furniture around him. Then everything turned white, and all sound vanished.

*   *   *

The sound was heard throughout Point Fire. It echoed down the streets and over the cobblestones. Over the balustrades and flying buttresses. Heat lines shivered in its wake.

Aren and Udar were sleeping at their lookout point, exhausted from the recent events, when the noise hit them. It vibrated deep inside their chests. They jolted upright, scanning their surroundings, ready to run at a moment's notice. No further noise came, and the battlefield far in the distance lay ever silent, ravaged by cold winds.

In that moment, both boys felt the same urge to return to their families and check if they were okay. Somehow, they both sensed that it was over.

After waving goodbye to Udar at an intersection of supporting walls, Aren ran as fast as he could back to Darch's tavern. When he arrived in the Hunters' district, he could already tell that something was different. People were stepping out of their homes, confused and afraid. They all felt it.

It's gone. The Darkness has left.

Aren rushed to the main entrance of the tavern and pushed his way past a couple of men furiously arguing near the door. The smell inside the establishment was already returning to its usual state – one of sweat and ale. Across the tavern, family members were regrouping, or sharing tearful hugs. There was a high proportion of Hunters inside the establishment, and Aren noticed Piet sitting at a table in the corner with a couple of them. They were deep in conversation, and the large man's brow was furrowed.

Good old Piet.

Darch was crouching down behind his bar counter, tending to someone. Aren knew immediately who it was.

"Mom! Mom, are you there?"

His mother stood up from behind the bar. Her hair was a mess. She seemed dazed for a moment, looking for Aren, but then their eyes met, and she scrambled over towards him. Darch looked on from behind, smiling.

"Aren!" She already had him in her arms and was squeezing him tightly. "You're safe! Thank the Seven! I woke up in the closet and you weren't there, and I was locked in and..." She started sobbing.

"I know Mom, I know. I'm sorry, I'm so sorry," Aren mumbled into his mother's clothes.

*   *   *

Avenir woke up to what he at first thought must be a dream. He was lying under a turquoise sky, bathing in warm light. There was no sound, only peace and tranquility. Slowly, his memories returned, like distant messages over the breeze. With this recollection came his sense of hearing. The tranquil silence was replaced by a shrill whining, which escalated until it reached a maddening pitch, before stopping altogether. His eyes refocused, and he was back in the cavern underneath the Cathedral.

Father.

His body attempted to jerk upright, but a sharp pain in his back caused him to roll to the side. He groaned, trying to make sense of his surroundings. He was suffering from some kind of shock, and he found he couldn't understand what he was looking at. Finally, objects began to reveal their true nature. He was lying in a pile of broken chairs and paperwork, most of it singed black. His dunerobe had also adopted a charcoal coloring.

He rubbed his eyes, trying to rid them of the green sparks that flashed in their periphery. The green lights moved to flutter around the center of his vision, drifting through the air slowly, like snowflakes would in the Frost.

Perhaps I'm dead, and this is indeed a dream.

The green lights were not disappearing, and he gave up trying to get rid of them. He propped himself up, looking around. The green lights were now everywhere, reflecting the turquoise glow that bounced

355

around him. Thick clouds of smoke, as well as more of the green dust, crowded the area where his father had been.

One of the green lights descended right next to him. He put out his hand, half-expecting it to land there.

It did.

His vision was still blurry. Avenir closed his eyes for a few seconds, hoping that it would help restore his senses. When he opened them again, he studied the thing in his hand.

It was a leaf. A *green* leaf, partially burnt. Its *greenness* stood out like a sore thumb against the concept of what a leaf should be. The ones in the North Side were grey and sickly. This one – besides the burnt sections – was alive with color. Then he realized that the rest of the green lights were leaves too, twirling lightly through the air.

Avenir finally managed to stand up. He clutched the leaf he had caught tightly in his hand, as if it were a great treasure. He moved across the cavern towards the smoke. The density of falling leaves increased as he approached. Some of them moved upwards in ragged gusts created by the ashy winds.

It's warm here, so warm.

He stepped through the smoking hole at the back of the cavern, passing through the azure wall. It was a sight...a sense...which was indescribable. A passageway led far away, downwards and into the depths below the cavern, further than he could see. Humid, warm air wafted upwards through it. Spread along the walls of this passageway were thousands upon thousands of phosphorescent mosses. And, illuminated beneath them, lay an undergrowth of countless luscious plants and shrubs, none of them the likes of which he had ever seen before.

It was a type of nature, one which Avenir...*which no one in Point Fire,* had ever conceived of. The succulent ferns bulged with nutrition, defying everything that lay above. The Frost...the grey skies... This green path was heavenly. A vision of the divine.

Another sense wafted upwards from this tunnel. It was earthy, alive even. It entered his lungs and it felt as if he were truly breathing for the first time in his life.

The warm air kept wafting from below. It seeped through his pores and flowed into his blood. In a brief, fleeting moment, he forgot about everything that had happened. It was a long-awaited peace...standing in a soft fall of burning leaves, feeling the alien warmth on his skin, and the unimaginable freshness in his nose.

Father. Where have you gone?

Among this brilliant new flora lining the walls of the passageway, Avenir noticed something. It was a small scrap of parchment. One of its edges was burned into the moss behind it, making it stick there. At first Avenir thought it was merely a fragment of the scrolls outside.

Perhaps sent here by the blast.

But then he saw a scribbled note at its corner, half-covering the original ancient writing of the manuscript...and a map next to it. He squinted his eyes, struggling to read the words under the phosphorescent light.

Avenir, my son. As I write this, you are lying in a pile of texts and burning wood. Some part of me hopes that you never read this, that you have in fact come to your end. I believe that to be a merciful future. I dare not check to see whether it is true – I have meddled with fate enough. But, should you wake to find this message, I beg you to never follow me down this passage, which must seem alien to your naïve eyes. Beyond it lies only ruin, and while I have already told you that I do not care much for ruin anymore, I know you do...

But I also know you are my son, and you will do it anyway. Here is what my eyes have seen. Many over the Few.

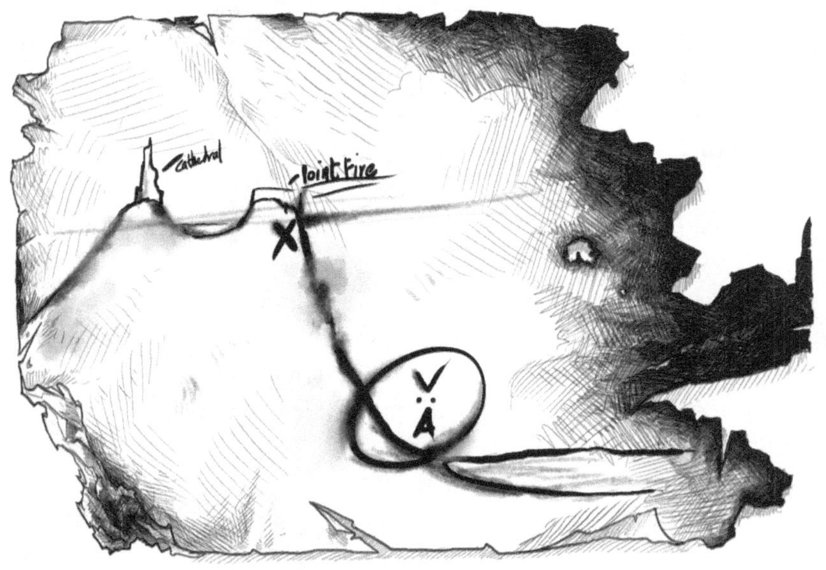

It was a simple map, clearly drawn by hand in haste. It depicted a mountain with two shining peaks. Each peak had some type of structure drawn onto it. They were labeled: *Point Fire, Cathedral.* At the base of this mountain lay a rough sketch of a magnificent lake. And at the shore of the lake, was a final label:

V

Ä

Avenir fell to his knees, tears rolling down his cheeks. It all felt so sudden, as if he had never even found his real father in the first place. The man was gone again, vanishing beneath the horizon like an ethereal Frost Storm. Leaving behind a trail of confusion and despair.

Yet Again.

And then he remembered.

Sen's death.
Aren.
Mom.

Wiping his eyes, he turned away from this otherworldly passage, tucking his father's letter and map into his dunerobe. He picked up Sen's Shard and placed it in his belt, trying not to look at the engraving of the closed fist. He left the caverns. He walked past Kreymar, who was still kneeling in disbelief. He stepped outside, back into the cold of the Frost, a feeling so familiar, but one that had now become so harsh in comparison.

Dusk was falling on the Point, and it was already beginning to glow orange against the dark sky. All those who had been standing in a daze had woken up, perhaps some time ago. Some were crying, others laughing hopelessly. Most were walking back to the distant walls of the city, confused, unsteady. It was their home...their families were there, waiting. The people walked silently past the dead who lay strewn across the snow, not knowing how to look at them. Luna stood out in the open, staring off into the distance.

Avenir looked at his hand as he opened it. The leaf lay tucked in his glove, mostly burnt away. He closed his fist tightly, so tightly that his knuckles burned and his muscles ached. He let the crushed ashes and green remnants flutter down onto the snow.

I will find you.
But for now, he just wanted to be with his family.
Aren would have kept her safe.

He merged with the crowd as they walked, joining them in their desire to return home.

For all those who believed in me and who were
willing to be a part of this amazing journey.

And especially for my mother, who has read this
story more times than I have.

ACKNOWLEDGEMENTS

My mom, for being the number one editor, fan, reader, and also everything else.

My dad, for his never-ending support and enthusiasm.

Stephen, for helping me visualize a dream.

Sarah, for being there for me (and for editing, of course!).

My teachers and professors, for encouraging my love of writing.

And all my friends and family, who never stopped asking: "When can I read it?"

ABOUT THE AUTHOR

Phillip Vorster was born in Cleveland, Ohio, but spent his childhood in and across South Africa. There, thanks to the many second-hand bookstores near Cape Town, he discovered his love for fantasy. He returned to the United States with his family to complete high school and graduated from Yale University with a B.S. in Cognitive Science.
Phillip now attends the University of Cincinnati Medical School.

The Novari Heptalogy is his first written fantasy series.

THE NOVARI HEPTALOGY

EMBR

YS

ECLIPSE

HOPE

WHISPR

PRAYR

NOVARI

www.ingramcontent.com/pod-product-compliance
Lightning Source LLC
Chambersburg PA
CBHW030831110726
47900CB00006B/1840